**CORDELIA WEPT.**

Somehow she was in his arms. He held her tight, stroking her back, murmuring soothing words.

"Hush, now, hush. You have been so brave, don't cry. Cordelia . . ." James hesitated. "Cordelia, I see no way to save you from the pasha but it might be easier for you if it were not your first time. Instead of giving your virginity to him, would you not rather give that gift to me?"

"Oh, James!" She was excruciatingly conscious of his hard, lean body pressed against her, the protective circle of his arms now disquieting, intoxicating. His mouth touched her forehead, kissed the corners of her eyes, licked the salt tears from her cheeks. "James . . ."

His name was more moan than protest. His lips met hers, firm and soft, sending a burning thrill shivering through her.

Outside, a rattling blast of sound rent the air.

James flung himself on Cordelia, flattening her.

The breath knocked from her body, she squawked, "Don't!" and struggled to sit up.

"Keep still!" he snapped. "Stay down! That's gunfire!"

# Scandal's Daughter

Carola Dunn

ZEBRA BOOKS
KENSINGTON PUBLISHING CORP.

ZEBRA BOOKS are published by

Kensington Publishing Corp.
850 Third Avenue
New York, NY 10022



First Printing: March, 1996
10 9 8 7 6 5 4 3 2 1

Printed in the United States of America

# One

*"Allahu akbar!"*

The cry of a muezzin at the nearby mosque, calling the faithful to the dawn prayer, woke Cordelia as usual. She rolled over on her back on the cotton-stuffed mattress, pulling the quilt about her for the night air held an autumnal chill.

*"Allahu akbar!"* A mournful, insistent wail. "God is great! There is no god but Allah. Prayer is better than sleep."

The sky still showed dark through the spaces in the elaborately carved wooden screen covering the glassless window. The bowl of roses beside it was invisible, though it perfumed the air. She'd give herself a few minutes more, until the muezzin had finished his call to all four points of the compass.

*"Allahu akbar!* Come to prayer."

She always felt a twinge of guilt at not heeding the call, even though Mehmed Pasha, her mother's lover, said few Turkish women were taught the prayers. A lifetime spent abroad, far from the Church of England she'd been baptized into, had left Cordelia with nothing but an echo from long-ago nursery days:

> Matthew, Mark, Luke, and John,
> Bless the bed I lie upon.

Who were Matthew, Mark, Luke, and John? Men, of course.

*"Allahu akbar!* Mohammed is the prophet of Allah."

Mohammed—another man. Religion was just one of the ways men ruled the world at the expense of women.

She threw back the quilt, shivering. A quick wash and she put on baggy trousers, a high-necked shift of fine gauze edged with embroidery, and a long-sleeved waistcoat. She checked the money in her leather drawstring-purse before fastening it at her waist. It was reached by a slit in the side seam of the garment she put on next, an ankle-length kaftan, close-fitting across the bosom and tied with a girdle. Pulling on soft leather socks, she hurried to the window for the best moment of the day.

The wooden houses opposite, their upper storeys projecting over the street, were still in darkness, but the sky was light now. Minarets and domes, ethereal as the fabled palaces of the Djinn, hovered above a golden haze of mist off the Bosporus mingled with the smoke of countless cooking fires. Cordelia watched as the sun's first rays added a rosy glow to the vista.

By then the men had finished their prayers and the street below her window was growing busy. Turbaned artisans and shopkeepers on their way to work; a string of heavy-laden pack mules with blue beads around their necks to ward off the Evil Eye; water-carriers; boys running to the mosque school; scavenging dogs and cats; porters bent double by the baskets and bundles on their backs; milkmen and yoghurt sellers shouting their wares; sherbet peddlers clinking tin cups; veiled women on their way to market—with a sigh, Cordelia turned from the scene, so much more picturesque and less smelly from here than when she was down there among them.

She crossed the richly patterned rug—Mama said Turkey carpets were much admired in England—to the mirror, where she rebraided her long fair hair. Since coming to Istanbul, she had been glad her eyes were brown instead of Mama's celestial blue. To the ignorant and superstitious, blue eyes were a sign of the Evil Eye. As it was, with a shawl to hide her hair and thrown across the lower part of her face, she could go to market without attracting notice, safely anonymous in her Turkish clothes.

No one would point her out as the daughter of the notorious Lady Courtenay, *divorcée* and kept woman, nor offer to take her into keeping. In some ways, Cordelia quite approved of Turkey.

She went downstairs. The two maids had made tea and set out on a low table a simple breakfast of bread, peaches, and fresh white cheese. Bare feet silent as a mouse, Aisha scurried up to Cordelia's bedroom to roll up the mattress, air the bedding, and sweep the carpet. Amina knelt on the floor beside the divan where Cordelia sat down.

Pouring tea, Amina chattered, giggling, about the handsome young charcoal seller who had brought his wares to the door earlier. Cordelia understood Turkish quite well enough to follow the girl's prattle, though the Arabic alphabet with which it was written still baffled her. Throughout the wandering years, her gift for languages had proved invaluable. Mama spoke only French, adequate for communication with her noble lovers but useless for everyday life, for shopping in Naples or arguing with landladies in Berlin.

Ibrahim, the eunuch, short and chubby in his dolman and loose, calf-length trousers, came in from the courtyard. Like the maids, he had been a slave, presented as a gift to his mistress by Mehmed Pasha. For once in agreement, Lady Courtenay and Cordelia had promptly given all three their freedom, thus earning their utter devotion.

Bowing to Cordelia, Ibrahim told Amina to cease her foolish nonsense. "If you had more sense," he said in his high-pitched voice, "you could be sent to market as Mehmed Pasha intended so the *Bayan* need not go."

"But I like to go," Cordelia reminded him. In Istanbul it was a special pleasure because each vendor arranged his goods in elaborate patterns to attract the attention of buyers. But ever since she could remember, she had enjoyed searching out the freshest fruits and vegetables, the best cuts of meat, at the lowest prices. When they were in funds, she always bought flowers. In the good times Mama teased her for her thrifty ways, but often enough, between lovers, every penny saved meant the wolf kept from the door a little longer—because Mama absolutely refused to sell a single one of her jewels unless the bailiffs were on the doorstep.

"I cannot go with you this morning, *Bayan,*" said Ibrahim.

"I have summoned a litter for the Lady." He used the English word. "She wishes to visit the Jewish jeweller before the heat of the day. There is a ring to be reset."

Lady Courtenay patronized Aaron the Jew because he spoke a little English, supplemented with a few words of French. Besides, she didn't have to keep her face covered in his presence. She was by no means so enamoured of Mohommedan modesty as her daughter.

Finishing her breakfast, Cordelia went upstairs to wish her mother good morning. Attar of roses vied with the fragrance of fresh roses in half a dozen vases. Drusilla Courtenay was just stirring, still-golden curls a-tangle amid the heaps of soft pillows, covered in rich brocades and velvets, with which her room was strewn. She gave Cordelia a sleepy kiss.

"Take care, my darling Dee, and do remember to buy some lokoum, the kind with pistachios. But don't go eating more than a piece or two or you will grow plump."

"I don't mind, Mama." After all, she had no prospect of attracting a respectable man, and the other kind she did not want. "I'll see you later."

She and the barefoot maid put on shoes and wrapped white muslin shawls about their heads. Carrying baskets, they set out, picking their way down the street between slops and heaps of rubbish, replenished as fast as the red-smocked sweepers cleaned.

The morning was still pleasantly cool, so Cordelia took her time. She stopped at a friendly bookseller's stall to see if he had any volumes in a language she could read. As usual, his stock consisted mostly of copies of the Koran, large and small, but he had something for her. He produced it diffidently, for the first thirty-four pages were missing and the rest stained by salt water.

"I had it of a sailor," he explained. "I would not have taken it but I thought you might be interested."

It was a collection of English poetry, so the missing pages scarcely signified. Cordelia gladly handed over a silver akche for such a prize to add to her meagre, often-read library, as fiercely protected as her mother's jewels.

At last, their baskets full, she and Amina turned homeward. The girl continued to scan the faces of the passersby and glance up every street, hoping to see her handsome charcoal-seller.

"Look, *Bayan,*" she said, pointing up one of the steep, narrow alleys as they stood aside to let a string of camels pass. "Isn't that our Lady's litter? I think I saw Ibrahim."

Cordelia turned away from the haughty, cantankerous beasts. A litter was coming down the alley, its bearers treading carefully on the mucky, slippery slope. If Ibrahim was there, he was hidden now by a porter with a huge basket of fish.

"Make way!" shouted the first bearer. The curtains of the litter parted as its passenger peered out.

The porter lowered his burden to the ground and stood aside, against the wall. Instantly a dozen half-starved cats appeared from nowhere, swarming towards the fish. Amina giggled as the porter grabbed for the basket. He caught up one handle but missed the other and a stream of fish slithered over the side, a torrent of reddish-silver scaled mullet rushing down the steep alley.

The front bearer tripped over a cat. The litter tilted flinging the passenger out head-first onto the fish. In a tangle of clothes she slid helplessly down the hill.

Mama! Cordelia sprang forward to catch her, slipped on a fish, fell over a cat, and on hands and knees saw her mother end up under the feet of the last camel in the train. Its hoof caught her golden head as it passed, and it passed on, haughty, oblivious.

Lady Courtenay lay still.

"What happened? I shall see those responsible punished, you may be sure."

Cordelia couldn't stand the man, his corpulent body in a kaftan richly embroidered in silver and gold thread, his shaven head beneath the tarboosh and turban, his eyes like prunes. How could Mama bear to let him touch her?

How could Mama have borne to let him touch her?

*"Allahu aalam*—God is all-wise—but tell me," said Mehmed Pasha impatiently. He sat down on the divan and beckoned her to join him.

She didn't want to sit beside him, nor to sit on the floor, in a position of subservience. As if he understood her silent rebellion, Ibrahim piled two cushions on top of each other and bowed her to the seat.

"It was an accident, no one's fault." In a flat voice, Cordelia recounted the absurd events leading up to the tragic end.

Through the haze of grief, she was aware of the absurdity. Nonetheless, never would she forgive Mehmed Pasha for his hearty laughter. Resentfully she finished the story, resenting Mama, too, for dying a death as indecorous as her life.

The maids wailed and beat their breasts. Faithful Ibrahim had tears in his eyes.

The pasha sobered. *"Allahu aalam.* God knows best and he is merciful. Drusilla was a fine woman, a beautiful woman. You are not so beautiful but you are younger and a virgin. I shall allow you forty days to mourn and then I shall come."

"No!" Cordelia sprang to her feet. "No, I shall never be your mistress, your concubine. I shan't be any man's mistress, ever!"

"Don't be foolish, girl," he chided indulgently. "You have no family to take you in, and no respectable family would take in the daughter of a whore anyway. You have no choice. Or rather, I allow you a choice: if not here in this house, then in my harem. In forty days, I shall come for you."

Signalling to Ibrahim to help him up, he strutted out, confident of his victory. A pasha of the Ottoman Empire need fear no defiance from a mere female, alone in the world.

If only Mama had left her baby behind when she ran away from her husband with that first lover! Cordelia stood with clenched fists, head bowed. Daughter of a whore—that was what she was. But it was no fault of hers. Need it mean she must become a whore in her turn?

# Two

Cordelia raised her head with proud resolve. She would not submit, would not give in to Fate as these Mohommedans expected, the two maids and the eunuch with their faces turned to the wall now so as not to witness her shame.

"I shall go home," she said in English. Her father had divorced her mother, not her. At home, in the England she had left as an infant, she would find the respectability she craved. "I have forty days to make preparations. I shall go home."

The three servants turned to stare, wondering at her vehemence in the language they could not understand. Dare she trust them?

Amina was a chatterbox, her veil no barrier to a good gossip with the peddlers who came to the door. However well-meaning, she might easily let slip word of her mistress's plans to be picked up by police spies and retailed to Mehmed Pasha. Best to keep her in ignorance as long as possible. Aisha was a quiet child, and good with her needle. Cordelia would need her help if things worked out the way she hoped.

As for loyal Ibrahim, his doe-like eyes red from weeping with her over her mother's body, without him she could do nothing.

She sent the girls to prepare the evening meal. "Ibrahim, walk with me in the courtyard," she requested.

The heat of the September day still hung over the city, but the small courtyard was shaded and the splash of its fountain gave an illusion of coolness. Waterlilies, pink, white, and yellow, floated in the marble pool. Cordelia and Ibrahim strolled for a while in silence while she collected her thoughts.

"I'm going back to England," she began, "to my father."

Ibrahim nodded, his soft, young-old face understanding. *"Inshallah*—if God wills it, it is good. An unmarried woman belongs in her father's house. But is it not a long journey?"

"A very long journey. That is why I need a travelling companion. Will you go with me?"

"Oh, *Bayan,* I am honoured that you ask me," the eunuch stammered, "yet I am afraid. I have heard, in Europe they do not make men like me."

"True." Cordelia frowned. She didn't want to drag him all the way to England, to a cold climate where he couldn't speak the language and would be regarded as a freak. "I know, come as far as Athens with me. Greece is part of the Ottoman Empire, so if I give you enough money you can easily come back to Istanbul."

"God is merciful, but to desert my kind mistress would be a sin. It is not right for a young lady to travel alone."

"In Athens I shall go to the British Resident. He will find someone reliable to go with me, perhaps even a party of English travellers. People come all the way from England to visit the ruins, especially now Napoleon has closed so much of Europe. So, you see, you need not worry about me. But, oh dear, will Mehmed Pasha find you when you return and blame you for my flight?"

Ibrahim drew himself up proudly. "The pasha is not my master. You are my mistress, and he cannot blame me for doing my duty to you. Perhaps I shall go to Cairo or Damascus," he added more practically.

"I'll give you as much money as I possibly can. That's the next thing. I shall sell Mama's jewels." At last all those useless baubles could be put to good use. "I'll go and sort them out now, and take them to Aaron the Jew tomorrow. Mama trusted him, and so must I."

She went up to her mother's room and lit a lamp. The muezzin was calling the faithful to the twilight prayer. Was it only this morning she had listened to his cry with nothing more on her mind than what to buy for dinner?

Since then her life was irrevocably changed. At last she was going to be respectable.

There were two jewellery cases, one of stamped leather, the other of sandalwood inlaid with mother-of-pearl. Shunning the luxurious, licentious bed, Cordelia sat cross-legged on the blue and red carpet and emptied onto it the wages of sin. Rubies, emeralds, sapphires, amethysts—Lady Courtenay had not been fussy—glimmered in the lamplight. The sparkling river of diamonds given her by the Margrave of Rennenburg put to shame the Polish Count Szambrowczyk's topaz bracelet.

Little chamois leather bags held delicate opals and pearls, some the gift of the Conte di Arventino, Cordelia thought. She had fond memories of the Italian nobleman, who had been a father to her for several years and taught her much about art and literature. He had even taught her to write English correctly, Mama's orthography being anything but orthodox.

Then his family had insisted that he marry; his mistress and her daughter had moved on.

At the bottom of the leather case, Cordelia found a simple string of quite ordinary pearls. Those were Mama's before her marriage and she hadn't worn them since. She had given them to Cordelia on her sixteenth birthday. Cordelia had had little occasion to wear them, none since coming to Istanbul, but she decided to keep them. Half ashamed of her sentimentality, she told herself they were not worth much. She clasped them round her neck and tucked them under her kaftan.

At the bottom of the sandalwood box, she found her baptismal certificate, her mother's marriage lines, and a letter.

"My Dearling Dee,

I know I have offen erked you by refusing to part with my Jewls. Now you are reading this you will reelise why and not blame yore foolish Mama—They are All I have to leave you. I know my wise child, so much wiser than her mama will make use of them wisely to ashure her Future. God bless you and keep you, my Dearling.

Your ever loving Mama."

Cordelia wept.

In the cool of the morning, Aaron the Jew sat on the bench outside his little shop. His yellow turban, as decreed by the authorities, proclaimed his faith. His shabby clothes proclaimed not his relative wealth, nor a superstitious fear of the Evil Eye, but a sensible wariness of arousing the envy of his Moslem neighbours.

Approaching, Cordelia studied his face, thin, lined, with deepset eyes and a sparse grey beard. All depended upon his willingness to help her. If he refused, or if she felt unable to trust him, she didn't know where to turn.

He regarded her with a gravity which inspired confidence. Standing up, he bowed and without a word held back the curtain across the doorway of his shop. She entered, followed by Ibrahim with the jewellery in a plain rush basket, wrapped in linen cloths. Aaron came in after them, letting the curtain drop. The light within was dim.

*"Shalom,* Meess Courtenay," he said, much to her surprise, continuing in broken English, "your visit honours to me. I hear the mother dies and feel much sorry. A lady of good charm."

"Thank you, Mr. . . . sir." Cordelia unwound the shawl from her face, though she left it over her hair. "How did you know who I am?" she went on in Turkish.

"I know your servant. Also, I have seen you with your mother, and though you wear Turkish clothes, you do not walk like a Turkish girl, if you will excuse my mentioning it."

Blushing, she glanced at Ibrahim, who nodded confirmation. So much for her prized anonymity in the streets! This might complicate her escape, but with luck no one would think twice about her visiting her mother's jeweller.

"You have come for the ring?" he asked. "It is in my workshop, not here. I have not yet done the work, but perhaps you want it left as it is?"

"Yes, thank you." She had forgotten the ring Mama brought yesterday to be reset—the reason for her fatal outing. "That is, it doesn't matter now. Mr. Aaron, I need your help, but I must beg your promise to keep my affairs secret. If you cannot promise, I shall have to . . . to think of something else."

"I promise not to disclose your affairs." As he spoke, the Jew lit a lamp. "Until you tell me what you wish, I cannot promise to help."

Cordelia looked around the small room. "I don't know," she said doubtfully, noting the bare furnishings. On the threadbare carpet stood two low, cushioned benches, and in a corner a plain wooden chest, not large, with an iron lock. A shelf on one wall held only writing materials. "Maybe I am expecting too much of you."

He smiled, his thin face wrinkling. "You must not judge my business by this place, meess. Most of my stock is at my workshop. Here I show prospective customers examples of my work and discuss their wants with them. If you care to sit, I shall send for coffee and we shall discuss your wants."

Still uneasy, Cordelia sat down. Ibrahim stood against the wall, clutching the basket to his chest, as Aaron stuck his head out of the doorway and called to an urchin to bring coffee from the coffee-house.

While they waited, he told Cordelia how much he had enjoyed talking about England with Lady Courtenay. "I have relatives there," he said. "I do not hear their news often, but now and then I am fortunate enough to be of assistance to them in some small matter of business. We Jews are found in every corner of the globe, like you English."

"I was too young when I left to remember anything," Cordelia told him, her trust in him increasing, "but I want to go back."

She fell silent as a ragged, barefooted boy came in with a brass tray holding a long-handled copper pot and three tiny china cups without handles. Aaron paid him the money for the coffee and a tip for himself, then poured the thick, fragrant liquid. "May your servant drink with us?" he asked.

"Oh, yes, of course. Ibrahim, you may put down the basket."

The eunuch sat cross-legged on the floor, the precious basket close beside him, and accepted a cup. They all sipped the hot, syrupy-sweet coffee.

"You wish to return to England, meess," Aaron prompted gently.

"Yes, and I must leave soon." She owed it to him to warn him that helping her might well offend Mehmed Pasha. "The trouble is, someone—a high official—does not want me to leave, so all must be arranged in secret."

"I understand. I am sure I can find a discreet ship's captain who will give you passage at least to Alexandria or Piraeus, the port for Athens, perhaps even to Italy."

"Can you really?" Cordelia had not even begun to consider how that might be accomplished, still less thought of consulting the jeweller. "That's wonderful. I can pay well—that is, if you . . . You see, I have very little money, but a good deal of jewellery."

She signalled to Ibrahim, who spread a cloth on the floor and laid out the glinting gems in their gleaming gold settings. Aaron's sharply indrawn breath told her he was impressed.

"You wish to sell all this?"

"I have no use for jewels, and much need of money."

He leaned down, picked up the Margrave's diamonds, and let them run in a glittering rainbow through his fingers. "These alone are worth a fortune, meess. If you turn them all to gold coins, it will make a heavy load, and one easily lost or stolen."

"What do you advise, then? That I sell some and take the rest with me?"

"No." He carefully put down the diamonds, sipped his coffee and stroked his beard. Cordelia watched him eagerly, convinced now of his good will. "No, such gems as these are not easily sold should you find yourself in need of further funds on the way. You must have some ready money, of course. For the rest, I suggest you exchange half for small diamonds. Sew them into a cloth which you can wind around your waist, under your clothes."

"That's what I was going to do with the gold coins."

"An excellent idea, but diamonds will give you more value for much less weight, and small, loose diamonds are not difficult to sell. I can give you the names of reputable dealers in the cities you are likely to pass through."

"You are most obliging, sir," Cordelia said gratefully. "But you say to change half for diamonds. What of the rest?"

Aaron spread his hands, indicating the shimmering gems laid before him. "This is worth a great deal. I cannot tell you how much without further examination." He turned to Ibrahim. "You had best put everything back in the basket for the present, lest anyone come in. Meess, I can only say I would not carry so much with me for fear of losing all. The world is full of accidents and thieves."

"What should I do?"

"If you wish, I can arrange for my relatives in England to provide you with funds to the value of half your goods. I will give you a letter of credit, and also notify them by other means so that losing the letter would not be a great disaster to you. Otherwise, I advise you to entrust the funds to the English Ambassador here in Istanbul, to be sent to England with the next returning diplomat on a vessel of the English navy."

Cordelia clasped her hands beneath her chin, closed her eyes, and thought hard. No doubt a Royal Navy ship was safer than most means of travel. No doubt the British Ambassador was an honest man. But he had been extremely rude when Lady Courtenay went to report their arrival in Istanbul. He might agree to take charge of her money yet not trouble to keep her departure secret. She didn't want to ask him, to have to explain Mehmed Pasha's plans for her future.

Aaron had not required an explanation. She had already decided to entrust the jewellery to him, and she would have to trust him to give her fair value, so she might as well trust him for the rest.

"Please," she said, "I leave it all in your hands."

"You honour me, meess." Rising, he bowed to her before fetching his writing materials from the shelf. "The first thing is to make two lists, one for me and one for you."

"I can't read Arabic writing," Cordelia confessed.

"In this country, few females can read at all. I do not know the English words, so I shall write the Turkish words in English characters as best I can."

He beckoned Ibrahim over to the chest in the corner, and turned a heavy key in the iron lock. One by one, as he listed them, the pieces were transferred from the basket to the chest: Count Szambrowczyk's topazes, the Margrave's diamonds, the Conte's pearls and opals, the Pasha's amethysts, one lover's rubies and another's emeralds. Each disappearance into the depths of the plain wooden box seemed to Cordelia to loosen the chains of her mother's past from about her heart.

At last the basket was empty. Ibrahim stolidly folded the cloths and stowed them away.

Giving Cordelia one list, Aaron said, "How soon must you leave, meess? It will take me several days, perhaps a week or more, to find the diamonds you need. Then you must sew, and it's no use to seek a ship before you are ready."

"Forty days," Cordelia whispered. "Forty days from yesterday."

It had sounded like plenty of time when Mehmed Pasha announced his intentions. Now it seemed all too short.

One more day. At dawn the day after tomorrow, the Greek ship Aaron had found would leave its berth in the Golden Horn and set sail across the Sea of Marmara towards freedom.

From the street below came the night-watchman's raucous

cry. Cordelia lay tossing and turning in the dark. Tomorrow night she and Ibrahim would sneak out of the house and down to the quay where Captain Vasiliadis expected them.

Everything was ready. Aisha, wide-eyed, had helped her sew the diamonds into a long strip of linen. Amina, at last let into the secret, had already packed the clothes she was taking into a bundle Ibrahim could carry. The rest she would leave for the two maids, along with enough money for dowries—Aaron had promised to take them into his house until he could find them either husbands or positions in comfortable households.

One more day. She'd never be able to sleep tonight, she was sure. Yet as the watchman's cry faded into the distance, she began to drowse off.

Then suddenly she was wide awake again. Someone was in her room. By the pale moonlight which now filtered through the carved screen, she saw a dark figure crossing the carpet towards her with slow, stealthy steps.

Starting to sit up, she took a breath to shout for help. The figure pounced. A hard hand clapped across her mouth.

"Hush, don't scream," hissed an English voice.

# Three

Flat on her back, petrified, Cordelia stared up into a veiled face. The eyes above the yashmak stared down. A woman? A Turkish woman who spoke English? An Englishwoman in Turkish clothes? But the hand crushing her lips had a masculine strength, the voice when it came again, though hushed, had a masculine timbre.

"Don't scream. Promise and I'll let go." The pressure eased fractionally.

She nodded. The hand was lifted and the intruder kneeling beside her low bed sat back on his—or her—heels.

"I wasn't going to scream," Cordelia whispered indignantly. "I was going to call for help. If I were the sort of female who screams I daresay I'd have swooned by now."

"I beg your pardon." The voice, now with an odious laugh in it, was definitely a man's. An Englishman's. It reminded her of her mother's first lover. To Cordelia he had always been kindly but remote. He had not reckoned on the girl he loved bringing her baby with her when she deserted her husband for his sake.

Drusilla Courtenay had not reckoned on losing him so soon. They had promised each other to live happily forever after, she told her little daughter, but after only six years, in a small town in Germany, he took a fever and died. Cordelia could scarcely remember him, confusing him with those who had followed until this Englishman's voice resurrected his image.

"I should have known from what Aaron told me that you aren't the screaming, swooning sort," he went on.

"Aaron?" Horrified, she sat up, hugging the quilt about her. "Who are you? How did you get in?"

"Climbed the wall into your courtyard."

"Why? What are you doing in my bedchamber? Leave at once!"

"Hush! I can't leave, I must talk to you."

"Downstairs."

"Your servant is sleeping in the room downstairs."

"I won't talk to a man in my bedchamber. I don't know why I should talk to you at all." Except that she was dying of curiosity. "I'd trust Ibrahim with my life."

"But can I trust him with mine?"

"If Aaron told you about me, you must be aware I can't afford a fuss with the authorities. Ibrahim knows it, too."

The man heaved a weary sigh. "Very well." In one lithe movement he rose, then stumbled as one foot caught in the hem of his robe. Recovering his balance, he ripped the shawl and yashmak from his head. "To the devil with these draperies! Come on, then."

"You go down. I have to dress," said Cordelia primly, clutching the quilt beneath her chin.

"I'll wait on the stairs." He was laughing at her again, the brute! Yet much as it annoyed her, for some reason his amusement made her feel quite safe with him. He went on, "I don't want to be down there without your protection if your Ibrahim wakes."

Silently he slipped from the room. Flinging back the quilt, she fumbled with the tinder-box and lit a lamp. She hurriedly pulled on her shift and caftan, but as the stranger was an Englishman she didn't bother with the loose trousers underneath. Lamp in hand, she went after him.

He sat half way down the stairs, his head rested against the bannister. His black hair was short, raggedly cropped. From above he no longer looked large and menacing, just unspeakably tired. His eyes must have been closed, for the light of the lamp didn't make him stir.

"Sir . . ."

Springing to his feet, he whipped round, his right hand flying to his girdle as if in search of a weapon.

"Oh!" His shoulders slumped and he passed his hand across his thin, fair-stubbled face. "I'm sorry, I forgot where I was. I was half asleep, I think." Standing aside, he bowed ironically. "Pray precede me, Miss Courtenay. Allow me to carry that lamp for you."

The light roused Ibrahim. Sitting up on his mat on the floor, he rubbed his eyes, then gaped at the peculiar figure behind his young mistress. He looked at Cordelia in dismay, obviously convinced she was following in her mother's footsteps—and no doubt wondering why she should choose a lover who dressed in homespun women's clothes when she had rejected the rich, influential pasha.

She hastened to disabuse him of this unthinkable notion. "This *English*man has *just* arrived and wishes to speak to me," she said sharply. The English had an occasionally useful reputation for eccentricity. "You will stay with us."

"Yes, *Bayan.*" He stood up, and bowed, then stayed standing against the wall, arms folded across his chest, hands hidden in his sleeves in the approved fashion.

"I wish you hadn't told him I'm English," said the stranger. "Still, no use crying over spilt milk. Do you mind if we sit? I'm a trifle fagged."

Cordelia waved him to the divan, but he did not seat himself until she subsided cross-legged onto the cushions Ibrahim hurried to pile for her. Despite his outrageous dress, still more outrageous behaviour, and unshaven chin, the Englishman apparently had gentlemanly manners. She studied him as he lounged back against the pillows, very much at his ease.

He was not particularly tall, though taller than Ibrahim. As far as she could tell, given his billowing female garment, his build was lean, his strength wiry rather than brawny. His face was thin, the sun-bronzed features regular, unremarkable, the bristling chin square and determined. It was odd that the sprouting beard was fair when his hair was so very dark, as were his eyebrows. His eyes looked black by the light of the single lamp, but she thought, from the quick glance she had given him as she passed on the stair, that they were dark blue.

She realized he was studying her, too, a slight smile on his face. "Neat ankles," he observed. "Neat as a new pin."

Belatedly, she became aware that her caftan was by no means long enough to cover her legs decently. Fiery-cheeked, she reached for the nearest cushion to hide her feet. "Ibrahim, fetch my shawl from my room," she ordered in Turkish. Glaring at the stranger, she continued in English, "You are no gentleman to notice. Who are you? What do you want?"

The smile became a grin. "I'd not have mentioned it," he said, "had they been thick. My name is James Preston. As to what I am, let us say a traveller in a foreign land. I can claim acquaintance with Lord Byron, if that is any recommendation."

Far from it. Lord Byron's besmirched reputation had not been enhanced by his recent sojourn in Istanbul. "And your jeweller is a relative of mine."

"Aaron!"

"My mother was Jewish, my father English. Since the Jews are matrilineal, they regard me as one of themselves, while to the English it is the paternal lineage which counts. So I belong to both tribes, a happy result, you must agree. And as for what I want: Uncle Aaron—I call him thus though he is more of a distant cousin—tells me you are leaving Istanbul tomorrow morning. I want to go with you."

Wordless, she took the shawl Ibrahim presented to her, but she was too stunned to remember what she had requested it for. "To go with me?" she said blankly.

"I also wish to leave Istanbul," he explained, as patient as if he addressed a halfwit, "as soon as possible. It seems to me I might be of assistance to you on the journey."

"You have come to offer your services? I don't believe it, Mr. Preston. Besides, I shall have Ibrahim to help me."

"Well, not exactly." His ingenuous tone instantly put Cordelia on her guard. "The fact is, I need your help more than you need mine. You see, if you cannot afford a fuss with the authorities, still less can I. They are after me, and I'm not likely to survive a meeting."

"What do you mean?"

"You must have seen what happens to those who run afoul of the law here in Turkey."

She had, from a crippling beating on the feet, to the loss of a hand, to death by stoning, or sentencing to the galleys, perhaps worse than death. But if that was what he feared, he was a criminal, scarcely a fit travelling companion.

Yet, looking at him, she knew she could not abandon him to such a fate. "I cannot see how going with me will help you," she said crossly.

"In the Moslem world, a woman cannot travel alone."

"That's why I'm taking Ibrahim." Only as far as Athens, she reminded herself uneasily. "But you're not a woman."

"They are looking for a man travelling alone. As your servant, I'd not be noticed."

"A woman with a manservant would most certainly be noticed!"

James Preston sighed heavily. "I know," he said with a wry glance at Ibrahim, "I shall just have to steel myself and pretend I'm a eunuch."

"You don't look or sound in the least like a eunuch."

"Thank you, you relieve my mind. Nor do I feel like one." As he rasped his hand across his chin, his dark, considering gaze made Cordelia bridle at the *double entendre.* His lips twitched. "Don't you think if I were smoothly shaved I might pass? My beard is very light in colour."

"They tend to be portly. We'll have to pad . . . I mean, you would have to wear padding, and pad out your cheeks as well."

"Thank you, Miss Courtenay." His eyelids drooped, his body relaxed, and suddenly he was asleep.

"Well, really!" Cordelia stood up and looked down at him. "We can't leave him here," she said in Turkish. "I must explain to Amina and Aisha before they see him. He'll have to sleep in Mama's room. Wake him, Ibrahim."

Half awake, he stumbled up the stairs behind her, Ibrahim bringing up the rear with a second lamp. She opened the door to her mother's room.

Preston paused on the threshold, glancing around the room, bleary-eyed. " 'So this is the love nest," he mumbled.

"Good night," said Cordelia frostily. To explain her plight, Aaron must have disclosed what he knew of Lady Courtenay, but she wished he had not. "Ibrahim, you will sleep in the passage."

"Yes, *Bayan,"* said the eunuch, much relieved.

Somewhat to her surprise, Cordelia sank into sleep as her head touched her pillow. Her last wispy thought was that there was something infinitely, if inexplicably comforting about having an Englishman to travel with, however much of a rogue.

Her first thought on waking to the muezzin's cry was that there was a strange man in the house and she must have been moonstruck to let him stay. Had she really agreed to let Preston travel as her servant? Not in so many words, she decided, but she had implied consent, and he had certainly taken it as such. If she now changed her mind and refused, he might complain to his Uncle Aaron, who had it in his power to ruin her.

Aaron! Cordelia sat bolt upright. Aaron knew all about the wealth she'd be carrying on her. She trusted him, but suppose he, trusting his relative, had mentioned the diamonds. Perhaps James Preston's tale of fleeing the authorities was nothing more than a ploy to gain her sympathy so as to rob her later.

Yet if he was not in trouble with the law, she had no reason to believe him to be a criminal. And surely if he had been deliberately playing on her sympathies he'd not have made those indelicate remarks about her ankles and the "love-nest" and not feeling like a eunuch.

Unless he thought her as immoral as her mother.

"Oh *drat!*" said Cordelia. She would have to make sure he understood his mistake.

Not that she cared a farthing for the opinion of a ne'er-do-well wastrel, but one way or another she seemed to have decided to take him with her. If she left him to be crippled or beheaded or whatever the ghastly penalty was for whatever crime he had committed, the horror would haunt her forever.

*"Inshallah,"* she murmured with a sigh. "As God wills."

She washed and dressed and went out into the passage. Ibrahim was still there, sitting cross-legged on his bed-mat. He beamed as he saw her, saying as he rose, "I have guarded the *Bayan* through the night. The Englishman is still asleep."

"Thank you, Ibrahim. Come down, now, and I shall explain to you and the girls."

Amina was in a great fuss because Ibrahim had not lit the charcoal fire to heat the water for the *Bayan*'s tea. "The last breakfast I shall make for the *Bayan,"* she cried, "and there is no tea prepared!"

"Cease your foolishness," he said grandly. "I had more important matters to attend to."

"What can be more important than the *Bayan*'s breakfast?"

Cordelia soothed her. "Ibrahim shall step out to find a yoghurt-seller and buy some *laban* for my breakfast," she said. "I can wait for my tea. Our guest will want some, I expect."

"A guest!" Amina gaped, and Aisha stopped on her way up the stairs. Ibrahim looked still more important. "What guest, *Bayan?"* Amina demanded.

"Aisha, come back, please. I must talk to all of you. An English gentleman arrived late last night."

The eunuch nodded smugly. "He sleeps still, in the Lady's room."

"He is returning to England," Cordelia went on, "and he will go with me."

"And I shall go to make sure all is proper," said Ibrahim.

Cordelia's thoughts raced. Only the rich had a eunuch slave or servant, only the very rich more than one. To appear on board the Greek ship with two in her train was bound to lead to gossip which might set Mehmed Pasha on her trail.

"No," she said gently. Ibrahim's face fell. "It was generous of you to agree to go with me, when I know you had much rather not. Now I don't need to ask it of you. You shall have the same money I promised you, enough to set you up in business as a barber, as you wish. The Englishman will escort me safely all the way to England." She could only hope it was true.

"To travel alone with a man who is not a relative!" said Amina, scandalized. Aisha and Ibrahim looked equally shocked.

Although they had been loyal to her mother in spite of her shameful behaviour, Cordelia realized, they had thought better of her. "These matters are regarded differently among the English," she said hastily. "Everything will be perfectly proper. Besides, he will travel as my servant, as a eunuch, in fact. We must try to make him look like Ibrahim."

Ibrahim was obviously pleased at the notion of the English gentleman pretending to be him. Aisha was dubious, still dismayed, but Amina at once started planning the transformation. All was in readiness by the time Mr. Preston came down.

Cordelia and Ibrahim had just come in from the market. She thought it best not to change her routine today, and in any case they had to eat—and feed the uninvited guest. Amina, who was a good cook, wanted to make *kadin budu,* a special delicacy, as a farewell dinner, but Cordelia considered the name—meaning "lady's thighs"—far too indelicate. Instead, she had bought lamb, onions, fresh mint, a lemon, and a large purple aubergine for her favourite stew. Lentils, pepper, turmeric, cinnamon, nutmeg, and garlic were all to be found in the store-cupboard.

As Ibrahim handed over the basket to Amina, and Cordelia unwound the shawl from her head, James Preston descended the stairs. There was a spring in his step, last night's fatigue forgotten.

His vigour, unmistakably masculine despite the female dress, alarmed her anew. How she wished she had not agreed to let him stay!

# Four

James paused near the bottom of the stairs as four pairs of eyes turned to stare at him. The two maids, caught without their veils, squealed and fled. His gaze fixed on Miss Courtenay.

By daylight she appeared younger than he had supposed, twenty perhaps, not more than two-and-twenty. The close-fitting bodice of her blue kaftan moulded a generous figure—on the plump side if one were not feeling generous. She had fine eyes, brown, with long lashes darker than the lustrous fair hair pulled back in a thick plait. Her face was too round for beauty, though she might be pretty if she ever smiled. As it was, the uncompromising set of her lips put him on his mettle. Admittedly he had rather thrust himself upon the poor girl, but she didn't have to regard him as if he were a particularly revolting cockroach.

Wishing he was decently clad in proper English breeches, he descended the last step and bowed. *"Selaam aleykum,"* he said, "peace be upon you."

*"Aleykum selaam,"* she responded, "but non-believers are not meant to use that greeting."

"Good morning, then, Miss Courtenay. I have been used this while to pass as a Turk, or at least, since my command of Turkish is far from perfect, as a good Moslem citizen of the Ottoman Empire."

"Why?"

"One can come to know the people," he said airily, "which makes travel much more interesting. May I beg a crust of bread to break my fast? I confess I am sharp-set, though Uncle Aaron fed me well last night." It had been the first decent meal he'd eaten in a week on the run.

She clapped her hands. The two little maidservants scurried in, properly veiled now and wide-eyed above their veils.

"Bring breakfast for the Englishman," Miss Courtenay ordered. Her Turkish accent was good, better than his. "Will you take tea or coffee, sir?"

"Tea, please. Turkish coffee is more like a sweetmeat."

"Amina knows how to make it in the Viennese style. My mother prefers . . . preferred it that way."

"Then coffee, by all means. Allow me to express my condolences on your recent loss, ma'am. A street accident, I understand. It must have been a terrible shock."

"Did Aaron tell you what happened?" she asked, giving him a suspicious look.

Curiosity aroused, he said on a questioning tone, "No, not the details."

Her mouth tightened and she turned to the maid. "Viennese coffee for the gentleman, Amina."

She drank tea and nibbled on a piece of Turkish delight while he consumed a substantial breakfast. Since she obviously, and naturally, did not wish to describe her mother's accident, he tried the subject of Vienna, but on this too she refused to be drawn. All she would say was that she and her mother had lived there for several years. His curiosity now running rampant, he wondered just what had brought the late Lady Courtenay from Austria to Istanbul as the mistress of a high official of the Ottoman Empire.

He found it difficult to believe the girl did not take after her mother. However, all he had seen of her so far went to confirm what Aaron had told him: though not innocent in the sense of ignorant, Cordelia Courtenay was uncorrupted. In fact she was as prim and prudish as any well-bred young miss newly emancipated from schoolroom to ballroom.

What was more, to judge by the way she looked down her

nose at him, she strongly disapproved of the tatterdemalion James Preston, Esquire.

"Have you changed your mind about taking me with you?"

"I never consented. However," she went on grudgingly, "I don't want your death upon my conscience. If you promise to behave with propriety, you may travel as my servant."

"I've no intention of robbing or ravishing you," he assured her, biting back a grin as she pursed her lips. "And I'll try to watch my tongue. I've been away from decent society for rather a long time, I fear."

She gave a long-suffering sigh. "Very well, then. Everything is prepared to make you look the part." She indicated a bundle in a corner. "Ibrahim will help you dress and shave. Aisha, the hot water, please."

The eunuch picked up the bundle and one of the maids dashed out.

"No hurry," said James, reaching for the coffee-pot.

"Yes, there is," she said impatiently. "The clothes may have to be altered, or a different sort of padding devised. Please go up with him now."

He had to admit the practicality of her concern, but he could not resist teasing her. "No need to go upstairs. I'll change here."

Drawing herself up, she said in an icy voice, "I fail to see why the maids and I should be forced to leave the room for your convenience. Thank you, Aisha, give the jug to Ibrahim."

Meekly James preceded the eunuch up the stairs to the luxurious bedchamber where the pasha had once disported himself with his English mistress.

The bundle contained clothing suitable for a male slave or servant, strips of quilted cloth of various lengths and widths, and a razor with a gleaming blade of Sheffield steel. This last a grim-faced Ibrahim proceeded to strop vigorously on a leather strap.

"I'll shave myself," James said firmly.

"I am an excellent barber. Even Mehmed Pasha says so. This is his razor."

"I prefer to use it on myself." He started to lather his chin at the wash-basin.

The eunuch bowed. "As you will, *Bay*." Handing over the well-honed instrument, he waited till James had set the sharp steel to his skin, then continued, "But if you harm a hair of the *Bayan*'s head, be sure I shall find out and come after you with such a blade, even to England if God permits."

With an effort of will, James contrived not to nick his cheek. He could not take the threat seriously, but the fervour with which it was pronounced impressed him. However priggish, Miss Courtenay had won the servant's devotion. He recalled Aaron telling him of the arrangements she had made for the two maids' welfare.

"Your mistress will be safer with me than without me, I expect," he said soothingly.

He shaved with extreme thoroughness, and then felt his chin. Not quite satin-smooth, but as he turned his head before the mirror he saw no sign of beard. The trouble was, he must keep it that way for several days.

"I'll have to pinch the pasha's razor," he mused aloud in English.

*"Bay?"*

"I shall need to take this razor with me," James said in Turkish.

"No! The *Bayan* has given it to me. It is a most superior blade and—*inshallah*—I am going to set up as a barber."

"You'll be better off without it. Suppose the pasha caught you with it? You'd be taken as a thief."

"It is true." Ibrahim was woefully dismayed. "My thanks, *Bay*. But how shall I find another such?"

"I'll give you a letter to my uncle, Aaron the Jeweller. He will help you. Now, let us see about the clothes. They are yours?"

"Yes, *Bay*. The *Bayan* will give me money for more."

With relief, James doffed his female garments. Ibrahim, quivering with ill-suppressed laughter, helped him pad his lean frame with strips of quilt, stabbing him with pins several times in the process. In no good humour, James climbed into trousers, shirt, and dolman, and tied the sash around his expanded waist.

The wide trousers, calf-length on the eunuch, reached only to the knee, but many men wore them thus. The too-short sleeves were more of a problem. Otherwise, regarding himself in the glass, he was quite satisfied, until he glanced at his face. Smooth enough, it was far too thin, in startling contrast to his now pudgy figure. He puffed out his cheeks.

*"Bay."* Ibrahim held out a small bowl. "To fill out the face."

Dried apricots! James tucked a couple behind his teeth on either side. The vision in the mirror of himself stuffing his cheeks like a squirrel struck him as exquisitely funny. He burst out laughing, only to half-choke on one of the apricots. Coughing and spluttering, he warded off Ibrahim's efforts to thump him on the back.

Miss Courtenay's anxious voice came from below. "What's the matter?"

"Nothing." Speech was not easy, either. "Just a little trouble with apricots. They'll work very well as long as I speak softly and remember not to laugh."

"Our situation will hardly be conducive to laughter. Are you ready?"

"Just the turban."

A few minutes later he waddled down the stairs. At the sight of him, Miss Courtenay was herself surprised into laughter. As he had surmised, she was really quite pretty when she forgot to look disapproving. He grinned.

Or tried to. "Dash it, I can't even smile properly . . ."

"Your voice is too deep."

". . . and I'll never be able to eat," he went on *falsetto.* "I think I shall be horribly seasick on board and have to stay in seclusion."

"If you claim seasickness, you will not be expected to want meals. We had best take a basket of supplies."

"Put in plenty of dried apricots. Will I pass?"

"Walk about a bit." She watched him critically, while the maids giggled. "Aisha will have to sew wider cuffs on your sleeves. And you are moving like a hobbled horse. Try taking smaller steps. Yes, that's better. Good enough for the Greek sailors, anyway, and we'll be going down to the quay at night."

"Most unwise," said James at once. "I've spent enough time in Istanbul to know women never go out after dark."

"No one will see."

"They will if we carry a torch, and if we're caught without one we'll be stopped, which is the last thing we want. No, we must reach the ship before nightfall."

"But if I'm seen, someone may tell Mehmed Pasha."

"I assume you're not planning to go unveiled? No one will know who you are."

She blushed and said crossly, "Your uncle says I don't walk like a Turkish woman."

"Aha, then what's sauce for the gander is sauce for the goose. If I can change my walk, so can you. Let me see."

Scarlet-cheeked, she crossed the room under his judicious gaze, then turned, glared at him, and demanded, "Well?"

"You move far too purposefully. Aisha, Amina, show your mistress how you walk. There, you see, they take three or four tiny steps to your one and it makes them seem to glide along. Try it."

"I don't need to try it, I can see what to do," she snapped. "If we are to leave at twilight, you had best go and take off that shirt at once so that Aisha can alter the sleeves."

"All right, but I hope you will practise." He gave the exasperating young woman an austere look. "Just remember this, Miss Courtenay. If something goes wrong, you may lose your virtue, but I shall lose my life."

# Five

Cordelia and her vexatious escort set out for the harbour just after the sunset prayer, leaving the house by the back door into a little used alley. She wore a proper yashmak instead of her usual shawl, and she pattered along with the smallest steps she could take without falling over. It was very tiring.

James Preston carried the bulky bundle containing her clothes, as well as the napkin-covered basket of food. He had been most sympathetic with her despondency over abandoning most of her books. She was quite in charity with him, until he complained at being nonetheless overladen.

"A hired porter might tell tales," she pointed out.

"You could take the basket."

"It would draw attention," Cordelia said stiffly. "A wealthy lady with a eunuch slave never carries a burden."

"Nor does an English gentleman."

"You are not a gentleman. You're a criminal fleeing the law."

The anger in his face made her quail internally, but he dropped a properly subservient pace behind and said no more. Glancing back, she realized that the awkward way he carried the unaccustomed load was quite likely to draw unwelcome attention anyway, but she was not about to back down. In any case, few people were about and they in a hurry to get home. The authorities discouraged movement in the streets after dark.

Descending the street towards the Golden Horn, Cordelia saw that the harbour was likewise tranquil. A forest of tall masts showed where the Turkish fleet was moored. The smaller ships were merchantmen from the Black Sea, the Aegean, and the Mediterranean. Then there were the local craft, clumsy barges and swift, light caiques. These plied the Golden Horn, the Bosporus, the shores of the Sea of Marmara, linking the European and Asian quarters of the great city. A few of the caiques were still out on the choppy waters, their oarsmen hastening homeward with belated passengers.

If Captain Vasiliadis had not drawn for Aaron a map of the quays with the *Amphitrite*'s berth marked, they would never have found it.

Under the stocky captain's vigilant eye, the last of a stack of sweet-smelling, resinous planks was being loaded as Cordelia and Preston arrived. A cargo of timber from Russia, he informed her in broken Turkish, ignoring her supposed servant.

"In Greece, not much forest left one thousand years, maybe two thousand." He shrugged expressive shoulders. "Much olive tree. My ship bring olive oil to Istanbul. I expect you later, *Kyria,* but is better now. Please, come aboard."

They followed him across the gangway as the day's last call to prayer sounded from countless minarets. A sailor handed him a pair of lanterns and he showed them to two tiny, adjacent cabins at the stern, beneath the poop deck.

*"Kyria,"* he said in a low voice, handing each of them a lantern, "my friend Aaron tell me you English, but my crew think you Turkish lady. So is best you stay like in hareem. Your servant will bring food, or what else you need, and poop deck is for only you use. Is good?"

"Yes, thank you, Captain," Cordelia agreed. If the crew discovered the truth, their gossip might endanger the captain, she realized as he went off to supervise the closing of the cargo hatch.

Then she recalled Preston's plan to feign seasickness as an excuse to keep to his cabin. He would not be able to fetch her meals. She turned to consult him, only to find he had deposited her bundle in her cabin and disappeared into his with the basket of food.

Angrily she knocked on the door. He opened it a slit and peered out.

"Oh, it's you. I've taken the apricots out of my cheeks—ate them, actually—so you'd better come in."

"Certainly not. You're not really a eunuch."

"My dear Miss Courtenay," he said with infuriating indulgence, "do stop imagining I have designs upon your virtue. Even if I wished to assault you, this padding would put paid to the notion, believe me. It's excessively wearisome and I want to take it off as soon as may be."

"Then I can't possibly come in. But you must not take it off yet. No one will believe you're seasick while we are tied up at the dock—and that's what I wanted to talk to you about." She explained Captain Vasiliadis's request for her not to mingle with the crew. "So you cannot stay in your cabin during the voyage."

"When I don't turn up, they'll soon notice something is wrong and come to find out. It won't hurt you to do without a meal or two," he added callously.

Cordelia felt tears fill her eyes. Biting her lip she turned away, suddenly very tired and frightened. For three weeks of plans and preparations, she had not allowed herself to dwell on the perils of the long journey ahead. Now she was utterly dependent on an unknown Greek sea-captain and an unkind English vagabond, the chances of reaching England safely seemed shockingly slight.

She went into her cabin, set down the lantern, and subsided onto the cushioned mattress which took up nearly half the floor. Burying her face in her hands, she huddled there, willing herself not to cry.

"Miss Courtenay." James Preston had come in without knocking, but she was too miserable to reprove him. "I'm sorry, that was unforgivably facetious of me."

"G-go away."

"Here, take this." He thrust a handkerchief into her hands.

"I d-don't need it. C-crying solves no diffic-culties."

"No, but it may relieve your feelings. We do have difficulties, don't we? We must put our heads together to solve them instead of sniping at each other. May I sit down?" Without waiting for permission, he lowered himself cautiously onto the mattress. "Dash it," he groaned, "sitting is even more awkward than walking with all this extra avoirdupois. I'm afraid I'm decidedly doubtful whether I can carry it off in broad daylight on the deck of a swaying ship."

Cordelia instinctively moved a little away from him, but she said, subdued, "We had best not risk it then."

"Never fear, I shan't let you starve. I'll fetch your dinner tonight and bring you something from the basket for the morning. I'm sure our good captain will come to speak to you by midday. If not I must just gird up my loins and stumble to the galley with a napkin held across my mouth, making the problem perfectly obvious."

She gave him a faint smile, unable to confess it was not the meals she cared about but his mockery. After all, he had already apologized.

"Cheer up," he said. "We shall contrive somehow. You have shown yourself remarkably courageous and pragmatic. Don't despair now. I'll be back shortly."

He hung up her lantern from a hook in the ceiling and went out.

Courageous and pragmatic? Cordelia sighed. At least he found something in her to approve, even if she was not the sort of female he admired. Which was, of course, precisely the situation to be hoped for. She did not want any man to desire her, let alone a good-for-nothing rogue like James Preston.

He returned with a tray. "Smells good," he said, setting out a jug, two tin cups, bread, and two bowls on the low table hinged to one wall. "Come and eat."

As Cordelia rose from the divan-bed, he took an armful of cushions and stacked them in two piles by the table.

"You can't eat here," she said.

"If anyone notices, which is unlikely, they'll just think I'm waiting on you."

"But . . ." She was too tired to argue about propriety. "Oh very well."

The bowls contained a delicious stew of fresh fish, carrots, and leeks cooked with olive oil, garlic, and lemon. Despite Preston's unwelcome presence, Cordelia enjoyed it until she recognized the fish as mullet. Reminded of her mother's accident, she pushed the bowl away.

"Not hungry after all?"

"I have had all I want, thank you."

"Then do you mind if I finish it? I'm still ravenous and I'm going to be on short commons for several days."

She watched as he tipped the remains from her bowl into his, scooping out the last drop of sauce with a piece of bread. Really, the man had no manners at all. How could she have taken him for a gentleman? He ate as if he were half-starved.

Catching her disgusted look, he grimaced. "Sorry. As I told you, I've been away from civilization for too long, and I'm not the sort to dress for dinner in a jungle clearing. I'll leave you in peace." He piled everything on the tray and departed with a terse "Good night."

Cordelia barred the door behind him, put out the lantern, and went to bed.

The cries of the muezzins woke James next morning. Devil take 'em, he'd never get used to the din. He could have done with another several hours of sleep.

Where the deuce was he? He blinked up at the low ceiling, felt the gentle up and down motion, and remembered. On board ship, Athens bound. Thank heaven, he would never again be wakened by the call to prayer.

Then he remembered his travelling companion and pulled a wry face. When Uncle Aaron told him about Miss Courtenay, she had sounded like . . . well, like the answer to a prayer. A young woman, the daughter of a lady of less than perfect morals, setting out alone on a journey of a thousand miles—not only could she provide the key to his escape, they might have a bit of fun together on the way. Uncle Aaron had helped her because he was sorry for her, but also because Lady Courtenay had been so friendly and amiable in his dealings with her. How could James have guessed the daughter would turn out to be a censorious, narrow-minded prude?

He had half a mind to attempt to seduce her, just to extinguish her holier-than-thou air.

From the near-dark outside came the slap of bare feet on the deck, the creak of ropes and the rattle of windlasses, mingling with the sailors' shouts and the screeching of seagulls. Captain Vasiliadis was as eager to depart as his passengers. James wondered how much Miss Courtenay had paid him to accept the risk of offending the pasha.

She had not said a word about his share of travelling expenses. He had borrowed money from Uncle Aaron, as little as he thought could get him to England if he were frugal, but he'd prefer to keep it for emergencies as long as she was willing to fund him. He'd pay her back when they reached home.

If she trusted him, on which he was not prepared to wager a China orange against all Lombard Street.

A China orange—he was hungry again. Sitting up, he delved into the basket. He had forgotten to take her anything from it last night, but missing breakfast would not hurt her, though he was truly sorry he had said so. As he ate, he wondered what she'd look like if she lost a bit of weight.

The *Amphitrite* slid away from the quay. Out into the choppy waters of the Golden Horn she sailed on the dawn breeze, down to the Bosporus, and out into the Sea of Marmara. She began to pitch and roll, not hard, almost playfully.

James did not feel like playing. In fact, he felt distinctly queasy. His stomach rediscovered what his mind had kindly concealed from him since last time: until his body adjusted he was going to be deucedly uncomfortable. For a day or two, he was not going to have to pretend to be seasick.

* * *

"Your servant is ill, *Kyria.*" The captain sounded unsuspicious. Cordelia had heard retching and a few groans next door and she was afraid Preston was rather overacting. "I have brought your breakfast," Captain Vasiliadis continued. "I'll set it down outside the door. When you are finished, just put the tray out, and . . . and anything else you wish to be rid of."

*"Thank* you, Captain." She had been wondering what on earth to do with the tin chamberpot, covered fortunately.

After eating her breakfast, she read for a while. She had brought her "new" poetry anthology, despite its tattered state, because its contents were still delightfully unfamiliar. Later, veiled, she sallied forth up the ladder onto the poop deck, glad to be wearing her Turkish trousers for the climb.

By then Istanbul was no more than a cloud on the horizon. A chapter in her life had closed—no, an entire volume. Surely the next volume must be an improvement. From now on she was no longer an appendage of a fallen woman, shamed by her mother's shameful behaviour. This journey was but the brief prologue to a new life as the respectable daughter of Sir Hamilton Courtenay, Baronet.

If only she did not miss Mama so much. If only James Preston were a real friend to whom she could talk, instead of an unrepentant villain, guilty of some nameless crime.

The day was too fine for vain regrets. The blue waters sparkled in the sun and seabirds wheeled and cried above as the *Amphitrite* forged westward, her sails billowing in the stiff breeze.

When she climbed back down to the main deck, Cordelia hesitated outside Preston's door as a particularly dolorous moan met her ear. It sounded most realistic, though unnecessary—maybe he had taken her footsteps for those of a sailor. She would have liked to talk to him, criminal or not. Would a genuine Turkish lady venture into her eunuch's quarters to enquire after his well-being?

Unlikely. Sighing, she went on to the confinement of her own cramped cabin.

By dawn the next morning the ship was approaching the Dardanelles. Cordelia went up on deck for a while, but as the straits narrowed the great fortifications on either side reminded her unpleasantly of the power of the enemies she and Preston were fleeing. Though Istanbul lay a hundred miles behind and more, they were still well within reach.

With a shiver, she returned to her cabin and her poetry. She was beginning to grow tired of her own company, as well as heartily tired of the fish stew which turned up yet again for luncheon. At least it had not been made with mullet after the first night.

Perhaps after dark she'd slip next door and beg a handful of dried apricots, except that the wretch was bound to laugh at her and make rude comments. He might even take advantage of her entering his cabin, whatever he said about his intentions. As Mama's experience had taught her, men only wanted one thing.

# Six

That evening they reached Cape Helles and emerged into the Aegean. Once on the open sea, the *Amphitrite* settled into a regular motion as she climbed and descended the waves. Cordelia went up for a last view of the Turkish mainland, fading away behind them in the east. Three islands added to the charm of the scene, a small one to the south and two larger, one to the north and one ahead, its hills silhouetted against the sunset.

Leaning back against the rail she watched the play of colours in the western sky. Rosy pink swiftly changed to burnt orange with streaks of pale yellow and green, and the first star appeared. Then, to her surprise and annoyance, James Preston joined her.

"You are supposed to be playing seasick," she reminded him sharply.

"I *am* seasick."

She regarded him more closely. Though smoothly shaven, otherwise he looked dreadful, pale and shaky, with dark circles under his eyes. His turban was wound crookedly around his black felt cap and his girdle was coming undone.

"Then what are you doing out here?"

"I should say I *was* seasick. Have you no compassion for my sufferings?"

"Yes, of course," said Cordelia, slightly abashed. "But it can't be so very bad."

"Ha! Have you never been seasick? Woman, you know not whereof you speak. For the past two days I've been praying for a quick death. However, my stomach seems to have settled a trifle at last, though I can't say I'm feeling in plump currant. I absolutely had to have some fresh air."

"Well, no one comes up here so I daresay you are safe enough for now. They will have seen you, though. They'll expect you to be up and about after this."

"Not after watching me stagger and stumble on the way up. I shall stagger and stumble back down to my cabin and no one will be surprised if I don't appear again. I must say, I feel better already."

"There is some colour in your cheeks. I—"

"Hush a minute." He gazed up at the lookout high above in the crow's nest on the mainmast, who was shouting something in Greek. Then he turned to stare back at the receding mouth of the Dardanelles. "Damnation, they're after us!"

"What? Who? I don't see anything."

"They are not visible from down here yet. The lookout says a naval vessel is signalling for us to heave to."

Cordelia peered up through the gathering dusk at the sailor on high with his spyglass. "How do you know?" she asked, hoping Preston was wrong.

"I speak Greek. Here comes our good captain, in high fidgets by the look of him."

Captain Vasiliadis's broad, swarthy face was agitated. *"Kyria,* alas, navy ship follows, orders we stop. For Greek to defy Turks is not good."

Her hands clenched, nails biting into the palms, Cordelia asked as calmly as she could, "Can you not outrun them?"

He spread his hands in a helpless gesture. "Impossible. Navy ships are fast, sail more close to wind."

"But it's nearly dark. Pretend you did not see their signal. Without a man with a glass up the mast, you would not have, would you? Surely at night we can evade them."

"Maybe." He shrugged. "But they know we go to Piraeus. They will sail ahead and wait."

Feeling helpless, she glanced at Preston. As he started to speak, an idea struck her and she interrupted. It was best for all concerned if Captain Vasiliadis continued to think him a eunuch servant. Time enough for him to intervene if the captain rejected her proposal.

"Suppose we don't sail straight towards Athens. Suppose you change course under cover of darkness and take us somewhere else. Then when they finally catch up with you, you can deny all knowledge of us."

"I don't know, *Kyria* . . ."

"Please," she begged. "They cannot possibly be certain we . . . I am aboard the *Amphitrite*. Of course, I will pay you for your lost time."

Rubbing his black-stubbled chin, he glanced up at the crow's nest then gazed back at the eastern horizon. No ships in sight. Already the last light was fading; the sky was indigo velvet spangled with stars; the *Amphitrite's* glimmering white wake frothed like lace against the black satin waters. He turned and stared to the north.

"Is possible," he said grudgingly. "We sail north between Lemnos and Imroz. Wind is good. Before daybreak we reach place for you go ashore. All right, *Kyria,* we try this, because infidel Turks are your enemies and enemies of all Greece."

Spitting over the rail, he swiftly crossed himself in the Orthodox fashion and hurried down to the main deck, shouting orders.

Slowly the stars above wheeled as the ship turned. Cordelia glanced back and saw the curving wake, faintly phosphorescent, marking their course. She touched Preston's sleeve.

"Look! They will see which way we went."

"We must hope it will fade before they reach this spot. They must be some distance behind. I wonder if it's your Nemesis or mine hot on our trail."

"Yours, I'm sure," she snapped, jerking her hand away from his sleeve, "since it's a naval vessel. Mehmed Pasha is a retired diplomat. I doubt he can call out the fleet, especially for so trivial a purpose."

"You don't regard yourself as a second Helen of Troy?" he drawled. As Cordelia stalked off towards the ladder to the lower deck, he called, "Wait! Once again I beg your pardon, Miss Courtenay. Do try to overlook my unfortunate levity, there's a good girl. It's more important than ever that we not come constantly to cuffs if we're to be stranded together on an unknown shore."

"It was the best plan I could think of." She heard her voice waver and made an effort to stiffen it. "I'm sorry it doesn't meet your approval, but you could have offered your own."

"It's a splendid plan, truly. My mind was a complete blank. All I could think of was to beg Vasiliadis for a good meal before I was shot at dawn."

Common sense won out over offended feelings. "You must eat, whether you're to be shot at dawn or not. You need to regain your strength before we are marooned." A horrid thought struck her. "Oh, Mr. Preston, the captain won't leave us on a desert island, will he?"

"I doubt it," he soothed her. "He'd have more to gain by stopping and turning us over to the Turks than by abandoning us in an uninhabited wasteland. Don't you think you might bring yourself to address me as James? In our situation, the formality of Mr. Preston has a displeasing ring to my ears."

"On the contrary," Cordelia retorted. An exchange of Christian names was the thin edge of the wedge. If she permitted the least laxity, the least hint of intimacy, he'd begin to think her as immodest as her mother. "To compensate for the impropriety of our situation, we ought to cling to every last possible vestige of formality. Pray excuse me, sir. I shall go to my cabin and pack up my clothes, since I hope to snatch a few hours sleep before we are put ashore."

"I only wish I had clothes to pack," said Preston ruefully.

"I expect when we reach land we can buy some clothes. Once we are in Greece it will be safer not to be dressed as Turks, do you not think?"

"Definitely! The sooner I can stop pretending to be a eunuch, the happier I'll be!"

As she descended the ladder, Cordelia attempted to analyse the words and tone of this last remark. Though she did not much care for either, she didn't believe him quite such a villain as to force her to his bed. Not that there was a great deal she could do about it, anyway. She had made her decision to allow him to travel with her, and now she had no choice but to abide by the consequences.

Once safe in the cabin with the door barred, she undressed down to the strip of linen fastened around her waist over her shift. This she unwound and, taking the little scissors she used for both sewing and her nails, she unpicked one of the little pockets she and Aisha had made.

The light of the swinging lantern made the tiny diamond sparkle as it lay in the palm of her hand. Its value was a lot to pay for Captain Vasiliadis's extra sailing time, but his risk had increased since the discovery that they were followed. Besides, a gem might be hard to dispose of in a village or small town. Better to save her ready cash for that. Perhaps she could persuade the captain to give her some Greek coins in change.

In fact, she had better try to drive a bargain. The Greek had treated her very well so far, but should he guess at the wealth she carried he might be tempted. How easily he and his crew could take possession of her diamonds and rid himself of the threat she and James . . . Mr. Preston posed in one fell swoop, by throwing them overboard.

She shuddered.

A knock on the door startled her. *"Kyria?"*

"Just a moment, Captain." She hurriedly dressed and opened the door. "Yes?"

*"Kyria,* you mention extra pay. I not like to ask, but I am poor man with wife and children, and to arrive late in Piraeus I lose money. Also, must help crew forget seeing you."

"I understand." She let him see the faceted stone twinkling in her hand. "I will give you this, which is worth much money, but I shall have to pay for passage to Athens on another ship, so I must ask for some drachmas in exchange."

"Of course, *Kyria."* He named a sum, which Cordelia promptly doubled. She had no idea how much a drachma was worth, but after two years in the Levant she knew a good deal about bargaining.

While they haggled amicably, Preston approached across the deck with a tray in his hands. He headed towards her cabin, so she stepped aside to let him pass.

Reaching an agreement with Captain Vasiliadis which left him satisfied but not gloating, she handed over the diamond and accepted the coins he took from a leather pouch hanging at his belt. With mutual good wishes they parted and she retired into her cabin, turning as she closed the door.

"You drive a hard bargain, Miss Courtenay." Preston rose from his pile of cushions at the table.

"What are you doing here? I thought you had gone on to your own room! What will the captain think?"

"That I am your eunuch. Just a few hours more. Do come and eat. I have contrived to remember my manners and restrain my appetite despite the heavenly smell of this fish stew."

"Fish stew again! I am heartily sick of the stuff. You may take my portion with my good will. I don't suppose there are any apricots left in the basket?"

"Haven't touched 'em, apart from the couple I put in my cheeks just now before I went to the galley. Here." From the breast of his robe, the Turkish substitute for pockets, he drew out a handkerchief which he spread open on the table. "I brought them for our dessert, and figs and hazelnuts too."

"Oh, good."

After that Cordelia could hardly be so churlish as to insist on his removing himself. While he silently and steadily ate his way through two bowls of fish stew and most of the bread, she nibbled on the dried fruit and nuts. She found she had little appetite.

Having escaped Turkey, she had expected to reach Athens in three or four days and then to be comparatively safe under the protection of the British Consul. Instead she was to be stranded on an unknown shore with a man she mistrusted, utterly at the mercy of strangers whose language she did not speak.

"I wonder how anyone found out we boarded the *Amphitrite*," she said unhappily. "I hope Ibrahim and the girls are safe."

"I expect so. You are probably right, the Turkish ship is after me, not you. I'll tell you what, we shall have Vasiliadis put me off and you stay aboard, go on to Piraeus. I'm used to fending for myself and you'll be better off without me."

She desperately wanted to agree, but the words stuck in her throat. Somehow she had come to depend on his presence, on having someone to talk to in English, on the link he represented between her past and her future. Boldly as she had planned to set out alone, the prospect of going on without a companion appalled her.

At least he spoke Greek, she reminded herself. What she said was, "I'd hate to disembark in Piraeus and walk straight into Mehmed Pasha's arms. He may be on board the ship, even if he didn't order it to follow us."

"I ought never to have embroiled you in my affairs," Preston said remorsefully. "I was at my wits' end when Uncle Aaron suggested it, but I should have known I'd be more of a hindrance than a help."

"I cannot blame you for all my troubles." Cordelia's simmering resentment came to a sudden boil. "It's my mother's fault. If she had no concern for her own reputation, she might at least have considered how it would ruin my life. Oh, how I wish she had left me behind!"

Preston looked dismayed. For a moment he was silent, then he said gravely, "You have had an exceedingly tiring time of it, and I'm afraid tomorrow is not likely to be any easier. Try to get some sleep."

He piled the empty dishes on the tray and departed. Barring the door behind him, Cordelia was filled with relief that he had not asked any questions about her outburst. Obviously he was aware of Mama's relationship with Mehmed Pasha but the last thing she wanted was enquiries into the past. Then she wondered whether he already knew all there was to know about the notorious Lady Courtenay. How much had her mother told Aaron about her history, and how much had the jeweller passed on to his young relative?

Too tired to care, she washed her face and hands and was asleep within minutes.

*"Kyria?"*

Cordelia struggled up through layers of sleep, certain she had only just laid down her head. "Captain? It's still dark!"

"Please, *Kyria,* best to go ashore in dark, so no one see my *Amphitrite.*"

She groaned as memory flooded back. "Yes, Captain. I shall get up at once. Give me ten minutes."

"Is good, *Kyria.* In fifteen minutes, boat ready."

So quarter of an hour later, in the chill of darkness before dawn, Cordelia scrambled down a rope ladder into a little row-boat. Once again she was glad of the Turkish trousers. Preston, gone before, steadied her as she reached the bottom and helped her to a bench.

For a moment the dinghy rose and fell alongside the *Amphitrite*, then, at a murmured order from above, the sailors in the stern and bow let go the ropes. With boathooks they pushed out from the wooden wall. They took their seats beside the other two, unshipped their oars, and pulled away.

The land they were heading for was no more than a black bulk against the still starry sky. It seemed to grow larger rather than nearer, but suddenly the keel grated amid a lacy froth. The sailors jumped out and pulled the boat up onto a beach.

*"Kyria."* With silent courtesy, one of the men handed Cordelia out. Preston followed with the bundle and the basket.

A sailor said something and pointed to his left. Then they all piled back into the dinghy and a moment later it was no more than a shadow on the water, growing smaller and smaller until it disappeared.

Away to the east, over Turkey, the sky began to pale.

Cordelia shivered. "What did he say?"

"Just what Vasiliadis told us, there's a village not far off, just beyond that headland."

Turning her head to follow his gesture, she gasped at the sight of a featureless rocky mass towering above them, its end cut off in a vertiginous fall to the sea. She swung round. The landward side of the cove was even higher, the eastern end perhaps a little lower. A hundred feet, two hundred, three, it hardly mattered. Unless they sprouted wings or fins, it was an impassable barrier.

# Seven

"Not far in a sailor's terms," James Preston said wryly. "Hop in a boat and row for a few minutes. Can you swim?"

"A little." Cordelia blessed the Conte di Arventino, who had let her learn. "Not well enough to swim right round that headland. Will the tide go down?"

"Not much. The Mediterranean, including the Aegean, has very little tidal rise and fall."

"At least it won't come up, then, and trap us against the cliffs," she said, trying to sound matter-of-fact. "What shall we do?"

"I know the first thing I shall do now I'm no longer a eunuch." With a grin he started to untie his girdle.

"W-what?" She backed away.

"Get rid of all this damn . . . dashed padding."

Cordelia turned her back. "I meant what shall we do about escaping from this horrible place."

"Don't despair. It's always possible a fishing boat may pass close enough to hear us call. At worst, I can try to swim for it and bring back help. But we won't try any desperate measures until we have had a look at the cliffs in broad daylight."

"You really think we might climb up?"

"I'm not making any promises, but in my youth I used to climb the cliffs in Cornwall for fun. Though they often looked impossible until one studied them closely, there was usually a way up."

"For fun!" Startled, she turned. Fortunately he was just retying his girdle, strips of cloth strewn around him on the beach.

"Regarded with the right attitude," he said, "many unlikely occupations can be enjoyable."

"Yes, it's true. I have always enjoyed marketing, which Mama considered an abominable chore. I shall endeavour to enjoy the climb if we decide to do it."

"Good girl! In the meantime, let's find shelter from this breeze, which feels as if it comes straight from the North Pole. I have breakfast in the basket."

"Thank heaven. I was beginning to think most uncharitable thoughts about Captain Vasiliadis rushing us off without a bite to eat."

Preston laughed. He picked up the bundle, she took the basket, and they found a spot in the lee of a big rock which was perfectly shaped to lean against if they sat on the sand. They had a good view of the sea, in case a boat should happen by.

Before she sat down, Cordelia took off her veil. "No more need for this," she said, half glad, half regretful.

"Wait, don't throw it away. We are still in Turkish country and sometime it may be convenient to hide behind it again." As he spoke he unwound his turban. "I shall keep this. The tarboosh is sufficiently like the cap some Greeks wear to pass, I hope. I shan't wear it to climb, though. It will only fall off."

"You still look rather Turkish. Tuck up the skirts of your robe into your girdle so that it looks more like a long shirt. That is better, but I hope we can buy new clothes in the village. If we ever get there."

"Don't think about that now. Look at that sky!"

As they ate, the eastern sky changed from green, to primrose, to gold, while above delicate pink puffs of cloud scurried before the breeze. Small crabs as pink and delicate as the clouds scurried about their feet, scavenging crumbs, until a gull landed nearby and frightened them off. The grey and white bird, head cocked, fixed Cordelia and Preston with an enquiring, hopeful eye and squawked.

"It's saying please," said Cordelia, and Preston threw it a crust.

"No more," she advised quickly, laying her hand on his wrist. "We may want the scraps ourselves before we reach civilization."

He nodded and touched her hand. She instantly withdrew it, her cheeks burning. It was all too easy to treat him just as a friend—the first real friend she had ever had—and to forget that he was also a man.

"It's light enough now to study the cliffs," she said, head bowed over the basket as she packed up the remains of their meal.

The gull flapped away with another squawk, indignant this time, as they stood up. They went around their rock and stared up at the cliff, now illuminated by the first rays of the sun. It no longer seemed a sheer wall. Instead it was a bewildering patchwork of sunlit rock and shadow, grey upon black upon grey, blotched, streaked, impossible to interpret. Here and there a small, wizened tree or a tuft of straw-coloured grass clung to a ledge.

Cordelia glanced at Preston. He stood very still, his eyes alive in his thin face, darting back and forth across the face of the cliff. Then he gave a sudden, decisive nod.

"We can do it. Whether we can manage the basket and your bundle I don't know. Have you any valuables stowed away?"

"No." Her hand went to her throat, where the pearls hung under her kaftan.

He grinned. "You carry your wealth around your neck? Good. We shall see how far we get encumbered but I don't want any nonsense about risking your life to save your clothes, or even your books. That shawl is going to be in your way. Have you a kerchief you can wear over your head?"

"Yes. Do you really think we can climb all the way to the top? I cannot see how."

"I'm pretty sure it's possible. The difficulty is always that once one starts one can no longer see the way. I'll study it some more while you kilt up your kaftan as you made me do. What a pity you're wearing those Turkish trousers."

Glaring at his oblivious back, Cordelia tucked the hem of her kaftan into her girdle. If it weren't for the trousers she wouldn't dream of doing so.

Except that it would be the height of folly to try to climb with her skirts tangling around her ankles.

She turned and stared at the cliff. The angle of the sun's rays had already changed a little, and the pattern of light and dark took on a three-dimensional aspect. It was still a formidable barrier and her heart failed her.

"Perhaps we should wait awhile to see if a fishing boat passes," she said hopefully.

"Conditions are perfect now. The breeze has died and it's not too hot. The sooner we start up the better." He glanced at her. "It's not so bad, truly, but if you prefer to stay until I can fetch you by boat . . ."

"No. I don't want to stay here alone." She took a deep breath and picked up the basket. "Let's go."

"Hold hard! Before we start, I want to point out to you what I think is the best route, just in case."

In case of what, Cordelia didn't care to consider. Listening carefully, she followed his pointing finger as he explained. Whether she was actually looking at the same formations he was describing she was not at all certain, but the marks began to make a sort of sense. She nodded as he indicated the spot where he hoped to reach the top.

"What about the other side?"

"We'll worry about that when we come to it. For all we know it's a gentle slope with houses built all the way up. We'd best abandon the basket, I think. The food can go in the bundle. I'll combine the water from the two bottles and hang the full one on my belt."

The leather water-bottles had loops for that purpose. While Preston threaded his girdle through, Cordelia transferred their meagre supplies to the bundle and knotted the four corners of the cloth tightly. He picked it up with a cheerful smile.

"On our way," he said jauntily.

The silvery sand ended in a jumble of rocks and shingle,

interspersed with pools. The bottom foot or so of the rocks was encrusted with barnacles, limpets, and mussels.

"Whatever tide there is, is low," Preston commented. "In my still earlier youth, before I took up rock climbing, I used to spend hours harassing sea-anemones and hermit crabs in the tide-pools."

"In Cornwall?" Cordelia accepted his proffered hand to help her over a ridge, before she remembered she had meant to refuse aid unless it became absolutely necessary. "Is that where your home is?"

"It was, until my father died." He stopped, gazing ahead with his hand shading his eyes. "That's where I want to get to. You see that ledge? I couldn't see the part below before. It'll be a bit of a scramble."

To Cordelia, the slab of rock below the ledge looked completely blank and practically vertical. Preston put down the bundle and scuttled up like a crab.

"Easy." Four feet, five feet, an infinite distance above her, he lay down flat on his front and reached down. "Pass me the bundle."

She picked it up, clutched it to her chest, looked up at him in sudden terror.

"Don't be a widgeon, I'm not going to rob you of your clothes and abandon you. If I intended anything of the sort, I'd have chosen a better time and more valuable booty. What a low opinion you have of my morals and my common sense!"

Equally abashed and annoyed at his percipience, she passed up the bundle. She had to stretch to let him reach the knot on top. He set it beside him and leaned over again.

"I can't do it!"

"Of course you can. The surface is covered with tiny knobs and ridges and grooves, and at that slope you don't need proper handholds. Let your fingertips cling where they may for balance and just walk up."

Biting her lip, she felt the rock just above her head. Little roughnesses, barely visible, met her touch. Surely not enough to support her!

"Shall I come down and give you a heave from behind?"

"No!" She set one foot at an angle on the steep slope, then the other. The leather of her shoes caught on the rough surface. Tentatively she raised one hand to feel above her again.

She promptly slid down.

"You can't do it slowly. Keep moving and your feet won't have time to slip. Come on, one more try."

One more try or else what? He'd go on and leave her wondering whether he would be able to find a boat to fetch her? Or he'd come down and lay hands upon her person to heave her up? She didn't like either alternative.

Fingers scrabbling for purchase, she swarmed up until she could grasp the edge of the ledge and haul herself the rest of the way. Preston grinned at her as she crouched beside him, a trifle breathless and feeling quite pleased with herself.

"I thought I was going to have to unwrap the bundle and use the carrying cloth as a rope. I told you it wasn't difficult. You shouldn't give up so easily."

"If I gave up easily, I should now be sitting at home in Istanbul awaiting Mehmed Pasha's visit," she pointed out coldly. "Why didn't you suggest making a rope, instead of talking about *heaving*."

"Oh Lord, have I rubbed you the wrong way again? You really are the touchiest female! I wanted you to get up by your own efforts to give yourself confidence in your abilities. We have a long way to go."

"Oh." To avoid looking at his exasperated face, Cordelia craned her neck to peer upwards. From here the top was invisible, which made it seem even farther away.

"You can stand up now. Careful, the ledge is narrow. Try not to look down. Do cheer up, Miss Courtenay. I'll tell you this much: You may take offense at the drop of a hat but there's no other female of my acquaintance I'd even consider taking along on such an adventure."

Why his praise should warm her from the crown of her head to the tips of her toes she could not imagine, but it did, and made her determined not to disillusion him. Not that she'd dream of telling him so. "I am ready to go on," she said.

"All right. I shall be ungentlemanly and go ahead . . ."

"I could not pass you here if I wanted to."

"True," he said with the patient air which always infuriated her. "The next little way is straightforward, but when we meet the next difficulty you must watch how I go and copy me exactly. If you cannot reach, tell me at once, or if for any reason you fall behind. Understood?"

Turning, he picked up the bundle and led the way. The ledge sloped upwards, steep and narrow but straightforward as he had said—for several yards. Then there was a gap of eighteen inches with nothing to break a fall to the beach, already an alarming distance below, before their path continued at a slightly higher level. Preston stepped across as if the gap was not there. *Don't look down,* Cordelia reminded herself, and she followed.

"Well done!"

The next obstacle was a vertical crack like a chimney, which had to be climbed. Then a wide, short ledge took them to a flat slab like the one down on the beach, less tall but terrifying because of the drop below. Cordelia made no protest when Preston told her to go first. His steadying hands on her hips let her get high enough to grasp the rim at the top, and his lifting grip on her ankles helped her over the edge. She had to lie still on her stomach for a moment to allow her heartbeat to slow before she reached down for the bundle. A moment later, he joined her.

"Have you no nerves?"

He laughed. "Not many. I've found them on the whole a useless encumbrance. Come on."

The climb became a blur of rock before her face, rock beneath her feet, rock between her clutching fingers. Her purse weighed her down and she blessed Aaron for suggesting she carry diamonds rather than gold. The weight of the gems was insignificant, but the cloth around her waist in addition to her clothes made her feel as if she was in the hot room of a Turkish bath. Sweat ran down her forehead into her eyes and she had to stop to wipe it away.

The moment her footsteps ceased Preston turned his head. "What . . . ? Oh, it's getting hot, isn't it?" He took out a handkerchief and blotted his own beaded brow.

"You were right not to wait any longer before we started up."

"Just a little farther and there's a shelf where we can sit down for a drink."

Cordelia had insufficient energy to object when the shelf turned out just wide enough for them to sit touching at shoulder, hip, and thigh. Gratefully she took a gulp of stale, lukewarm water from the leather bottle. "I've never tasted anything better," she said, handing it back. "Oh, look at the view!"

The sea spread below them, aquamarine in the nearby shallows, cobalt-blue further out, into a distance dotted here and there with sails, white or rusty-red. On the horizon floated smudges which might be clouds or islands. Gulls wheeled above, and Cordelia realized she had heard their cries all along without consciously noticing. A flight of white pelicans skimmed the water, wings blazoned with black, their clumsy beaks so heavy-looking one expected them to topple headfirst into the waves.

"It almost makes the climb worthwhile, doesn't it?" Preston swallowed a mouthful of water. "Not yet mid-morning by the sun. It's going to get hotter. Why don't you take off that kerchief?"

"A lady never permits a gentleman to see her outdoors with her head uncovered." Oh, the irony of quoting her mother on the subject of ladylike behaviour!

"I distinctly recall your telling me I am no gentleman, so you need have no qualms. You might be more comfortable without the kaftan, too."

"Certainly not!" she snapped, then admitted to herself that he could not know her shift was of the finest gauze, almost transparent.

Her response let him guess, however. He gave her a long, slow look which burned all the way from her shoulders to her waist, as if he saw through both kaftan and shift. But he said only, "Well, I shall take off my dolman, if you wouldn't mind sitting with your . . . ah . . . limbs over the edge to give me a little more space."

She complied, turning her back on him. He stuffed his robe into the bundle, along with her kerchief, which he accepted without comment. They set off again.

At first Cordelia wished Preston had kept his dolman on. She was uncomfortably conscious of the way his white shirt revealed his muscular shoulders, back, and arms. But soon she had to concentrate on where he put his hands and feet, so as to follow him over a steep, awkward ridge. After that she was too tired to think of anything but the protest of her own muscles at each new effort.

She was taken completely by surprise when he stopped, turned, and said quite casually, "Well, here we are."

Gaping up at him, she saw he was silhouetted against a brassy sky. The breeze had risen again, ruffling his short, unnaturally black hair. She could not stir, simply could not take the last step.

He dropped the bundle, reached down to take her hands, and pulled her up beside him. Her legs promptly gave way. She sank to the ground.

Preston sat down beside her. "Water? And I think we deserve a little something to munch on." He handed her the water-bottle and delved into the bundle. She tried not to think of the intimate garments therein. "Here, nuts and raisins and a bit of cheese should keep you going."

"Going! I shall never move again."

"Yes, you will, and we must not sit here too long or you'll stiffen up."

Cordelia groaned. "Is it much farther?"

"I haven't really had a chance to spy out the land," he said cautiously.

"At least it must be downhill from here!"

"You're full of pluck, Miss Courtenay. I'll admit I wasn't sure you would make it."

"That climb must be ten times worse than your Cornish cliffs."

"Oh no. A bit higher than most, but easier in some ways. In Cornwall the rock is often slick with spray or rain, and some of it is brittle shale, tends to break off in your hands. What's more, your hands are usually cold."

"Then if that was so easy," she said waspishly, "why did you think I couldn't make it?"

"I didn't say 'couldn't,' I said 'wouldn't.' " His dark blue eyes met hers in a steady look. "I was afraid you might decide it was impossible, which tends to be a self-fulfilling prophecy. I beg your pardon for misjudging you." He paused, as if waiting for a similar apology from her, then sighed. "Time to go."

Standing up, he reached down to offer his hand, but Cordelia struggled to her feet without it. She didn't misjudge him, she assured herself. He was the one who had told her he was fleeing the law.

The ground sloped gently upward from where they stood, a mixture of bare rock and pebbles. Here and there pockets of soil supported stunted grey-green shrubs, prickly weeds, and tussocks of dry grass. A flock of twittering goldfinches with scarlet faces and flashes of yellow on their wings flitted from thistle to thistle, tearing the silvery puffs apart to eat the seeds. As Cordelia and Preston started up the slope, a small goat with long, shaggy, dark-brown hair came over the crest. It stared at them, amber-eyed, before it returned to cropping the unrewarding herbage.

"We must be near people!" Cordelia exclaimed.

From the top, they looked down on a village of whitewashed, flat-roofed houses, built around a small harbour sheltered on the far side by another rocky headland. The nearer end of the village was hidden by a slope like that they had just walked up. Less than a quarter mile ahead, the ground ended in an abrupt edge with nothing but air beyond.

"Meh-eh-eh," said a second goat mockingly and turned its matted back.

As one, Cordelia and Preston swung round to look inland.

"It never rains but it pours," said Preston philosophically.

Their headland was joined to the rugged, mountainous mainland by a neck of land no wider than the goat track which ran along its top. On one side, the cliff they had climbed fell sheer to the deserted cove. On the other, a low, equally precipitous cliff ended in a steep slope of scree, which petered out in terraced fields and olive groves, dotted with a dozen or so houses, outposts of the village.

The loose mass of earth, pebbles, stones, and boulders looked as if a touch would start a landslide. Half way down lay a dead goat.

Cordelia shuddered. If the sure-footed beast had fallen, what hope had they?

# Eight

"Shall we try that cliff over there?" Cordelia gestured hopefully. The terrors of climbing a precipice suddenly seemed insignificant compared to the prospect of walking a tightrope between two precipices.

"I cannot study it properly from above," James Preston pointed out. "I would not want to start down a cliff without having some idea of what I'm going to find on the way, and at the bottom."

"No." She looked again at the knife-edge ridge. The longer she gazed, the narrower it looked. "I can do it," she said with grim determination, "but let us go now, before I have time to think about it."

"And before this breeze grows any stronger. If you have the slightest feeling you're going to lose your balance, down on your knees and crawl. I shall, I promise."

The near end of the isthmus was below them. As they descended towards it, Cordelia saw it was nearer two feet wide than the six inches she had guessed. A perfectly adequate path—were it not for the drop on either side. If only she could traverse it with her eyes shut!

Might James Preston allow her to hold onto his girdle?

"You go first, this time," he said, as promptly as if he had read her thoughts. I want to be able to grab you if you falter."

That stiffened her spine. "I shan't," she snapped, and started across.

For some distance the track continued downward. At the bottom, it narrowed to less than twelve inches. Cordelia hesitated. Then, feeling his critical eyes on her back, she marched on, her gaze glued to the ground before her feet, trying to ignore the void on either side.

To her right, in the corner of her vision, a seagull floated by. Distracted, she saw the jumbled rocks far below, dark fangs hungrily waiting for her. Quickly looking the other way, she saw the dead goat, a horrid warning of the perils of overconfidence. A gust of wind caught at her kaftan.

In an instant she dropped to her knees.

"Thank heaven," Preston remarked in a conversational tone. "Call it masculine vanity if you will, but I wasn't going to go on hands and knees until you did. No, don't look round. I assure you I'm right behind you, my nose to those charming ankles of yours."

Bristling, she held her tongue and crawled doggedly onward.

The path widened as it began to rise. Soon Cordelia forced her weary limbs upright again. Then, miraculously, they were walking side by side.

She stopped and stared back. "I cannot believe we crossed that."

"We did. But I'm afraid your bundle didn't. The wind pulled at it and I had to let go. I'm sorry."

"It doesn't matter." Gazing down, she discovered it was true. The bundle had caught on some snag and ripped open. The scree slope about the goat's pathetic carcase was strewn with clothes. Shifts and shawls, richly embroidered kaftans given her by the pasha and elegant, high-waisted gowns given her by the margrave. Another link in the chain of her past was broken. "No, it doesn't matter."

Turning away, she found him regarding her with surprised approval, as though he had expected her to kick up a great fuss over her lost possessions. She frowned and quickly looked away, towards the village. The sun glinted on a gold cross where the dome and belfry of a small church stuck up among the low, rectangular cottages on the slopes above the harbour. A boat approached the quay, propelled by a man waggling a single oar at the stern. Bent black figures worked in the terraced, pocket-handkerchief fields, punctuated with the dark exclamation marks of slender cypresses.

"The only thing is, what shall we say to the village people, arriving with nothing but the clothes on our backs?"

"A good question." As he spoke, he led the way along a goat path which seemed to lead in the right direction, though it wound about a good deal between fragrant myrtle bushes. "Not that the lack of luggage makes a great difference, but I've been pondering what tale to tell and still haven't come up with a good answer."

"Then perhaps we should not try to explain our presence. They will not believe we are Greek anyway, since I don't know the language."

"I don't speak well enough to be taken for a native."

"Suppose you pretend you understand well but speak only a very little, just enough to make our wants known, and perhaps a word or two of explanation. 'Lost,' say, and maybe 'ship,' and a great deal of waving of arms. No, I have it. Tell them we were on a Turkish ship when the captain robbed us and set us ashore. I daresay they will believe any evil of a Turk!"

"And be glad to help us. Splendid! Let's see, the *Amphitrite* sailed north, so the nearest sizable port is probably Thessaloniki, if I recall my geography correctly. I'll tell them in shockingly fractured Greek that we were on our way to Thessaloniki. It's just as well you don't speak any at all. You won't be able to contradict my story by accident if we are separated."

"Separated! Oh no!"

"It's not likely," he soothed, "not for long, anyway, since we shall have to pretend to be husband and wife."

"We what?" Scarce able to believe her ears, she stopped and glared at his back. Sometimes she almost forgot he was a rascal, but one way or another he always reminded her. She had guessed right, for all his denials he had designs on her virtue. "Never!"

He turned to face her, the patient expression she found insufferable combined—still worse!—with amusement. "My dear girl, the modern Greeks don't keep their women segregated like the Turks, but we cannot expect them to receive with cordiality an unmarried man and woman travelling together."

"Fiddlesticks! You must tell them we are brother and sister."

"I hadn't thought of that," he said regretfully, then brightened. "You will have to call me Iakov, then, the Greek equivalent of James. You cannot call your brother mister."

She frowned.

They went on. James heard the girl stumbling along behind him. She must be exhausted after the unaccustomed exertion, but he'd be damned if he would offer her his arm. She'd probably cry rape.

How determined she was to believe him a villain! That was bad enough, but what really annoyed him was her certainty of her own superiority. She even despised and resented her mother, with no attempt to understand or forgive that unfortunate lady's fall from grace.

James did not know the full story, only what little Uncle Aaron had told him. Lady Courtenay had found herself at low ebb in Prussia, of all places, with a daughter to support. Without resources or friends to turn to, she had accepted the protection of Mehmed Pasha, in Berlin to court an alliance with King Frederick William against Russia, or Napoleon, or both.

Lady Courtenay was not the first—nor doubtless the last—beautiful widow to be forced by circumstances to veer from the straight and narrow. James felt nothing but sympathy for her. Yet her daughter, whom she had kept in comfort, held her in contempt and blamed every difficulty on her.

It was practically his duty to seduce Cordelia Courtenay, he mused. She depended on him as Lady Courtenay had depended on the pasha. Let her learn what had driven her mother to succumb to the Turk's blandishments.

Though he'd no more force her than rob her, he would do his best to win her favours, he decided. For the present they were brother and sister, but England was still a long way off.

The goat track he was following twisted and turned downward until it ended at a gap in the stone wall of a small vineyard. Autumn-yellow vine leaves drifted to the ground under the assault of the strengthening wind, but bunches of purple grapes still hung here and there.

Cordelia plodded up behind him as he paused at the tumbledown wall. "Do you think anyone would mind if we ate a few?" she said longingly.

"I doubt it. The vines look abandoned to me, all overgrown and tangled as if they haven't been pruned in years, and most of the grapes are wrinkled."

"And there's a fig tree in the corner, look, with figs on it."

James gave her his hand to help her over the fallen stones in the gap. She was tired enough to accept his aid, and he no longer minded if she fancied he intended to seduce her. Now it was true.

He smiled at her. "Sit here against the wall in the shade, Miss Courtenay, and I'll bring you some fruit."

"Thank you." She sank wearily to the ground. "It is dreadfully hot for the time of year."

When he returned a few minutes later, his hands full of grapes and figs, she was leaning back against the wall with her eyes shut.

At the sound of his footsteps, she opened her eyes and sat up straight. "It is a little cooler in the shade, but the wind is hot. Is my nose sunburned?" she asked as he dropped to the ground beside her.

"I think not. We had our backs to the sun most of the time." He studied her round face, pink-cheeked from heat and exercise. Her fair hair escaped in wisps from its severe braid, and small, pearly teeth, slightly uneven, bit into the rosy flesh of a juicy fig. Despite dust and dirt she was quite attractive. Making love to her would be no penance.

"My nose freckles horridly. I wish I had a bonnet."

"We haven't a head-covering between us. They disappeared with your bundle."

She stared at him, dismay in her brown eyes. "I forgot."

"Fortunately it's only the Moslems who regard a woman's bare head as not merely indecorous but sacrilegious."

"So the villagers will never believe even the wickedest Turk stole the kerchief from my head!"

"Oh Lord, I daresay you're right," he said, and started to laugh. "So much for our story."

After a startled moment, Cordelia smiled. "Ah well, it wasn't much of a story anyway. You will just have to make sure your Greek is so shockingly bad they do not try to ask personal questions."

The hot wind continued to rise as they rested, and the sky turned a leaden hue. When they went on they caught a glimpse of sullen grey waves rolling white-capped into the harbour, where a number of boats were now tied up at the quay. On the other side of the vineyard, they found a cart track which ran between stony cultivated fields and vineyards, groves of oranges and lemons, olives and figs, all deserted.

"Nap-time," James said when Cordelia wondered at the absence of the toilers she had seen from above. "What the Spanish call siesta. Everyone and everything comes to a halt for the hottest hours of the day."

Everything except the dogs. As they came to the outskirts of the village and started walking along a crooked street no wider than the cart track, a bony mongrel sprawled in the gutter raised its head and the alarm.

Springing to its feet, the cur let fly an ear-shattering volley of barks. Instantly a half-dozen, a dozen, a score of canine voices joined the cacophonous chorus.

Cordelia stopped dead. "It's not going to attack, is it?" she said. "It's just barking, not growling or snarling."

"I see you know dogs. I—"

Above them a pair of green shutters crashed back against the wall. A man stuck his head out, his leathern face decorated with a huge black moustache, and bellowed a demand for silence. He followed his roar with a missile which crashed in shards beside the dog, sending it scampering off with its skinny tail between its legs. Then he looked down at the strangers and said mildly, *"Kalespera."*

*"Kalespera,"* James responded to the greeting. He continued in deplorable Greek which would have appalled his schoolmasters, "Us lost. Ship captain Turk he rob us."

"Filthy Turks." The man turned his head and spat sideways into the street.

Encouraged, James continued, "Me and sister go Thessaloniki now."

He did not need to pretend to have difficulty understanding the man's speech. The local dialect was a far cry from anything he had ever heard, but helped by vigorous gesticulations he contrived to get the gist of it. He turned to Cordelia.

"We're not on the mainland," he said, "we're on an island. I'm afraid this fellow reckons we'll be here for several days, at least. This wind is a sirocco, and they're expecting it to blow up a storm."

# Nine

Cordelia wished she had been able to learn some Greek from Captain Vasiliadis. All around her in the cool, dim, low-ceilinged room, men and women and children chattered to Preston, giving her an occasional smiling nod. After a meal of fried octopus washed down with a rough red wine, she was drowsy. She leaned her elbows on the table, her head drooping.

A hand tugged on her arm. She blinked up into a kind, wrinkled face, the mother of their host, Kostas, as she had managed to gather. The old woman said something and tugged again.

"Iakov?" She had to admit she could not very well call him Mr. Preston when she was pretending to be his sister.

"She is saying something about a bed and sleep. You look as if you can do with both."

"You won't leave, go to another house?"

"I'll be here when you wake up, I promise. By then I'll be able to tell you the name of every boy taken from the village to join the Turkish army in the past three hundred years. Sleep well, Cordelia, and don't fret."

Her Christian name sounded shockingly familiar on his lips, but she was too sleepy to care. She followed the old woman up stone stairs to a room where a huge bed with an elaborately carved head and foot awaited her. Her hostess patted the headboard proudly, and with great care folded back a coverlet of woven wool, patterned in colours bright in spite of the closed shutters. Beneath were reasonably clean, if not fresh, cotton sheets over a mountainous featherbed. It looked like heaven to Cordelia.

As Mrs. Kostas—for want of a better name—started to help her take off her kaftan, she remembered the purse she wore beneath it. Had James told people everything they owned had been stolen? If so, he would just have to pretend they had misunderstood. Surely it would not seem odd that a Turk had failed to search a woman as thoroughly as a man, had even failed to envisage a woman carrying a significant sum.

Besides, she would feel guilty not paying the villagers for any goods they were able to provide. Mrs. Kostas was quite neatly and respectably dressed in a widow's black, but many of those Cordelia had seen below wore clothes scarcely better than rags. It must be a poor island, she thought, recalling the tiny, stony fields and the rugged interior.

With obvious admiration, Mrs. Kostas fingered the heavy silk of the kaftan before draping it neatly over a stool. She tactfully looked the other way while Cordelia untied the purse and dropped it on top. She kept the long waistcoat on, however, to hide the bulge of the diamond cloth about her middle.

"Thank you, *Kyria,*" she said, as she climbed into bed.

The old woman patted her shoulder and said in a sympathetic voice, *"Bulgar, bulgar,"* then went away.

The sirocco wailed around the house, whistled through the gaps in the shutters and made them creak and tap against each other. From below came a murmur of conversation and an occasional laugh. The sounds faded from Cordelia's consciousness and she slept.

When she woke, she was so stiff that putting her kaftan back on was a struggle. She untied her braid and shook out her long hair before she remembered she had no comb. Time to start making a list of all the things she needed to buy, for both James and herself. It wasn't at all proper for her to be paying for clothes for a gentleman, but she would have to, after the story he had told.

She realized she had not the least idea whether he actually

had any money or not. She had paid for Ibrahim's passage on the *Amphitrite*, and James had not suggested reimbursing her. Had he planned all along to hang on her purse strings all the way to England?

If so, she decided, she would just have to let him. Any travelling companion, even one more scoundrel than gentleman, was preferable to going on alone. Without him, her arrival in this village would have been greeted with suspicion at best—if she had ever arrived. She shuddered as she remembered the cliff.

The room below, lamp-lit now, was as crowded as before. A black-robed priest with a long grey beard sat at the table with James, Kostas, his two grown sons, and three other men. As Cordelia entered, they all looked up and called out greetings, as did the huddle of women in the corner. Before the battery of eyes, she felt herself blushing.

James jumped up and came towards her. "Your hair is beautiful," he murmured. "Time I washed the lamp-black out of mine, though I cannot match your glorious gold. You should wear it loose more often."

The warmth in her cheeks increased. His back was to the light and she was not certain whether he was teasing, genuinely admiring, or buttering her up for some reason of his own. "I have no comb," she said.

"I'm sure that can be remedied." Turning to the young woman who had emerged from the group, he made gestures as if combing his hair and pointed at Cordelia. "This is Kostas's second wife," he told her, "consecutive, not simultaneous. He's the wealthiest man in the village, and the most important apart from the priest. Be nice to her."

"Of course! How do I say thank you?"

*"Efcharisto."*

The young woman nodded. With a shy smile, she beckoned to Cordelia and led her back upstairs. She insisted on combing and plaiting her hair for her. Cordelia discovered that her name was Ioanna and that she was pregnant, an easy concept to convey by sign language.

She was a gentle creature, very much under her mother-in-law's thumb but adoring of and adored by her vigorous if middle-aged husband. In the days that followed, he would beam with pride when he came upon her sitting with Cordelia, carding wool from their small flock of sheep as she taught the foreign woman the rudiments of Greek.

One word Ioanna was unable to explain was *"Bulgar,"* as used by the elder Mrs. Kostas. Cordelia asked James what it meant.

He grinned. "Just what it sounds like: *Bulgar*—Bulgarian. They decided that's what we are, chiefly because of our hair." He ran his fingers through his light brown crop. "I see no need to disillusion them. The Greeks have their differences with the Bulgarians, but they're all Orthodox Christians under the Ottoman heel, so it suits us well enough."

English or Bulgarian, they were both dressed as Greek peasants when at last the wind dropped and they went aboard Kostas's fishing yawl. They had changes of clothes, too, as well as other necessaries, all packed up in two sturdy baskets with hinged lids. Yet Cordelia's purse was very little lighter, for the villagers refused to accept payment. She had given the priest, Father Georgios, some money to help those in need, and with difficulty she had persuaded Ioanna to take the kaftan.

Her Turkish shift, waistcoat, and trousers she kept. The shift protected her delicate skin against the coarse homespun of the peasant garments; the waistcoat would help keep her warm—winter was approaching; and the trousers were to wear in case she again found herself having to climb ladders or cliffs.

Settling forward of the single mast of the small vessel, Cordelia glanced up at the headland, towering over the village, as precipitous on this side as the other.

"I still have not thanked you," she said to James as he seated himself beside her. She had not seen much of him in the three days since their arrival. The Greek men and women were not strictly segregated like the Turks but they tended to go their separate ways.

"For what?" he asked, surprised.

"For my escape from the next cove. I could not have climbed out alone, nor with only Ibrahim to help."

"I expect you would have done it somehow. I don't believe I have thanked you for my escape from Istanbul. *Efcharisto."*

She smiled. *"Efcharisto."*

"We need each other," he said, gazing deeply into her eyes. His were such a fascinating dark shade of blue, like the sea on this cloudless morning but warmer.

Too warm. Cordelia tore her gaze away and waved to Ioanna, who stood on the ancient stone quayside wiping tears from her cheeks with her shawl. Half the village was there to bid them farewell, even Father Georgios, with his pectoral cross raised in blessing.

Kostas kissed his young wife and jumped aboard, roaring an order. Pushing off, his sons raised the sails. With Kostas at the tiller, they sailed out of the harbour before a gentle breeze, westward-bound for Stavros.

In Stavros, Kostas had explained, they might find a ship going to Piraeus. If not, they could hire horses to take them to the great port of Thessaloniki, an easy ride forty or fifty miles farther west, across the peninsula. Cordelia was not sure she regarded fifty miles of even the flattest country as an easy ride. An hour or two was the longest she had ever spent on horseback. But they could not expect Kostas to leave his beloved Ioanna for long enough to sail south around the peninsula and up the Gulf of Thermai to Thessaloniki.

Sighing, Cordelia wondered what it was like to be so loved.

Beyond the shelter of the headlands, the breeze was stiffer. The yawl cut through the sparkling waves with a lively rocking motion. A school of silvery flying fish soared across their bow, followed by several porpoises which leapt and cavorted as if the pursuit was more for fun than food.

"Oh, are they not marvellous?" Cordelia cried, turning to

James. He gave her a wan grin and swallowed. "You are feeling seasick? You poor thing! Would it help to lie down?"

He shook his head miserably. "Not much," he groaned, then suddenly dived across to the side of the boat. Leaning over, he was violently sick.

Cordelia reached for the nearest water-bottle and went after him. She damped her handkerchief, gently wiped his greenish face, and held the bottle to his lips. He rinsed out his mouth, spat over the side.

"Drink a little," she urged.

"I'll only bring it up."

"It is better if you have something in your stomach to bring up. Just a sip or two."

Meekly he obeyed. "A fine escort I am," he croaked.

"I have heard Lord Nelson was always indisposed at the start of a voyage," Cordelia said consolingly.

"Indisposed!" He clutched the side with both hands and leaned over again, retching.

Cordelia glanced astern to see what Kostas and his sons were making of poor James's agonies. All three were gazing southward, shading their eyes and looking worried. She followed their gaze. Not the Turkish Navy! she prayed.

Far to the south, the sky was no longer blue. The line of slate-grey clouds looked alarmingly familiar.

Kostas handed over the tiller and came forward, ducking under the boom as it swung. Hands on hips, balancing with the tilt and roll of the boat, he stared down at the oblivious James. A smile tugged at the corners of his mouth as he shrugged his shoulders and turned to Cordelia.

*"Kyria,"* he began. He spoke slowly and carefully and aided by his gesticulations she picked up a word here and there. As she had guessed, another sirocco was blowing up, or perhaps the present calm had proved to be only a lull. The voyage to Stavros had become dangerous, maybe impossible. He pointed ahead, and she realized they had already turned northward, flanking the island instead of sailing away from it.

"Do you understand what he's saying?" she asked James urgently.

"Yes," he grunted. "He's taking us to a mainland town, a small port, and it's much closer than Stavros. Thank heaven!"

With the sirocco chasing them across the steely waves under a louring sky, they reached the town by mid-afternoon. Leaving his sons to guard his precious boat, Kostas took them to a taverna just beyond the harbour. He sat them down at a table, their baskets at their feet, and embarked upon a spirited discussion with the landlord, involving as usual much waving of arms. They both spoke much too fast for Cordelia to follow.

When he returned to their table, he slowed his speech, but she still had to turn to James for an explanation.

"He says we are in luck, there is a mule train leaving for Thessaloniki in the morning. Or we can wait until the storm blows over and hire a boat." He faltered momentarily but went nobly on, "The choice is yours."

Regarding his still pallid face, the arms clasped protectively about his middle, Cordelia set aside her qualms at the prospect of an even longer ride. "You have had enough of the sea for the present. Let us try the mules."

James looked distinctly relieved, but he warned her, "It will probably take several days longer."

"Perhaps we shall at least get where we are going!" she said tartly. "Aesop was Greek, was he not? I daresay he modelled his fable of the hare and the tortoise on the swift ship and the slow mule train."

He summoned up a weak laugh. "I daresay. We've not had much luck, have we? I'll find out how we go about joining the mule train."

Kostas would organize all. They must wait here and he'd return shortly to give them the details. He had already arranged beds for them for tonight, here with his good friend Spiro—he waved at the plump innkeeper, who nodded and bowed and beamed.

"What was it he whispered?" Cordelia asked as Kostas strode out.

"He's telling everyone we are 'foreign Greeks,' settlers from Anatolia, because here on the mainland many people are prejudiced against Bulgars."

"How I should like simply to be English again! Would it not be easier just to admit it? Surely England is too far away for prejudices to have arisen against us."

"And too far for easy explanations of our presence here, besides which, the Turks are looking for an Englishman."

"They know you are English? I did not realize that."

"Yes, that's why they . . . uh, why I regretted your telling your servants I'm English—remember?—and why I have to pose as absolutely anything else."

What had he been going to say? Cordelia was about to demand to know when the innkeeper came over to ask if they wanted something to eat or drink. Still queasy, James rejected the offer with a shudder.

"You will feel much more the thing if you eat," Cordelia advised him. "Something simple like bread and fruit, and tea to drink, if they have it, rather than coffee or wine."

"I don't think there's a Greek word for tea, but I'll see what I can do."

The tea turned out to be neither Indian nor China but a fragrant, greenish mint brew even better for settling an upset stomach. After drinking several cups, James devoured bread and an apple. Having lost his breakfast, he was ravenous. He was about to order a more substantial repast when Kostas returned, very pleased with himself. He had arranged all with the leader of the caravan and had even, with the rest of the money Cordelia had provided, bought them blankets and provisions for the journey.

"Invite him to dine with us," Cordelia urged James, "and I expect one of his sons might be spared from guarding the boat. We can send a basket of food to the other. We owe them such a great deal."

"An excellent notion."

James passed on the invitation in his wretched Greek. Kostas was delighted. He helped to order the best the house could provide and then went to fetch his son.

"That's all settled, then," James said contentedly. "I must admit, the longer I can put off going back to sea the happier I shall be. Oh, but good lord, I hadn't thought. You do ride, I take it?"

"Yes, though not since we . . . not for some time, never for so long a distance, and never on a mule."

"It's much the same as a horse. For a different sort of a ride, you should try a camel!"

"I detest camels!" Cordelia burst out.

"You have tried one, have you?" said James, surprised. "A deucedly uncomfortable mount."

"No, I have not ridden one." She fought down the memory of the camel striking her mother's golden head with its hoof and stalking on, indifferent, unconcerned. "I just dislike them."

"How fortunate we don't have to cross any deserts on the way home!"

Spiro's daughter brought a jug of wine and a vast plate of *meze.* The hors d'oeuvres included olives, pickles, *hummus,* stuffed vine leaves, cubes of fresh white cheese, little meatballs, and *taramasalata.* The fish roes of the latter must have been what attracted the cat. With a hopeful miaow, it rubbed against Cordelia's leg.

The cat's sudden appearance startled her. Already on edge after the talk of camels, she sprang to her feet, clapping her hand to her mouth to stifle a scream. The bench crashed against the wall.

James jumped up. "What the devil?" Circling the table, he reached for her arm, then he looked down and smiled. "Don't tell me the intrepid Miss Courtenay is afraid of cats?"

"Not afraid. I cannot bear them," she said fiercely, her eyes closed tight to try to shut out the vision of the swarm of cats, the litter-bearers stumbling, herself tripped, falling as she tried to save Mama.

"You're shaking like a leaf." He righted the bench and made her sit down. "Here, drink a drop of wine. I'll see that the beast is shut up while we are here."

Spiro's daughter had already scooped up the cat. Giving Cordelia a curious glance, she said something to James in an apologetic voice and carried the animal out.

James's gaze was equally curious. He must suppose she was mad to let a cat disturb her so. She wanted to explain, but she was dreadfully afraid the story of her mother's accident would make him laugh, and that she could not endure.

She pushed the glass of wine away. "I don't want this. I'm not hungry anymore. I think I shall go to bed so as to be rested for tomorrow."

His gaze became searching. "As you choose. However, I must remind you that our guests will arrive any moment, and they will expect you to act as hostess."

Cordelia had an odd feeling that he was testing her, though she could not imagine why a wastrel should care whether she behaved like an English lady. If, indeed, an English lady would be expected to help her brother entertain male friends at an inn, which she rather doubted. She doubted still more that a Greek lady would attempt anything of the sort. Perhaps if she agreed James would take it as another sign she was no lady.

Yet Kostas and his wife and mother had offered them such generous, unstinting hospitality. She did not want to risk affronting him, to have him return home and tell Ioanna she was too proud now to sit at table with him.

"I'll stay."

"Splendid. You may find you are glad to have eaten a last decent meal before we go on travelling rations, even if you are slightly less rested. But I shall see them well plied with wine, so you will have every excuse to make an early night of it."

True to his word, he seemed to be refilling a glass every time Cordelia looked up from her food, and fresh jugs of wine arrived at frequent intervals. She began to fear that James would grow fuddled and arouse suspicion with his command of the Greek language, or even reveal their true identities. However, when she ventured to remonstrate, he told her brusquely not to fuss.

Knowing from experience how useless it was to argue with a bosky gentleman—Count Szambrowczyk had been particularly difficult in that regard—she took this as a signal to retire. Not until then did she discover that the night's lodging Kostas had arranged for her was to share Spiro's daughter's bed.

Too late to make other plans. Huddled on the very edge of the lumpy, straw-stuffed mattress, Cordelia tried in vain to close her ears to the carousing below.

# Ten

Joining in the chorus of a Greek sea shanty, James tried in vain to close his mind to the thought of Cordelia tucked up warm in bed above. He was not in the least bosky, and he resented her tight-lipped advice not to lose control of his drinking and his tongue. At the same time, the few glasses of the harsh, resinous wine he had actually consumed had awakened his desire. Despite her shapeless peasant clothes, her figure retreating up the stairs enticed him. He ached to make love to her.

The fact was, she was still a mystery to him. Sometimes prickly, sometimes amiable, often as disapproving as the highest stickler though decidedly unconventional in so many ways, she was bold enough to set out on a long journey with a stranger, brave enough to climb a sheer cliff, yet apparently terrified of a cat. Cats and camels, he mused, pouring more retsina for his guests. What had happened to give her such a horror of both? Would she ever trust him enough to tell him?

When at last his guests staggered back to their boat and James fell asleep on a palliasse in a corner of the room, cats and camels waltzed around him in his dreams. But the partner in his arms was Cordelia.

It was still dark when Spiro shook him awake. By the time he had washed his face and hands, Cordelia had come down. Kostas, his hard head apparently unaffected by his hard drinking the night before, arrived to escort them to the mule-train's starting point. They drank coffee and ate a bit of bread with olive oil, then set out.

The sirocco was still blowing, but in fitful gusts rather than a sustained blast. It had rained in the night, just enough to lay the dust in the streets, and the air was damp and chill.

Cordelia was unwontedly quiet. In the grey light of dawn she looked wan and despondent. James wondered whether it was excessively unfair of him to drag her on a long ride through increasingly wintry weather instead of taking a ship. Then they crossed a street leading to the harbour. Glancing down at the boats bobbing on the storm-tossed waves, he gulped, nauseated by the very sight, and hardened his heart.

They came to a Turkish-style caravanserai on the edge of the small town. In a courtyard surrounded by galleried chambers, some forty pack mules stood patiently as they were loaded amidst a milling throng of shouting people. There were a score of riding mules, too, and half a dozen horses. The scene reminded James of a stage-coach setting out from one of the London inns.

Undaunted, Kostas pushed through the crowd, forging a way to the caravan-master. Impatiently the muleteer pointed out two saddled riding mules and an as yet unladen pack animal before turning back to a vociferous argument with a fat merchant.

Kostas helped James to tie their two baskets and the sack of blankets and provisions onto the back of their pack mule. An assistant muleteer, a villainous-looking, snaggle-toothed fellow in a sheepskin coat, promptly came over and reloaded to his own and—James hoped—the mule's satisfaction. The mule ought to be satisfied; its load was a quarter the size of most.

"I hired saddles for you," Kostas pointed out, a little anxious. The peasants rode their donkeys with nothing more than a rug over their backs. "One man's saddle, one for a woman. It was expensive, but for the *Kyria* . . ."

"Is good," said James firmly. Though he might have contrived without, Cordelia was going to find days in the saddle difficult enough. At best a side-saddle was awkward and uncomfortable. The sea safely behind him, he glanced at her dubiously, no longer doubting her resolve but belatedly concerned as to her strength and endurance.

"Why are so many men carrying guns?" she asked nervously, in a low voice.

Looking around, he saw at least a dozen muskets and shotguns slung over sturdy shoulders. He passed on the question to Kostas then relayed the answer. "To shoot game, to vary the menu en route. Kostas says bandits are not a problem as troops patrol the shore road regularly."

"Turkish troops?"

"Yes, but watching for bandits, not for us. They have their uses."

She seemed unconvinced, but saying no more she went over to her mule, stroked its nose, and fed it a crust. It twitched its long ears at her, nuzzling in hope of more. Thank heaven she had no aversion to mules!

He was relieved to notice that she was not to be the only female. Joining her, he pointed out three riding beasts with sidesaddles.

Cordelia brightened at once. "Oh, I am glad. Do you think Kostas might find the women, or at least one of them, and present me?"

"I shall ask him." James was ashamed not to have realized how alone she must feel. She really was an extraordinary, an exceptional girl. However unconventional her upbringing, it could not possibly have prepared her for her present situation.

He consulted Kostas, and a few minutes later was pleased to see Cordelia's smile as she was presented to a stout merchant's wife.

Somehow the confusion in the courtyard was sorted out. The sun's first rays broke through the clouds to gild the eastern sky as James and Cordelia bade a grateful farewell to Kostas. James lifted Cordelia into the saddle, saw that she was properly settled, and mounted his own animal. They took their places in the line filing through the gateway.

"Give my love to Ioanna!" Cordelia called back.

Kostas understood his wife's name if no more. He waved and nodded vigorously as they rode out into the new day.

The coast road was a stony track winding between sea and mountains. They passed few signs of habitation, an occasional tiny fishing hamlet around an inlet, or a shepherd's hut clinging to a hillside. In places the road was carved into cliffs of solid rock, braced here and there with masonry which looked so ancient it might have been Byzantine, or even classical Roman or Greek. Elsewhere the track clung precariously to unstable slopes, or crossed a stream by bridge or ford.

The rainy season was just beginning. A few of the stream beds were still dry but for a trickle of water; others tumbled seaward in muddy brown torrents, already knee-deep. These the caravan forded with care, the animals linked by ropes in long lines so that if one stumbled the others might save it. The mules plodded through with their usual stolid, sure-footed patience, which James admired the more since two of the horses skittishly baulked at every crossing.

He admired Cordelia, too. Though her hands clenched white-knuckled on the reins, she made no complaint, never reminded him it was for his stomach's sake they had taken this roundabout way. He made sure he was always beside her when they came to a ford.

When the path was wide enough, she often rode beside the merchant's wife, with whom she had quickly made friends.

"Kyria Agathi is bent upon improving my Greek," she told James as they walked along together, leading their mules. The side-saddle cramped her limbs if she rode for too long at a stretch, so every now and then he lifted her down. The caravan's slow pace was easy to match for a mile or two. "My island accent horrifies her."

"You learn quickly," he said.

"I have needed to. But I enjoy it, too. There is something very satisfying about being able to communicate in a foreign tongue."

"Is there not? I have given up pretending to speak no more

than a few words of Greek, since these people don't know how badly I was bungling it yesterday. I've been talking to your Agathi's husband, Mr. Miltiades. He's a fellow-sufferer."

"Seasick?"

"Yes, which is why he went by land to Istanbul when business took him there, sensible man."

Among the train, James had found two or three interesting people besides the fat merchant to chat with, all happy to talk about their own affairs and not enquire into his. He would have thoroughly enjoyed the ride had they moved at more than a snail's pace. The clouds blew over; the sun shone. The azure sea smoothed to gentle swells—and he was not on it. New grass was already showing green after the first rains, a confusing sign to an Englishman, especially as the balmy air felt spring-like.

The mules eagerly cropped the green shoots when the caravan stopped near the mouth of a river at midday to rest and eat. Kostas had provided bread, cheese, apples, dried fruit, and nuts, but the Miltiades invited James and Cordelia to share a roasted chicken so they lunched well.

James tried to resign himself to the two hours lost by the time the mules were rested and everyone was packed up, ready to take to the road again. Travelling on his own on horseback, he'd expect to make sixty or eighty miles a day. While he had known mule trains were slower, he had not realized how slow. At this rate they would be lucky to cover five-and-twenty miles.

Of course, it did not really make much difference. The authorities would be waiting for him in Athens anyway, and this gave him plenty of time to devise a plan to circumvent them.

When he said as much to Cordelia, she responded hopefully, "Or perhaps they will have lost interest in us by then. Perhaps we should go all the way by land."

"No, I'll be brave and sail from Thessaloniki or we shan't be home till midsummer."

"Home!" she said longingly, but when he asked about her home, she flushed and returned to the subject of the authorities. "You don't think they will forget about us?"

"About you, possibly. Not about me, I'm afraid."

Her mouth tightened. "Ah yes, of course, you are wanted for breaking the law. It slips my mind occasionally."

She returned to Kyria Agathi and he cursed himself for reminding her of her unshakable belief in her own invincible superiority.

When the caravan stopped to camp that evening, James suffered in silence a thorough scolding from Kyria Agathi for not providing a tent for his sister. Cordelia was invited to share the Miltiades' tent, quickly set up by their two efficient menservants. She ate with them, too, while James joined a group of men around another campfire.

Later, wrapped in his blankets out under the stars, he renewed his resolve to take her down a peg or two. Seducing her would not only be a pleasure, it would put a hefty dent in her armour of insufferable self-satisfaction.

He would have liked to wait until she missed his English conversation, if not himself, and came to him. However, she could not well seek him out among all the men, and besides he was supposed to be her brother and protector. So when the camp stirred at dawn he went to wish her good morning and take her a share of their provisions for breakfast. She seemed to have thought better of giving him the cold shoulder, especially as the Miltiades greeted him with pleasure and invited him to join their meal.

Content to let bygones be bygones, James treated her no differently from the day before, unless his hands lingered a little longer at her waist when he helped her mount and dismount.

They were riding together along a wide stretch of track after the midday break when the drumming of horses' hooves approaching brought the cavalcade to a ragged halt. Around the curve of the hillside ahead came a detachment of soldiers, riding at an odd but speedy shuffling walk. James recognized them as Janissaries by the curious flaps of white cloth sticking up above their tarbooshes.

The Janissaries were once elite troops of men taken in boyhood from Christian families and raised as Moslems fiercely loyal to the sultan. Now more of a hereditary caste, they had actually overthrown Selim III in 1807 when he attempted to reform the army, and Mustafa IV a year later. However they were still, especially under a good officer, formidable fighters not to be despised.

Their leader shouted an order and the troop drew rein. Her eyes enormous, Cordelia reached across the space between their mules to clutch James's arm.

"Our protection against brigands, remember?" he said lightly.

The officer started to move slowly along the mule train, asking questions, while one of his men rode along the other side with his rifle cocked. In no time the news travelled back along the line.

"They're looking for two outlaws, a man and a woman, foreigners."

# Eleven

"They are Turks." Cordelia had to force the words past the tightness in her throat. She felt cold all over and she did not dare look at James in case he saw how much she wanted him to deny what she was about to say. "They will not be able to guess from your speech that you are not a Greek. Tell them I bribed you to pretend to be my brother. They will let you go."

"What the devil do you think I am?" He sounded furious, not grateful. She looked up and his glare confirmed his fury. "Do you really think me capable of hiding behind a woman's skirts?"

"I didn't m-mean . . ." she stammered.

"No." His face and his voice gentled. "And if you did you had every right. I should never have come to you in Istanbul."

"Don't you think it might work?" she asked eagerly. "It would be silly for both of us to be taken unnecessarily. Then maybe you could rescue me later."

"From armed soldiers?" He shook his head. She followed his gaze to where the two Janissaries approached along the line of mules, slowly but inexorably. "If I thought there was even half a chance . . . But in any case, any moment someone is going to point us out as foreigners. Did you know our word for barbarian comes from the Greek for foreigner? The ancient Greeks had a low opinion of the rest of the world."

Recognizing his attempt to distract her from the inevitable, Cordelia tried to smile. "Like the English," she said. "Even Mama . . . Oh James, I don't want to be his mistress!"

"Courage, dear girl. You're English, remember. Stiffen the

sinews and imitate the action of the tiger. Since we cannot escape them, shall we go to meet them?"

Cordelia saw the officer turn his head to stare at them as one of the travellers pointed, his companion nodding. The two soldiers started towards them.

"Yes," she said, raising her chin. "Let us go to meet them."

He took her hand and side by side they rode forward. Suddenly James squeezed her hand urgently then dropped it.

"We have no reason to assume . . ." he started. "Damn, too late. Just follow my lead."

Puzzlement warred with Cordelia's fear. Did he hope the soldiers were chasing two different people? Did he mean to try to persuade them he and Cordelia were someone else? She did not know what, if any, papers he had on him, but hers clearly identified her as the woman wanted by Mehmed Pasha. If James gave a false name for her, it would soon be disproved.

"You are foreigners?" the officer asked in bad Greek. He was a tall man, made taller by his peculiar headdress. His long, swarthy face, adorned by a waxed moustache, had a mournful air, but his brown eyes were bright and watchful. "You speak Turkish? Follow me, please," he went on when James assented.

He turned his mount and the second man fell in behind them, his rifle still at the ready. Cordelia suppressed a sudden urge to dig her heels into her mule's flanks and flee. There was nowhere to go.

As they reached the head of the mule train, the muleteer called out in Turkish, "Excellency, we have long journey. We may go on?"

"No."

The Greek scowled but did not protest.

The Janissaries had spread a rug on the ground beside the track. Dismounting, the officer courteously helped Cordelia down and invited her to sit. With a gesture he brought James to join them.

"I am Captain Hamid." He addressed Cordelia: "And you are?"

Before she could answer, James interrupted. "My name is Preston," he drawled. "I persuaded this lady to allow me to travel as her brother. Otherwise she has no connection with me. Let her return to the caravan."

The captain heard him out but at once turned back to Cordelia. "Did this man force you to accompany him?" he asked.

Cordelia hesitated. James had told her to follow his lead, obviously hoping—she now realized—that Mehmed Pasha had nothing to do with the soldiers' search. If so, and if she agreed that James had compelled her to travel with him, she might go free. Even if they were looking for her as well as James, she might avert from her own head Mehmed Pasha's wrath at her departure. On the other hand, she would add a charge of abduction to whatever offenses James had already committed.

She looked at him. His intent, urgent gaze told her to say yes, to seize the chance of freedom. But he had refused to save his own skin at her expense and she found she could do no less.

"No, he did not force me to take him with me. I felt I should be safer with an English gentleman as my escort."

Captain Hamid glanced from her to James with a knowing look, and she realized he assumed they were lovers. She refused to dignify his assumption with a denial—which he would disbelieve anyway, no doubt.

"It is most fortunate that you have come to no harm, Meess Courtenay," he said urbanely. "His Excellency, Mehmed Pasha eagerly awaits your arrival in Thessaloniki."

So he had followed her trail! Inside her a last tiny seed of hope shrivelled.

"How did he find me?" she asked numbly, afraid for all those who had helped her escape.

"I do not know, *Bayan*. I was told only to search for you and Mr. Preston on the coast road and to bring any foreigners to Thessaloniki to be identified. Come, we must be on our way."

He stood up and snapped out an order. The Janissaries had dismounted to let their horses graze. Two of them led over a pair of saddle-less mounts and transferred the saddles from the mules onto their backs.

"I don't suppose the captain would be interested to learn those saddles don't belong to us," James said, helping Cordelia to stand, "though he seems a decent enough fellow, on the whole. Polite to us, at least. Don't despair."

She recalled other occasions when he had said the same. He had proved right then, but now they were well and truly in the briars, entangled beyond any hope of extricating themselves. "Do you never despair?" she said drearily.

"A singularly useless thing to do," he said with severity. "It stops you thinking. I daresay our muleteer will be relieved not to have lost the two mules along with the saddles." He cocked his head with an expectant look.

"Two mules?" she gasped. "We hired three! What about our baggage? I must have my comb and a change of linen, if nothing else."

James grinned at her. "Aha, you have started to think again. We shall need our blankets, too."

"Captain Hamid." Cordelia spoke in Turkish in a determined tone. "I cannot travel without my clothes and other things."

"Of course not, *Bayan*."

He bowed and sent a man to fetch the baskets and bundles. They were added to the burdens of the soldiers' pack-horses, while Cordelia's side-saddled horse was fastened by a leading rope to Hamid's mount, James's to that of his second-in-command.

"Permit me to help you up, *Bayan*," the captain requested politely.

Much as she would have liked to, it was not a request she could refuse. He lifted her into the saddle.

As James in his turn mounted, he said, "Captain, Miss Courtenay is a lady. She cannot be expected to ride for hours on end like your men."

"I will remember." His smile was surprisingly charming. "*Bayan*, you must tell me please when you grow tired." In a low voice he added, "You will have troubles enough, I think, when we reach Thessaloniki. I do not wish to cause unnecessary suffering before. Only, I must do a soldier's duty."

"Thank you, Captain," said Cordelia, grateful despite her heavy heart.

The rest of the troop was already on horseback. Captain Hamid swung into his saddle. At his signal, the Janissaries and their prisoners set off towards Thessaloniki.

Hamid was as good as his word. He let her rest or walk whenever she asked, and even let her disappear behind bushes without an embarrassing escort—after all, there was nowhere to run to. However, she was reluctant to try his patience and by the time they stopped for the night she was exhausted.

"I am almost used to being too tired to move," she said wryly to James, flopping down on the rug spread for them. To her relief, he was being treated as honourably as she was, not like a common felon.

The road had wandered away from the sea and the camp was set up on the bank of a stream in a valley between two rocky hillsides. Between huge boulders and outcroppings of the mountain's very bones grew enough grass to pasture the horses, while a belt of dark green firs higher up the slopes provided firewood. As the last light faded from the sky, fragrant blue-grey smoke curled upward from a circle of camp-fires. Soon the appetizing odour of *shish kebabi* browning on skewers wafted through the still air.

"Positively idyllic," James murmured wryly as a Janissary brought them sizzling meat wrapped in rounds of flatbread. "The Turks really know how to put on a picnic." He took a large bite.

"I'm not hungry," Cordelia said. She caught his minatory eye. "All right, if you insist, I'll eat to keep up my strength."

"It's what you told me, and very good advice too."

After a day of fresh air and exercise, the first bite restored her appetite and she ate hungrily. Captain Hamid nodded his approval and called for more.

When they finished eating, a soldier brought water from the river for them to wash their hands. What Cordelia really wanted was a hot bath, or better still a Turkish *hammam.* She would have to do without until they reached Thessaloniki, and then it would be a prelude to a night with Mehmed Pasha.

The thought appalled her. Not that she was afraid of the sex act itself. Mama had never pretended not to enjoy her lovers' attentions. But to be degraded to her mother's infamous level, to lose her last chance of respectability, and worst of all to suffer the intimate touch of a man who disgusted her . . . resting her forehead on her knees, Cordelia sat hunched in silent misery.

"You are tired, Meess Courtenay," said Hamid kindly. "I shall have my tent put up for you at once. By Allah's bounty it is a fine night and I shall be happy to sleep under the stars."

Looking up to thank him, by the ruddy light of the fires she saw him exchange a glance with James. They must be worried about her ability to endure another day in the saddle. Perhaps she could postpone the evil day by pretending to be weaker than she really was, though in truth she felt limp as a dishcloth.

As the captain shouted for his subaltern and issued a stream of orders, James said, "He's not a bad chap in his way. An officer and a gentleman."

"Yes, I suppose we are lucky in that, if unlucky in everything else."

He patted her back. "You'll feel better in the morning."

The small tent was pitched in the centre of the ring of campfires, and a soldier brought their baggage. As Cordelia retired into the tent, she saw many of the Janissaries already rolled in their blankets. Others stood about on sentry duty, a few beyond the fires facing outward, most inside the ring, facing inward, guarding the prisoners. Orange firelight cast the sentries' flickering shadows on the tent walls, looming over her like ghosts, insubstantial yet threatening.

She shivered, although the heat of the fires made the air quite warm.

Spreading her blankets, she sat down, untied her head-kerchief, and pulled off her boots. After a moment's thought, she took off the knee-length tunic and ankle-length petticoat Ioanna had given her. She still had on a stout cotton chemise, as well as her Turkish gauze shift underneath, not to mention the diamond cloth.

The rough woollen bedding was cosy, but little protection against the hard ground. Last night Mrs. Miltiades had lent her a pallet. Lying on one half of the blankets, the other folded over her, Cordelia was not at all comfortable. She wriggled and turned, then pushed back the top blankets to reach into the basket for her Turkish trousers to make a pillow for her head.

She froze, her heart standing still, as the tent flap opened and a man stooped to enter.

"Who . . . ?"

"It's only me."

James's voice eased her fright but made her angry. She grabbed the corner of the blankets and covered herself. "You cannot come in here."

"I'm afraid I have no choice. Our gallant captain says it's too difficult to keep an eye on me if I'm just another body rolled in blankets, one among many."

"Oh."

"He kindly offered to tie me hand and foot if you prefer."

"Oh!"

"Well?"

"Well . . ."

"I promise on my honour to do nothing against your wishes."

"Oh . . . well . . . I daresay it would be excessively uncomfortable to be tied up all night," Cordelia said dubiously.

"Excessively!"

The odious laugh in his voice reminded her of their first meeting, when he had appeared in her bedchamber in the middle of the night. He had not assaulted her then.

"Oh, very well, then, stay."

Reaching with care for her trousers and rolling them into a pillow, she watched James's silhouette. He seemed to scoop out a small, shallow dip in the ground before he laid out his bedding on top of it and sat down to remove his boots.

"Why did you do that? Dig, I mean."

"It's an old trick, making a hollow for one's hip-bone when sleeping on the ground. You'd be surprised how much difference it makes."

"I was just thinking I'm going to be stiff as a board in the morning."

"Move over a bit and I'll do the same for you. I imagine a woman needs it even more than a man."

Cordelia frowned at this uncalled-for reference to the contrast between male and female anatomy. Then she remembered he could not see her frown—and it would be foolish to lie in discomfort all night because of an indecorous remark.

Incautiously she rolled over, exposing herself from head to toe. If the dimly lit sight of her in her chemise inflamed James's passions, he gave no sign of it but flipped the other edge of the blankets over her and dug her a hollow.

"Thank you."

She shuffled back to occupy the dip. It was much more comfortable, but she found herself considerably nearer to James's bed. And he was taking off his outer clothes.

"T-talking of being stiff," she said nervously, "this afternoon you said something about stiffening sinews and a tiger . . ."

"Henry V, drumming up the courage of his troops going into battle. Shakespeare, like you."

"Like me?"

"Cordelia was one of King Lear's three daughters, the only one who did not betray him. As you refused to betray me, this afternoon."

"*I* am no liar, to let them believe you had abducted me. But you should not have told them your name. They might have let you go."

"They knew I was a foreigner and I have no papers. They were bound to take me with them to be identified, so I might as well admit who I was. No, there was no chance of escape for me, but there might have been for you if the search had no connection with your pasha—"

"Not mine! I loathe him!" Cordelia wept.

Somehow she was in his arms. He held her tight, stroking her back, murmuring soothing words.

"Hush, now, hush. You have been so brave, don't cry. Cordelia . . ." He hesitated. "Cordelia, I see no way to save you from him, but it might be easier for you if it were not your first time. Instead of giving your virginity to him, would you not rather give that gift to me?"

"Oh James!" She was excruciatingly conscious of his hard, lean body pressed against her, the protective circle of his arms now disquieting, intoxicating. His mouth touched her forehead, kissed the corners of her eyes, licked the salt tears from her cheeks. "James . . ."

His name was more moan than protest. His lips met hers, firm and soft, sending a burning thrill shivering through her. Almost involuntarily she ran her fingers through his hair, pressed the back of his head, holding him close as if she *wanted* his tongue to tease her mouth in that agonizing, heavenly way.

His hand under her chemise cupped her breast through the thin gauze of her shift, stroking, playing, gently rolling the nipple between his fingers. His mouth moved down to her throat, dropping little kisses all the way. She moaned again, wantonly, as he pulled up chemise and shift.

"How soft your skin is." His lips, his tongue were on her breast, kissing, caressing. His hand ran down her side towards her waist. "What's this?" A laugh in his voice, a tender laugh. "Don't tell me I have to tackle a corset!"

"Bribes!" Cordelia sat bolt upright, tearing herself from his embrace. "My diamonds. We can bribe—"

Outside, a rattling blast of sound rent the air.

James flung himself on Cordelia, flattening her.

The breath knocked from her body, she squawked, "Don't!" and struggled to sit up.

"Keep still," he snapped. "Stay down! That's gunfire!"

# Twelve

All thought of love-making had vanished from James's mind. As Cordelia ceased to wriggle, he was unconscious of her luscious body beneath him—well, nearly. He listened.

The ragged volley of musket shots was answered by screams, groans, yells, running feet, and a return volley. The light on the tent walls dimmed as soldiers kicked out the betraying flames of the camp-fires.

"Bandits?" Cordelia whispered.

"I don't know." James frowned in the darkness. "Bandits have little to gain by an attack on armed troops. Merchant caravans are their natural prey."

"Then who?"

"I don't know," he repeated, coming to a decision, "but this may be our chance. Get dressed, quickly, but for heaven's sake keep your head down."

He rolled off her and, still lying down, reached for his clothes. The pandemonium outside continued, the ragged exchange of shots, shouted orders in Turkish, and now cries in Greek, coming closer.

"Freedom or death!"

"St. George for Greece!"

"Kill the infidels!"

"Partisans," said James. "Fighting for independence. Are you dressed?"

"Nearly. I can't find my boots." Cordelia sounded more breathless than frightened. To his surprise, as he felt around for her boots she said, "I thought St. George was England's patron saint."

" 'God for Harry, England, and St. George.' Yes, but he was a Greek, I believe, so I suppose the Greeks have first claim. Here are your boots." His elbow knocked against hers. "Can you pull them on?"

"I think so. I've never dressed lying down before."

"Undressing is more fun. Keep down. We've been lucky so far, not a single shot has hit the tent, but it can't last." Rising on hands and knees, he collected such of their provisions as he could find in the dark and rolled them up in his blankets. As fugitives in those barren hills, they would need everything he could carry. If he managed to carry anything at all. If they escaped.

"What are we going to do?" Now she sounded nervous.

"First I shall rashly stick my head out to see what is going on. Hand to hand fighting now, I think."

The gunfire had given way to grunts, gasps, thuds, and the clash of steel. The Janissaries must have drawn their yataghans, the curved swords they always carried along with their modern rifles.

As James crawled forward to peek under the side of the tent away from the river, a glinting knife-blade stabbed through the cloth above his head. Drawn swiftly downwards, it split the fabric like the skin of a ripe peach, revealing a dark, bulky figure.

"Come," commanded a rough voice, in Greek. "Quickly."

James grabbed Cordelia's arm and came.

They stumbled through the slit. The man took Cordelia's other arm and between them they half helped, half dragged her away from the tent. All the fighting seemed to be on the far side, but James had no time to look around. By starlight their rescuer urged them onward, up the hill, through bush and briar and the inky shadows of the massive rocks. They came to a clear space where a score of mountain ponies were tethered.

"Wait."

The Greek disappeared downhill at a run, and a moment later they heard a piercing whistle.

"James, I cannot ride one of those horses. They have no saddles. Don't let them leave me behind."

He put his arm around her shoulders, felt her trembling tension. "After the trouble they have gone to to rescue us, I hardly think they're likely to abandon you. You shall come up with me. It's easier if you can ride astride, though."

"I put on my Turkish trousers. I'll try."

"Good girl. It's a pleasure to travel with so practical a companion." He laughed. "But I'm afraid once again we haven't a hairbrush or comb between us."

"Just now I cannot bring myself to care!" she retorted, and he laughed again, full of admiration for her spirit. "Do you really think they attacked the soldiers just to rescue us? How could they know the Turks held us captive?"

"Perhaps they watched from the hills and saw our mounts on leading reins, and the sentries set to guard the tent. As to why they attacked, the way they went about it seems to argue that their chief purpose was to rescue us, but as for why, I cannot imagine. Unlike the Serbs', the Greek uprising against the Ottomans is young yet, poorly organized, and hardly ready to take on troops at random."

"I'm glad they—Oh!"

All around them, silent figures flitted into the clearing. Below on the hillside James heard shouts in Turkish, but the Greeks made no sound except the groans of a wounded partisan carried between two others. A pony whickered and was swiftly quieted.

A man appeared beside James and Cordelia, leading two ponies. James could not tell if he was the same who had brought them up the hill.

"We lost four," he said tersely in a low voice. "Hurry, mount."

"They have good horses," James whispered as he obeyed. "They will follow."

The man's teeth gleamed white in a mirthless grin. "The way

we take, if they find it at all, is not fit for good horses. And we loosed their horses before we attacked." He turned to Cordelia. "Come now, *Kyria,* we must go."

"The lady will ride with me. Please help her up. I'll lead the other pony for when this grows tired from the double load."

James thought the partisan gave him an odd look, but the light was too dim to be sure. At any rate, without further ado he lifted Cordelia onto the pony's crupper and hurried off.

One arm around James's waist, Cordelia hissed, "He has put me on sideways."

"Damnation! You'd be much safer astride. Can you slide back a bit and get your leg . . . limb over?"

Removing her arm, she clutched at his clothes on both sides and shuffled back. The pony sidestepped restively. A knee hit James in the kidneys.

"Ouch!"

"Sorry. I'm caught up in my skirt. I'll have to—"

"Too late. Get yourself straight and hang on."

The partisans were beginning to file out of the clearing at a trot. A rider came up behind them and waved them on. James suddenly noticed that the shouts of the Janissaries were much nearer—he could only hope they had not yet found their dispersed horses. He kicked the pony's sides, hoping his youthful skill at bareback riding was not entirely forgotten.

Having Cordelia clinging to him with desperate determination was not a help.

He followed the rider ahead between a rocky outcrop and a huge boulder. For a hundred yards, hooves rang on stony ground. An outburst of shots came from behind, but none whistled near. Then they were among the firs, winding through the trees in black darkness, fallen needles deadening hoofbeats. James let the pony have its head until another outcrop loomed ahead, white stone reflecting just enough starlight for him to see the others veering left.

He followed. Abruptly the trees ended and the night seemed

almost light in contrast. Nonetheless, the leaders had slowed to a fast walk.

"James, I'm slipping. There's a fallen tree I can use as a mounting block. Let me settle properly."

He listened. The ring of hooves on stone once more came from ahead, but from behind no shots, no shouts. At least temporarily they had lost the soldiers. He turned aside to the tree-trunk.

Cordelia slipped down, hitched up her skirts, and quickly remounted. "Ready." Her arms encircled his waist and her soft bosom pressed against his back.

He allowed himself a sigh of regret for the interrupted seduction as he urged the pony forward again.

One of the partisans rode over to them and said angrily, "What are you doing? They will be after us soon enough."

James made no answer but trotted on to catch up with the rest. He soon found out why they had slowed. Their path lay across a steep, treacherous slope littered with loose pebbles. The sure-footed mountain ponies picked their way across it slowly but unhesitating, while the Janissaries' great troop-horses would have a devil of a time following, even if they found the trail. On this ground, few marks of their passage would remain even in daylight.

"I'm glad it's dark," Cordelia murmured, "but I think I shall close my eyes anyway. It is an awfully long way down."

"As long as you don't fall asleep."

"Small chance of that!"

He felt her lay her cheek against his back, and wondered again at the odd mixture of trust and mistrust she showed towards him. Only last night she had once more accused him of being a criminal. This afternoon she had expected him to save his skin and abandon her to the Turkish soldiers. This evening she had cringed when he entered the tent. Yet how sweetly responsive she had lain in his arms, and how still more sweetly she relied on him now to keep her safe in the midst of danger.

It *was* a long way down. He concentrated on the horseman ahead.

After a while the way turned uphill and they rode through a mountain pass. Before they started down the other side, James stopped to change ponies. Cordelia slid down with a whimper.

"I cannot go on," she moaned as he dismounted. "I'm so sore I shall never walk again, never mind ride."

Himself weary after all day and half the night on horseback, James let an edge of annoyance creep into his tone. "Come on, we cannot stay here. I have not the least notion where we are. We have no choice but to go on."

"I know." She turned towards the other pony and waddled two awkward steps, her legs far apart.

The tender skin of her inner thighs must be rubbed raw, James realized. Unaccustomed to riding astride, she was not merely stiff and tired like him, as he had supposed, but in pain. When he had suggested her riding astride, he'd expected a short, fast ride not this endless jog.

"You had best come up before me, seated sideways," he said, hoping his own strength would hold out. "If we continue at a walk, as I expect we will since we have wounded among us, it won't be too difficult."

He lifted her up on the pony's withers and mounted behind her. With one hand entwined in the mane, her other arm—at his insistence—around his waist, she sat quite straight, balancing with apparent ease as he urged the pony forward.

"That's much better," she said gratefully.

At first James found it easier too, without the drag of her hanging onto him behind. But as they rode on, her shoulders drooped and soon she slumped against his chest. Without stirrups to compensate, he had only the grip of his tired thighs and knees to keep him from sliding backwards. The ride became a nightmare of endurance until at last he was forced to call to the nearest partisan for help.

*"Kyrie,* will you be so good as to take up my wife before you for a while?"

Unfortunately Cordelia recognized the Greek word for wife. She stiffened in outrage. "I'm not your wife!"

"For the present you are," he said with what patience he could muster. "They saw us together in the tent, remember."

Silenced for a moment, she again protested as the obliging Greek stopped beside them, dismounted, and reached up to lift her down. "You cannot expect me to ride with a man I don't know."

James ran out of patience. "Better a noble patriot you don't know than an unprincipled scoundrel you do," he snapped. "Stop arguing, woman, unless you prefer to ride by yourself."

He might as well have saved himself the trouble, since the partisan, uncomprehending, set her on his pony's back and mounted behind her even as they spoke. They rode on.

Down they rode into woodland, and out into dew-drenched meadows as the sky began to pale. A flock of sheep and goats scattered bleating before them, the bellwether's bell ting-tonging. A ragged shepherd boy, seated on a rock, lowered his pan-pipes to stare. His wild, airy aubade followed them as they paused by a shallow, stony stream to let the ponies drink, then splashed through.

Before the sun rose, they came to a flat-topped, grassy knoll crowned with gnarled, silver-green olive trees and the dark, slender spires of cypresses. James was bone-weary. He had dismounted and tied his pony's bridle to a sapling before he noticed the ruins.

The sapling was forcing its way between cracked flagstones, companioned by thistles and dandelions and willowherb. Nearby a toppled pillar lay where it must have fallen an age ago, for ivy entwined it and moss grew thick on the north side. Scanning the scene with tired eyes, James thought he made out four rows of pedestals where pillars had once stood. The partisans used them as convenient stools.

By daylight they were not a prepossessing group, tattered, grimy, unshaven, some with bloodstained bandages to indicate their hastily bound wounds. As they arrived at the ancient temple, they tethered their mounts and piled their muskets before the man who must be their leader. Seated on a truncated pillar, he sent several of his followers to stand guard among the trees. Two men levered up a paving stone and began to stack the muskets in the hole revealed beneath.

"James!"

He swung round as Cordelia slid down from the pony. Her knees buckled and he just caught her before she subsided to the ground.

*"Efcharisto,"* he said to the partisan who had taken her up.

*"Efcharisto,"* Cordelia echoed.

The man nodded, his face surly as he turned away to tie his mount. He strode off to speak to the chief. James supported Cordelia to the nearest pedestal, cushioned with a mat of dead leaves and ivy, and she sank down onto it.

"I cannot believe I thought I was tired before." Her face was drawn, her hair uncovered after their hurried departure, dusty and coming loose from its braid.

He grinned. "Amazing what one can do if one has to, is it not?"

"Amazing, but I *pray* we don't have to go any farther for at least a few hours."

"You stay here. I'll go and see what their leader has to say."

"Pray give him my heartiest thanks. He may have made us ride a thousand leagues in a single night, but when I consider the alternative . . ."

"Complaining would appear churlish," he agreed lightly, forgiving her snappishness in the night. She was burned to the socket.

As he started towards the chief, the man stood up and beckoned impatiently. He was burly, and taller than most of the others. James thought he was the one who had cut open the tent and led them up the hill. For someone about to be thanked for a daring and courageous double rescue, he looked to be in no good temper.

The partisan who had carried Cordelia on his pony stood

beside the chief, looking as disgruntled as his leader. If he had not wanted to help, he should have said so before, James thought.

The chief stepped forward. "Stavros here says your wife is not Greek, and he suspects you are not either. I myself thought your speech odd, but there are many dialects in our country. Are you one of us?"

"I admire your struggle for freedom from the Turks."

"Are you Greek?"

"No, I and my wife are Swedish."

"By the gods of the underworld," the ancient oath exploded from his lips, "you are right, Stavros! We lost four comrades and risked all our necks to save a pair of foreigners, may Christos forgive me. Enough is enough. Let them fend for themselves now. Time we went home."

And within a very few minutes, James and Cordelia found themselves alone in the ruined temple, with no horses, no baggage, no food, and no idea where they were.

# Thirteen

The patter of rain on the leaves overhead woke Cordelia. Beside her, James stirred in his sleep, brushed a spider from his cheek, and rolled over. His arm settled across her breast.

She removed it, placing it firmly by his side. He need not think that because she had been forced to pretend to be his wife she was going to succumb to his undeniable charm. Last night he had taken advantage of her despair at the prospect of being forced to join Mehmed Pasha's harem. She had responded only out of a need for comfort. She was *not* a wanton like Mama.

Green light filtered down through the canopy above. So far no raindrops penetrated the thicket of ivy, bramble, and laurel roofing the corner where a tree had fallen across a tumbled pillar. The bed of dry leaves underneath her smelled faintly musky, a fox's den, James said. If so, the fox had not disturbed their sleep.

The leaf-bed rustled as Cordelia shifted. The sting of her skinned inner thighs cut through the overall ache of her abused body. She did not want to move, to get up, to walk in search of help.

Nor did she want to lie here getting wetter and wetter while the light faded until they had no choice but to spend the night in their borrowed shelter. She watched a drop gathering on a leaf, growing, collecting the insidious leakage until it was heavy enough to trickle down and splash, plop, right on James's eyelid.

He shot up, clapping his hand to his eye as if he'd been hit by a fist, not a drip. "What . . . Ouch!"

"You've got your hair all entangled with the briars. Keep still. There . . ."

"Ouch!"

"And there. Now lower your head, carefully. That's right."

"Did you hit me in the face?"

"Certainly not. It's raining and a drop landed on you."

"I dreamt I was King Harold at the Battle of Hastings, being shot in the eye with an arrow. Just a *rain*drop? Are you sure?"

"Quite sure. I watched it fall. That was a quick dream."

"Thank heaven. I did not enjoy it. Couldn't you have stopped the drip, or at least diverted it?"

"I didn't want to move. But I suppose we will have to." Another leaf disburdened itself on her sleeve. She sat up cautiously, hunched over. If her long hair mixed itself up with the brambles she'd have to cut it off—not that they had anything to cut with. She was hungry and thirsty, too.

"I daresay we had best be on our way," James agreed reluctantly. "We shan't stay dry here for long. I wonder how late it is. It's much darker, but perhaps that's because of the rain."

"It's all very well saying we must be on our way, but which is our way? The partisans went off in every direction."

"Sneaking home to their various villages, I imagine. At least it suggests there *are* a number of villages around. We'll go downhill and follow the first stream we come to."

"As we are on a knoll," Cordelia pointed out, "every way is downhill. And the first stream is right this minute flowing down my neck."

"Then let's go," he said with infuriating cheerfulness. Twisting onto hands and knees, he crawled out into the downpour. "Come on—no, wait. Take off those trousers first."

"What!" she gasped. What he had said of the pleasures of undressing lying down returned to her. Surely he had not decided to assault her here and now?

"The less Turkish you look when we find a village, the better. And sore as you are, you'll probably find it easier to walk without the cloth rubbing your skin."

How did he guess she was so sore? He should not be thinking about that part of her at all! He was right, though; she'd do better without the trousers. Kneeling, she reached under her petticoat, untied the drawstrings at knee and waist, and pulled them off.

With the trousers rolled up under her arm, she crawled out of the fox's den. The rain slashed down, a chilly, autumnal downpour. James was already bedraggled, his brown hair plastered to his head. No more than she had he contrived to bring a headdress from Captain Hamid's tent.

He pulled her to the slight shelter of the nearest olive tree and looked her up and down. "Respectable, no, but at least not Turkish. It's a pity you have no covering for your head. Could you wind your trousers into a turban?"

"Then I'd look Turkish again. Which reminds me, why on earth did you tell them we are Swedish?"

"The Turks are looking for an English couple. If I'd said we were Macedonian, or Croatian, or Albanian, in the first place someone might know the language, in the second they'd probably hold some ancient grudge against the people. Sweden's far enough away for them very likely never to have heard of it."

"Next time say Polish. At least I speak that."

"You do? You continually amaze me. Well, perhaps we can pretend Polish girls never wear a headdress."

"Oh, just a minute, I have an idea."

James watched, puzzled then amused, as she arranged the waistband across her forehead and tightened the drawstrings at the nape of her neck. Her hair was inside the trousers, rather insanitary but she was so filthy anyway it hardly mattered. The wide legs hung down her back like a cloak. At least the rain would not run down the back of her neck for a while.

"If we were in London, you'd set a new style," James said with a grin. "I'd say we have a couple of hours of daylight left. Let's go."

The heavy rain prevented any view of their surroundings from the top of the knoll, so they set off down the slope at random. The short turf had curious horizontal ripples, as if it had once been a wide staircase. At the bottom the old approach to the temple continued in a track comparatively clear of undergrowth, so they followed it.

As she plodded along, the rain began to seep through Cordelia's clothes, thick homespun though they were. The top of her head was sodden, but the quadruple thickness of the trouser-legs still protected her back somewhat. James, with no such protection, must have water running in a constant, clammy stream down his neck. She glanced at him, ready to commiserate, only to find him walking jauntily, as unconcerned as if he was strolling through an English meadow on a summer's day. Infuriating man!

Soon the track met another, wider and well-used though rough and stony. On its far side, a line of yellowed willows marked the course of a stream, beyond which rose a steep hillside.

"Downstream," said James firmly, so they turned left, picking their way between pothole puddles, their shoes squelching. Cordelia's limbs ached, her sores smarted and she was growing more and more soggy and chilled when a rumble and squeak behind them made them both turn. An ox cart loomed through the rain, lumbering down upon them at a speed minimally faster than their slow walking pace.

The driver, a withered old man with a red nose and a toothless grin, reined in his great, stolid beasts. He gestured wordlessly to James and Cordelia to climb up.

*"Efcharisto!"*

James lifted Cordelia up onto one of the solid wooden wheels and she scrambled into the back of the cart among earthenware jars packed in straw. Some smelled of pine resin and alcohol, others had greasy splashes on their lips—retsina and olive oil, she guessed.

James joined her. The old man grunted at his team and off they rumbled, jolting over the stones. The squeaky wheel was music to Cordelia's ears.

"This is heaven!" she said, scrunching down into the straw.

James looked at her. Looking at him, wet, cold, dirty, his

forehead scratched by the brambles, she had a very good idea of what he was seeing. They both burst out laughing.

The old man glanced round, grinned his toothless grin, and shrugged his shoulders.

"If this is heaven," James said, "where are the manna and honeydew? I could eat a horse and drink a lake."

"Perhaps you can persuade him to let us roast one of his oxen. At least ask him if he has a water-bottle."

This James did. The old man mumbled something, shrugged again, and passed back a bottle. James handed it to Cordelia, who took a long swig.

"Aargh!" She coughed and spluttered as the liquid set fire to the back of her throat, burnt its way down to her stomach, and brought tears to her eyes.

James rescued the bottle. "Not water, I take it. Are you going to survive?" He sipped. "Ouzo! Well, it would warm us but I don't think it's a good idea on an empty stomach, especially when we're so thirsty. How much did you swallow?"

"Quite . . . ughaa . . . a bit," she gasped. "What's ouzo? It's certainly warming!"

"A local type of brandy. In about thirty seconds you will be bosky, if not drunk as a wheelbarrow."

Cordelia giggled. "I do feel a bit odd. Why a wheelbarrow? *I* shall be drunk as an ox cart."

"I hope not!"

That was the last thing she remembered clearly when she woke up with her head on his shoulder. She had a vague impression of having found their plight uproariously funny. Returning to a cold, wet, twilight world, with a crick in her neck, a slight headache, and a raging thirst, she could no longer see the joke. She groaned.

"With us again?" James's smile was far too amused and insufficiently sympathetic. Just let him wait until next time he was seasick! "Good. We have reached a village at last."

"Water!" Cordelia croaked.

"My throat is as dry as the rest of me is wet. I hate to think how you must feel. Ah, here we are, wherever here is."

The oxen halted in a small, muddy square with a church on one side, a taverna opposite, and a well in the centre. James thanked their driver and vaulted over the side of the cart. His energy made Cordelia feel limper than ever. Bleary-eyed, she watched him turn the crank of the well, listened to the clank and creak as the bucket went down. The liquid sound of the splash as it hit the water roused her to action.

Clambering down, she did not clank but she could have sworn she heard her joints creak. She trudged over to reach him just as the bucket reappeared, full to the brim.

"Heaven!" She never would have believed plain, cold, clear water drunk from her cupped hands could taste so good. "Sheer heaven."

"Fire and food next."

The old man had disappeared, and the wooden benches and tables under the huge pine outside the taverna were deserted, but lamplight and the sound of voices came from within. Cordelia followed James into the low-ceilinged, smoky room.

Every voice fell silent, every head turned to stare. In the hush came a whisper: "The foreigners."

One of them must be a partisan, which meant James and Cordelia had to go on claiming to be Swedish—and claiming to be man and wife.

The only woman in the room, Cordelia quailed beneath their combined gaze, half curious, half hostile. Then James said, *"Kalespera!"* and some of them responded, "Good evening," before turning back to their wine, their backgammon, their pipes, their conversations, low-voiced now.

A tall, stout man in an apron came forward, looking them up and down with a disparaging expression. "What do you want?" he asked in a grudging tone.

Cordelia grasped very little of what he and James said to each other, but she understood the change in the man's demeanour when James mentioned money. They were ushered into a back room. In here the air was steamy and smelled divinely of frying onions and garlic and spices. Five children seated around a table stared, while the taverna-keeper explained the situation to an equally large woman stirring a pot over the fire.

"My wife, Marika," he said, and returned to his customers.

Clucking and tutting, Marika waved James to a bench beside the fireplace and tugged Cordelia through another door into a tiny room filled with a huge bed. The only other furniture was a wooden chest, from which she produced a voluminous black garment. This she laid on the bed and, with words and gestures, urged Cordelia to put it on in place of her wet clothes.

Fortunately she then returned to her cooking, as otherwise Cordelia would have had no space to turn around. She stripped off everything except the diamond cloth. Its outer layer was damp but somehow the inner layers had stayed dry.

Over it she put on her kind hostess's gown. It was rather like wearing a tent. Folds bunched about her feet and there was room for three or four of her inside, while the neckline drooped almost to her bosom. She rolled up the sleeves to her wrists, with both hands raised the front of the skirt above the floor, and waddled back to the other room.

Marika, who was chattering volubly with James, took one look at Cordelia and laughed heartily. She produced a shawl for a girdle, a beautifully embroidered kerchief for a fichu. Then she sat Cordelia down at the table with the silent, wide-eyed children and set bread and a bowl of thick, savoury bean soup in front of her.

She beckoned James into the bedroom, returning with Cordelia's wet clothes. These she hung on a rope tied across the ceiling, among braided strings of onions and garlic. James's wet clothes joined them when he reappeared in a shirt and breeches several sizes too large, eliciting another guffaw from Marika.

Grinning, he said to Cordelia, "I don't mind being a figure of fun as long as I'm fed. Is that as good as it smells?" He sat down beside her.

"Just as good, though I should have been happy with dry bread."

"Those *shish kebabi* seem an awfully long time ago," he agreed, gratefully accepting the bowl of soup Marika brought him. Half of it disappeared before he spoke again. "Ah, that's better."

Cordelia finished her soup. Marika promptly refilled her bowl, but the edge was off her appetite and she started to think ahead. "They haven't room here to put us up for the night, have they?"

"Unless we want to sleep in a cow-byre, I gather, only one house in the village is large enough, and that belongs to a cantankerous widow. She has no children and no aged parents. Luckily she's as renowned for piety as for ill-temper, so Marika has sent her son to fetch the priest, in hopes of persuading him to persuade the widow Eleni to accommodate us."

"In separate rooms."

"What, you don't want to spend the night with your dearly beloved husband?" he mocked.

She scowled at him. "Separate rooms."

"We'll be lucky to get any room at all."

Before he finished his second bowl of soup, the priest came in. A thin, nervous young man with a sparse black beard and liquid black eyes, he seemed bowed beneath the dignity of his sacerdotal robes and headdress.

According to James's translation, he was perfectly willing to do his best for them. However, as he shyly confessed, while Eleni was undoubtedly devout and had followed the least suggestion of his predecessor, he himself had yet to win her wholehearted approval. Still, the gospels had something to say on the subject of taking in strangers. He would try.

Marika encouraged him, and he went off looking determined.

The children were asleep on palliasses on the floor by the time the young priest returned. The widow Eleni refused point-blank to have a man in the house. If they did not object to separating, he said apologetically, Cordelia might go to Eleni and he would find a corner for James.

Cordelia breathed a sigh of relief.

Her relief was compounded the next morning when she discovered her monthly courses had begun. Explaining *that* to James would have been even more difficult than convincing him she did not want him to make love to her, whatever she had allowed in Captain Hamid's tent. As it was, explaining her needs to her hostess was far from easy, but at last Eleni understood and, grumbling, provided the necessary cloths.

Now all Cordelia had to do was delay their departure until her menses finished. Thank heaven the flow had not started sooner! She could not possibly travel with James for a few days.

Which brought to mind the question of whither they were to travel. Mehmed Pasha awaited her in Thessaloniki. Soldiers hunting for them on the coast road surely meant other nearby ports were being watched. Where could they go?

# Fourteen

"James, thank heaven you have come!"

"Now that's the kind of welcome I like to hear." With a grin, he sat down beside Cordelia on the courtyard bench sternly indicated by Eleni. The wood was damp, but the sky above was blue again, washed clean by yesterday's rain. "Has your hostess been browbeating you?"

"I think she has tried, but since I don't understand more than one word in three she has not had much success."

"She appears to have succeeded in cowing her plants," said James, glancing round the small courtyard. The mulberry tree in the centre was pruned to a few stubs and the small baytrees in terra-cotta pots had round-cropped heads which would have done credit to Oliver Cromwell's soldiers. In a raised bed, onions, garlic, and herbs grew in strictly serried ranks, beneath a clothesline laden with dripping laundry. "Lucky it's a fine day or I daresay she'd make me sit out here in the rain to talk to you."

"I could have met you elsewhere if I had anything to wear besides Marika's tent. My clothes dried overnight but they were so filthy I could not bear to put them on, so I washed them and now they are wet again." She waved at the clothesline.

"Mine too. Father Stephanos's wife found me these, which fit more or less, and washed mine, though I gather it's not normal to launder until Easter."

"Oh, is *that* what Eleni was trying to tell me? I just wish the

Greeks had adopted the Turkish custom of frequent baths. What would I not give for a *hammam!*"

"No such luck. I've put word about that we wish to buy clothes, as well as provisions and mules and a tent."

"Tents. I shall give you a diamond to pay for everything." She seemed unaware of the incongruity of handing out diamonds yet washing her own laundry. Other matters were on her mind. "James, it's all very well buying mules, but where shall we go? Mehmed Pasha is in Thessaloniki and the Janissaries will surely be watching the other nearby ports. Can we go directly west to the Adriatic?"

"In summer perhaps, but I'd rather not attempt it at this season. It's mountains all the way, snowbound in winter, populated chiefly by Albanian brigands. You are right about the Turks guarding the ports, though, so I believe our best hope is to travel by land to Athens."

Cordelia smiled. "Anything to postpone the agonies of a sea voyage?" she said teasingly.

"If you suffered as I suffer! But they cannot question every traveller on every road so if we avoid Thessaloniki and the main highways we should be safe. However, that will make a long journey still longer. The sooner we start the better, tomorrow at dawn if I can obtain all we need by then."

"Oh no! I mean, I need a few days to recover. You may be accustomed to adventure but I am not!"

He eyed her critically. Her cheeks were rosy, brown eyes bright, if anxious, her flaxen hair escaping in exuberant wisps from her braid—she must have washed it in spite of the lack of a bath. "Adventure seems to suit you. You look delightful, in spite of that extraordinary garment."

"I am not fishing for compliments, I assure you," she retorted sharply. "Indeed, I need to rest before we set out."

"Don't tell me your hostess is pressing you to stay?"

She grimaced. "Hardly. Oh, please, James, what difference will two more days make in the end?"

"None, I suppose. It may even allow the Janissaries' vigilance to decline." He shrugged. Game as she was, it must be difficult to face exchanging the comparative comfort of Eleni's house for a week or more on the road. Her thighs would be stiff and sore for some days, too, making even a sidesaddle devilish uncomfortable. "As you wish. Now, Eleni seems to be as well to pass as anyone in the village. Let me have a diamond and I'll see what she will offer."

Blushing furiously, she jumped up. "Yes, I'll go and . . . and fetch one," she said, and ran into the house.

James pondered Cordelia's blush. He remembered her sudden notion of bribing the soldiers with her diamonds. That, not the partisans' gunfire, was what had abruptly curtailed his seduction attempt. And the thought had struck her when his questing hand came to the unexpected obstruction about her waist. Ergo, she was probably carrying the diamonds wrapped around her, and a very good thing too or they would have been lost in the attack with the rest of their belongings.

So she would have to undress to give him a diamond. No wonder she had blushed. A curious combination of practicality and primness, passion and prudery, Miss Cordelia Courtenay!

He had never known a woman like her. He wanted her, but he also wanted to know what had made her the way she was. He was going to have plenty of time to find out, he reflected, on the long road to Athens.

Hearing her footsteps returning he looked up to see Eleni peering at him suspiciously from a window. Talking to the Greek woman was unlikely to make Cordelia view men with a more favourable eye. No doubt the widow had her reasons, but he wished Cordelia had not insisted on staying with her an extra couple of days. And that was odd, too. He did not believe she needed to rest and he would have expected her to be as eager to move on as he was. He frowned.

"What is wrong?"

"Nothing. Let's see." Taking the diamond from the palm of her hand, James held it up to the sun. Though small, its fiery glitter set rainbows dancing about the courtyard. "We'll never get its true worth here," he said regretfully.

"I just hope it will pay for what we need. I do have some cash left but if we spend it all here we may find ourselves wishing for it later."

"Very likely. I'm glad you were able to retain it in the confusion. Is your Greek up to asking Eleni to come out here, if she still refuses to let me into the house?"

"I'll try." She returned in a few minutes, shaking her head. "I think she understood, and I think she said she won't speak to you without the priest. I could not explain what you wanted."

"No matter. I shall try elsewhere first and come back with Father Stephanos if necessary."

"Come back anyway."

"Of course. I'll have to tell you what goes on, and I should not dare purchase any clothes for you without your approval! Once you have something decent to wear, you can go about paying morning calls on Father Stephanos' wife and Marika at the taverna. Unless you are too tired?"

"Not at all. I should like to get out of the house for a while."

So much for her need for rest. "I shall be happy to escort you. Well, I'm off." He kissed her cheek and stood up, smiling at her startled expression. "I'm your loving husband, remember," he said and strode off with a jaunty spring in his step.

Cordelia put her hand to her cheek, where the impression of his lips seemed to linger, burning. It reminded her all too clearly of her disgraceful behaviour in Hamid's tent. *His* disgraceful behaviour, she corrected herself quickly. She did not want to think about it but she had no occupation to distract her, not even a book. Perhaps she could persuade Eleni to help her improve her Greek.

Eleni could not be described as a willing teacher. Once coaxed into agreeing, she went about the business with a grim thoroughness which taught Cordelia as much in a few hours as she had learned from Ioanna and Mrs. Miltiades in several days. Those two amiable ladies had been so delighted when she mastered a new word that they had never attempted to correct her grammar. Eleni, having taken on the task, never let an error slip by. Uneducated as she was, nouns, verbs, adverbs, and adjectives meant nothing to her, but she knew when what she heard was wrong.

Cordelia's head was a-buzz with pronouns and prepositions by the time James returned.

"No luck," he said ruefully as Cordelia went out to join him in the courtyard.

"No one would buy the diamond? You did not try to drive too hard a bargain, did you?"

"I didn't bargain at all. As a matter of fact, I'm no hand at haggling—the fault of a gent . . . an Englishman's upbringing, I expect."

"No doubt," said Cordelia defensively. "Mama was always ready to pay the first price named, which is why I took over the marketing at an early age whenever she was between . . . whenever we had no servants. Haggling may be unladylike, ungentlemanly, but it is expected in a marketplace."

"And a way of life here in the Levant," James agreed with suspicious meekness. "I'm at a severe disadvantage, I admit. Let me hasten to explain that in this case I did not bargain because no one was interested in my wares."

"I suppose they are too poor."

"Oh, they live well enough, but as I feared, there is very little cash used in the village, and that goes about equally to the taverna and to taxes. They sell a little excess olive oil and wine—our friendly carter takes it to the nearest town along with the produce of the next village up the valley. Mostly they grow just what they need for themselves. A diamond is a useless bauble."

"Yes." Cordelia sighed. "When Aaron suggested diamonds, he assumed I should be travelling from city to city, not village to village."

"Cheer up. Eleni is generally reputed to sleep on a mattress stuffed with gold, which sounds deuced uncomfortable but may turn our trick. Father Stephanos is on his way."

However, whether the bed of gold was a myth or Eleni was just too crossgrained to help, the young priest's intervention failed. As she pointed out, she could not use the diamond to pay the wages of the men who tilled her vineyard or the women who picked her olives. Nor, as James had found, could she sell it to anyone else.

With an apologetic shrug, Father Stephanos went off, and Eleni withdrew into her citadel.

"Ah well," James said philosophically, "one cannot blame her. You had best let me have some cash. Already several people have brought goods to the taverna in hopes of selling to us."

"Then I shall just have to come as I am," said Cordelia, standing up. "We cannot afford to buy without haggling!"

He looked her up and down and laughed. "Gad, no! I cannot permit my wife to be seen in public looking like a perambulating marquee."

"I'm not your wife," she snapped. "And if I was, we are far enough from England for your credit not to suffer. If you have any credit."

"Which you most reasonably take leave to doubt. I beg your pardon, I ought not to have laughed, but it was at that garment not at you, I assure you. You look singularly pretty this morning."

Mollified in spite of herself, Cordelia grumbled, "Spanish coin will get you nowhere."

"On the contrary, any coin will serve as well to get us where we wish to go. I doubt they care whether our money is Greek or Turkish or Spanish, so it be gold. If you want to come with me, and I own your bargaining skill is needed, at least let us check whether your laundry is still damp."

He crossed to the line and felt her chemise, as though he could not just as well have tested a less intimate garment, she fumed. Sometimes he seemed quite determined to irk and embarrass her.

"That's dry," he said cheerfully. "With it next to your skin, the rest will soon dry on you. Go and change quickly, there's a good girl."

Not deigning to reply, Cordelia gathered her clothes and swept past him into the house. The dignity of her exit was somewhat marred when she tripped over a bit of hem she had not tucked high enough and had to reach for the doorpost to regain her balance. Fortunately, when she sneaked a peek backwards, James had his back turned and was gazing at the sky. Bother the man!

Even with Cordelia's skill at bargaining, three days later her purse was alarmingly light although they had not contrived to obtain all they needed.

"That poor little donkey will never carry everything!" she said gloomily as she and James checked their food supplies, a goodly stock since the less they had to speak to people on the way, the less trail they would leave for the Turks to follow.

James sounded not much more cheerful. "There's not another donkey to be spared for love nor money, and they have no mules or horses. He'll do it, and carry you as well according to his old master."

"I shouldn't dare ride. It would be too dreadful if he was injured."

"True. We'd have to carry everything ourselves."

"Oh, dear, yes. I was thinking of him, not us. The one thing I should wish to add to his burden is a tent."

"Most of the villagers have only the vaguest notion of what a tent is. The trouble is, no one ever goes farther than to the next village, and that only for weddings and funerals, except for the carter."

"And at least one partisan," she reminded him, "the man who told everyone we were foreigners when we had scarce arrived and not yet opened our mouths. But it does not help, since he has not offered to sell us his pony, and if he did I daresay I could not afford it."

"Perhaps we should go first to the nearest town, though it's considerably out of our way. We might find someone to buy a diamond and sell a horse or two and a tent."

"Or two. But we might not. It is very likely only a larger village at best."

"We can decide later. There is only one road out of the village and we don't have to make up our minds until we come to the first fork in the road, which is a good few miles, I gather. By then we shall have some idea of how well you go on on foot. We leave at daybreak, agreed?"

"Yes," she said, wondering miserably whether she would make it as far as the crossroad. She *had* to.

"All right, let us pack the baskets with food and the bundles with blankets and clothes. We must hang roughly equal weight on each side of the pack-saddle."

When the baskets were full of food and water, Cordelia could not shift them a single inch. James picked up one in each hand, to make sure they were evenly balanced. He was much stronger than he looked, she thought, reluctantly admiring. She could only hope the donkey was twice as strong.

At cockcrow next morning, James knocked on the shutter of her window. Already dressed, she slipped out to open the court-yard gate. He led in the donkey and she took the halter, stroking the skinny little beast's nose apologetically while James began to tie their mountains of baggage to the pack-saddle.

Reaching down for a basket, he groaned.

"What is the matter?" Cordelia whispered. She did not want to wake Eleni, having made her farewells the night before.

"My head. Some of the fellows spent a good part of what we paid them to give me a farewell party at the taverna."

"You should not have drunk so much."

"Don't be sanctimonious," he growled. "If it had been a good claret, the amount I drank would not have had the least effect. I just didn't make allowance for the local rot-gut."

In offended silence he finished loading the patient donkey, and they set out through the still somnolent village.

In spite of James's megrims, Cordelia enjoyed tramping along. Overhead, a brisk breeze blew puffs of white cloud across the sky, but down in the valley the air was still, though chilly. The road meandered between olive groves, leafless orchards, and neatly pruned vineyards, sometimes running along the stream for a while. Flocks of small birds twittered as they searched for seeds and insects, and from a distance came the bleating of sheep and goats, the tinkle of their bells.

As the sun rose higher, the day grew warm. Cordelia took off her head-kerchief, then her shawl. Without stopping, she tucked them through one of the ropes holding the donkey's load.

Her feet were tiring and her hurried breakfast began to seem a long time ago, but she refused to ask James to pause for a rest. He plodded on, lost in taciturn gloom, taking frequent swigs from a leather bottle which she hoped contained only water. The donkey plodded stolidly behind.

The valley narrowed and the orchards fell behind. The road curved around the base of a bluff, then crossed the stream by an old stone bridge. James stopped on the bridge and looked up at the sky, and Cordelia seized her chance to sit down on the low parapet.

"At this rate," James said sourly, "we shall be a month or more on the road to Athens."

"A month!" She jumped up. "Oh no! I shall try to walk faster."

"It won't help if you exhaust yourself. I'm sorry, we should have stopped for a brief rest sooner." He gave her a rueful smile. "I was afraid if I sat down I'd never be able to force myself to get up again."

"Is your head still aching?"

"Not much, and I actually feel I can face something to eat. You must be thirsty. Pray resume your seat, madam, and I'll dig out another water-bottle."

"Heehaw!" said the donkey.

"Oho, are you thirsty too? I'll take you down to the stream when— What's that?"

Around the curve behind galloped half a dozen ponies. Each rider had a cloth across the lower part of his face and waved a musket. Another three appeared from a clump of bushes on the hillside ahead and plunged down the slope, yelling.

"Oh hell!" said James. "Not again!"

# Fifteen

"Stop or we'll shoot!" shouted one of the riders, as though a woman, an unarmed man, and a laden donkey neatly trapped on a bridge had anywhere to go.

James found Cordelia in his arms. He was unable to savour the moment properly.

"Bandits?" she whispered, shivering.

"I find it hard to believe they are soldiers or partisans. Chin up, little one."

This advice proved impracticable as she was torn from him and flung face-down over a pony's withers.

"James!"

It went against the grain to let them take her, but he could do her no good if he was shot or clubbed insensible. A moment later he met the same fate. As his stomach hit the pony's bony shoulders, he was glad he had not eaten or he'd surely have cast up his accounts.

"What about the donkey?" someone cried.

"Bring it, you fool. Who can guess where they've hidden the diamonds?"

They knew about Cordelia's diamonds! Someone in the village was passing information to the brigands—or was one of them. Very likely, James thought cynically, the same young fellows who fought as partisans to free Greece also sought excitement in robbing travellers.

The ground beneath him wheeled as the pony swung round. Giddy, nauseated, he shut his eyes. Hooves pounded into a gallop and the jolting became well nigh unbearable. James's headache returned with redoubled force. The blood drummed in his head, echoing the pony's hooves, but worse still was the knowledge that Cordelia was suffering the same torment.

Soon thought became impossible. With every last scrap of strength, James struggled to stay conscious. The ponies surely could not keep up this pace for long, and when they stopped he must be ready to seize the slightest chance to protect Cordelia.

"The cursed donkey can't keep up!"

They slowed to a canter.

"Unload it and turn it loose. Don't leave anything behind or by St. Spiridion I'll slit your gizzards!"

Galloping again, on and on and on, just two sets of hooves now.

Yet when after an eternity they stopped and James was hauled off the pony's back, dizzy as he was he noted the sun still high in the sky. He stood swaying on the hillside. The turf at his feet, beginning to green after the summer's drought, sloped gently to a steeper, rocky drop. Beyond, a green plain crossed by a pale ribbon of road and a dark ribbon of river stretched into a blue-grey distance bounded by far-off hills. To the north, not far off, clustered the roofs of a small town.

One of the men lifted Cordelia down and set her on her feet. Her legs failed her. She sank to the ground, her face deathly white beneath a coat of dust. Her eyes fluttered open and her lips moved. No sound emerged.

A killing fury rose in James but the barrel of a musket swung to cover her and he gritted his teeth, his nails digging into the palms of his hands.

"Bring her," the man with the gun grunted at him.

The other was already leading the two ponies away somewhere behind him. He turned and saw the mouth of a cave, half concealed by bushes.

Cordelia moaned as he raised her to her feet. Despite aching ribs and head, his strength was swiftly returning, but he was afraid he might drop her if he tried to pick her up and carry her. He slung her arm across his shoulders, gripping her limp hand in his, and put his other arm around her waist. Staggering and stumbling, they followed the ponies into the cave, the man with the musket close behind.

The roof of the small cave was not far above their heads. Reflected sunlight showed it to be empty, the uneven limestone floor trackless.

The man in front led the ponies straight to the back and disappeared. Then the ponies' heads disappeared. James realized they were going round a wall of rock into a chamber beyond. No one simply glancing into the cave would notice the concealed passage or guess that the shallow, empty cave hid a den of thieves.

James stopped, blinded, as he passed from sunlight into dark. The gun-barrel instantly poked him in the back and he moved forward again, his eyes adjusting to lamplight.

The single lamp left burning on a broken stalagmite illuminated only a fraction of the inner cavern. Listening to the echo of their footsteps and the clop of the ponies' hooves, James reckoned it was huge. Somewhere water trickled and plopped. The vast, chill, impenetrable blackness made the nearest corner with its rugs and cushions and sooty hearth seem almost homey.

The first man led the two ponies off to the right, tethered them, and took off their saddles. As James gently lowered Cordelia onto a rug, the rest of the band of brigands filed in with their doughty steeds. They brought all the baskets and bundles taken from the donkey, even the pack-saddle and Cordelia's shawl and kerchief. With a challenging look, James retrieved the shawl from the heap and wrapped it about her shivering shoulders.

She gave him a pitiful smile. "Do you think the poor donkey will be all right?"

"I expect he will find his way home. They're clever beasts, even if we humans tend to use them as a model of stupidity. How are you feeling?"

"A bit better now. It hurts to breathe."

"Don't I know it! Bruised ribs, but that's the least of our worries, I'm afraid."

"They will kill us, won't they? We know their hiding-place."

A quick death was the best they—or at least she—could hope for, James thought grimly. He wondered whether he might provoke their captors into shooting them, by grabbing one of their guns, perhaps. But the muskets were stacked over by the ponies. In the unlikely case he reached them without being stopped, they would kill him long before he could return to Cordelia, leaving her at their mercy.

"It is like Ali Baba's cave, in the *Thousand and One Nights,*" she said, a hint of wonder in her tone.

James looked around. One of the brigands had lit more lamps while another fetched wood and built a fire on the ashes in the makeshift hearth. The added light revealed brass-bound chests, casks, wine-jars, sacks, bales of silk and brocade, the booty of the bandits' raids on merchant caravans. The grimy carpets they sat on were of the finest Persian make. The bandit chief, when he came over to them, was drinking from a chased silver tankard with an elaborate handle.

Setting it down, he growled, "Let's have your purses."

As he weighed the leather pouches in his hands, the others gathered round. Several of them were young men in peasant dress, no different from any to be found tilling the fields but for the gleam of excitement in their eyes. Four older men, including the chief, wore clothes which would not have disgraced the richest merchant had they been clean and well-kept rather than filthy and torn.

"This is the gems," said the chief. "Too light to be gold." He sat down cross-legged and emptied Cordelia's purse on the rug.

A groan of disappointment rose as her few remaining coins rolled about. Angrily the chief emptied James's hoard. The glint of gold pleased his followers, but he scattered the coins with his fingers, hunting for diamonds.

"Not here. We'll have to search their baggage."

"Time we was getting back to work," one of the young men said reluctantly. "We'll be missed."

"If them diamonds aren't a pipe dream, you won't need to work much longer."

"My cousin wouldn't make up a story like that," said another of the peasant lads, injured.

"He'll be sorry if he did. You be off then. Come back at dusk. You'll get your share of the loot and you can take the bodies to dump in the river."

"Don't knock the wife on the head till we've had our share of the fun, too. I kind of fancy that yellow hair."

"We'll keep her alive for you, never fear."

James glanced at Cordelia. He knew her grasp of Greek had vastly improved over the past few days and he feared she might have understood their plans for her, if she had not already guessed. However, though still pale and frightened, she looked no more appalled by their situation than before.

"They know about the diamonds," she whispered, as the younger men led out their ponies, "and they think I'm your wife, don't they? Someone in the village must have told them."

He nodded. An idea began to germinate in his mind, a possible way to save her from degradation before death.

She watched the remaining brigands start to search the baggage. "They will be furious when they cannot find the diamonds. I'll explain that I have them and hand them over." As she spoke, she stood up and took a step towards the men.

"Wait!" said James, jumping up as he realized what she was about, too late.

One man grabbed her and two seized James by the arms.

"Better tie 'em up," grunted the chief.

"That's not necessary," James protested.

"Wouldn't be, maybe, if you could keep your wife in order."

"She's not my wife." He saw Cordelia wince as her hands were wrenched behind her back and her wrists bound. Lord, he hoped she wouldn't understand what he was about to say!

"That's what I heard," the brigand said, uninterested.

"We've been travelling as man and wife. It's easier that way. But she's really my doxy."

"Don't make no matter to me."

"Oh, but it does. When I say she's my doxy I don't mean she's my bed-mate." He attempted to smirk as a stout cord tightened painfully around his ankles. He was trussed like a chicken, dammit. "Leastways, not any longer. I sell her services, and believe me, with her looks I was onto a good thing."

The brigand chief showed no sign of contempt at James's revelation that he was a pimp. "High-price whore is she? All the better. P'raps she'll show us a trick or two afore we wring her neck." Then James's words registered. "What d'ya mean, you *was* onto a good thing? And why not any longer?"

"Disaster struck. She caught the Persian pox."

"Persian pox? What's that?"

He lowered his voice dramatically. "A horrible disease, like the plague and leprosy rolled into one, only worse. It don't show in a woman, not for years and years, but in a man the symptoms come out in just a week or two."

All four men stared at him, mouths agape. "W-what happens?" one gasped.

"First sign's when your balls turn blue. Well, sort of purplish. Then the colour creeps slowly down your prick and up your belly till it comes to your belly button. That's when it starts to change to black, and you piss black, and your balls swell up big as a pig's bladder. At the same time, your prick begins to wither like a dead vine. And when it's all withered, it falls off."

"Aargh!"

"And then you die?" breathed the chief, shuddering.

"Some do. It's the ones that don't I'm sorry for." Though proud of his command of colloquial—not to say vulgar—modern Greek, James decided it was best not to embroider on that statement. "Like the pasha who was her last customer. That's why we had to hop it from Istanbul in a hurry, only the bastard sent the Janissaries after us." A nice touch of the truth, there.

"Taki's cousin said the Turks arrested them, chief."

"That's right. They caught us when we were peacefully on our way to find customers some place where we're not known."

"Why are you warning us?" demanded the chief suspiciously.

"I thought you might be grateful and let us go, seeing we can't afford to peach to the authorities."

"Ho, you did, did you? Think again. What's to stop you telling someone else where to find us and leaving it to them to peach? No, dead men tell no tales, that's my motto. Nor dead poxy whores, neither." With a malevolent glance at Cordelia, he turned away. "It's going to take a while to go through this lot properly."

They dumped the contents of the bundles on the floor and on their knees started searching through the heaps of clothes, running their fingers along every seam.

"What did you tell them?" Cordelia asked James. She lay curled on her side, her eyes huge and dark in the lamplight.

"I hoped if they knew about the Turks chasing us, they'd realize they could safely let us go, but no such luck," he said regretfully. By gad, they wouldn't be raping her though, he exulted. It wasn't worth the risk, even if they doubted his fantastical tale. The farrago of nonsense had scared them half out of their wits. He could not quite suppress a smile.

"If they are determined to kill us why are you grinning?"

Some day when she was being annoyingly prudish he'd tell her—if they survived, which seemed impossible. Perhaps the story would serve to take her thoughts off their imminent fate. He had not quite made up his mind when running footsteps sounded in the outer cave.

One of the peasant lads appeared, panting. "The Turks!" he cried. "They're coming! Taki's dead and they've nabbed the others. You've a chance, but hurry!"

As the brigands sprang to their feet, he swung round and raced out again.

James watched with bated breath as the four men sped to grab their muskets. If they chose to they could easily withstand a siege, which their captives would undoubtedly not live through.

But they cut their ponies' tethers and hustled them out of the cavern, shouting as they got in each other's way. A moment later, the drumming of hooves faintly penetrated through the outer cave.

And then gunfire.

James wriggled across the rugs till he could briefly touch Cordelia's cheek with his in a gesture of comfort. "While there's life there's hope," he said.

"Out of the frying pan into the fire," she retorted.

"Come now, even the pasha's bed must be preferable to a knock on the head followed by drowning in the nearest river. Or perhaps they will not find us."

"In which case we shall starve quietly to death, unless your bonds are looser than mine."

"They are devilish tight," James admitted. "Hush, someone is coming."

A man stepped into the cavern and paused to regard the scene. The Janissary's tall headdress was unmistakable. So was the glint of lamplight on the pistol in his hand.

"Well, well, well, fancy meeting you again," said Captain Hamid, transferring his pistol to his left hand. "I shall be happy to report finding you dead at the hands of the bandits." He drew his yataghan.

# Sixteen

Cordelia stared up at the soldier, wondering whether having one's throat slit by a Turkish sword was a less painful way to die than being hit on the head and drowned. The diamonds, she thought frantically. She could bribe him—no, he could easily strip them from her dead body.

"Anyone else in here?" he asked, peering into the heavy darkness.

"No, they're all gone," said James cheerfully. What did he see to be cheerful about? "Like rats deserting a sinking ship."

"My men will take them." Captain Hamid holstered his pistol as he approached. "This time we weren't the ones caught napping."

"How did you find this place?"

"We were on patrol on the road down there." He waved his yataghan at the cave entrance, then bent down towards Cordelia.

She tensed, only to catch her breath on a sob of relief as he sliced through the knotted cords around her ankles.

Turning to perform the same service for James, Hamid continued, "We knew the brigands had a hiding place somewhere nearby. I'd like to claim cleverness, but it was by Allah's will I happened to look this way through my spy-glass just as they carried you up the hill. Four people and two ponies disappeared into what I had been told was a very small cave, followed by another six or seven men and as many ponies."

"Aha, you said to yourself, something fishy there. I say, my dear fellow, it might be a good idea to use a smaller blade to free our wrists. Were you looking for us?"

"Yes." He sheathed his sword and drew a knife. "The Greeks took you north and west. You wish to go south to Athens, and this is the only good north-south road. Meess Courtenay, if you will please roll over so that your hands are in the light, I shall be less likely to draw blood. That is good."

She felt the strands part one by one, cold steel against her skin, then the painful throb of blood returning to her veins. Her arms were free. She sat up and chafed her wrists, thankful they had not been tied for more than a few minutes.

*"Thank* you, Captain," she said, as he freed James.

"My pleasure, *Bayan.* Now we must make plans before my men return. These are your goods?" He gestured at the tumbled heaps of clothes, the baskets and rolled blankets, and the coins strewn on the rugs. "You must move them further into the cave, out of the light and well away from the robbers' treasure."

"You'll be taking that with you, I suppose?" said James, taking one of the lamps and moving off into the darkness.

"Yes, I must have evidence against the brigands, and there will be a reward for me and my men. Whatever can be identified will be returned to the owners—those who ran off fast enough when they were attacked. However, if that is all the money you have left, you had best fill your purses." He crossed to a pile of small leather sacks, opened one, and grunted with satisfaction. "Here, Meess Courtenay. This will help you on your way."

"Thank you, Captain, you are very kind. But I don't know how we are going to carry all our stuff."

"There is a donkey outside. Is it not yours?"

"A donkey! James," she called towards the distant light, bobbing among stalagmites and stalactites, "the donkey must have followed us. I'm so glad, I was worried about it."

"You have a good heart, *Bayan.* I shall try to leave a pony or two, but our own pack-horses cannot carry all this treasure, so it depends upon how many of the brigands we take prisoner and how many we leave to feed the buzzards."

Returning without the lamp, James said cheerfully, "Speaking of which, are you going to need to show your men our dead bodies?"

Hamid grinned. "They must see something. When you have moved your baggage, go right to the edge of the circle of light, where it grows dim. Lie down flat on your backs and pull a rug over you, faces and all, as if I had covered you. Meess Courtenay, try to arrange your beautiful hair so that it shows. This will convince them of your identity, *inshallah.* It is fortunate that you are infidels. They will not think it sinful to leave you to the wolves instead of taking your bodies for proper burial."

"You seem to have thought of everything!" James said with admiration.

"If not, I shall be in bad trouble." Hamid drew a finger across his throat.

"It's deuced good of you to take the risk for us."

"The prophet forbids the persecution of women. Also, England drove the French from Egypt and I believe the time will come when England and Turkey will be allies against the Russian bear. I hope you will speak well of my country when you reach home. Now I must go and see what is happening outside, and you must move your belongings. Do not delay."

Cordelia hastily bundled up the clothes while James lugged the baskets to where he had left the lamp. Then she scooped up the spilled coins.

"You had plenty of money all the time," she accused. "I thought you were destitute."

"A loan from Uncle Aaron." He looked down at her, half abashed, half laughing. "Though I doubt I shall ever be able to repay it. I didn't know about your brilliant haggling. For all I knew you were an extravagant female who would waste the ready as if it grew on trees. Besides, it seemed a good idea to sell your diamonds where we could and to save my funds for emergencies."

"In the village we could not sell a diamond."

"No, but by then revealing my hitherto concealed wealth

would have made you angry. I hoped if I waited until we were in desperate need, you would be more pleased than annoyed."

"Perhaps," she grudgingly admitted.

He went off with the last load and she took the opportunity to tie her purse around her waist under her clothes, a much more complicated manoeuvre than taking it out. It was heavy again, with the bandits' gold, and the sack the captain had given her was still three-quarters full.

James came back with the lamp. She gave him his purse and the sack of gold. "We'll keep this with us for the moment," he decided. "Is there anything else?"

Cordelia glanced around. "No . . . Yes, look, they left several muskets!"

"Splendid! We'll take a couple of those, one to shoot and one to load. I'll teach you to load while I fire."

"I know how to load. A pistol at least and it cannot be very different."

"Good gad, how on earth . . . ?"

"Count Szambrowczyk taught me to shoot."

"We'll take four of these, then, though I'd rather have a rifle and a brace of pistols, and a shotgun for game. And here are powder and ball. Bring a light, will you?" His arms full, he started off towards their cache, asking over his shoulder, "Who the devil is, or was, Count Whichik?"

She wished she had not mentioned the count, talk of whom could only lead to the revelation of her mother's disgraceful history. "Captain Hamid may return with his soldiers at any moment," she pointed out, following him with a lamp. "We must go and lie down. Do hurry."

"Don't want to break an ankle. Careful now!" he said, as she stumbled. The swinging lamp cast monstrous shadows of strange limestone formations. "This place would be worth exploring."

"Not now!"

"No, right now we'd be better off dead."

"Oh James, what a horrid way to put it! I was sure the captain was going to kill us himself when he spoke of reporting us murdered by the brigands. How did you guess he meant to pretend?"

"Hamid is a natural gentleman. Being one myself, I recognize the breed."

"Indeed," said Cordelia sceptically. Captain Hamid might qualify but she was far from persuaded James Preston did.

They returned to the brigands' nest. James picked up a dirty blanket and regarded it with disgust. "Squalid, and probably verminous. Still, beggars can't be choosers."

"We should have kept one of ours. Too late now. Just pray it doesn't make us sneeze."

"Nor squawk when the fleas bite. You take this and I'll bring a carpet to lie on, or we're going to be devilish uncomfortable."

Even with a carpet under them, spread on the flattest space they could find on the murky outskirts of the circle of light, they were vastly uncomfortable. Ridges and bumps obtruded themselves beneath Cordelia's spine. One slight pressure she had grown used to, though, failed to make itself felt on the back of her neck: her pearls were gone.

The string must have broken while she was head down over the bandit's pony. The pearls were not valuable in comparison to the diamonds, but it hurt that she had lost her last memento of Mama.

"Is your hair sticking out?" James asked.

"No, I forgot." Reaching up to arrange her braid, she turned her head and held it at an awkward angle. The blanket smelled abominable.

"Faugh!" said James, flipping back the edge covering their faces. "We'll pull it up when we hear them coming. Listen."

She lay rigid, straining her ears. The distant gurgle and plink of water was suddenly loud. Their breathing soughed like a sirocco and her heart thumped a drumbeat against her still aching ribs. Her wrists and ankles hurt where they had been bound. She did not dare stir.

"Relax your muscles," James whispered. "Let your feet flop sideways. Corpses don't stay heel to heel and toe to toe."

"How did you know my toes were pointing up?" said Cordelia, letting her feet flop.

"I can feel how stiff you are."

"We are not touching." Even so, she was suddenly shamefully aware of his intimate closeness. A fiery spark quivered to life deep within her. *I'm dead,* she reminded herself. *He's dead. We have to convince the soldiers we are dead or we really will be.*

"You radiate tension," he said, silently laughing at her, at a moment like this!

All the same, when he took her hand in a warm, strong clasp, she held on tight.

It seemed like forever they lay there. Cordelia developed an itch between her shoulderblades, another on the back of one knee, whether from fleabites or sheer fancy. Just when she was sure she had to scratch or scream, the thud of booted feet came from the outer cave, then Hamid's raised voice.

"Those who checked this cave before must have just glanced in from the entrance," he said loudly. "Sheer carelessness!"

James flipped the edge of the blanket over their faces and quickly pulled his arm back beneath it. This time Cordelia reached for his hand.

The Janissaries tramped in, exclaiming over the vast cavern and the brigands' hoard. A hush fell when Captain Hamid pointed out the supposed corpses of the couple they had been seeking.

*"Allahu aalam,"* they murmured. "God is all-wise."

No footsteps approached. No one questioned the captain's assertion, nor suggested removing the bodies, for burial or to show to their superiors.

"Take only the valuables," Hamid ordered. "We have no use for old clothes and bedding and filthy carpets. Sergeant Abdullah, you have the keys taken from their leader? Let's get those chests out into daylight and see what's inside. Maybe we can transfer the contents into sacks, which will be easier to carry with us."

Listening to the thumps and rattles and clinks as the Janissaries carried off the spoils, Cordelia now itched to turn her head and observe. At least it took her mind off those other itches. In fact she found they had vanished, which she hoped meant she had not been attacked by fleas or bedbugs.

A muffled snort came from James and he let go of her hand. She held her breath. If that was a swallowed sneeze, he was now desperately pinching his nose, but a sneeze suppressed had a way of escaping with an even greater explosion. Her fists clenched and she realized her toes were pointing straight up again in a thoroughly uncorpselike fashion. Should she keep still or let them flop?

Who would have believed it was so difficult to play dead?

James gasped and she nearly jumped out of her skin. She was sure she must have jerked like a hooked fish, but if so, no one was looking.

Or no one but Captain Hamid. Cordelia was excessively glad to hear him say, "That looks like the last. I'll just check around and make sure there is nothing else worth taking. Start loading the goods, but remember, I don't want to take more ponies than absolutely necessary. It's just more to be fed and watered." The footsteps of several men receded, then one set approached. "All right, you can come out now."

James flung back the blanket, sat up, and sneezed hugely. The echo ricocheted round the invisible walls of the cavern, mingling with the sound of running feet. James hurriedly lay down again and pulled up the blanket.

"Captain?"

"All's well, Sergeant." Hamid spoke from the far side of the pool of light, where he was bending over a pile of clothes. A fast and silent mover, Captain Hamid. "I was just checking these sheepskins and the smell made me sneeze."

"Filthy bastards, these Greeks, sir."

"The first thing I'll do when we've delivered the loot and

the prisoners is visit the *hammam.* Go and get on with the packing. I'll be with you in a moment."

"Yes, sir." Once more the sergeant's footsteps receded.

"Are you going to do that again, Mr. Preston?" the captain enquired.

"I don't think so." James sat up more slowly this time and gave Cordelia a hand. "Anyway, they'd just think it was you again.

"It sounded like a barrel of gunpowder exploding," said Cordelia. "They must have thought Captain Hamid had been blown up."

Hamid grinned. "God is merciful. But I have no time to waste. Meess Courtenay, I must ask a favour. The four who stayed in the cave are all dead and unable to deny having murdered you. But be so good as to give me a little of your hair to show Mehmed Pasha as 'proof' of your demise, or at least of your identity."

"You can cut it all off!" James declared. "From now on Cordelia will travel as a boy, as my younger brother."

"Certainly not!"

She blushed as the captain looked her up and down and raised sceptical eyebrows. "You think it wise . . . and possible?" he asked.

"If you had heard what those bandits planned, you would agree it's essential, Captain."

"W-what?" Cordelia faltered.

"I am too much the gentleman to tell you, but I promise you I never want to go through a moment like that again. Let the captain cut off your braid. It should convince the pasha."

Biting her lips, Cordelia turned her back and bowed her head. A gentle tugging was all she felt as her one claim to beauty vanished.

"With your permission, Meess Courtenay, I shall keep a lock as a memento of a brave and charming woman."

"Please do, Captain." Blinking back tears, she turned to smile at him. "I shall never forget a generous and chivalrous soldier."

"Nor I." James shook his hand, then frowned as he regarded Cordelia. "I must say you still look rather female. I hope a change of clothes will help."

"There are sheepskin coats and hats and warm cloaks over there," said the captain. "They will help the disguise and you will need them in the north."

"North!" James exclaimed. "We are going to Athens."

Hamid tilted his head back in the Turkish gesture of negation. "I am sorry, this I cannot permit. Even if the hunt for you is called off, in the south patrols are frequent and foreigners are often asked to show their papers. You will be caught and I shall die with you. Even Meess Courtenay—when we last met I had not personally spoken to Mehmed Pasha. I now believe he pursues you more in anger than in passion. If you are caught, we shall all three die unpleasantly."

Shuddering, Cordelia recalled stories of concubines sewn up in sacks and thrown into the Bosporus to drown. "James?" She touched his arm.

"Perhaps you're right, Captain," he acknowledged. "Better the furious winter's rages than the furious pasha's rages. I've heard death by freezing is not unpleasant. North to the mountains it is."

# Seventeen

"Two ponies!" James stood among the bushes at the mouth of the cave, gazing down the slope in the dusk. "I must say, Captain Hamid has done us proud."

"Is everyone gone?" Cordelia hovered inside the mouth of the cave, ridiculously self-conscious in male clothing though she told herself it was not so different from a Turkish woman's. For the hundredth time she touched the ragged edges of hair at the nape of her neck. Her head felt strangely light.

"Not a soul in sight. We must be off first thing in the morning, though. The local people will probably come to see if anything worth having has been left behind. I'll bring the animals in for the night."

She ventured out as he started down the hillside. The steep, rocky drop beyond the meadow had discouraged the ponies and the donkey from wandering off. All three raised their heads as James approached. The donkey, its pack-saddle still on its back, gave a welcoming bray and trotted towards him as if delighted to find it had not been abandoned again.

Cordelia looked out over the wide valley as the last crimson sliver of sun set beyond the hills on the far side. High over her head an eagle soared—or a buzzard. She turned to the north. There the setting sun still blushed on mountain peaks, the mountains they must cross to reach Ragusa on the Adriatic coast, and a ship to Italy. Three hundred miles as the crow flies, Hamid said, but they were not crows and winter was coming. She shivered.

On the near edge of the valley, not far off, lamps began to shine in the little town. A Turkish bey resided there, the governor of the rich agricultural lands of the river basin. They had not needed the captain's advice to avoid it and the highway leading to it. They'd find plenty of cart tracks running through the fields and groves and orchards.

James returned and handed her the donkey's halter. "I can't take all three at once through the inner entrance."

"I'll bring him." She stroked the velvety nose and led him after the ponies. "You ought to have a name, faithful as you've been."

"Call him Achates."

"Oh, yes, that's the perfect name."

Glancing over his shoulder, James said in surprise, "You know who Achates was?"

"Aeneas's faithful companion, in the Aeneid."

"You have read it?"

"Not in Latin," she said defensively. "Only in Italian. I thought it was horridly bloody but *Zio* . . . the Conte di Arventino said it is a classic everyone should know."

"Another count and another language! You still have not explained the Polish chap."

To her relief, he disappeared around the rock wall as he spoke so she did not have to answer. She lingered a moment in the outer cave, looking back at the bands of lemon and green in the western sky. Then suddenly it was dark and she had to feel her way forward until the brigands' lamps came into view. The vast cavern seemed positively cosy, particularly when she considered the prospect of crossing the wintery mountains without a tent.

"I have an idea!" she exclaimed, leading the donkey over to where James was tethering the ponies. "At least," she went on doubtfully, "do you suppose Achates could carry two carpets on top of the rest?"

"He may stop loving us quite so much but I don't believe it would hurt him. You've seen the enormous loads the peasants make donkeys carry. A carpet *would* be more comfortable to sleep on than the ground, and warmer."

"Yes, but I was thinking we might use them above us, stretched over sticks perhaps, like a tent to keep off the rain."

"Not to mention snow. That is a splendid notion! We'll take two, one for under us and one for on top."

She instantly objected. "Two tents, one each."

"You cannot expect poor little Achates to bear four carpets," James pointed out. "Fetch me a lamp, will you? There's a leather bucket here and I'd better give these fellows a drink."

Cordelia brought a lamp and he went off towards the sound of water. Watching the light bobbing away, she decided there was no point arguing over the number of tents. She did not want to overload the donkey. As long as the weather held fine, they could each have a carpet to sleep on, and with luck they might be able to buy a proper tent—*two* proper tents—before they needed them. Only, would Achates be overloaded with two tents?

She was *not* going to share a tent with James ever again. And what about tonight? There was plenty of space but would he observe a proper distance?

Returning with a full bucket, he said with a sigh, "I daresay I ought to sleep in the outer cave tonight."

"You think someone might come? Or wolves?" she asked in alarm, remembering what Captain Hamid had said.

"No, not really. But if we are to rise early one of us needs to be where daylight is visible and I am far too gentlemanly to suggest that it should be you."

"Thank you," she said gratefully, forgetting that a moment before she had regarded him as a far from gentlemanly seducer.

By noon next day they were well past the town, having seen no one but peasants, few of whom turned their heads from plough or pruning hook to observe the travellers. They had forded the river, fortunately not yet swollen by autumn rains. Now the day grew hot, and Cordelia hotter.

"It's all very well saying this cloak makes me look more like a boy," she said crossly as they stopped on the riverbank to eat and rest, "but it will not help if I expire from a heat fever before we reach the mountains."

"Very true, and you must be tired, too. We'll stay here through the hottest hours. There is plenty of grass for the animals, and the bushes will both give us shade and hide us from anyone who passes."

Already dismounted, James watched critically as she descended from her pony's back. She wished he wouldn't—swinging one's leg over a horse's rear end was neither elegant nor ladylike—but sooner or later she would have to do it before more eyes than his. And she was pleased when he said, "Not bad, not bad at all, if more like an old man than an active lad."

"I am a bit tired, though not as much as I expected. Riding astride is much easier than side-saddle when one has the right clothes." Especially with drawers under her breeches. With a sigh of relief she discarded the heavy woollen cloak.

"Just don't forget to tell me if you start to get sore." James started to unload the donkey and she went over to help. "It will waste much less time to stop right then and take a rest than to have you laid up for days unable to ride at all. Here, take Achates down to the water, but don't let him drink more than a mouthful or two until he has cooled off a bit."

"How do I stop him?"

"Just pull on his halter and lead him out."

Achates had other ideas. Instead of rejoining Cordelia on the bank when she pulled, he jerked his head and she joined him in the river.

It was sheer bliss. Leaning back on her elbows in the shallows, Cordelia let the cool water run over her, washing away road dust. The sun on the bushes filled the air with the fragrance of myrtle and bay. Beside her Achates swigged to his heart's content and beyond him the two ponies drank deep.

James stood on the bank, holding the ponies' reins and laughing at her. "Let's hope donkeys have less sensitive stomachs than horses," he said. At that moment, both ponies decided to wade out a bit deeper. Not concentrating, he followed them with a mighty splash.

"Let's hope ponies also have less sensitive stomachs!" Cordelia said as he came up spluttering.

He looked ruefully at the happy pair, muzzles deep in the river. One came up for air, snorting and shaking his head. Silver drops flew.

"Too late to worry. They ought to have names, don't you think? Since we already have Achates, how about Dido and Aeneas?"

Though she agreed, Cordelia did not like the names. After all, Aeneas had callously deserted Dido, and it seemed a bad omen to name her mare after the unhappy queen. But if she mentioned her qualms, James might think she still feared he would desert her, which would offend him. And she was *not* afraid of that any longer, or at least only when she awoke in the small hours of the morning in a vast, empty cavern.

She returned to practicalities as Achates decided he had had enough to drink and hauled her out of the river. Sodden, dripping, she let him lead her to the lushest patch of grass where she hobbled him, as James had shown her at their earlier stop. Then she fetched dry clothes from a bundle and disappeared into the bushes to change.

When she emerged with an armful of soggy garments, James was hobbling Dido and Aeneas. "I'm going to wash these properly," she said, "or at least as well as I can without soap, and the cloaks too. They should dry fast if I spread them over the bushes. Get changed and give me yours."

"It's only fair that I should do my own. You shall show me how. What about the sheepskins? Are they too heavy to dry?"

"Probably, but more important I'm afraid washing may spoil them. You cannot wash furs." She had learned that in the affluent days with the Margrave of Rennenburg, but she was not about to mention another foreign nobleman to James.

He groaned. "You mean we have to go about stinking all winter? They have been airing on top of Achates' load all morning and they still smell."

Inspiration struck Cordelia. "We shall roll them up with myrtle and bay leaves inside and hope the scent will counteract the stink. But later. I'm hungry and I want to do the laundry before we eat."

Much refreshed by their impromptu baths and an hour's sleep, they set off again as soon as the worst of the midday heat had passed. Soon they turned west through a gap in the hills. According to the map Captain Hamid had quickly sketched for them, this would bring them to the River Vardar, which they could follow northwest as far as Skoplje. Beyond that, he could not advise them.

Long before reaching the town, he told them, they would leave the Greek provinces of the empire. In the provinces to the north, such a mix of peoples and languages was found that they were unlikely to be recognized as foreigners, or rather as non-subjects of the Ottomans. A good road ran up the Vardar valley and he thought there was little danger in their taking it.

This they did. After the first day, the weather turned damp and chilly, and Cordelia had no further objection to wearing a cloak. Her notion of using a carpet as a makeshift tent, draped between rocks or bushes, worked well as long as the wind did not blow too hard. To her relief, though they shared its shelter James made no attempt at unwanted familiarities, thanks, no doubt, to weather too inclement to invite unnecessary undressing.

Despite the cold rain, they avoided seeking lodgings in the villages they passed through. They bought fresh food to supplement their supplies, but if they stayed questions were bound to be asked to which they had no satisfactory answers.

On the road, they met Macedonians, Albanians, Greeks, Serbs, Gypsies, and Bulgars, as well as Turks. Each had their own national costumes and languages. For the most part Greek and Turkish served well enough when James and Cordelia needed to communicate, but she was delighted to find her Polish came in useful. A Slavic language, it had much in common with Serbian. As they were likely to meet more and more Serbs, she started to teach it to James as they travelled.

However, they never rode along with other travellers, always falling behind if they could not pull ahead after an exchange of greetings.

The valley narrowed as they continued north. Often hidden in mists, the bleak hills on either side boasted few trees but the rains brought fresh grass springing, to the delight of ponies and donkey alike. Between the plentiful forage and their new, shaggy, winter coats, their once visible ribs disappeared.

Cordelia, on the contrary, began to feel her ribs for the first time in an age. Even with the occasional quail, pigeon or rabbit James shot, their travelling rations were spartan fare. Together with constant exercise, they proved a more effective reducing diet than any her mama had recommended over the years. What was more, she felt full of energy and she was growing much stronger. Soon she could ride all day with only brief rests, as much for the animals' sake as hers.

"If anyone had told me I should positively enjoy spending day after day on horseback in the rain, I should have thought them tottyheaded," she said to James when they set out on the day they expected to reach Skoplje. "But I have enjoyed it."

He grinned. "Must be the company."

"Yes, Dido and Aeneas and Achates are excellent company," she retorted with a smile. "All the same, I shall be glad to spend the night at a caravanserai if you really think it's safe."

"Hamid said it is large enough for anonymity if we only stay one night."

"As long as we stay in the town long enough to visit the *hammam.*"

"He did say it's one of the most splendid in the empire, but we are not travelling to see the sights."

"Wretch! It's a bath I want and for all I care the building

may be built of wattle and daub. I cannot visit it as a boy, though, James. I shall have to turn back into a female for a few hours."

"A delightful prospect!"

She looked at him severely. "It is lucky we have plenty of funds to take two rooms, thanks to Captain Hamid and the brigands."

"Yes," he agreed with a sigh, "I cannot pretend we are short of money. However, we have a long journey ahead of us, with no more large towns on our way. If you will entrust a diamond or two to me, I shall seek out a jeweller."

"Aaron did not give me the name of a trustworthy jeweller in Skoplje. Neither of us could have guessed I might pass this way! You won't take the first price you are offered?"

"Nothing less than double," he promised, laughing.

By mid-afternoon the sky cleared and ahead of them the sun shone on the domes and minarets of Skoplje. Next the red-tiled roofs appeared. Riding across the ancient Roman Vardar bridge they entered the town.

The first person James accosted directed them to the caravanserai. The season being advanced, many routes were already closed by snow so the huge inn was not busy and they had no difficulty taking two rooms next to each other. James tipped the ostler in the stables to ensure good treatment for Dido, Aeneas, and Achates. Then they picked up such of their belongings as they could carry and followed a servant burdened with the rest.

The great courtyard was surrounded by two stories of galleries with rounded arches on square pillars. Their rooms were upstairs, each with a barred window to the gallery, another to the outside, and a door with a hefty lock.

"Travelling merchants would soon cease to frequent a caravanserai where their valuables were not safe," James said. "You can leave your diamonds and money here when we go to the *hammam*."

"Good. Let's go right away. I shall change my clothes and meet you in ten minutes."

He escorted her to the *hammam*'s women's entrance and went off to the men's side. She entered the windowless, multi-domed building rather nervously, since she had never before taken a Turkish bath without Aisha or Amina to attend her. The thought of letting strangers wash and massage her body embarrassed her. However, the hired attendants were so matter-of-fact about the whole business that she soon relaxed and enjoyed the process of ridding herself of weeks of dirt.

The only awkwardness came when one of the women exclaimed over her hair. Cordelia explained vaguely that the colour was because she came from the north, and that she had had to have it cut off because of a recent illness. She was overwhelmed with sympathy. As if to compensate her for its shortness, they all gathered round to praise its fairness.

James was waiting for her when she emerged, glowing, into the chilly dusk.

"I've got the name of a Jewish jeweller," he said triumphantly. "I'll wager he's at least heard of Uncle Aaron. Let's get those diamonds and I'll go and knock him up."

"If he is Jewish, I shall come too."

"You're the haggler," he agreed, grinning. "Shall you be my brother, my sister, my wife, my mother . . ."

"Not your mother!"

"No, he'd never believe it. You are too pretty. Be my wife."

Cordelia nodded, but a curious pain twisted her heart. She did her best to disregard it. It was not as if she wished him to ask her seriously to be his wife. The last thing she wanted was to be wed to a ne'er-do-well scamp, even if he was a wonderful travelling companion.

They fetched two diamonds from her chamber and found the jeweller, who turned out to have actually done business with Aaron of Istanbul. He bought the jewels at what seemed a fair price, then invited them to dine with his family. Despite grumbling about the short notice, his wife provided a magnificent meal, while he provided advice about the journey ahead of them.

As a result, next morning before setting out they bought a

tent, a compass, a cooking pot, and a tin bucket to melt water for the animals to drink. They also hired the guide he recommended.

Dinko was a blithe young Macedonian who had left his isolated village to make his fortune in the big city of Skoplje. He scraped a living guiding travellers along the mountain tracks to his home, which lay on the most direct, if not the easiest, route to the Dalmatian coast.

He agreed, for a modest sum, to lead James and Cordelia the thirty miles to his village and as far beyond. After that, they must rely upon finding in each village a guide to the next.

Besides his knowledge of the way, Dinko's chief virtues were cheerfulness and a total lack of inquisitiveness. He expressed no interest whatever in his clients' affairs. If he guessed that Cordelia was not the boy she tried to appear, as seemed probable in the circumstances, he considered it none of his business. Having discovered her excessive modesty in regard to bodily functions, he was careful always to disappear behind a rock or a bush to relieve himself. Nor did he wish to share the tent, an effeminate invention, however cold it was outside.

And it was cold. Soon after leaving Skoplje, they started up a single-file path zigzagging across a steep, rugged slope. Before they had gone far, a glance across the river gorge at the north-facing crags on the south side revealed snow clinging in patches wherever the rock was flat enough to hold it. The brigands' cloaks and sheepskins were now necessities without which they'd have fared badly.

As the beasts plodded upward, Dinko's estimate of ten miles a day began to look optimistic, not meagre, as James had supposed. Worse, he reckoned ten miles on the ground equalled at most three in a straight line. The two hundred miles on the map between Skoplje and Ragusa—Dubrovnik the Slavs called it—might easily stretch to a thousand.

James kept his conclusions from Cordelia, but she was no fool. She stopped talking about Christmas in Italy. Had he been mad to let Hamid persuade him to bring her this way?

The zigzag climb ended in a plateau, inches deep in snow and littered with boulders. The few, leafless bushes were stunted, for lack of soil, according to Dinko. Without him they would never have found the track which meandered for several miles to the start of the descent.

Barren plateaux cut by deep, narrow, wooded valleys; paths carved into the sides of ravines or climbing dizzying precipices; tiny, hospitable villages of thatched huts perched on the sides of mountains, between riverbank winter pastures and high summer pastures; now and then the distant howls of wolves. James and Cordelia learned to choose a camp site sheltered from the biting north winds, to build a campfire that would burn all night. She never complained.

She need not have worried about sharing a tent with him. Though no more snow fell, it was far too cold to contemplate removing anything but his boots, and those he often kept on. He watched her face grow thinner, wondering about the figure hidden beneath layer upon layer of clothing.

Heartily welcomed by Dinko's family, they spent a night in his home village, then pressed on. Three days later, when another, indistinguishable village came into view a half a mile ahead, he announced he could take them no further.

"Those people Albanian Moslems," he explained in the hybrid tongue they used. "Don't like Christians, don't like Macedonians, but for travellers from far away no trouble." With that he left them, turning back alone as jauntily insouciant as he had started out.

The Albanians proved dour, but quite willing to sell bread and sheep's milk cheese for gold. Several of them spoke a little Turkish, just enough to understand that James and Cordelia wished to hire a guide to the next village and to explain that no guide was available. All the younger men were either down in the valley with the flocks or out hunting. However, the way to the next village was easy, as it ran along the side of a gorge with no side turnings to lead them astray.

"Perhaps we should stay here until the hunters return," James said doubtfully.

"They say they may be gone for days, and it's only six miles. Let's go," Cordelia urged.

An old man led them to the edge of the village and pointed out the path. It looked quite straightforward, so they rode on.

Within an hour James heartily wished they had not. First the sky swiftly clouded over, then big, feathery flakes of snow began to fall. A fierce wind swirled along the gorge, blowing snow in their faces and trying to pluck them from the path. There was no shelter in sight, not so much as an overhanging crag. Soon he could scarcely see his pony's ears ahead, and behind him Cordelia was no more than a dark blur.

Drawing rein, he called back against the howl of the wind. "It's not safe to go on. We'll have to stop." Not that sitting still in the middle of a snowstorm was exactly safe, he reflected wryly.

# Eighteen

Behind a barricade composed of two ponies and a donkey, James and Cordelia huddled against the cliff. He put his arm around her waist and pulled her closer to his side. She looked up at him, nothing but her eyes visible between the sheepskin hat, topped by her cloak's hood, and the shawl across her lower face. A snowflake landed on her eyelashes. He wanted to kiss it away before it melted, but his own face was equally swathed.

"Cold?"

"No, not really, not yet. I daresay I shall be if we have to sit for long." She laughed, to his astonishment. "Do you recall telling Captain Hamid death by freezing is not unpleasant? I hope you are right."

"We are not going to find out. If there is no sign of the storm abating soon, I shall go on and fetch help. On foot I can feel my way, and the village cannot be very far ahead."

"Three or four miles. You are not going without me, James."

"My legs are longer, to plough through the snow, and I'm heavier, less likely to be blown over the edge."

"But if you were blown over, I'd rather fall with you than be left to freeze alone. With you going ahead, leading Aeneas, you will trample a path in the snow for me."

"I suppose so."

"Don't agree with me! Arguing is very warming."

James laughed. "Boys should have more respect than to argue with their elder brothers," he said provocatively.

"Never having had a brother, I cannot offer an opinion. But

I'm glad you didn't say ignorant females should not argue with men."

"No one could call *you* ignorant, though as a general principle I support that opinion."

They disputed the subject in a bantering way for several minutes before Cordelia fell silent. The wind had slackened somewhat, but the snow fell thicker than ever, drifting against the animals. James could not see how deep it was beyond them.

"I should hate to be stuck here in the dark," Cordelia said softly.

James stood up and peered into the swirling flakes. Though visibility was already minimal, he supposed darkness might make it worse. Even without the wind tugging at them, one false step on the narrow track would be fatal. He wished he had a good, solid wooden staff to probe the way ahead. If only he could guess how much longer it was going to go on snowing.

"James, look!"

He swung round, reaching for the nearest musket. A tall, black figure loomed through the white obscurity like a monster from a nightmare, an afreet, an ogre, a cyclops, or a troll.

The troll raised a hand and spoke in a deep, reassuring voice, in Serbian. Something about children?

"Be at ease, my children," Cordelia translated, continuing in Serbian-flavoured Polish, "Who are you?"

"Father Josif."

"A priest!" she exclaimed in English.

They exchanged a few more words, James catching bits and pieces, then the priest said in excellent Greek, "It is not good to be benighted on the mountainside in the snow. If you will follow me, I shall lead you to the monastery."

"Monastery!" James offered Cordelia a hand to help her struggle to her feet. "We were going to the next village."

"So was I, but in such weather the nearest shelter is the best. The village is a good eight miles off, the monastery not more than one."

"We were told six miles village to village," James said indignantly, "and no one mentioned a monastery at all."

"The Moslems would not think to direct anyone thither." Father Josif gave Cordelia a searching glance as she bent down to take Dido's cheekpiece, urging the pony to rise. "And even in such weather, alas, I cannot be sure the monks will admit a woman to their cloisters. Their rule against it has stood for half a millenium."

"This is my little *brother,*" James said firmly, grabbing Achates' mane as the donkey followed Dido's example. He was alarmingly close to the edge, even for so sure-footed a beast.

"Then you must be St. Francis." Father Josif's laugh was an echoing boom. "No, no, I know what you meant. Allow me to help you load *this* little brother." Leaning a stout staff—the sort James had just been wishing for—against the cliff, he picked up a basket as easily as if it were empty.

Though no troll, he was a head taller than James and brawny beneath the long black robe flapping about his ankles, with a pack on his back adding to his bulk. He seemed oblivious of the cold, sandals on his feet and his head bare but for a dusting of snow. His long, full beard was untouched with grey.

"You are not a monk?" James asked, tying the basket to the pack-saddle.

"I am a humble parish priest. Few of the villages hereabouts are Christian, and fewer still are large enough for a church, so I make my rounds, winter and summer. I daresay I could walk this path blindfold. The ascent to the monastery is a little tricky, but if you follow me closely we shall have no trouble."

Father Josif agreed that it was safer not to ride, so they gave part of Achates' burden to the ponies. Leading Aeneas, he strode confidently ahead through the drifting snow, two large feet and four hooves tramping out a path for Cordelia, who followed with Dido. James brought up the rear with the donkey. To him the priest was invisible, Cordelia a dark patch veiled with white. The wind had died and the flakes fell straight down now, a slow, unceasing, mesmeric cascade. He kept his eyes on Dido's bobbing rump.

"Please, not so fast!" Cordelia called out in Greek, a phrase she knew well from her lessons.

The priest's booming laugh came back to James. "My apologies, little *brother.* I walk so often alone, I forget the good Lord gave me extra-long legs to help me carry out my duties."

James translated into English for her. "I'm afraid he has guessed you are a woman," he went on. "Did you understand what he said about the monks?"

"Monks! What monks?"

"He's taking us to a monastery."

"I thought we were going to the next village."

"Apparently the monastery is much closer. The trouble is, no women are allowed."

"And you think Father Josif has guessed? Oh James! Will he tell them?"

"I believe not, to judge by the way he called you little brother. As a village priest—and Orthodox priests marry, remember—he's probably more tolerant than a bunch of celibate monks shut away from the world on a mountaintop."

"And surely they would be less likely than he to suspect I'm not a man."

"That would depend on the monastery's . . . er . . . conveniencies."

"You mean they may have communal . . . ?"

"Privies," he said, deciding to give her the word without the bark. "Dormitories for visitors, too, rather than cells."

"Oh no! And if they find out, what will they do? Throw me out in the middle of a snowstorm?"

"We'd be no worse off than before Father Josif came along," James pointed out.

"And no better. I . . . What did you say, Father?"

"Be careful here. We turn off the main track and there are steps. Soon it will grow steep, too steep for horses perhaps, but pack-mules come up with supplies in the summer so your animals will not find it too difficult, I trust."

James translated.

"Off the track?" Cordelia exclaimed in English, stopping. "The Albanians said there was no way off. Perhaps we should go on to the village after all."

"Father Josif says it is much farther than we were told, and if there is one side path there may be others. We might easily lose our way."

"Suppose we ask him what the accommodations are?"

"We'd have to explain. As long as he doesn't know for sure I doubt he will give you away, but if we told him he might feel obliged to inform them. I would prefer to go on to the monastery, but I leave it to you to choose."

After a moment's silence, she said with a sigh in her voice, "Very well, the monastery. At least we may get a little rest and shelter and a hot drink before we are ejected."

"Courage, little brother. I shall think of some excuse to—"

"Are you in difficulties?" Father Josif called in Greek, then repeated the query in Serbian, having apparently worked out that Cordelia understood it better.

"No, we are coming," they assured him multilingually.

James was beginning to appreciate being a native of an island where—apart from the Gaelic and Welsh fringes—everyone spoke the same language. More or less, he amended. A Yorkshireman and a Cornishman were pretty near mutually incomprehensible.

Thereafter, Father Josif gave his warnings in both languages. The way grew steep, the drifts deeper, and the wind picked up again. The falling snow swirled and eddied, sometimes clearing so that James could see Cordelia plodding on with bent head, and the tall shape of the priest in the lead. Once a gust parted the white curtain just long enough to reveal a masonry wall of smooth stone blocks, seemingly growing out of the sheer rock from which it rose.

Catching a glimpse of the vertical drop to his right, James was glad when the curtain of snow closed down again.

Not long after, they came to a stone archway with a weathered Greek *chi-rho* carved on the key-stone. Its heavy, iron-barred gates were closed, the scarred wood suggesting they had withstood more than one siege. There was no room outside them for battering ram or cannon, James noted grimly, always supposing besiegers could get either up the hill. The flat space, enclosed on the outer side by a low wall, was crowded with three people and three beasts.

Father Josif tugged on an iron handle set in the wall beside the gates. As a bell jangled within, he hastily reached into the bosom of his robe and pulled out a black, cylindrical cap.

"One must strive not to give offence," he said cheerfully, teeth gleaming white in the midst of his black beard as he jammed the cap on his head. He had to hold it on with one hand against the wind.

In the wall above the bell-pull, a panel swung open behind a small, square grill. "Father Josif! Welcome!" cried a disembodied voice in Serbian, which Cordelia translated as he spoke. "You have brought us guests?"

"Two storm-buffeted travellers, Father, with two ponies and a hard-working donkey. Pray let us in before we turn into six monstrous icicles."

"Ha ha," the voice uttered uncertainly, as if the porter laughed seldom and expected jokes from Josif but was not sure whether this was one. "I come, I come."

"Cordelia, pretend you're ill," James said quickly as the gates creaked open. "Not at death's door, but bad enough to need to spend a day or two in bed."

After a startled glance, she nodded. She took a step backwards and put her arm around Dido's neck, leaning heavily on the mare. "A day or two in bed would not come amiss," she said wryly in a failing tone.

"Father Josif, my brother is unwell! He was ever sickly, child and youth, and I fear the cold wind has made him ill."

The priest swung round. He gave Cordelia a shrewd look and his dismay changed to amusement. Shaking his head reprovingly, he winked at James, then turned back to the porter, a tiny greybeard with a cowl over his round cap. Father Josif's explanation made him wave them hurriedly through the gates, into the shelter of a cloister.

The gates closed behind them, shutting out the biting wind.

In no time Cordelia was ensconced in a tiny, stone-floored cell with walls of whitewashed plaster, the only decoration a simple wooden crucifix. The small, high window had no glass, just an iron grating, but as it overlooked the cloister the draught was not too bad, and the abbot gave special permission for a brazier. In fact the room was much warmer than their tent. The furniture consisted of a low bed, a wood frame laced with leather thongs supporting a thin mattress.

"*Much* more comfortable than a carpet on the ground," Cordelia declared. Curled up in most of her clothes, with two blankets, her cloak, and her sheepskin coat on top, she fell asleep before James, playing the anxious elder brother, left the cell.

Father Josif awaited him in the passage, with a stout monk he introduced as the infirmarian. Father Nikola was eager to get to the patient, but with the priest acting as interpreter, James said firmly that his brother was sleeping. The infirmarian agreed disconsolately that sleep was the best medicine.

"When my brother awakes," James said to Father Josif, "I think he ought not to visit the privies, which are doubtless cold and draughty. Would it be possible to procure a chamber pot for him?"

The priest eyed him with mischievous understanding. "You are an excellent brother. I shall see what I can do." He explained to Father Nikola, who brightened at the thought that he could be of some help. He hurried off. "When he returns," said Father Josif severely, "I believe it would be politic for you to attend the church service which is about to begin."

The monastery's church was an astonishing contrast with the austere quarters James had seen so far. Candlelight revealed richly coloured frescoes of saints covering every inch of the walls, gleaming with gold-leaf haloes, and bejewelled crosses, statues, and icons sparkled.

Ignorant of the service, James stood at the back watching and listening. In constant motion, the monks lit candles and snuffed them again, bowed, prostrated themselves, kissed icons, swung a censer which filled the chilly air with the pungent smoke of incense. Endlessly, tirelessly, they chanted and read and prayed.

James made no claim to be tireless. After a while the fascination wore off, the incense stung his eyes, the chill crept up from the stone floor and his legs began to cramp from standing still. He considered prostrating himself, just for the sake of a change of position, but he feared it would appear the sheerest hypocrisy. Yet he did not want to walk out and offend his hospitable hosts.

To his immense relief, Father Josif appeared beside him and whispered, "The abbot excuses us weary travellers from the rest of the service, may the Lord bless and keep him."

They slipped out. The sound of chanting followed them down the corridor.

"You are not Orthodox?" Father Josif enquired.

James had been properly brought up in the Anglican Church, though he seldom thought about it. He didn't want to introduce complications by mentioning England. "I'm afraid I'm a Protestant," he said.

"Better than a Roman, Moslem, or Jew, but best not to mention it. Let us go to the kitchens. There is bound to be a pot of soup on the fire and I do not belong to an ascetic order!"

"I'd like to go first to make sure our animals are well cared for, and to see whether my brother is awake and as hungry as I am."

Cordelia was awake, hungry, and bored. Fetching bread and two bowls of thick lentil and vegetable soup from the kitchen, James sat on the edge of her bed to eat with her.

"I was sorry to leave Father Josif to eat alone," he said. "He's an excellent fellow, and discreet, but I'm sure he is curious about us and the less opportunity for questions the better."

"And I thought you were eager for my company!" she pouted.

James grinned. "That too, of course."

"What have you been doing?"

He told her about the church service. "For all I know it will go on for hours yet," he finished.

But when he left to return the empty bowls to the kitchen, he met Father Nikola hurrying down the passage towards him. In a mixture of Polish, Serbian, and sign language, he did his best to convey that his brother had gone back to sleep after eating a little, a very little—luckily only Father Josif knew Cordelia's soup bowl had been nearly as full as his own.

Looking grave, Father Nikola said several times, "Tomorrow, tomorrow," and patted James's shoulder sympathetically.

Before James retired to his cell for the night, he warned Cordelia about the persistent infirmarian.

"What if he comes to see me in the morning before you are up?" she fretted. "He will want to examine me and he is bound to guess I am a girl. I shall be thrown out."

"Then we shall go on to the next village as we should have if Father Josif had never found us, having had a hot meal and a good night's rest."

"It is not so easy. We are no longer on the direct route to the village."

"Oh Lord, you're right! I'd forgotten. Well, we'll just have to see that Father Nikola has no chance to examine you. Shall I spend the night with you?"

"Oh, yes, please!"

"Splendid." He could not resist teasing. "I have been longing for this moment but I thought you'd never agree. The bed is a trifle narrow for both of us, but where there's a will there's a way."

"James, please!" she said crossly. "That's not what I meant, as you know very well, and besides, this is a monastery."

"But I am no more a monk than I was a eunuch before. No,

no, you don't need to throw your boots at me! Remember you are ill," he begged, laughing.

"I wish I had never pretended to be ill!"

"But you did, and you might take a turn for the worse in the night, so no one will wonder if I share your room. Not, please note, your bed. I'll fetch my mattress."

Though he slept well, periodically James half roused to hear a bell pealing and he knew the monks were once more on their way to prayers. Waking at last to a pale half-light, he went to the window and stood on tiptoe to peer out. Beyond the cloister snow still fell. He began to fear that by the time it stopped the monastery would be snowbound, perhaps for the rest of the winter. What would they do if they were ejected but could not get to the next village?

He turned to look at Cordelia. Her head pillowed on one hand, dark lashes kissing rosy cheeks, a slight smile on her thoroughly kissable lips, she looked very feminine and not at all ill.

Someone knocked on the door. Her eyes opened, full of alarm.

"Pull the covers up," he hissed. "You're still asleep."

He slipped out. This time, Father Nikola had brought another monk to interpret, a tiny, wizened old man with a grey beard to his waist and ink-stained fingers. No doubt he had a superb grasp of old Greek ecclesiastical texts, but his modern spoken Greek was decidedly shaky.

It suited James very well. He announced that he now thought his brother was not ill but simply overtired from their long journey. This took the elder such an age to translate, with many consultations back and forth, that Father Nikola did not attempt to ask questions. The infirmarian said he would put up a restorative potion, but if the lad was not much revived by the next day, and eating well, he feared there must be more amiss than mere exhaustion.

Cordelia took one sniff at the potion and refused to taste it.

However, she was perfectly willing to eat a huge breakfast, luncheon, and dinner.

"Which is all very well," she pointed out, "but though he won't insist on examining me if I'm not ill, I cannot go on hiding in my cell if I'm no longer tired. They will expect me to join in their communal life as much as you do. I know I shall be discovered."

"I'll think of something," James promised. But his mind was a complete blank when, next morning, he woke to the expected knocking at the door.

# Nineteen

"It's a glorious day," declared Father Josif. "I trust your little brother is well enough to travel?"

"Yes, indeed!" James sagged against the cell door in his relief. "She . . . he has completely recovered, thanks to Father Nikola's tonic."

The priest's eyes twinkled. "I shall tell the good father he has effected a marvelous cure. We shall leave as soon as we have broken our fast, for the going will not be easy."

Their departure from the monastery was an ominous portent of the difficulties ahead. The wind had piled snow against the gates almost to the arch above, and when the porter opened them, he was knocked down by a minor avalanche.

Father Josif was undeterred.

Monks with shovels cleared a way for them through the monstrous drift. As they emerged at the top of the track, a vast white panorama spread before them, mountain beyond mountain dazzling in the sun, beneath a clear blue sky. Surprised at the warmth of the sun, James reminded himself he was in southern climes in spite of the wintry view.

The track proved steep enough to have shed most of its burden of snow, but the footing was decidedly slippery, with a sheer fall of several hundred feet to one side. Even the intrepid Father Josif, in the lead again, crept downwards with extreme caution. Dido and Aeneas did not care a bit for the descent, though Achates took it in his stride with his usual patient aplomb.

With several anxious moments but no mishaps, they reached

the main track along the ravine. This was less dangerous—easy it was not. In places the snow was over the animals' heads, but Father Josif bulled his way through the drifts with inexhaustible energy and good cheer. Well-rested and well-fed, Cordelia tramped along happily behind him leading Dido. Luck had truly been on their side for once when they met the priest.

Behind her, James echoed her thoughts. "It was our lucky day when Father Josif found us. Without him we'd never have reached the next village. I could not march through snowdrifts without turning a hair as he does, loath though I am to admit myself bested."

He sounded so disconsolate, she had to comfort him. "He knows the path, and he is big as an ox, besides. I daresay it would have taken us longer without him, but you would have contrived somehow. You always do."

"My thanks for your confidence in me, though not all of our escapes have been my doing." He laughed. "One way or another, we have always succeeded in scraping through by the skin of our teeth, have we not?"

"More often than I care to recall!" Cordelia said tartly. "We have had more than our fair share of adventures."

"Just think of the tales we'll have to tell when we get back to England. That is . . . Oh Lord, I hadn't thought."

"Thought of what?"

"I'm not going to be able to tell any tales which involve you, and you are going to have to keep quiet about this journey altogether. Otherwise your reputation will be in shreds."

"Why?" Turning her head to stare, she stumbled.

"Careful! We cannot discuss it now. You must watch where you're going."

"But James—"

"Not now."

He said no more. Glancing back a moment later, she saw he was frowning.

Why should her reputation be in shreds? Cordelia thought rebelliously. She had not done anything to be ashamed of, not like Mama. Not quite—thanks, admittedly, to the unwitting intervention of a band of Greek partisans. Hot all over at the memory of a certain brief interlude in Captain Hamid's tent, she determinedly turned her attention to her surroundings.

For some way the track had been slowly but steadily descending. Now she realized the ravine had widened. Not far below, trees grew on the valley floor and grass was visible through rapidly melting snow.

Father Josif looked back at her and grinned. "Soon we shall stop to rest, and to eat. I am hungry. Fighting the snow takes much energy. You walk well, little sister."

She smiled at him. He had known all along!

Over luncheon, the priest advised them that Cordelia would do well henceforth to resume her own sex.

"Among the Albanians," he said, "a woman alone may travel safely without fear of molestation. Indeed men often take a female relative with them on a journey to reduce the chance of being attacked, for the Albanians are a quarrelsome people, much given to blood feuds. The Montenegrins, on the other hand, have an immense respect for sisters, much more so than for mothers or wives. The love of a sister, they say, is pure and unselfish and much to be prized. I do not know, and I do not ask, what is your relationship, but I suggest you travel as brother and sister."

"It is much easier to ride astride, in breeches," Cordelia said doubtfully. "In fact, we have no sidesaddle."

Father Josif waved his hands. "Ride astride. Wear breeches, but wear a skirt over them."

"I don't like it," James said in English, frowning again. "Those Greek bandits were all set to ravish you."

Cordelia winced at his frankness. "If I'd been dressed as a boy, sooner or later they would have searched us for the diamonds and found out. And not all guides will be as accommodating and uninquisitive as Dinko about my . . . my need for privacy. Truly, James, I'd rather not have to worry about betraying myself."

"The Turks are looking for a man and a woman," he reminded her.

The priest caught the word "Turk." "Montenegro is not part of the Ottoman Empire," he told them. "It is ruled by the Prince-Bishop Petar. Nor do the Albanians love the Turks, though both are Moslems."

James gave in, and Cordelia donned a skirt before they went on their way. Very soon the track narrowed and climbed again, and she had no chance to talk to him about his unnecessary fear of damage to her reputation. After all, the Greek brigands had *not* ravished her; she had *not* succumbed to James's caresses; Mehmed Pasha had *not* made her an inmate of his harem. She was chaste, so she had nothing to fear.

Father Josif brought them to the next village as the sun set. Under his aegis, they had no difficulty hiring a guide for the morrow. The villagers killed and roasted a sheep to celebrate the coming of their peripatetic priest, and the feast went on long into the night. When Cordelia and James at last retired to their tent, they both fell asleep at once.

The days that followed offered no better opportunities for serious discussion. Winter was settling on the wild country; the way was hard. After riding and walking from dawn to dusk, then finding pasture or fodder for the animals, lighting a campfire, and setting up the tent, dusk to dawn was for exhausted sleep. At least they always found a guide and never again were caught on a narrow path in a snowstorm.

Most of the villages they passed through were Albanian. Cordelia never had the slightest reason to fear for her virtue—though she soon discovered virtue was the only aspect of women the Albanians did respect—and no one glanced twice at her costume of trousers under a skirt, any more than they had in Istanbul.

Sometimes she imagined what her life would have been had she stayed in Istanbul: her own house, three servants to take care of her, warm rooms, plenty to eat, clean clothes, a *hammam* five minutes walk away. Then James would smile at her, or take her hand to help her over an obstacle, or give her the best bit of a goose he had shot. And then she remembered Mehmed Pasha, who would have visited whenever he fancied, to paw her and undress her and make her his whore.

She turned her imagination instead to what life would be like when she reached England, as the respectable daughter of Sir Hamilton Courtenay, Baronet, of Hill House, Fenny Sedgwick, Norfolk. It sounded very grand. In her mind, she furnished it with all the most beautiful objects she had seen in Italy, Germany, Austria. The garden would be full of roses—Mama had loved roses.

But Mama had never talked about her father. Cordelia could not picture him, only his eyes, brown like her own, filled with tears of joy at the return of his long-lost child.

Anticipating that happy day did not stop her dreaming about baths, from the *hammam* to the tin-plated tub in front of the fireplace, laboriously filled with buckets. The only washing she did these days was to scrub face and hands with snow melted over the campfire. James was sprouting a beard perforce, fair and curly, and itchy, he complained.

As for laundry, rinsing out her shift and drawers occasionally and drying them at the fire was the best she could manage. That was embarrassing enough. She was grateful that James always washed his own intimate garments.

Thank heaven her monthly flow was late. She was sure of it, though she had lost track of days and weeks long since. Her mother had told her the timing could be upset by emotional disturbance, of which she had certainly suffered plenty in the past month! Perhaps being usually cold and often tired and rarely having quite enough to eat had some effect, too. She could only hope it would last until they reached civilization.

She was out of luck.

That day they stopped for their midday meal by a stream which, in the strange way of the country, emerged full-fledged from underground. After running several miles along the pleasant valley, it very likely disappeared into a hillside again. Of course that meant the valleys did not interconnect, or they would have reached the coast long since.

James had explained the phenomenon: the mountains were limestone and water tended to dissolve it rather than carving a way through it—hence also the caves where they sometimes took shelter. The limestone produced little soil, accounting for the lack of vegetation on the stark, rugged peaks.

However, today their campsite was sheltered from the north wind by leafless woods. For once there was plenty of frost-yellowed grass for the animals, all three lean now, with shaggy winter coats. Their guide, Bashkim, told them the flocks and herds of his mountainside village grazed this valley during the winter. While the sheep, goats, and cattle were still fat from summer pastures, the herdsmen drove them to the far, north-west end, then they slowly moved along as the grazing was exhausted. They had not yet reached this point.

While James and Cordelia unloaded Achates and hobbled him and the ponies, Bashkim went off to gather firewood. They had discovered that a hot drink at midday, even if they had only a pinch of herbal tea or coffee to add to the water, revived their spirits and energy. When possible, it was worth the extra time.

Cordelia retreated into a thicket of evergreen bushes, emerging a few minutes later with a bundle of linen carefully wrapped so that the bloodstains were hidden.

"I must wash a few things," she said to James.

"Good idea. I'll change my . . . ah . . . ultra-unmentionables and join you."

Kneeling on a stone on the bank of the stream, Cordelia scrubbed and squeezed her drawers and her monthly cloths in the icy water. The worst was done by the time James came over, but for the next few days she was going to have to launder frequently, whether there was a stream available or not.

Her head bent, she asked, "I don't suppose we could stay here for a day or two?"

"My poor girl, are you dreadfully tired?"

"Not really," Cordelia said honestly, and then wished she had seized the excuse. "At least, not more than usual and not as much as I used to be."

"Just tired of getting up every day and hopping into the saddle? It grows tedious, I agree, and this is a pleasant spot—considering the time of year—but I doubt Bashkim will agree to a delay. He's already nervous about having agreed to take us within sight of a Montenegrin village."

"Who can blame him? It was in his own great-grandfather's time the prince-bishop ordered every Moslem in Montenegro slaughtered."

"Not I, and I comprehend his wanting to get it over with and return to his herdsman friends here in the valley as soon as may be. In fact, if we delay I fear he may renege."

She sighed. "I suppose so. It's just that . . . I mean, I . . . that is . . ."

"What is it, Cordelia?" James asked patiently.

Peeking at him, she saw he was smiling. "You know about . . ." Her cheeks felt hot enough to warm her hands by their glow. "You know that women, every month . . ."

"Is that your trouble! Of course I know, dear girl. Do you feel unwell? Or is riding astride too difficult?"

"No, it's uncomfortable but I can manage. Only, you see, there is a stream here for washing . . ."

"Ah, I do see. But we can easily melt enough snow in the bucket for you to do your laundry when there is no river nearby."

She nodded, eyes still cast down. "I know, but I could not without you seeing. I did not want to have to . . . to discuss it with you."

"I'm sorry you are still shy with me after all we have been through together," James said soberly. "Particularly since, after trying for days to come up with another answer, I have concluded that the only way to preserve your reputation is for us to be wed."

"Wed!" Cordelia turned to stare at him.

He was concentrating on his washing, his profile anything

but happy, not looking in the least as if he wished to marry her. Well, even to save her reputation, which she didn't consider endangered, she was not going to marry someone who did not want her. Not, she reminded herself fiercely, that she had any desire whatsoever to tie herself for life to a penniless scapegrace.

"Oh no," she said, "I cannot possibly marry *you*."

James gave her an exasperated glance. "My dear girl, don't be stubborn. I tell you, I have thought and thought and I cannot find any way out of it. We shall never be able to keep this journey secret from everyone. We simply have no choice."

"Of course we do. I have not lost my virtue. I don't want to marry you and I shan't."

"Just attend to me a minute, will you? You don't understand. It's not a matter of whether your virtue is intact, it's what people—"

"Hush!" She held up her hand to silence him, trying hard to believe she was imagining the distant thunder of hooves, the shouts and yelps and gunshots. "Listen! Bandits? Soldiers?"

He cocked his head, then grabbed her hand. "Quick, into the bushes. It's not much of a chance but it's the only one we have!"

# Twenty

Like hunted animals, they crouched in the bushes. Cordelia turned a pale, wide-eyed face to James and he put his arm around her shoulders.

"Perhaps the Montenegrins are slaughtering Moslems again," she said, in a whisper although the racket of hooves and men's raised voices and barking dogs would cover a shout. "Bashkim said they covet the grazing."

"If so, while I hate to think of them murdering the poor chap, maybe they would let us go in peace."

"No, listen, I'm sure they are shouting in Albanian."

Concentrating, James agreed. Between them, they had picked up quite a bit of the language and though he made out only a few words, those were plain. Unfortunately, given the Albanian propensity for blood-feuds and brigandage, that did not mean either the guide or he and Cordelia were safe.

A sudden hush fell, so quiet James heard the bushes rustling in the wind. No, not the wind. The sound was coming directly towards them.

"Dogs?" Cordelia breathed.

As he shook his head, his finger to his lips, a massive, ugly head parted the leaves a few yards away. Long nose snuffing the air, vicious tusks, small, angry red eyes, the wild boar took a few more steps forward. James noticed blood on its flank.

Then it smelled them. It stopped, the mane of grey-black bristles along its spine standing erect, making it look even huger. Five feet nose to tail, James was prepared to wager, and thirty stone if it weighed an ounce. And unfriendly.

It swivelled to face them, pawing the ground.

"I'll try to distract it. You go that way." Moving slowly, he took off his hat and held it out at arm's length, away from Cordelia. Then he waved it vigorously up and down. The boar snorted and turned its head to watch.

Cordelia inched to her knees and started to creep away. With a squeal of fury, the boar charged her.

"Run!"

She jumped up and ran, pushing wildly through the bushes. James leapt to his feet. As the boar passed, he flung himself full-length on its back.

The beast charged on, barely staggered as his weight hit it. He got one arm round its throat, grabbed a handful of coarse bristles with the other hand, clung to its flanks with his knees, and hung on like grim death. They burst into the open hot on Cordelia's heels.

She stumbled, fell, rolled aside. The boar altered course. Miraculously hands were there to pull her out of the way.

Surrounded now by shouts, barks, the smell of its tormentors—men, dogs, horses—the boar sped on, intent on escape. But James was on its back. He didn't dare let go, sure he'd be trampled beneath the sharp hooves, gored by the hideous tusks. He tightened his grip on its neck, pulling its head up with some vague idea of throttling it at least enough to slow it down, though what he would do then . . .

It reacted by jerking its head downward and charging on at full tilt, straight into a tree trunk.

Half stunned, the boar shook itself. James ignominously fell off. Then the hunters arrived. Yelling men dragged him aside. Dogs darted in and sprang back. A dagger gleamed and plunged. The dazed boar gave a shudder, toppled, raised its head, lay still.

"Poor thing," said Cordelia as she arrived panting. "James, you were simply *splendid!*"

James was a hero. Not that his exploit had been of much use

to anyone, but for sheer derring-do none had ever seen the like. No one had ever ridden a wild boar before, the Albanians declared, for if any had a song would surely have been made upon the feat to make sure it went down in history.

He and the boar were borne off in triumph towards the hunter-herdsmen's encampment, despite his protests. Left behind, Cordelia managed to persuade Bashkim not to desert her, and to help her reload Achates. Rescuing her and James's laundry from the bank of the stream, she fastened it to the load to blow dry in the wind. Modesty be damned, she thought crossly.

Plodding along with the laden donkey, long before they reached the camp, the odour of roasting pork wafted to their nostrils. At least James was watching for her. He came grinning to meet her, the anise scent of *raki* on his breath.

"There's a feast in preparation," he said, helping her down from Dido's back, "to celebrate my reckless idiocy and the successful hunt. We're invited. That is, I am. They don't really invite women to their feasts, but of course I insisted."

"We were hoping to reach the next village by nightfall," Cordelia protested, rather feebly as the smell of pork made her mouth water. Not to mention the sight of the carcase, sizzling on a spit over red-hot coals in the space between the thatched stone huts.

Bashkim had ridden ahead to speak to his friends. Now he came back and said firmly in his broken Turkish, "Tonight we stay here. Tomorrow to village."

Cordelia capitulated. She kept discreetly out of the way of the masculine festivities, settling herself against the side wall of one of the huts. James brought her hunks of juicy pork with chopped onions and seasoned yoghurt for a sauce, wrapped in bread baked on hot stones. There was fresh goat's milk to drink, the nannies thriving better than ewes or cows on the poor winter pasturage.

The men were not drinking milk, however. Muslims they might be, but no more than they scorned pork did they follow the Prophet's dictates with regard to alcohol. Cordelia watched as the fiery anise-flavoured brandy poured down their throats like water, not least down James's throat. Whether he'd be fit to ride in the morning remained to be seen.

The revellers grew noisier. Cordelia didn't dare go among them to ask James to help set up the tent, but as the dusk deepened she found it impossible to keep her eyes open. Rolling up in a couple of blankets, she fell asleep to the strains of a fierce song about a long-ago battle.

She awoke to bright moonlight.

"Cordelia!" James shook her, his *raki*-laden breath on her face, his voice slurred. "Wake up. They insist on delivering us to the village, to prove they're not afraid of the Montenegrin infidels. Hurry or they'll go without us, taking our baggage with them."

Throughout the wild ride along the valley and up the mountain track, the Albanians let off musket shots at random. When they reached the village, they fired a fusillade at the stars and yelled defiance at the moon, since not a single inhabitant showed his face to be defied.

Their impetuous escort dropped off the travellers' belongings in a heap in the middle of the village. With a farewell salute of a second fusillade, they galloped off into the night. It was none of their concern just how the villagers would react in the morning to the hair-raising midnight arrival of strangers in their midst.

The icy night air had sobered James enough to help Cordelia hobble the animals and set up the tent, fortunately as it was bitterly cold at that height. She crawled in and settled down while he went off to relieve the pressure of vast quantities of *raki*. When he returned, she was already nearly asleep. She was quite unprepared to fend him off when he lay down close beside her and took her in his arms, blanket cocoon, sheepskin coat, and all.

Lying half on top of her, he pressed ardent, spirituous kisses on her mouth. She struggled in vain to free her arms to push him away, not daring to cry out lest she bring down vengeful villagers upon them. Not wanting to cry out. His lips burned her skin. He fumbled clumsily with the blankets, amorous but inept, and she was dreadfully tempted to help him.

Then he fell asleep.

His warm breath teased her ear; the weight of his body crushed one breast, his arm the other; his knee rested intimately, achingly against her private parts . . .

How could she have forgotten her menses! In that condition, she had been on the verge of giving herself to a drunken wastrel! Was that how her mother's lovers had made her feel, that urgency which made everything else unimportant?

But Drusilla Courtenay had a husband to make love to her. She'd had no excuse for wickedly running off with a lover and ruining her daughter's life. If she had stayed properly at home, Cordelia would not now be stuck in a tent in a primitive village in the middle of nowhere, striving to evade the embraces of a good-for-nothing sot.

So far, despite the difficulties, she had succeeded in preserving her virtue intact and she was not about to give up the struggle. She tried to sit up but James's arm moved down to her waist and tightened about her. Turning her head she stared at his face as if her gaze could pierce the pitchy darkness.

She knew that face so well, always thin, thinner now, its bronze deepened by sun reflected off snow; the square, resolute chin hidden beneath his new beard, fairer than his hair and even curlier; the dark blue eyes, laughing, teasing, serious, concerned . . .

This was only the second time he had been in his cups, and he was not really altogether a good-for-nothing. Whatever the outcome, she knew his foolhardy exploit with the wild boar had been an effort to save her life. If only he were respectable, if only he really wanted her for his wife, she would marry him like a shot.

Cordelia had just reached this dispiriting conclusion when the tent collapsed.

Enveloped in its heavy folds, she once again fought to sit up.

Once again his strong arm tightened around her waist, and he muttered something.

"James!" she hissed furiously.

He had said himself he was half seas over when he helped her put it up. Now, instead of helping her escape from its toils, he was actually hindering her. Every time she tried to move, he held her tighter without, apparently, rising any nearer to consciousness. Wrapped up in her blankets, the tent weighing her down, she was quickly forced to concede to superior force.

Fortunately, some fortuitous arrangement of the poles kept the tent's fabric off her face. She could breathe quite easily, but for all James cared she might be smothered to death.

She lay there fuming. She wouldn't marry him if he went on bended knee, if he were the last man in the world!

At some point she must have fallen asleep, for she awoke to the sound of muffled laughter. James had somehow managed to roll away from her. She freed one hand and poked him in the back. He grunted.

A moment later the tent began to stir. Voices called to each other in Serbian. Serbian! They were in Montenegro, beyond the Ottoman border, safe from Mehmed Pasha, safe from the Turkish authorities' unexplained pursuit of James.

Safe from the Montenegrins, whose peaceful sleep their rackety escort must surely have shattered?

As helpful hands folded back the fabric, grinning faces reassured her. The collapse of the strangers' tent was a good enough joke to excuse their unmannerly midnight arrival. James's slumbering through the rescue only added to the hilarity.

Cordelia arose with what dignity she could muster and did her best in Serbo-Polish to explain. That they were fleeing the Turks was enough to persuade the villagers to extend a warm welcome.

The hamlet was tiny, the cottages no more than windowless huts, each a single room divided by a woven willow screen into space for beasts and space for people. As usual in this harsh land, most of the flocks and most of the men were away at the winter pasture. Cordelia noticed that the remaining men were all armed; at least one always kept a wary eye on the still sleeping James, stretched out beneath the blankets she had thrown over him.

He continued to sleep while the women fed Cordelia on bread and sheep's-milk cheese and helped her do her bit of washing. All their water came from melted snow. In fact they told her they spread straw matting over the snow and ice in early spring to preserve the supply as long as possible. James was lucky not to have arrived in midsummer, since he woke tormented with a raging thirst.

"And a splitting head," he groaned when Cordelia arrived, tugged by the hand by an excited small boy. "What the deuce happened?"

"You remember riding the wild boar?"

"Of course I do." He gave her a pallid, rueful grin. "It's because we were celebrating my folly that I couldn't refuse to swill *raki* with them. Wild boar, wild revelry, wild ride, but after that?"

Some of "after that" was best forgotten, Cordelia decided. "The tent fell down," she said primly. She gestured at the villagers, gathered again in a circle around them. "These people rescued me shortly before I expired for want of air."

"Oh lord, I'm sorry! I must have been a trifle foxed when we put the damned thing up."

"So you informed me." She couldn't help laughing at his comically guilty dismay. "I wasn't really near to expiring. Come on, come and eat and assuage your thirst or we shall cover no distance today."

Tenderly he pressed his fingers to his temples. "I'm afraid if I try to ride, either I shall fall off Aeneas or my head will fall off my shoulders. Please, dear Cordelia, may we not take a holiday?"

"Well, I'd rather not have to try to stick your head back on, nor to recover your body from the bottom of a cliff."

So they stayed the rest of the day and set off again early the next morning. Winter had well and truly set in. As the weather worsened, the mountains grew more rugged, the fertile valleys rarer, the villages sparser and poorer. The people rarely had much food or fodder to spare, even in exchange for gold, and firewood was a treasure almost more precious.

Amazed and admiring of Cordelia's stamina, James sometimes wondered if they shouldn't stop in one of the larger villages and wait for spring. But however hospitable, the villagers' resources were strained by their presence and they were always relieved to see the travellers depart.

At least they had no difficulty finding youths or old men irked at being left behind with the women and happy to act as guides. With painful slowness the uncounted miles fell behind.

Wherever the track was wide enough, James and Cordelia rode side by side. As if to persuade themselves that the rest of the world still existed somewhere beyond the endless snow-covered mountains, they talked of places they knew. Cordelia spoke of Vienna, Berlin, Warsaw, the forests of Germany and the sandy Baltic coast. But more often James told her about England. He described the wonders of London, highways with comfortable inns every few miles, fruitful woods and fields, provincial towns with shops and markets, pretty villages where even the poor grew flowers as well as vegetables in their gardens.

Cordelia had endless questions about England. He answered them as well as he could. However, if she was curious about his way of life or his family she restrained her curiosity, and she never mentioned her own. Though itching to learn more of her history, James tactfully followed suit.

He realized he did not even know at what age she had left her native land. To judge by her ignorance, she must have been very young—and for some reason her mother had told her next to nothing.

When places palled, they talked of food. Cordelia was explaining the differences between various German sausages when she suddenly stopped and said, "Grass. James, look, grass!"

They had just reached the crest of a pass, bare limestone crags on either side. Down in the valley, instead of the usual blanket of white—or at best white patched with ochre—a haze of green met their gaze.

Two days later, from the top of another pass, they looked down a rugged hillside speckled with fresh green growth at the Adriatic.

The indigo sea was fringed with vivid turquoise along the rocky shore and around a small, dark-green, offshore island. In startling contrast, the brick-red tile roofs of Dubrovnik lay enclosed by the ancient wall which had helped the city keep its independence from Hungarians, Venetians, Serbs, and Turks.

"Dubrovnik!" sighed Cordelia. "Now all we have to do is find a bath, and then a ship to take us to Italy."

"A ship!" groaned James. "The very notion makes me shudder. To think I failed to appreciate ponies and snowy mountains while I had them!"

Their guide, Pero, apparently appreciated his mountain fastnesses better than the prospect of going among the Ragusans. "They are Dalmatians," he explained, spitting eloquently on the stony track. When James and Cordelia looked blank, he elaborated: "Croats. Roman Papists. Almost as bad as Turks. Still, they have many goods for sale and you will pay me when we reach the city. I will take you all the way."

They followed the zigzag trail downward. The gentler slopes near the sea were intensively cultivated, with apricot trees in bloom. Spring had come to the coast though not far inland harsh winter would linger on the heights for weeks yet. The midday sun was warm. Sheepskins already abandoned, Cordelia flung off her heavy cloak and fastened a simple cotton kerchief over her head.

Her blond hair, nearly shoulder-length by now but still too short to tie back, hung in lank strands around the hollow-cheeked face in which her eyes looked huge. Without the bulky clothes, she appeared painfully thin, a veritable waif, despite the diamond cloth wound about her middle. Finding it hard to believe he had ever considered her too plump, James decided the next most important thing after a bath was a good meal, or two or three.

Anything to put off going to sea.

They made their way around the outside of Dubrovnik's white limestone ramparts. Ahead, their road joined another leading to the drawbridge approach to the arched and crenellated city gatehouse. Sentries stood guard at either end of the bridge, smart in white breeches and dark blue, gold-laced coats, with white-plumed shakos on their heads and rifles slung on their shoulders.

Pero turned and looked James and Cordelia up and down. "Better tell 'em you're Slovenes," he grunted. Before James could ask why, Pero swung down from his pony and started to lead it forward.

James dismounted and turned to help Cordelia down from Dido's back.

Her face was aghast. "James," she gasped, "those soldiers are French!"

# Twenty-one

All too well, Cordelia remembered the inexorable tide of Napoleon's armies sweeping across Europe. By sheer chance, she and her mother had never been in the neighbourhood of a battle. Nor, as insignificant women protected by powerful men, had they ever been molested by the invaders. Yet she had grown up always aware that she was English and, whatever the gyrations of the German states, of Austria, Prussia and Russia, England was at war with France.

The years in Istanbul and the months crossing the Balkan peninsula had allowed the French peril to slip to the back of her mind. Now, after escaping the amorous pasha and surviving the journey across the mountains, here she was faced with the old enemy again.

If they asked for her papers, they would find out she was English. And her only protector was James, who had no papers at all.

As she automatically accepted his hand to help her dismount, he hissed at her, "Pretend we're Slovenes. Pero seems to think it will help."

Too late to discuss what to do. Already the sentries were gazing at them with obvious curiosity. Their clothes must appear odd, especially combined with her fair hair and James's fair beard. "Slovenes," she murmured. "What language?"

"Who knows?" He gave her a crooked grin. "Try Polish. And we're husband and wife."

She had no time to object. Ahead of them, Pero approached the first sentry, speaking volubly and waving his hand northward.

The soldier, his nose wrinkled, turned to his fellow and said, *"La Slovénie, c'est l'une des nôtres?"*

*"Je crois."* The other shrugged, apparently not merely unsure but uninterested in whether Slovenia was now part of the French Empire. His nose, too, wrinkled as James and Cordelia led the animals towards him. *"Slovénie, Slavonie, parbleu, j'en sais rien, sauf que ça pue comme le diable, ces montagnards! Laisse aller, mon vieux."*

Cordelia had never expected to be glad she stank like the devil. Her own nose was inured to the accumulated dirt of bathless weeks, but the two soldiers hastily waved them on, drawing back fastidiously as they passed. She exchanged a wry smile with James as the second pair of sentries also stepped back without attempting to stop them.

Across the bridge, through the arch, at last they reached the goal of so many weary miles. They were inside Dubrovnik. The limestone-paved streets, polished to a marblelike shine by centuries of feet, rang to the hooves of Dido, Aeneas, and Achates. On either side, three-story buildings of the same pale stone crowded upon each other, shops and taverns below, dwellings above, varied here and there by a clock-tower or a church.

French uniforms were few and far between. Not heeding their presence, people went about their business in a leisurely way, stopping to chat or to stare at the strangers. Most were dressed in local costume. The women wore long white dresses with embroidered bodices, the skirts covered by bright coloured aprons, spotted or striped. On their heads they had elaborately starched white kerchiefs. Cordelia envied them, until she noticed one in Western European clothes.

The lady in question strolled up the street on the arm of a French officer. She wore a charming high-waisted gown of apricot sarcenet, with ruffles around the hem and lace at the neck and the cuffs of the long, full, gauze sleeves. But it was her hat Cordelia most coveted. A wide-brimmed Leghorn, it sported apricot silk roses around the brim and a curly ostrich feather dyed to match, which bobbed enticingly with every step.

After the sheepskin cap she had worn so long, it was a bit of delectable, irresistible, feminine frippery.

"James, I *must* buy a hat!"

Following her gaze, he laughed. "So you shall, *after* a bath and a meal and a visit to the jeweller's shop I just saw back there. My pockets are pretty much to let, and I don't imagine yours are in much better case."

"Not much, and of course it's all foreign coins, which they are bound to discount. I hope we have enough left between us to persuade an innkeeper to give rooms to us stinking mountain folk. You understood what the sentry said?"

"Yes, and I must say I feared worse of those soldiers than insults! Why on earth did Pero not tell us the French had taken Dubrovnik?"

"He probably assumed we knew, and Captain Hamid probably did not know himself. He said it was an independent city state, not part of the Ottoman Empire, so news of it would not be of any great interest."

"About as much interest as those fellows at the gate had in Slovenia," James agreed. "Where the deuce is Slovenia?"

"I haven't the least idea, and I suspect Pero would be hard pressed to tell us, but at least he appears to have found us an inn," Cordelia said as the guide stopped before an archway and beckoned them on.

A hurried consultation revealed that Slovenia was somewhere to the north, and that its people spoke a language similar to Serbian—which was the same as Croatian though no one would admit it. Cordelia and James decided their Serbo-Polish would serve nicely.

In fact, the landlord understood them quite well enough. His face rigid with the effort to conceal his disgust from those who might yet prove to be good customers, he listened to their explanation of goods to be sold to replenish their purses. In exchange for stabling for the animals and a single room, he took every coin they possessed, leaving nothing but promises for Pero. Fortunately the Montenegrin guide was not only willing to trust them but quite happy to bed down in the stables.

Cordelia was not at all happy at having to share a room with James. A chamber in an inn was utterly different from a tent in the wilderness, especially a bitterly cold wilderness where a great many clothes had to be worn. However, there was no choice until they had sold a diamond, and they could not visit a jeweller in their present state without arousing acute suspicion.

"I shall want a bath at once," she told the innkeeper, "and my *husband* will take one when I am finished."

The man's face brightened and he forbore to demand further payment for the extra service.

"In the meantime," Cordelia continued in a firm voice, avoiding James's eye, "he will go out and see the sights of your beautiful city."

"Don't you want me to scrub your back?" James murmured in English. "I was counting on your scrubbing mine."

She glared at him. "He will be gone for at least two hours," she announced.

"I must find a barber," he said obligingly, stroking his beard. "Time this came off."

The tin bath came with a kindly chambermaid, Jula, to scrub her back and help her wash her hair. Her short hair and scrawny frame suggested to Jula that Cordelia had recently recovered from some dreadful illness during which the doctor had forbidden her to wash. She was all sympathy. Cordelia made no attempt to disillusion her, nor to explain why her clothes were as dirty as her person.

The water had to be changed half way through, or washing her hair would have been an exercise in futility. She heard Jula arguing with the innkeeper outside the chamber. The maid won. Fresh hot water arrived.

At last Cordelia was as clean as two tubfuls of water and a bar of soap could make her. Wrapped in a towel, she looked at the clothes she had taken off and those the maid had unpacked.

Of them all, the only thing she could bear to put on was her Turkish shift, washed in a mountain stream since last she wore it. The strip of linen with her worldly wealth so carefully sewn up into little pockets was badly in need of laundering before she wrapped it around her again.

Jula, in her neat red and green striped apron, arms folded beneath her ample bosom, regarded the heap of clothes with a disdain quite equal to Cordelia's. "What will you wear?" she enquired.

"I must buy new clothes, but I don't want to wear those to the shops."

"I'll lend you my second best dress, dear." The maid had evidently decided to take Cordelia under her wing. "Shall I send this stuff out to be cleaned?"

"No, will you give it to the church, for the poor?" Her thrifty soul rebelled, and she remembered James wondering whether she was an extravagant female who spent money as though it grew on trees. Of course, it was *her* money, but all the same . . . "I'll keep one or two things," she said quickly.

A shawl and two kerchiefs, plain but useful, her spare shift, a petticoat—she hesitated over her breeches, so comfortable when riding astride, but she was not going to play a boy's part again, and from here on they would travel by sea. The warm, hooded cloak might come in handy on board.

Since she could not let anyone else handle the diamond cloth, she asked Jula to bring her water to wash her undergarments. While the maid was gone, she dropped the towel and looked at herself in the mirror. She groaned. The last looking-glass she had consulted had agreed with Mama that she was too plump, but now she was about as pretty as a skeleton. Hastily she pulled on the shift over the horrid sight.

Clad in Jula's gown, Cordelia washed out her bits and pieces and draped them over a chair to dry. The cloak and shawl, well brushed, she hung up to air. Then she sat down on the edge of the bed to await James's return.

A real featherbed, with clean sheets, a bolster and two fat

pillows, and a blue quilt, it was so inviting she simply had to try it. She didn't want to crush Jula's second best gown, so she took it off and slipped between the sheets. After sleeping on a carpet on the ground for so long, it felt strange at first, but she rather thought she could easily reaccustom herself to such luxury.

She yawned. Where was James? He had left a good two hours ago and he was as eager for a bath as she had been. Surely the French soldiers hadn't . . . There was something about the French she must . . .

Cordelia awoke from a dream of filling the ponies' water bucket at a waterfall. The splashing noise continued, and someone was humming, very softly and out of tune, a tune she did not know. Opening her eyes, she saw James's naked back protruding from the tin tub scarce a yard away. Hurriedly she shut her eyes again.

Behind her closed eyelids, the image remained. His ribs were as prominent as her own, below the sharp bladed but muscular shoulders. His water-darkened hair, curling irrepressibly though dripping wet, had long grown out of its ragged crop though it did not quite hide the nape of his neck—why did she suddenly want to run her fingertips down that nape? She clenched her hands in denial.

Concentrating on his thinness, she sneaked another peek at his ribs and resolved to make sure he ate well before they sailed from Dubrovnik. Until he regained his sea-legs, he would starve on board. She wasn't sure how long it would take to reach Italy.

Italy. She frowned. There was something about Italy . . .

A sudden whoosh made her eyes fly open. She bit back a gasp. James had stood up to reach for a towel, exposing his lean flanks to her fascin—horrified gaze. She buried her fiery face in the pillow.

James knew she was awake. Her slow, deep, even breathing had suddenly ceased and then, as he stood up, from the corner of his eye he glimpsed the sudden movement of her head. Swiftly he dried himself. Wrapping the towel around his waist, he went to sit on the edge of the bed.

She stiffened. Very gently he stroked her hair, still damp but soft as silk.

"I don't want you to be afraid of me, Cordelia."

"I'm not afraid," she muttered into the pillow.

He cursed himself for those drunken kisses he had forced upon her after the wild boar-inspired carousal. By the next morning he had forgotten, but when he asked her what had happened, her hesitation before she told him of the tent's collapse had made him rack his memory. Her distaste for him was not to be wondered at.

But it was before that she had adamantly refused to marry him. No matter; when they reached England she would understand the necessity. He knew his duty as a gentleman and he had every intention of doing the honourable thing, so why not anticipate a little? His body ached for her. He had not had a woman in months.

Under his gentle, unthreatening stroking, her tautness relaxed. He moved his hand down to caress the back of her neck. A quiver ran through her, and she didn't seem to notice when he folded back the covers.

Every bone in her spine was visible through the fine gauze of her shift. Soon—oh, in an hour or two . . . or three—he'd take her to find the finest food Dubrovnik could provide. In the meantime, he leaned down to drop featherlight kisses on her neck while he licensed his roving hands and let them go, one to slowly, softly smooth the gauze down her back, the other to graze the side of her breast, slowly, softly, don't rush, don't frighten her, though his pulse raced, his blood cried out for urgent haste.

"Oh James!" she moaned, and half turned towards him.

Rat-a-tat. He froze.

Rat-a-tat again. A pause. Thump, thump. Bang. Cordelia's huge eyes.

"The French?"

An irritable tattoo. "You there!" Croatian, accented. A French accent? "You want go to Italy?" Fractured, shattered Croatian. "I Italian captain. Have ship. Sail tomorrow. You want?"

James sprang up, the towel falling to the floor. "Yes! I come. *Venio!"* Latin was the best he could do. Cordelia spoke Italian, but she was in no state to interview the sailor. She had pulled the covers up, nothing but a blond lock visible. "While I was out I put word about," he explained, hurriedly pulling on breeches and a shirt. "Most of the traffic is local, coastal, so we're lucky to get something so soon."

Lucky? He suppressed a groan at the thought of how nearly he had tasted her sweetness. But so much time had been lost since their departure from Istanbul! However reluctantly, he must seize the chance to speed the journey.

He detoured on the way to the door to kiss the top of her head.

When James returned to the bedchamber, Cordelia was fully dressed. In Jula's gown, with her shawl draped protectively over her shoulders and bosom, a kerchief on her head, and her mountain boots—for want of other footwear—she felt safe from James's temptations . . . attentions, she meant. Especially as they had a great deal to accomplish if they were to sail tomorrow.

She did her best to act as if the disgraceful episode in the bed behind her had not occurred. Though she could not quite meet his eye, she asked with tolerable composure what he had settled with the Italian captain.

"We sail at dawn. A deuced restless lot, these sea captains, always weighing anchor at daybreak," he grumbled, amazingly cheerful considering his sufferings at sea. Cordelia could not help recoiling a little from the alcohol on his breath. He grinned at her. "Never fear, just a single glass of slivovitz to seal the bargain, though it's gone to my head a little for want of food in my belly to absorb it. Come on, we'll eat before we approach the jeweller."

"I have two diamonds in my purse."

"Splendid. We've the ponies and Achates to sell, too."

"Oh dear, I suppose so. I hadn't thought, but of course we cannot take them with us, the dear, faithful creatures. I shall miss them," she sighed.

"So shall I. Dido and Aeneas have none of the points I've

ever required in a mount, but they have served us well. As for *fidus Achates,* I shall regard donkeys with a new eye since being honoured with his acquaintance."

Somehow they fitted all their business and two hearty meals into the remaining hours of the day—fortunately Dubrovnik did not shut up shop for the night at dusk. Wearily they returned through the well-lit streets towards the inn, Cordelia clutching a hatbox she refused to entrust to an errand boy.

They had both purchased new clothes: breeches, shirts, and a swallow-tailed coat for James; high-waisted muslin gowns for Cordelia. James complained that the fit simply could not compare with London's tailors, hardly surprising since they had to buy second-hand goods for want of time to order new. Cordelia was just happy to have what she regarded as normal garments, ribbons and ruffles instead of coarse homespun, and the glorious new hat with its wreath of white silk roses.

Her pleasure in her purchases began to fade as she contemplated the night ahead, sharing the chamber with James. They had enough money now to take a second chamber, but to do so would look most odd and they could not afford to arouse suspicion. What was the good of a new nightgown trimmed with lace if she did not dare put it on?

It didn't seem fair to insist on his sleeping on the floor instead of in the first comfortable bed they had come across since Skoplje.

As they reached the inn, James said, "I believe I shall stroll on down to the harbour. It will be just as well in the morning to know exactly where to find the ship, and if Captain Pascoli is about, I shall pay him something on account. You go on up. I shan't be long."

Cordelia scurried up the stairs. In no time she was ensconced in bed, on the far side from the door. She had on her nightgown over her shift, and drawers underneath, and her cloak wrapped around her. With the quilt pulled up to her chin and the bolster carefully arranged down the middle of the bed, she turned her face to the wall, her back to James's side.

When he came in, she was determinedly asleep. As the light of his candle shone pink through her eyelids, as his weight jounced the bed, as the bolster pressed firmer against her back, she did not stir a muscle.

He gave a tiny sigh. Then his breathing slowed and evened, Cordelia relaxed, and the next thing she knew was Jula knocking on the door to announce it was time to rise.

The eastern sky was just beginning to pale when Cordelia and James passed under the city walls by the arch leading to the harbour. Fishing boats were already sailing out of the narrow exit to the sea, others coming in with a night's catch, unloading at the quayside.

Captain Pascoli welcomed them on board the *Donna Maddalena*, a small merchantman almost a twin to *Amphitrite.* Delighted to discover that Cordelia spoke fluent Italian, he congratulated her on coming from that corner of Slovenia which had been for so long a part of the Venetian Republic.

"But I do not go so far north, *signora,"* he said anxiously. "I told your husband, but I am not sure he understood. I sail to Bari."

"Bari! Perfect." She had not asked James whither they were bound, as crossing the Adriatic had seemed the most important goal at present. What a stroke of luck that they were to land within a few miles of Arventino! The count always spent the spring months on his country estate. Surely *Zio* Simone would be glad to see her and ready to help them on their way.

Captain Pascoli shouted orders to his men to cast off, then showed them to their cabin.

"Yes, one cabin," said James wryly as the captain left. "I had to tell him you are my wife, as the inn servants were within earshot. Besides, as far as I could gather, he only has the one cabin for passengers. Don't fret, I shall be in no condition to trouble you."

By the light of a lantern, barely swaying as the *Donna Maddalena* reached the harbour entrance, Cordelia regarded him critically. "You already look unwell, and we are scarcely under way. Why don't you lie down?"

"I believe I shall." He thankfully subsided on one of the two bunks.

"Did the captain tell you how long it will take to get to Italy . . . Oh James, Italy! I knew there was something I ought to remember. Mama and I left Italy years ago, when I was only fourteen, and it had already been invaded. It's ruled by the French!"

The only response was a groan.

# Twenty-two

Cordelia soon ceased to worry about the French and started to worry about James. Hastily fetching the basin from the washstand, she held his clammy forehead while he lost what little breakfast she had persuaded him to eat. She wiped his face with a cloth damped with water from the ewer. There was a carafe of drinking water, too, so she brought that for him to rinse out his mouth.

He lay back weakly in the bunk, his eyes closed. "Thank you, it's amazing how much a supporting hand helps."

"Mama used to hold my head thus when I was a child." She had almost forgotten those long-ago happy days when she uncritically adored her gentle, loving, beautiful mother—before she realized the meaning of the succession of temporary uncles.

"But you must not feel obliged to nurse me. I have survived before, however desperately I may wish to die, and I shall survive . . . Aagh!" He leaned over the bowl again, retching helplessly.

When the bout was over, Cordelia went off to make some tea for him with the dried mint she had bought in Dubrovnik. A sailor directed her to the tiny galley. Uncovering the brazier, she put a pot of water on to boil.

While she waited, she went up on deck. The *Donna Maddalena* was sailing northwards between the mountainous coast and an archipelago of small islands. Puzzled and uneasy, Cordelia gazed astern. A reddish streak between mountains and sea might be the roofs of Dubrovnik, but the walled city was no more than a blur. Surely they should be well out into the Adriatic by now.

Frowning, she returned to the galley, infused some leaves of mint, and took the brew to James. He drank a little. Though it came straight back up, at her urging he took a little more, which stayed down, at least temporarily.

She did not want to disturb him needlessly about the ship's unexpected course. Pleading a desire for fresh air, she went in search of Captain Pascoli.

"Is Bari further north than Ragusa?" she asked, using the Italian name for Dubrovnik. She thought perhaps for some reason he had decided to sail up the coast before turning west so as to have a shorter distance across the sea.

"No, *signora,"* he said, surprised, "further south."

"But we are sailing north."

"North-west. I explained to your husband. Perhaps he did not understand."

"Very likely."

"So you will tell him, *signora."*

"It depends what there is to tell," said Cordelia, a trifle impatient. "He suffers badly from seasickness."

"Ah, the unhappy *signore!* In my cabin I have mineral water, which is helpful for this affliction. Mineral water and dry bread is best, a little at a time."

"Thank you, captain, but first, please tell me why we sail north when Bari is to the south!"

"Because of my cargo, of course, *signora!"* Captain Pascoli appeared astonished at her lack of comprehension "I have wheat, the best Apulian wheat, some for Ragusa, some for the islands, some for Spalato. When it is all delivered, then we go home to Bari."

"I see. How far is Spalato?"

He shrugged. "Three days, or four. It depends on the winds and on how fast we can unload at the islands."

Armed with a bottle of mineral water, Cordelia went to break the news to James. "I have been talking to the captain," she said brightly. "It seems we shall be stopping at several islands, and you will be able to go ashore."

"Islands?" he mumbled weakly, a ray of hope in his eyes. "There are islands in the Adriatic?"

"Well, in a way."

"In a way? Cut line, Cordelia. What's the hitch?"

"The islands are actually along the Dalmatian coast," she confessed. She explained the *Donna Maddalena*'s itinerary. "So I'm afraid the voyage will be lengthened considerably. But the first few days should not be too dreadful as we shall go ashore several times. Then by the time we set out across the Adriatic you will have grown accustomed to the motion, as you did on the *Amphitrite*."

"If I don't die first," he moaned, and reached for the basin.

The mineral water helped a little. At least he kept most of it down, though it did not help the unrelenting nausea. Cordelia bought the captain's other two bottles and hoped to find more in Spalato, if not on the islands.

James stumbled ashore on the first island with a sigh of relief. He managed to eat some soup and bread, but he lost it all an hour later, as soon as they returned on board. On the second island, Korcula, following Captain Pascoli's advice, he ate only a little dry bread. They stayed on Korcula for nearly four hours, so he had a chance to digest it before the next bout of sickness. At Hvar, too, he had some bread, but as they approached Spalato, Cordelia was growing very anxious about him.

He was not absorbing nearly enough nourishment, and he had been too thin when they left Dubrovnik. His cheeks were sunken, his eyes dull. Worse, they had been at sea three days, and instead of growing accustomed he was as unwell as ever. It seemed to her that the hours on solid ground, though bringing a brief respite, set him back to the beginning again.

At Spalato—Split to its Slav inhabitants—Captain Pascoli had to load a return cargo and he promised them a full day ashore, from midday till the following morning. James looked forward to it with such pleasure, Cordelia hadn't the heart to suggest he might be better off in the end staying aboard to be gently rocked on the placid waters of the harbour. At least she'd be able to get three good meals into him.

As soon as the *Donna Maddalena* tied up in the ancient port's splendid harbour, Cordelia asked directions to the nearest decent eating place. However, James still felt too queasy to do justice to the excellent food.

"I'm well enough to enjoy watching you eat, though," he said, smiling. "You are beginning to lose the famished look."

"Am I getting fat again?" she asked in alarm.

"Good Lord, no! Not that you were fat before. It will take more than a sennight of guzzling to restore—"

"I'm not guzzling! Only I seem to get hungrier the more I eat. I wish you did, too. Won't you try a bit more of this chicken with peppers? It's simply delicious."

He shook his head, a spasm of nausea crossing his pallid face.

A stroll through the town restored him somewhat. They found Diocletian's vast palace, fifteen centuries old and still housing thousands. At the market in its courtyard, Cordelia bought tidbits, delicacies, and sweetmeats from every vendor. James consumed somewhat less than his fair share, but he began to look a trifle less wan. By dinnertime, he was ready to confess to a rapidly reviving appetite.

They dined at the inn where they had reserved two chambers. Over the meal, James for the first time expressed an interest in their destination in Italy.

"I didn't understand much of what Captain Pascoli said," he admitted. "I concentrated on the essentials: when he was sailing and how much money he wanted for the passage to Italy."

"Oh James, I've been so worried about you I'd forgotten again that Italy is under French rule!"

"I know, but there isn't much we can do about it!"

"You don't think we should wait here for a ship going somewhere safer?"

"We might wait forever, since Split is also under French rule.

Travelling within the French Empire is reasonably safe, I dare-say. It's when we leave . . . What port did you say we are bound for?"

"Bari. It's in Apulia, right down in the south, and oh James, such luck, it's quite near Arventino."

"Arventino? That sounds familiar. Why do I associate it with Achates?"

"I told you I read the *Aeneid* with the Conte di Arventino e Grassano. I'm sure he will help us."

"How did you come to know him?"

Foreseeing humiliating explanations, Cordelia began to wish she had never mentioned Arventino. "He was . . . he was a sort of uncle to me, when I was a child."

James frowned. "I cannot think it advisable to apply to some-one who knows you are English."

"He would never give us away," she fired up in defence of *Zio* Simone.

"But the less time we spend in Italy the better. You are right, though, that we are lucky to be going to the south. From Bari I hope it will not be difficult to reach Sicily or Malta, which are under British occupation. What a relief that will be!" He yawned enormously. "Gad, I'm tired. I'm for bed."

The misery which had kept him awake the past few nights had not spared Cordelia. She slept soundly.

So did James, as he declared over an enormous breakfast. "I've been at sea for three days now," he said cheerfully. "I shall do very well now."

Alas, Cordelia's unvoiced misgivings proved justified. He lost his breakfast as they left the harbour, and was miserably sick throughout the following three days. When they reached Bari, he was so weak he had to be helped ashore by a couple of sailors.

A few French soldiers were visible, but none seemed inter-ested in the return of an Italian vessel to her home port from another part of the French Empire. Cordelia hired a carriage. With the wretched James ensconced inside, his feet up on the seat and his eyes closed, she ordered the coachman to drive to Arventino.

*Zio* Simone would look after them.

In spite of her concern for James, Cordelia delighted in the once familiar landscape. At first their road ran along the flat shore. On one side the neat rectangles of salt-pans reflected the sky's azure hue, or sparkled white, as if frosted with diamonds. On the other side lay the reed-beds and tussocky grass of the marshes which made the coast unhealthy.

They turned inland amidst groves, orchards, and vineyards. Everywhere fruit trees in pink and white bloom stood out against the silver-green of olive foliage and the emerald of fig leaves. The sweetness of orange and lemon blossom hung in the air. Cordelia recalled the Apulian spring as a brief but glorious time between the winter rains and the parched heat of summer.

The dusty road began to rise. Now they drove between drystone-walled pastures where newly shorn sheep grazed on rich green grass, all too soon to turn to straw, shrivelled by the fierce summer sun. Here and there stood *masseria,* farmhouses built around a courtyard used as a sheep-pen. The peasants lived in hamlets of *trulli,* whitewashed cones of unmortared stone, like giant beehives, Cordelia had always thought.

The road levelled again, with the blue-green of sprouting wheat on either side. "We're nearly there," Cordelia said, sitting up straight and hanging on to the strap as she peered out of the open window in her excitement. Nothing had ever been quite the same since she and Mama left Arventino.

James opened his eyes and feebly hauled himself up to a sitting position, waving away Cordelia's anxious offer of assistance.

"Arventino?" he asked with the ghost of a smile. "I thought we had agreed not to trouble your friend."

"You said we should not. I never agreed. Indeed, I cannot imagine anywhere safer while you are so ill."

"I confess I've never felt so deuced invalidish in my life.

Weak as a newborn kitten! But I shall soon come about with a few good meals."

"This is the best place to get them without strangers asking awkward questions," Cordelia said firmly. "Oh look! You see that row of poplars? That's the beginning of *Zio* Simone's gardens."

"*Zio* means uncle?"

"Yes. Don't worry, he was once a diplomat and he speaks both English and French."

"That's not what is worrying me. Your uncle . . ."

"He's not really . . ."

"Your honorary uncle, then, but having known you as a child he will never believe I am your brother. And I doubt whether in these circumstances we can convincingly play husband and wife, unless . . ."

"No!" Cordelia felt herself blushing at his amused look. "I mean no, it's no good pretending you are my brother or . . . or my husband. I could claim you as cousin, except that I don't know whether I have any and I don't know how much my mother ever told him about our family. I think it will be best to say you are a hired courier."

"A superior kind of servant."

"I think it will be best," she repeated. As a servant, however superior, he'd not have intimate chats with the count, and not speaking Italian, he could not gossip with the servants. No one would explain to him the nature of Lady Courtenay's relationship with the Conte di Arventino. "If you don't mind."

He burst out laughing. "I suppose at least a hired courier is a step or two up from a eunuch slave!"

His laughter exhausted him. He slumped back, eyes closed. Watching him, disquieted, Cordelia missed the gardens she had once loved and was taken by surprise when the carriage stopped.

"You stay there," she commanded, tying the ribbons of her new bonnet. "I shall fetch help."

As she descended from the carriage, James forced himself to rouse from the limp stupor that engulfed him. By no means so certain of their welcome as she appeared to be, he strove to compel his weary limbs to follow her, to be there to comfort her if she was rejected. The effort was beyond him.

Her voice, gabbling in fluent Italian to the driver, seemed to come from a vast distance. James watched her disappear under a classical portico with slender, fluted, Corinthian columns of pink-veined marble.

Cordelia had taken charge. With a faint smile, he abandoned himself to his mortifying weakness.

A very few minutes later, she returned with two menservants.

"Your name is Prestopoulos. I've told them you are a Greek gentleman-courier," she warned him as they supported his shambling steps into the villa, followed by the coachman with their baggage. "Barzetti, the dear old majordomo, was so glad to see me. He has gone to tell the count we are here."

In the ornate but airy vestibule, the lackeys assisted James to a marble bench inlaid with an elaborate mosaic. As he sank onto it, a slim, handsome gentleman, his black hair barely frosted with grey at the temples, strode into the hall.

"Cordelia? *Cara mia!*"

*"Zio* Simone!" Cordelia ran into his welcoming arms.

The Conte di Arventino was a good deal younger than James had imagined. Suppressing a quite unexpected and utterly nonsensical—but nonetheless painful—pang of jealousy, he turned away his gaze. A plump, dark young lady in mulberry silk had paused on her way down the elegant staircase to stare at Cordelia and the count.

After his own rush of irrational feeling, James had no need to understand the torrent of Italian which poured from her rosy lips to interpret the jealous fury in her face.

# Twenty-three

"I'm sorry." Cordelia stared miserably round at the familiar library, where *Zio* Simone had taught her to love books as much as he did. Everything was the same, the shelves of leather-bound volumes, the white-and-gilt French writing table, even the three chairs by the window. How often she had read aloud to the count there, while Mama's golden head bent over her embroidery, uncomprehending but happy in the amity of her loved ones. Yet everything was different. This was no longer her home. "I should have realized the contessa . . ."

"Lucia will do as she is told, my dear." He was just the same, too. The touch of grey in his hair simply made him look distinguished rather than dashing. Before, she had never thought about his age, but he could not be past his early forties. "She is nearer your age than mine," he continued, "so I hope you and she will become friends."

"I hope so," she murmured doubtfully as Barzetti, beaming, ushered in a young maid with a tea-tray.

"Lemon, sugar, just as you always liked it, *signorina,*" the old man said, bowing an apology to his master for venturing to speak. "Excuse me, *Eccellenza.*"

Cordelia smiled at him. "Thank you, Barzetti. It's a long time since I had a proper cup of tea."

The servants left and she poured, for herself and for *Zio* Simone, who used to insist on his cup though he seldom drank it.

"You look as if it's a long time since you had a proper meal," he said, frowning.

"Oh, no, I have eaten very well this past week. It's poor . . . Ja . . . Signore Prestopoulos who is half-starved. He was so dreadfully seasick, I was afraid for him."

"A seasick courier is not of much use to anyone!" said the count astringently.

"He could not help it. The servants do understand that he needs frequent small meals at first, do they not?"

"They will follow your orders, my dear. Most were here in your time and they remember you with fondness, and your mother also. I cannot believe my poor Drusilla is dead. Tell me what happened."

Cordelia shuddered as the memories she had so carefully banished to the hidden corners of her mind came rushing back. "It was an accident," she said reluctantly, "a street accident. It was horrible!"

"You witnessed it?"

"Yes." She had always confided in him, and now almost against her will the whole sorry story came out, the fish, the cats, the heedless camel.

Unlike the hateful Mehmed Pasha, the count was not in the least amused. As he expressed his horror and sympathy, Cordelia remembered how rarely he had laughed. Passages they read together which she thought funny, he had treated with utmost seriousness. Believing her youthful lack of understanding at fault, she had always deferred to his judgment. Yet now, grateful as she was for his gravity, his inability to see the least humour in her mother's accident perversely brought an inane giggle bubbling to her lips. She swallowed it—and burst into tears.

"Poor child." He moved to the chair beside her, gave her his silk handkerchief, and patted her back. "Drusilla loved you dearly. Never would she have willingly abandoned her 'darling Dee.' "

"I know." Cordelia dried her eyes, the brief storm over.

"Yet there you were stranded in Istanbul with no parent to advise you. Naturally you decided to return to England."

"To my father."

"England, and your father, are a long way off. How came you to hire that useless fellow Prestopoulos as your courier?"

"He was recommended to me." In a way, by Aaron the Jew. But the last thing she wanted to discuss was her travels with James. "You are a father now, are you not? I believe I heard the contessa mention *bambini?"*

"One son and three daughters," the count said proudly.

"I should so like to meet them!"

He took her to the nurseries, where she was delighted to discover that the children's nurse was the old woman who had looked after her for six years. The children were another delight: the roly-poly baby gurgling in her cradle; the toddler staring with great black eyes from the safety of his father's arms; the two little girls fascinated by Cordelia's blond hair.

Yet another joy awaited her in the gardens. Amidst the rigid formality of balustraded terraces and parterres, classical statuary and fountains, symmetrical avenues and walks, her mama's English garden had survived. Behind a row of sternly clipped cypresses, colour and scent exploded. Here roses ran riot, clematis spilled over trellises and bowers, butterflies mobbed the buddleia, and fat, furry bees bumbled through the honeysuckle.

Here Cordelia spent much of her time for the next few days. As often as Nurse could be persuaded to bring them out, she had the children with her. She rocked the baby in her arms, admired shiny pebbles solemnly presented by the little boy, helped the girls make garlands of rose-petals, and wished she were their sister.

Or at least really their cousin. After that first exclamation she no longer called the count *zio.* She was grown-up now, not a little girl in need of an uncle because her mother had torn her away from her father.

She still regarded him as an uncle, though. They walked often in the formal gardens, talking of old times. She knew the young countess resented their closeness. Lucia di Arventino seemed to have little in common with her husband, the marriage having been arranged in the usual Italian fashion, for the benefit of the two families. She was coldly polite to Cordelia when the count was present, ignored her otherwise. Since she spent a good deal of time in her boudoir, lounging on a sofa with a stack of French fashion magazines, they rarely met except at meals.

James was less willingly confined to his chamber. Cordelia made frequent enquiries about the health of her "courier" and the servants assured her he was slowly regaining his strength. However, by the morning of the fourth day, she simply had to see for herself.

It was not that she missed him, she told herself. Their having lived in each other's pockets for so long was no reason for a mere three days separation to seem like forever. She had to see him because she was concerned about his well-being and because they must plan the next segment of their journey. Though she was enjoying the peace of Arventino, the good food and the cossetting, they could not stay here forever.

As he had not yet left his room in the upper servants' quarters, she had no choice but to visit him there. Though such an attention to a sick hireling—however superior—might be considered remarkably condescending, there surely could not be anything improper in it.

Nonetheless, Cordelia did not wish to give the count even the slightest cause to suspect her of impropriety. He must not have the slightest excuse to mention to James that Lady Courtenay had been his mistress, so she must not be seen.

Picking a time in the middle of the morning when everyone was busy, she peeked round the corner, crept down the deserted corridor, and listened at his door. No sound of voices. He was alone. She tapped softly.

"Come in," he called in Greek.

"James, how are you? Are they taking proper care of you? Oh, you are up. Good!"

"I'm very well." Fully dressed, he stood on the far side of the small, bare room, at a window overlooking a courtyard. Though shockingly thin, he had some colour in his cheeks and his stride as he moved towards her was steady if without his usual vigour. "All the better for seeing you."

"I would have come sooner, only . . ."

"Only you are an honoured guest and I am a mere minion. Are they taking proper care of you?" He took her hand and stood back, surveying her. "Yes, you are blooming."

"Pray don't talk fustian, James." Blushing, she disengaged her hand. "The count is very good to me, just like in the old days, and Arventino is so beautiful in the spring. But should you not sit down?"

"What, leaving a lady and my employer standing?"

"You must be better. You have not teased me this age." Cordelia took a seat on a low stool, and James perched on his narrow bed. She thought guiltily of her own luxurious apartment.

"Actually, I was just thinking it's time I took a turn outside. I need more exercise to regain my strength than I can easily take in here. I'm not quite strong enough yet to face our next adventure."

"No more adventures!"

"I trust not. Have you asked the count's advice about how we should proceed?"

"Not yet. I wanted to talk to you first. I must tell you that he considers you a shocking failure as a courier!"

James laughed, but he said wryly, "So I am. I have a lowering feeling I'd not have survived that voyage without my kind and indomitable nurse."

"All I did was pour mint tea and mineral water into you," she disclaimed, trying to forget the dreadful moments when she had feared he was about to expire in her arms. "But that is past. What shall we do next?"

"I believe we should discuss that out in the gardens. Walls have ears, and besides, you ought not—"

A sharp rap on the door interrupted him. As it swung open without waiting for an invitation, Cordelia jumped up from the stool. The Conte di Arventino stood on the threshold, dark eyebrows raised.

"I was just leaving," Cordelia declared. "I must thank your servants, sir. They have taken excellent care of . . . of Signore Prestopoulos."

"I am glad to hear it," the count said suavely. "I was just coming to assure myself of that fact, when I heard voices." He turned to James and said in English, "I congratulate you on your recovery."

"Thank you, sir."

"Is it not convenient that Mr. Prestopoulos speaks a little English?" Cordelia babbled. "Of course that is one reason why I hired him."

"Of course. Well, now that I have satisfied myself that my people have done their duty, will you join me for a stroll, my dear?"

He offered his arm. Having announced her imminent departure, Cordelia took it perforce. She cast an apprehensive glance backwards. The sight of James biting his lip with a frown was not calculated to lessen her dismay.

Nor was the count's unnatural silence on the topic of her courier as they returned to the vestibule. There, he sent a servant scurrying for the parasol Lucia had lent her, at his insistence. Not until they were a good hundred yards from the house, strolling along a gravelled avenue of poplars, did he broach the subject.

"For a Greek," he said, "Prestopoulos speaks excellent English. And for a servant, he appears to be on excellent terms with his mistress. Is he your lover?"

"No! I am not my mother!"

"I beg your pardon, my dear. My relationship with your mother somehow never stopped my regarding you as a daughter, and perhaps foolishly I once again feel myself to some degree *in loco parentis.*"

"Oh sir," cried Cordelia, "I shall never cease to look upon you as the best and dearest of uncles."

He smiled at her gravely. "Then you will understand why I interest myself in this man of mystery to whom you have entrusted yourself."

"I do understand, and I would not have deceived you but that it seemed safer not to let your household know who he is. I am an insignificant female—and besides, I hoped I might rely upon their old fondness for me—but he is a man and a stranger."

"He is English?"

"An English gentleman, travelling as my companion, not my servant," she admitted.

"An Englishman is not safe in Italy with the parvenu Buonaparte's family and lackeys set over us. Why did you come here from Istanbul? Happy though I am to see you, you should have gone to Malta or Sicily, somewhere occupied by the British."

Concealing James's brush with the law, which was not her tale to tell, Cordelia told him of her flight from Mehmed Pasha. "I had no chance to seek out the best ship," she explained. "Mr. Preston and I had to take what we were offered."

Her highly edited story of their subsequent misadventures made no mention of James's attempts upon her virtue. For all his gravity, the Conte di Arventino was a fiery Italian who might take it into his head to avenge the insult to his honorary niece.

"So we ended up in Ragusa, in French territory," she finished, "and it seemed unlikely we should find a ship to English territory from there."

"Most unlikely," the count agreed, "unless a neutral ship happened to call, American perhaps, though few sail the Mediterranean these days despite the end of their embargo."

They came to the end of the walk and stopped at the balustrade to gaze out over the gently sloping fields to the blue line of the Adriatic in the distance.

"Did Mama ever tell you anything about my father?" Cordelia asked suddenly.

"Nothing but his name and that he had divorced her. Had she been a widow, I might have defied my family and married her, and you would be my daughter in truth." He put his arm around her shoulders. "But the church does not recognize divorce."

Cordelia felt tears rise to her eyes. She blinked them back.

"I wish . . . No, I am going back to England, to be the respectable daughter of the respectable Sir Hamilton Courtenay, Baronet, of Hill House, Fenny Sedgwick, Norfolk. But as long as I live, I shall never forget Arventino."

They stood in silence for a moment, then he sighed and dropped his arm, and they turned to return to the house.

"Has Mr. . . . Preston, is it? Has he a plan to get you to England?"

"No, except that he spoke of Malta or Sicily, as you did. We agreed to consult you."

"I shall be glad to assist," said the count, clearly pleased.

His expression changed as he looked ahead and saw his wife waiting on the steps at the end of the avenue, her foot tapping impatiently. He was resigned, Cordelia had realized long since, but not happy in his marriage.

Lucia gave her a brittle smile and turned to her husband. "Simone, I wish to go into Bari. With the warm weather coming, I must purchase muslin for new dresses. Besides, it is so dull here, I am sure the *signorina* must be bored to tears. I shall take her with me."

Cordelia was reluctant to reject this first offer of friendship, though she knew she must. Fortunately the count did it for her.

"Impossible, Lucia. It would be most unwise for an Englishwoman to venture into town unnecessarily."

"Thank you, *Contessa,*" said Cordelia, trying to ignore the black eyes full of malice. Whatever Lucia's reason for the invitation, she did not believe it was to give her pleasure. "I wish I could safely go with you, though I truly do not find Arventino dull."

"Well, I do," she said petulantly. "I shall tell Barzetti to order the carriage for me."

"It is too late today," the count pointed out. "By the time you reach Bari you will not have the leisure to linger over your choice of muslins, as I know you like to. Tomorrow is Sunday, and Monday is a saint's day holiday, so you may go on Tuesday."

Pouting, Lucia began to argue, and Cordelia made her escape into the house.

After being once discovered in James's room, she did not dare risk going back. She decided to take the children to the English garden in the hope that he would find her there. It was close enough to the house not to overstrain him, she thought.

Meanwhile, James waited impatiently in his little room. He had to talk to Cordelia, to discover what the count was saying to her about him, but he did not want to come face to face with them both together. When he guessed they must surely have finished their stroll, he would go out to look for her, hoping she remembered what he had said about meeting in the gardens.

He was about to leave when once more a rap on the door announced the count.

"A word with you, if you please, Mr. Preston," he said in excellent English. "Be so good as to come outside with me."

James grinned at him. "You, too, fear walls have ears, my lord?"

"Walls . . . ? Ah, this is an English saying?" The count nodded sober assent. "My people are loyal, but what is not known cannot be told. Come."

With the haziest memory of what he had seen on his arrival, James was impressed by the elegant house and the immaculately tended gardens. As, in deference to his recent debility, they sat down on a marble bench on a wide terrace, he said sincerely, "You have a beautiful place, sir."

"Thank you. It is particularly pleasant at this season, but even in summer Arventino is high enough for the cooling breezes, and far enough from the coast to avoid the malaria. I used to spend more time here but I regret we are too isolated to please my wife. Cordelia and her mother always enjoyed to stay."

"Cordelia was very keen to see Arventino again. To see you again. She has not mentioned how you came to be acquainted?" By using the phrasing of a statement with the intonation of a question, he hoped to avoid being damned for impertinent prying. Which would be justified, he admitted to himself.

"It is not secret. Her mother was my dearly loved mistress. We met in Berlin when I accompanied a diplomatic mission to the King of Prussia. Lady Courtenay has left her previous protector when he wished to send the child to an orphanage."

If Lady Courtenay's dissolute history shocked James, this long-ago averted threat to her daughter outraged him. "An orphanage!"

"Drusilla did not allow. She was greatly fond of Cordelia, and I became greatly fond also. This is why, like any fond papa, I wish to know what you mean for her."

"Whether my intentions are honourable?"

*"Sí.* I do not expect that you will marry the daughter of such a one as my unhappy Drusilla. Cordelia tells me you are not yet her lover. It is best this does not happen, that she goes safe to her father."

Her father? James had assumed Lady Courtenay was a widow. This news put her conduct in a still more scandalous light. "I shall do my best to deliver Miss Courtenay unharmed to her father," he said stiffly.

"But nature is powerful." The count shrugged. "And Cordelia has chosen to put herself under your protection. I ask only that you remember this. When we drive the French innkeeper's son from the throne of Naples, I shall seek her, and if you have seduced and abandoned her, be certain I shall avenge her."

"Sir, I am a gentleman!" Seduce her he might, but never would he abandon her. Yet he did not announce that his intentions were still more honourable, that he did indeed mean to marry her. What the devil would his uncle say if he arrived home with the daughter of an adulterous courtesan as his affianced bride? "I give you my word Miss Courtenay shall not suffer through me."

"The word of the English gentleman is not to be doubted," said di Arventino, "especially as Cordelia has told me of your care for her on your journey from Istanbul."

"And hers for me, sir," James said soberly, thinking of the uncomplaining way she had soothed his agonies and cleaned up his messes in the cramped cabin of the *Donna Maddalena.* Come to that, if it weren't for her his body might now be rotting on a

Turkish impaling hook. At least the French guillotine was quick—not that he had any desire to try it. "In a few days I shall be strong enough to continue our journey, thanks to your hospitality. Will you be so kind as to give us your advice on how to proceed?"

"By sea, I fear."

James groaned. "As I feared."

"Though the Straits of Messina are scarce a league wide, I cannot advise you to travel there by land. In Calabria are many French troops, in the mountains to fight the peasants' uprising, and on the coast to guard against invasion from Sicily."

"Will it not be difficult to find a ship to take us to Sicily?"

"My yacht is at Taranto, on the south coast of Apulia, not much farther from here than Bari to the north. It will carry you to Siracusa, where there is an English garrison. You will be glad to hear," the count added dryly, "that it is a swift vessel."

"Very glad. Thank you, sir."

"All I ask is that you take with you some papers and give them to the English commander to be conveyed to King Ferdinand in Palermo. He is a Spaniard, but at least he is of royal birth."

James assented. They settled on the following Wednesday for the departure, since di Arventino had promised his wife the use of the carriage on Tuesday. "I shall have to consult Cordelia," James said, "but I doubt she will object. Do you know where I may find her?"

"Try the English garden. It is her favourite, as of her mother." With a sigh, the count pointed out the way.

He returned into the house and James set off. He was glad to find his limbs more than equal to the short walk. For the next few days he would eat like a horse in preparation for the coming voyage.

Turning the end of a row of cypresses, he saw Cordelia seated in the shade of a thoroughly English honeysuckle bower. Glorious roses, crimson and white, pink and yellow, added their perfume to the scented air, which rang with the happy chatter of two little bonneted girls playing at her feet. She had a baby on her lap, and a small boy with black curls, scarce out of short coats, stood beside her, earnestly showing her something.

She glanced up and saw James. A smile lit her face.

James's breath caught in his throat. A vision rose before him of Cordelia in a real English garden surrounded by her own fair-haired children. Hers and his. He was going to marry her, come hell or high water. Not because it was his duty, not just because he wanted to make love to her; but because he wanted her for his wife, and because he loved her.

To the devil with her mother and his uncle!

Then he recalled her reaction when he had asked her to marry him. "I cannot possibly marry *you,*" she had said, and how that stress on *you* had rankled! "I don't want to marry you and I shan't," she had gone on. "I don't have to, I have not lost my virtue."

There was no help for it, he'd have to seduce her to convince her she had no choice but to become his wife.

But not here in the house of her protective honorary uncle, he decided. He had no more desire to experience Italian vengeance than a French guillotine. Joining her, he acquainted her with the plans for their departure.

After three restful, well-fed days, James felt himself almost ready to face the horrors of a sea voyage again. Sitting with Cordelia and the count on a shady terrace after a hearty luncheon, he was about to tell them so when Barzetti, the old majordomo, scuttled out of the house.

*"Eccellenza,"* he cried, "the outrider of Signora la Contessa is come. He says she has reported your English guests to the French and they are close on his heels!"

# Twenty-four

The open carriage, intended for leisurely jaunts about the countryside, bounced along the stony track. Cordelia clung to the side. Clouds of white dust rose from the horses' hooves and the wheels, to coat the occupants and hang in the air behind them.

"Like the pillar of cloud leading Moses through the wilderness," James said grimly, "except this is leading the French after us. Tell me what happened. I did not understand the half of it."

"The outrider said Lucia's maid told one of the footmen this morning that Lucia had muttered something about informing on us to the French. The footman told him but he did nothing as he did not really believe it. Also he had been sent to escort the countess and he did not dare desert his duty. But then Lucia ordered the coachman to take her to the French *comandante.* The outrider decided he was as likely to land in the suds through not warning his master as through deserting his mistress."

"So he raced back to Arventino at once? That would explain why the troops did not arrive before we left. It's even possible the contessa thought better of betraying us when he departed in such a hurry."

"I hope so," Cordelia exclaimed, "but pray don't suggest to our driver that he need not go so fast!"

"I shan't." James grinned wryly. "Loath as I am to set sail, I shall be most insistent on the count's captain putting out to sea the moment we arrive, ready or not."

Captain Rutigliano needed no persuading. Their driver knew his habits and quickly ran him and two of his sailors to earth at a *trattoria* near the old harbour. He scanned the count's brief note and promptly hustled Cordelia and James aboard.

The other two crew members were there, guarding the yacht, a graceful vessel gleaming with white paint, polished teak, and brass fittings. The count had sent word days ago of their coming on the morrow, so all was in readiness. As the last red sliver of sun slid into the Gulf of Taranto, the *Bella Drusilla* slid away from the quay.

The captain and his men were too busy to show James and Cordelia to their quarters. James sat hunched on a coil of rope, hugging his middle, while Cordelia stood at the rail admiring the western sky.

Turning away from the sunset, she looked back at the ancient city with its fortress, cathedral, and episcopal palace. *"Zio* Simone told me Taranto began as a Spartan colony," she said in an effort to distract James from his unhappy insides. "The Romans and Carthaginians fought over it, then Lombards, Saracens, Greeks—let's see—and Normans, Austrians, Spaniards, and doubtless a few I've forgotten."

"And now it belongs to the kingdom of Naples, reigned over by Joachim Murat, the son of a French innkeeper and, to give the devil his due, a brilliant cavalry commander."

"Oh heavens," cried Cordelia, "here come some of his cavalry now!"

The thunder of hooves on cobblestones resounded through the gathering dusk as a troop of soldiers galloped out of the narrow, twisting streets and onto the quay. James pulled Cordelia down behind a windlass. They huddled there as the French officer bellowed, *"La* Bella Drusilla, *halte-là!"*

The gap of smooth, dark water between the yacht and the pier continued to widen. Captain Rutigliano came to the rail with his speaking trumpet.

"Impossible," he shouted in Italian. "I take my orders from *Sua Eccellenza, il Conte di Arventino e Grassano,* and he wishes me to sail to Bari. Perhaps we shall meet there." Turning away, he ordered his men to raise more canvas.

A few more yells followed them, but no bullets, though James made Cordelia stay crouched behind the capstan for several minutes more. Perhaps the Frenchman was impressed by the count's title, or he was not sure enough of his quarry to fire, or he simply thought it futile to shoot at a ship fast disappearing into the night. Cordelia hoped Captain Rutigliano would not find trouble waiting when at last he reached Bari. She supposed she would never know.

"At least we did not go dashing across the countryside for nothing," she said.

"And the excitement took my mind off my interior."

"How do you feel now?"

"Not *too* bad," James said cautiously. "Do you think that last ghastly voyage has cured me?"

"Very likely," Cordelia encouraged him, forbearing to point out that they were still within the harbour basin.

The captain came to usher them to their luxurious cabins—two, as the count had told him they were brother and sister. One of the sailors would act as their steward when not needed on deck, he explained. This would relieve Cordelia of the unpleasant tasks associated with James's sickness, but she had every intention of nursing him through his torments.

However, though queasy he was not desperately ill, and he was even able to eat a little as long as he walked about the deck for an hour afterwards. The narrow-beamed *Bella Drusilla* cut smoothly through the glassy waves with a minimum of pitch and roll. By the third day, James had found his balance, and on the fifth he was beside Cordelia at the rail as they sailed into the beautiful harbour at Syracuse.

On the citadel, beside the flag of the Two Sicilies, the Union Jack flaunted its red, white, and blue. Cordelia's heart lifted at the sight. For the first time since infancy, she was about to step onto . . . well, not quite British soil, and it was still a long way home. But at least she did not want to hide from the scarlet-tunicked soldiers on the dock!

There were British sailors, too, in blue pea-jackets. James pointed out two frigates and a sloop flying the White Ensign, the Royal Navy's flag with its red cross of St. George and a small Union Jack in one corner.

"Do you suppose we might sail on that sloop, all the way to England?" Cordelia said longingly.

"Too much to hope for, though I daresay we'd be shockingly uncomfortable on her. The navy isn't set up to carry passengers. I see several merchantmen among the fishing boats. Perhaps we shall be able to leave before I lose my sea-legs again, but first I must speak to whoever is in charge here."

In that he had little choice. A sergeant examined Captain Rutigliano's papers minutely, and politely invited him to take himself and his crew back to the mainland *subito.* With equal polite minuteness he studied Cordelia's papers, somehow preserved through thick and thin, with the ink running a little in places. Over these he nodded his approval. Then he came to James and discovered he had no papers at all.

"I'm afraid I'll 'ave to take you to see the major, sir," he said. "You sounds like English gentry orl right to me, but I can't take it on meself to let you pass. Never fear, sir, I'll 'ave one o' me men escort miss to a respeckable inn. *Albergo*, these 'ere Eyeties call it."

"Thank you, Sergeant," said James.

"But had I not better look about for a ship to take us onwards?" Cordelia protested.

"Don't you fret 'bout that, miss," the sergeant advised her. "The major's got everything you could want to know 'bout every vessel in the 'arbour. 'E'll direct Mr. Courtenay right, never you fear."

"Mr. . . . ?" Cordelia looked at him blankly for a moment, before she realized he had reached a natural conclusion. She and James claimed to be brother and sister, and her papers declared her surname as Courtenay, so obviously he must be a

Courtenay, too. They had used so many names, that complication had never crossed her mind, nor James's, judging by his equally blank look.

The soldier's eyes narrowed in suspicion. Cordelia hastened to give him the first explanation that came to her lips.

"Oh, this is Mr. Preston. We are *half*-brother and -sister, you see."

"Beg pardon, Mr. Preston, sir, I'm sure," said the sergeant, but his doubts had been aroused. He sent James off between a corporal and a burly private, under surveillance if not precisely under guard.

Cordelia nearly insisted on following. However, James appeared unworried. Her presence at his interview with the major was as likely to raise awkward questions about their relationship as to help. Besides, she reflected, she really knew remarkably little about his past, and what little she knew in his favour could always be told later if he ran into trouble.

A local porter was summoned to carry their baggage, and a young private was detailed to escort Cordelia to the inn. He blushed to match his scarlet tunic, making visible a youthful moustache so fair it was previously almost invisible against his fair skin.

"Please to step this way, miss," he said shyly.

Private Eddings seemed uncertain whether to lead the way, walk beside her, or fall back a few feet like a servant. Cordelia adjusted her pace to keep him at her side, enchanted to have a real Englishman for her guide after all the swarthy, black-haired foreigners.

"Is it long since you left England?" she asked.

"Nay, miss, 'tis just six months sin' I took the King's shilling, and then there were marching drill an' rifle drill an' that afore we was shipped out."

"Took the King's shilling?"

"Enlisted, like, miss. They gives a bloke a shilling to enlist. 'Tis a sight better nor being pressed to the Navy."

"Pressed? Forgive my ignorance, it is a long time since I was in England."

"Don't make no matter, miss," he muttered, blushing furiously. "The press gang goes out taking men for the Navy, see, and you don't get no choice to go or not."

"How dreadful!"

Private Eddings shrugged. "Otherwise there wouldn't be no one to man the King's ships, miss. 'Tis a hard life, much worser nor the army. This way, miss, if you please."

As they turned a corner into a narrow, crooked alley, Cordelia saw a jeweller's shop. A good deal of the proceeds from the Dubrovnik jeweller had been spent on their passage to Bari and tips for the count's servants and crew. There was no knowing when she would have another opportunity to replenish their funds.

"I should like to go in to that shop," she said, then remembered that her wares were swathed around her waist. "Oh no, I must go to the inn first. Will it be difficult to find my way back?"

"No, miss, but you oughtn't to walk about the streets alone, a lady like you," the soldier said anxiously. "These Eyeties, they haven't got a mite o' respect for decent females."

They blushed at each other as Cordelia recalled that once, in a crowded Naples street, her mama had been pinched on the bottom by an overenthusiastic unknown admirer.

"Then will you be so kind, sir," she said, "as to wait just a minute or two and escort me back?"

"That I will, miss."

"The sergeant will not scold you for being gone over long?"

"I'll tell him you was tired an' walked desp'rate slow."

They exchanged a grin of complicity and hurried to catch up with the porter.

The jeweller turned out to be a Jew who had done business with Aaron of Istanbul, though he had never met him. Among the Italian, Spanish, and Portuguese gold coins he gave Cordelia for her diamonds were several English guineas. She examined them with interest, feeling more and more as if she were nearly home though in miles at least two thirds of the journey still lay ahead.

"I have given you one American gold dollar as a makeweight," the jeweller told her, "but if you prefer I shall exchange it for silver."

"American? How did you come by that?"

"For several years, you English let the American navy use Siracusa as a base for fighting the Barbary pirates. Now, alas, you are no longer friends. It is bad for commerce when friends fall out and enemies go to war." He shook his head despondently, then cheered up, adding, "But lovely ladies will always wear diamonds. I shall have no difficulty disposing of these, *signorina*."

At a good profit, no doubt, Cordelia thought, but she did not really mind. Somehow she had never quite regarded the proceeds of selling the diamonds as real money to be scrimped to the last penny.

Her soldier-lad had insisted on waiting outside the shop to shepherd her back to the inn. He refused a tip.

"I were only doing my duty," he said, the ready scarlet rising in his cheeks like a reflection from his uniform. " 'Sides, 'tis an honour to walk wi' a pretty lady."

She thanked him and, as he turned reluctantly away, enquired of an inn servant whether her brother was come. The man was quite sure no Englishman had arrived.

"Oh dear!" she exclaimed aloud in English, beginning to worry about James.

Private Eddings at once turned back. "What is it, miss?" he asked eagerly. "Is summat wrong?"

Cordelia was not sure what to do. If the British Army, in the shape of his commanding officer, was detaining James, then the young soldier could not be relied upon as a friend. On the other hand, he had risked his sergeant's displeasure to guard her from indelicate advances, and he was the only friend she had.

She wanted James. She needed him—how could she ever

have been so foolish as to believe she could manage the journey on her own? But more than his assistance, she wanted his presence, merry, serious, plaguesome, or even in the ghastly throes of *mal-de-mer.* If she had to lie like a trooper to convince the major of his respectability, then lie she would.

"My brother is not yet come," she told Private Eddings. "I must go and find him. Will you direct me to the major's?"

"I'll take you, miss," he said firmly.

As they walked, she wondered just what lies would best suit her purpose. Then she wondered what James had told the major, and how she might find out so as not to contradict his story. It seemed impossible, and she began to envision James being clapped up in irons or even shot at dawn. She was working herself into high fidgets when they turned a corner to see James and a scarlet-coated officer strolling towards them, laughing.

Relief was succeeded by fury. Marching up to James, she snapped, "Where have you been all this time?"

"Has it been long? I beg your pardon for keeping you waiting," he said soothingly.

"I thought . . . I was afraid . . ." She bit her lip.

"Allow me to introduce Major Saunderson. Major, my sister, Miss Courtenay."

"How do, ma'am." The stalwart officer made a flourishing bow and preened his flourishing moustache. "Beg pardon for keeping your brother. He's been telling me a bit about your adventures. B'Jove, ma'am, you'll be glad to get aboard an honest Portuguee merchantman."

"We are in luck, the *Flor do Campo* leaves tomorrow, bound for Lisbon," James explained. "That's well on our way. I came to tell you before going back to the harbour to book passage."

"I shall go with you," said Cordelia decidedly, not about to let him out of her sight again so soon. "Major, I should like to commend Private Eddings, who has been a most kind and zealous escort."

Stiffly at attention, his face crimson, the young soldier gave a smart salute.

"At ease, Private. Eddings, is it? I'll make a note of your commendation, ma'am. Back to your duty now, lad."

Casting a glance brimful of gratitude at Cordelia, Private Eddings departed on the double.

"You have won a heart there," James observed.

"Yes indeed, haw haw," Major Saunderson chortled but he continued gallantly, "Only to be expected with such a beautiful young lady. May I tell my wife, ma'am, that you and Preston here will dine with us this evening?"

James nodded, so Cordelia accepted with due gratitude, and they parted from the jovial major.

"Do you think it wise?" Cordelia asked as they headed for the harbour. "There is so much we must conceal."

"He did not doubt my word. Just leave the talking to me."

As it turned out, James and Cordelia had no need to guard their tongues since the intrepid Mrs. Saunderson was too eager to relate her own adventures in India to want to hear theirs. They left soon after dinner and went aboard the Portuguese merchantman, *Flor do Campo.*

Though the ship remained tied up in the harbour, James passed an uneasy night. When they set sail next morning, his hopes of having retained his sea-legs were dashed. The merchantman was a clumsy, lumbering tub which wallowed in each trough and rocked on each crest before plunging sickeningly to wallow again as the wheat it carried shifted. Once again, he wanted to die.

Cordelia nursed him faithfully, leaving only when he snatched a little sleep, and for her meals. Over these, she reported, she studied Portuguese with Captain de Castilho, who spoke some English and Italian. Between bouts of nausea, James wondered at the evident delight she took in learning. She would come in her face bright with pleasure at the discovery of some similarity or intriguing contrast between Portuguese and Italian. To him the study of languages was a means to an end, but she obviously enjoyed it for its own sake.

What luck to have found her! he thought as she wiped his

brow and tried to distract him from his sufferings with the Portuguese word for handkerchief. If he survived, he *had* to persuade her to marry him.

The *Flor do Campo* floundered on, past Malta, through the Strait of Sicily, between the southern end of Sardinia and the North African coast. Eventually James's stomach grew used to the motion. As he recovered, he and Cordelia spent a good deal of time on deck for it was stuffy in the cabins—and she refused to enter his now that he was well.

At these latitudes the sun was fierce even so early in the year. The captain had a canvas awning rigged for them at the stern, behind the poop deck structure, out of the way of the business of the ship. In its shade they were invisible from anyone not seeking them out. James decided to take advantage of their privacy.

Cordelia sat on a cushion, earnestly penciling in a new addition to her list of Portuguese words and their English equivalents. "Do you recall whether Captain de Castilho said it has an accent?" she asked.

"Let me look. If I see it I may remember." James moved to a cushion close beside her and leaned still closer, his breath stirring the blond tendrils at her temple.

She edged away, moving back right into the curve of the arm he had carefully arranged behind her. She fitted very nicely.

"Is that the word?" he asked softly, pointing at the last in the list so that if she moved forward her breast would encounter his hand.

"Y-yes," she said in an unsteady voice. "I . . ."

*"Palmeira,"* he read. "Palm tree. Easy enough. 'And palm to palm is holy palmers' kiss.' "

"What . . . ?" She turned her head.

He kissed her, his arms closing about her. Her mouth was soft and sweet, responsive—momentarily.

"What's that?" She jerked away. "Listen!"

James had been distantly aware for some time of more shouts from crew to captain and back than usual. Since he did not understand, he took no notice. But now a new urgency had entered their voices.

The prow of a ship slid past, slowing, parallel to the *Flor do Campo* and no more than ten yards distant. As the deck of the brigantine came into view, black-whiskered men in turbans poured yelling from hatchways, brandishing daggers, scimitars, and pikes. Some whirled long chains about their heads and let fly grappling hooks to thud into the merchantman's planks.

Clasping Cordelia close, James uttered one terrifying word. "Corsairs!"

# Twenty-five

Inexorably the two ships drew together. When their rails were a yard apart, the whooping corsairs swarmed aboard the merchantman. There was no resistance.

"What will they do?" whispered Cordelia, cold despite the southern sun.

"I don't know," James said soberly, standing up and giving her a hand. "The British have a treaty with the Dey of Algiers, but he disregards it when it suits him."

"Let us hope it does not suit him at present!" She tried to smile. "At least Major Saunderson provided papers for you."

Two fearsome black-robed pirates, scimitars in hand and pistols in their belts, came round the corner to their little shelter. Two others with pikes appeared from the opposite direction.

"Go! Go!" bawled one of the pike-men in Turkish, jabbing at them with his weapon.

"You don't need to shout," Cordelia reproved him without flinching. A little British dignity could not come amiss, she felt. "We will go. Do stop waving that nasty thing about."

Dumfounded, the man gaped at her. "She's Turkish," he blurted out.

"No, we are English, and the English have a treaty with your ruler. You will be sorry if you treat us with discourtesy."

*"Allahu aalam!* Please, *Bayan,* our captain wishes to see you."

Cordelia nodded graciously. The scimitar-wielders parted before her as she led the way forward. She glanced back at James. His eyes were warm with laughter and admiration.

The Portuguese crew huddled under guard amidships. Captain de Castilho rose as his passengers appeared. Spreading his hands in helpless apology, he said, "It would have been useless to fight them. We are traders, not military men."

"We don't hold you to blame, Captain," Cordelia assured him.

"Don't we?" James muttered disgustedly in English.

*"Bayan?"*

Turning, she found herself face to face with a huge, hook-nosed corsair. His thumbs in his girdle, he looked her up and down.

"I am told you speak Turkish, *Bayan."*

"Yes." Though she refused to be intimidated, she tucked her hand into the crook of James's arm. "I lived in Istanbul for some years, but I and my brother are English. You have a treaty with the English. You had better let us go."

"I regret, *Bayan,* but if you are truly English . . ."

"We are English! We will show you our papers."

He waved this offer aside. "I do not read your alphabet. In any case, it is for Haji Ali Dey to decide. Besides, you cannot leave without a ship, and Reis Hammida would have me bastinadoed did I lose an unarmed Portuguese vessel. I must take you to Algiers."

"But the *Flor do Campo* carries wheat, not treasure."

The pirate laughed, white teeth flashing in the midst of his black beard. "The ship itself is of value, for we have little wood in our land suitable for ship-building. More important, there is always a need for infidel slaves. And if the Dey is not minded to please the English at present, a young, fair virgin will fetch a fine price."

In the circumstances, Cordelia was more than ready to claim she was no virgin. However, before she could speak, the corsair captain turned away to give orders to his men.

The merchantman's crew were to be deprived of their clothes

and locked up below deck while a small crew of corsairs in Portuguese dress sailed her to Algiers. Cordelia, James, and Captain de Castilho were confined all together in the latter's cabin next to theirs beneath the poop deck, to make it easier to guard them.

"Not that they will need to set a guard," James said grimly, scanning the comfortably furnished cabin. Its two windows, one opening forward onto the main deck amidships, the other to starboard onto the narrow gangway to the stern, were built small to withstand crashing waves in a storm. "Even if we escaped from here, there is nowhere to go and two of us unarmed cannot overcome a dozen armed pirates."

"Three," said Cordelia, then glanced at the captain, seated at his table sunk in hopeless gloom, his head in his hands. "Two. You followed what that man said about the crew? You did not look as if you understood."

"It might come in useful if they didn't realize I know Turkish, but yes, I understood most of it."

"About . . . about me?" Her gaze fixed on a brass barometer on the wall, she willed herself not to blush.

"About fair virgins, yes." His voice was studiedly casual.

"Do you think . . . do you think I should tell them I'm not?"

"It might make things worse. I don't know much about the Barbary corsairs."

"Will you ask the captain? While I pretend not to listen?"

"You are the one who speaks Italian and is learning Portuguese," James pointed out.

She glared at him. "I cannot ask him *that!* Perhaps he will understand if you ask in English. Or try Latin—he is a Roman Catholic, after all, so he must know some, and Papists are always talking about the Virgin Mary."

"I'll try," he said, the corners of his lips twitching. He had a truly abominable sense of humour!

Cordelia stalked the two paces to the open starboard window and peered out at the narrow strip of deck and the dark blue sea beyond. Doing her best not to hear the garbled mishmash of English, Latin, Italian, and Portuguese behind her, she concentrated on possible ways to escape. She might be able to squeeze through the window; conceivably, if the key had been left in the outside of the lock, she might be able to open the cabin's door for the men; but there would still be the corsairs to deal with.

"Better remain a virgin—for the present," James interrupted her thoughts. "As far as I can make out, de Castilho says you would be sold into a harem anyway but not treated so well."

"Oh." Her shoulders slumped and she sat down opposite the captain. "What about you?"

"I doubt any harem would want me," he said dryly. "You know very well I'm not really a eunuch."

She frowned at him. The captain was looking from one to the other as they spoke. Cordelia addressed him in a mixture of languages and passed on to James what she gathered in reply.

"If the Dey does not release us because we are English, he will ask for ransom. But until the ransom is paid, you will be treated as a slave. That means labouring in chains in the quarry or on the breakwater in the harbour. He says the breakwater at Algiers has been under construction for centuries because the winter storms destroy it as fast as it is built. Hundreds of thousands of Christian slaves have died . . . James, we *must* escape!"

He reached across the table to take her hand. "We shall," he said gaily. "We have had plenty of practise, after all. Just give me time to think." But his eyes were sombre.

They were given all the time in the world to think. No one came near them the rest of that day. Captain de Castilho relapsed into silent gloom, rousing only to fetch from a locker a crock of dried figs and apricots, and a bottle of Madeira wine of which he consumed the greater part. In the hot, stuffy cabin, Cordelia was too thirsty to eat the sweet fruit. She and James both tried calling through the forward window for water, but they were ignored so they had to ration out the contents of the one small pitcher.

All too much time to think—Cordelia began to wonder whether she would not have done better to stay in Istanbul as Mehmed Pasha's mistress rather than to be sold into an unknown harem. Mama had seemed quite content with him. He was generous, and kind enough as long as matters went his way.

Mama's lovers had all been kind to her, and all but one, quickly dismissed, to her daughter as well. *Zio* Simone had loved Mama, even wished it were possible to marry her. Had Mama loved him, too? When the moment came to part, had she bitterly regretted that her chosen way of life made the parting inevitable? Poor Mama, she had paid for her shameful behaviour even before her ignominious death.

That death played out before Cordelia's mind's eye in images as clear as if it had been yesterday, overwhelming her with the same helpless despair.

James shattered the mirage. "Don't look so blue-devilled. While there's life there's hope."

"I was thinking about my mother's death," Cordelia blurted out.

"I'm sorry. If I had known I'd not have spoken so abominably tactlessly."

"How were you to guess? I was sure the memory must have faded after all this time, but I can still picture the accident as if it were taking place in front of me all over again."

"My dear girl, you were present? I did not realize!"

"It was horrible." She shuddered.

"Talking about it might help to exorcise the memory, if you would like to tell me."

His gentleness decided Cordelia. Mehmed Pasha's reaction had infuriated her; *Zio* Simone's left her dissatisfied, because he did not comprehend that part of the horror lay in the sheer absurdity of her mother's end. Perhaps James would understand.

Once again, haltingly, she told the tale. James showed not the least disposition to laugh, but as she finished, enlightenment coloured the sympathy in his face.

"Cats and camels: that explains your detestation of both. My poor dear, what a dreadful business! Quite apart from a natural reluctance, I can see why you shrink from speaking of it. Such preposterous mischances would be apt to arouse as much levity as pity in a thoughtless listener."

"Mehmed Pasha laughed like a hyena."

"Which must have added vastly to the pain of losing your mother." He touched her hand as she nodded, immeasurably soothed by his discernment. "Well, you are safe from that hyena now. Have you any more notion than I of how to escape these Algerian beasts?"

"None." Brought back from the dreadful past to the dreadful present, Cordelia found herself thirstier than ever and no nearer a solution. "When shall we reach Algiers?" she asked the captain.

"Tomorrow, *senhorita,*" he grunted morosely, "or the next day."

Cordelia was given the captain's brass bedstead for the night. Though she would just as soon have slept on the floor, for his sheets were hardly pristine and she had grown unaccustomed to dirt since Dubrovnik, she could scarcely tell him so. He took the only easy chair and James stretched out on the Turkey carpet.

None of them slept well, but both the men were in the arms of Morpheus when the first light of dawn stole into the cabin. Cordelia could not bear to stay abed any longer. Stepping over outflung arms and legs, she crept to the starboard window and peered out.

A shifting mist hung over the smooth, dark, undulating waves. Within it appeared the silhouette of a ship. A reflection of the becalmed *Flor do Campo*, Cordelia thought.

But it moved slowly through the fog, its lean, swift lines all wrong for the tubby merchantman, its sails catching the least wisp of breeze. Had the pirate ship returned to escort them for some reason? No, the brigantine's deck had been bare, and surely that was the glint of a cannon's barrel she saw.

"James!"

She spoke softly. The captain snored on. James woke instantly and was beside her in one lithe movement.

"What is it? Are you all right?"

"Look! Is that the Algerian ship?"

"Not the one that took us. It's a frigate, I'd say. It may be one of theirs . . ."

"But it may not. Suppose . . ."

At that moment a hail rang across the water. "Ahoy, there! What ship?" English, oddly accented, yet not foreign.

"Americans!" James breathed.

No response issued from the merchantman.

"Should we not shout for help?" Cordelia begged.

"They might not hear us at this distance without a speaking trumpet, but our captors surely would. Lord knows what they'd do."

"Ahoy!" The frigate's sails were coming down and she was losing what little way she had.

"*Flor do Campo*, bound for Lisbon," someone shouted in mispronounced Portuguese from the deck outside the cabin. "Who are you?"

"*Columbia*, frigate, out of Boston."

"They will go," Cordelia moaned. "We *must* attract their attention. Help me climb out!"

"But—"

"There's no time to argue." She swung round to face him. "Lift me up so I can go feet first."

Without further ado, James picked her up, hoisted her over his shoulder, and manoeuvred her feet out of the window. Her skirts caught on something and ripped, then bunched up around her waist. With a squirm and a wriggle she squeezed her hips through. Her bare feet hit the deck.

The window's inflexible frame caught her by the shoulders.

"Let go my neck, cross your arms, and hunch your shoulders." James kissed her nose.

"But I might fall backwards. The gangway is very narrow here."

"I've got you. I shan't let you go," he promised. "Don't give up half way. You don't want them to catch you like this."

"No!" Of all the ignominious defeats!

With a twist she was out. There was the ladder she remembered, leading up to the poop deck.

"Give me a sheet. Hurry!"

She did not dare look to see what the *Columbia* was doing. A distant voice shouted an order. Nearer, amidships, she heard the corsairs in muttered consultation. Any moment they might decide to check on their prisoners.

The sheet slung around her neck, she scrambled up the ladder. She turned to see, through rapidly dissipating mists, the frigate's sails creeping slowly back up the masts.

If only someone were watching! Madly she flapped the sheet.

A faint shout. The sails stopped rising. Cordelia flapped and flapped until she thought her arms would fall off.

A loud shout, nearer. Much nearer. The corsairs had spotted her. She had nowhere to run to, nowhere to hide, so she went on flailing desperately with the sheet. A swarthy face rose above the edge of the roof, dark eyes gleaming as bright as the dagger clenched in its grinning teeth.

Another shout from below, in Turkish: "They are lowering a boat!"

The grinning head turned, then abruptly disappeared. Letting her exhausted arms sink to her sides, Cordelia watched the *Columbia*'s boat splash down. The spray rose sparkling in the sun's first rays. Sailors swarmed down ropes into the gig and set to the oars.

A moment later, a ragged rattle of musket fire erupted from the deck of the *Flor do Campo*. A hail of bullets whizzed across the waves to greet the Americans.

The *Columbia* promptly responded with a disciplined volley. A hole appeared in Cordelia's sheet. As she dropped flat on the deck, a scream came from below. More shots rang out, followed by the boom of a cannon.

Cordelia snaked her way to the far side of the ship and down the ladder. Huddled on the narrow strip of gangway, she at last had time to be frightened.

Quaking, she heard the cannon roar again. Were the rescuers going to sink the corsairs' prisoners with the ship? And if they survived, would she and James be any better off with the Americans than with the corsairs? For all their talk of liberty and justice, Americans also kept slaves, she recalled, and the Syracuse jeweller had said America and England were at odds. They might simply end up as two slaves on a cotton plantation instead of one in a harem and one quarrying rock.

The deck beneath her shuddered to a sudden shock.

If she was about to drown, she wanted to be with James. What was going on? She crept to the corner and peered around.

# Twenty-six

The ship shuddered.

"Direct hit," James muttered to the carpet in front of his nose. Were the overenthusiastic representatives of a youthful nation trying to rescue them or to sink them?

Where was Cordelia? If it was her antics which had led to this bombardment, surely the Americans would try to avoid shooting at her, but a stray shot might hit her. Or the corsairs might have grabbed her. His heart stuck in his throat, choking him.

" 'A plague a both your houses!' " he swore.

Unable to escape the cabin, he could do nothing to help her, or himself, but if he was about to drown anyway, he wanted to know what was going on.

Cautiously he raised himself far enough to peep out of the forward window.

Behind him Captain de Castilho, flat on the floor by now, spoke sharply: *"Cuidado, senhor!"*

No doubt advising him to keep his head down. Since he did not understand, it was easy to ignore.

Outside, the pirates had taken cover behind capstans, coils of rope, water-barrels—to add to his troubles, James remembered he was dying of thirst. Every now and then a man would raise his head and his musket and let off a shot. Answering shots from the *Columbia* gouged the planking. One corsair sat slumped, groaning, in the shelter of the mainmast's base, a bloody cloth tied around his upper arm.

Of Cordelia, nor sight nor sound. Without sticking his head out to make a nice target for both sides, James could see no more.

But he heard the splash of oars. Thuds and thumps followed, somewhere below. A boarding party? The corsairs reached for pikes, loosened scimitars in their belts, gripped daggers between their teeth.

While they were distracted and the Americans not shooting—he hoped—for fear of hitting their own men, James decided to risk a quick look about. He inched his head out through the window until he could see the frigate. She had launched two more boats, which were rapidly rowing towards bows and stern of the merchantman. He turned his head to look the other way.

The motion caught the eye of a corsair. Swift as thought, he flung his dagger.

Even as James ducked, he saw Cordelia's fair head peeking around the corner of the poop deck structure. She was all right! But what the devil did the little peagoose think . . . ?

A yelp behind him told that the dagger had found an unintended mark. Captain de Castilho clutched his thigh, staring at the blood staining his breeches in a circle spreading from the protruding blade. "I am not a military man," he moaned, and fainted.

However much James wanted to see what was going on outside, he could not leave the captain to bleed like a stuck pig. Making no attempt to bring him round, he ripped open the leg of his breeches. In a locker he found clean linen, which he fashioned into a bandage. Then he carefully drew out the dagger. Blood welled up. He pressed a pad to the wound and sat on the floor holding it, listening to the clash of steel against steel just beyond the cabin wall.

Cutlass struck sparks from scimitar. Cordelia watched, frozen in place by competing instincts. Half her mind told her to hurry forward to succour the wounded. The other half strongly advised removing her person as far and as fast as possible from the battle.

An abandoned pike slithered across the swaying deck to her feet. That convinced her she was much too close for comfort. She was about to perform a strategic retreat when she noticed the corsair who had been shot earlier.

Crouched behind the mast, he had so far taken no part in repelling the boarders. What attracted Cordelia's attention was the flash of sunlight on the blade of his scimitar as he raised it. Following his gaze, she saw that one of the American sailors had penetrated through the ranks of the pirates and was fighting with his back to her. The wounded man was in a perfect position to take him by surprise from the rear.

As the corsair sprang forward, Cordelia seized the pike at her feet. It was heavier than she expected, but after the travails of her travels she was stronger than was quite proper in a young lady.

She dashed after the corsair, swung the pike haft in a wild arc, and whacked him on the side of the head. He slumped to the deck just as a score of Americans swarmed from bows and stern to the aid of their comrades.

Cordelia stood with the pike in her hands, staring down at the man she had felled. One of the Americans, a black man—a slave?—gently removed the weapon from her grasp and led her away from where the others were rapidly disarming the corsairs.

"Well done, lady," he said.

"Did I kill him?" She looked back.

"Dunno, lady. You hit him with the blunt end."

"I could not bring myself to stab him. Not that I had time to think."

"And don't you think no more about it. Here."

She found he had taken off his jacket and was draping it over her shoulders. The top of her gown had torn as badly as her skirt in her scramble through the window, she realized.

"Heavens, I must change! That's my cabin, there."

The sailor escorted her to the door, gravely accepted the return of his coat, and said in parting, "You take it easy, lady. You're safe now."

Cordelia did not feel safe. Was he a slave? Had he been so kind and sympathetic because he guessed she too was bound for slavery in America? She locked the cabin door and sat down on her bunk, shivering though the early morning air was already warming. If she stayed quietly in here perhaps the black man would not mention her and the Americans would let the *Flor do Campo* sail on with her still aboard.

But what about James? They would find him when they released the captain.

Someone battered on the door. She shrank back.

"Cordelia, are you there?" James sounded frantic. "Cordelia! Oh lord, where is she?"

"James!" She flung herself across the cabin, unlocked the door, and fell into the safety of his arms.

"My dear girl," he murmured into her hair. "My dear girl."

She rested her forehead against his shoulder, feeling the fear drain from her body. Then she looked up at him and said proudly, "I did it! They saw me and they stayed."

His smile was a trifle wobbly. "You did it. But I have been scared half to death for you. You are not hurt?"

"Not a scratch. And you?" Remembering the dagger thrown at him, she pulled away a little to see him properly.

"Not a scratch, but de Castilho . . ." His gaze fell on her ripped bodice and his eyes widened. "Who the deuce did . . . ?"

"That was the window," she said defensively, crossing her arms over her breast. "I forgot, I must change."

He glanced back over his shoulder as if he half expected to see sailors of every nation gathered to enjoy the sight of her dishabille. The corsairs sat in a sullen group under guard, makeshift bandages evident on both sides. The near-naked Portuguese filed sheepishly up from their prison. A young American, an officer by his coat, came out of the captain's cabin, looked around, and started towards James and Cordelia. She fled.

Before putting on a fresh dress, Cordelia drank every drop of water in her pitcher. She was still thirsty, and hungry now also. She hoped the Americans at least fed their slaves well.

Perhaps they were not to be enslaved. James had not seemed concerned about having jumped from the frying pan into the fire—but he had been too worried about her to think ahead. Suddenly she needed desperately to be with him, to find out what lay in store. She hurried into her pink muslin with white ribbons, and to give herself confidence she donned her white rose trimmed hat.

Taking a deep breath, she was about to venture forth when James called her name and tapped on the door. She opened it.

"Are you ready? Yes, and dressed up to the nines!" He grinned. "Trying to impress our American cousins?"

"Cousins? James, they keep slaves, don't they?"

Looking puzzled, he nodded, then his look changed to enlightenment. "Are you afraid they will make slaves of us? No, my dear, unlike the impartial Mohammedans, they keep only black slaves these days. Besides, the *Columbia* is from Boston, in Massachusetts which is, I believe, a free state."

"Then they will let us stay on the *Flor do Campo*?"

"Better than that. At least, Lieutenant Carmichael, the excellent fellow who led the boarding party, thinks his captain may allow us to sail with them. They are westward bound, whereas de Castilho intends to put into Sardinia for repairs to himself and his ship—there's a whacking great hole in the bows, above the waterline, fortunately. Poor chap, his wound has put him quite out of humour and he is almost as annoyed at the damage to the ship as grateful for the rescue."

"How on earth was *he* wounded?"

"He was hit by a knife meant for me," James explained dryly.

"When you stuck your head through the window? How could you have been so muttonheaded!"

"Quite as muttonheaded as a certain young lady who was peering round corners when she should have been hiding! But never mind that now. Pack up your things quickly and Carmichael will take us over to the *Columbia.* He says Captain Barlow is signalling for them to return posthaste as a breeze has come up and he's in a hurry to sail. If we are there, the chances are he will take us."

"What about the corsairs?" Cordelia asked, hastening to pack the few things she had out.

"De Castilho is taking them to Sardinia to be tried. With his evidence and his crew's, they shan't escape justice."

"Good. I'm feeling vengeful, if only because I'm excessively hungry and thirsty!"

"Remember not to ask for tea," James advised with a grin.

"Whyever not?"

"It's a sensitive subject to Bostonians. They boast of having tossed several shiploads into their harbour. Though it was over thirty years ago, I've met those who still think tea and King George III are practically synonymous."

In the boat crossing to the *Columbia*, Cordelia mentioned the pangs of hunger and thirst to Lieutenant Carmichael, a fair young man with a round, boyish face. Beaming, he promised breakfast as soon as Captain Barlow had pronounced their fate.

"We took on fresh stores at Palermo, ma'am," he said. "How's about all the hot-cakes you can eat? And just for you, ma'am, I'll open up the last of my private stock of gen-u-wine maple syrup, though there's no more to be gotten this side of Vermont."

Expressing proper gratitude for this sacrifice, Cordelia wondered what hot-cakes and maple syrup were. They sounded good, and she was ready to eat practically anything.

Captain Barlow was by no means so amicable. Tall, gaunt, and lantern-jawed, he scowled at Carmichael as the lieutenant explained the arrival on board the frigate of the two Britishers. Cordelia was sure he would send them back to the *Flor do Campo*, but he gave an indifferent grunt, waved a dismissive hand, and turned away to give the order to raise sail.

Then he swung back and looked James up and down. "I'll see you in my cabin in five minutes, Mr. Preston," he announced, ignoring Cordelia.

"I guess breakfast will have to wait," Carmichael apologized, leading them to the captain's cabin. Since he appeared to assume Barlow meant both of them, Cordelia did not suggest she might at least have something to drink while waiting for James.

The lieutenant ushered them into the small, austere cabin and went off. In contrast to Captain de Castilho's comparative comfort, there was no easy chair, no carpet on the floor, and the narrow bedstead was of black iron. Tired after a restless night and an energetic, not to mention frightening morning, Cordelia sat down on one of the stiff wooden chairs at the table. James went over to the wood-cased barometer on the wall, tapped it, and contemplated its response.

"Set fair. One can only hope it's not referring solely to the weather."

It certainly did not seem to refer to Captain Barlow's mood. He arrived promptly, frowned at Cordelia, then once again ignored her and studied James with what looked inexplicably like grim satisfaction.

"So you're British."

"Yes, Captain. We are homeward bound."

"One of your ships impressed three of my men."

"Then they must have been deserters from our navy."

"And they refused to return two of my men who deserted to them."

Perplexed, Cordelia wondered why sailors would desert in both directions. Perhaps it was a case of the grass always being greener on the other side of the fence.

"The result," said Captain Barlow heavily, "is that my crew is five men short, without considering those wounded in going to your rescue. I shall deliver your sister to Gibraltar, but to take the place of one of my lost seamen, I'm enlisting you."

To her own mortification, James's consternation, and the captain's all too plain exasperation, Cordelia burst into tears.

# Twenty-seven

"But you never cry!" James exclaimed, dashing to Cordelia and thrusting his handkerchief into her hand. He stood protectively at her side, his hand on her shoulder.

"I'm s-sorry," she wept, blotting her eyes. "I-it must be because I thought we were quite s-safe at last. You said the Americans are our c-cousins, and I know Americans are supposed to believe in l-liberty, like the French, even though they keep slaves. Yet he's going to make you his prisoner and force you to be a common seaman!"

"He won't be a slave," growled Captain Barlow, determined though a trifle uncomfortable. "He'll draw his pay like the rest of the men."

"But he's an English gentleman. You cannot simply abduct him," Cordelia said passionately. "Besides, he gets dreadfully seasick, so he would be no manner of use to you."

"He'll be in good company. Believe me, these milksops soon stop feeling queasy when they're whipped up into the top-mast shrouds."

"No wonder they desert if you whip them for being ill!"

"I'll thank you not to criticize the way I run my ship," shouted the captain in a fury. "My mind is made up, he goes with us."

The tears chased from her eyes by her anger flooded back. "Don't take him! How can I travel all the way to England alone? You cannot be so cruel!"

"Hush, my lo . . . sister dear," James soothed. "It won't come to that. Captain, as my sister says, I am a gentleman, not a nobody. I have influential connections. Were you indeed to abduct me, your government would very quickly hear from mine. It could cause a nasty—"

"My mind is made up, I say!" bawled Captain Barlow, but he began to look distinctly uneasy.

"May I suggest that when you call at Gibraltar, you ask the Governor to—"

A sharp rap on the door cut him off.

"What is it?" snapped the captain.

Lieutenant Carmichael stuck his ingenuous head around the door and saluted. "Excuse me, sir, I thought you were finished with our *guests*." A patent untruth as he must have heard Barlow's quarterdeck bellow.

"Well, what's the matter?"

"It's Petty Officer Potter, sir." With a brief glance at Cordelia's tear-stained face, Carmichael fixed his earnest gaze on his commanding officer and gabbled, "Seaman Bailly just told him he saw Miss Courtenay save his life—Potter's that is—at risk of her own, and I thought you'd want to know, sir, besides which he's so keen to thank the lady he's waiting right here for her to come out so as to be sure to catch her before she goes to breakfast." Running out of breath, he stopped.

Captain Barlow glowered at him, then turned to Cordelia and asked sarcastically, "And how, pray, ma'am, did you contrive to save Potter's life in the middle of a fierce hand-to-hand battle without receiving a single scratch?"

"I hit a pirate on the head with a pikestaff when he was about to slice off your man's head with his scimitar. I'm very happy to have had the chance to save Mr. Potter's life. Dare I hope that, since I preserved for you a sailor you would otherwise have lost, you will reconsider taking my brother from me?"

"Take her brother?" Through the open cabin door a rising mutter of indignation came from the passage outside. "Take the young lady's brother?"

Over Carmichael's shoulder, Cordelia saw the friendly black seaman and several unknown faces. Of course the captain also saw and heard. His face turned red. He clenched his fists and took a stride forward, opening his mouth.

"Sorry, sir." The lieutenant hastily shut the door behind him. "Petty Officer Potter's popular with the men and they got up a sort of delegation to present their thanks to Miss Courtenay. There's a lot of admiration for her in the ranks, sir. They know she was the one I saw signalling, too, that made me figure there was something wrong aboard the Portuguee."

"The window was too small for me to squeeze out," James explained. "My sister is an amazingly brave girl, but to expect her to travel alone to England is too much."

"Alone!" Carmichael's astonishment was so overacted as to confirm Cordelia's suspicion of his having set up the whole scene. "A respectable young lady travel alone? Unthinkable! Folks back home would be mighty shocked to hear such a thing."

"Unthinkable," Captain Barlow agreed sourly. Whether persuaded by the threat of rumour flying, and doubtless growing, "back home" in Boston, or by the prospect of unrest amongst his crew, he tacitly backed down. "You'll be wanting your breakfast and I've work to do," he growled, sitting down at the table and reaching for pen, paper, and inkstand.

Cordelia hurriedly abandoned her seat and preceded James and the lieutenant out of the cabin. Somewhat to her relief, the group of vociferous sailors had discreetly vanished.

"*Thank* you," she said to Carmichael in low but heartfelt tones.

"He's an excellent officer in the main, ma'am, if a bit of a Puritan, which doesn't endear him to the men. But he tends to take odd notions into his head. I figured something was up by the way he acted when you came aboard. All it takes is a little coaxing to make him see straight."

"Masterly!" said James. "You are a fast and effective intriguer, Lieutenant. I expect to read one of these days of your being elected to your Congress."

Carmichael grinned. "My uncle hopes I shall step into his

shoes. He's there in the Senate already," he went on seriously, "doing his best to muzzle Clay and Calhoun and prevent a war with England which will do no one any good."

"I've an uncle who . . ."

Cordelia heard no more as they turned a corner and encountered her admirers. Though respectful, they were clamorous, each determined to get his word in until Lieutenant Carmichael said laughingly, "Enough, fellows! Let Miss Courtenay proceed to her breakfast."

Even before taking a desperately needed drink, Cordelia asked him, "Is Seaman Bailly a slave?" She had some vague notion of buying the man's freedom, small return for his part in preserving James.

"No, ma'am, that he is not," said Carmichael emphatically. "Slavery was banned in Massachusetts thirty years ago. Coffee?"

"Yes, please. James says it is no use asking a Bostonian for tea."

The lieutenant laughed heartily.

In the days that followed, Cordelia could not appear on deck without being saluted by every sailor in sight. She did not, however, venture from her cabin—actually Carmichael's, vacated for her use—during the captain's watch. They were not invited to dine at the captain's table, but, as Carmichael assured them, the officers' mess was a darn sight merrier.

Fortunately he was on duty when the Rock of Gibraltar came into view, for that was a sight not to be missed.

Tinted pink by the rays of the rising sun, the limestone cliffs towered against the blue sky. "Fourteen hundred feet," the lieutenant told her, "and pretty much sheer from the sea at the north end."

"Are you not glad we did not have to climb *that?*" James teased.

"I would still be sitting on the beach," Cordelia said with conviction.

"So would your brother," Carmichael assured her. "The Rock

is unclimbable on this side. It's riddled with caves, though, and you British have been digging tunnels through it since the great siege of thirty years ago. I've been into one of the caves, big as a cathedral and full of natural pillars. You must see it while you are here."

Cordelia shuddered. "Not me. I have had enough of caves to last a lifetime."

"No Greek brigands in this one, I promise," he said with a smile, "though you might find smugglers."

They had told the amiable American something of their adventures. He and James had become great friends. They held long political discussions which Cordelia was too ignorant to understand.

She had not known James was interested in the international situation, except as it affected their journey. Some day when they were alone, she resolved, she would ask him to explain his opinions to her. In Carmichael's presence, she was too ashamed of her ignorance to display it, though she had a sneaking suspicion he would be less shocked by that than by her desire for enlightenment.

In many ways he seemed a rather conventional young man. While complimenting her courage and spirit, he treated her like a delicate hot-house bloom. His admiring solicitude was prodigious flattering, of course. Yet it made her rather uncomfortable, accustomed as she was to James's matter-of-factness—when he was not tempting her to lose her virtue.

In fact, unlike the scapegrace James, the lieutenant was a true gentleman, thoroughly respectable. What a pity, then, that though she liked Carmichael very well, she found James so much more attractive!

They stood on either side of her at the quarterdeck rail as the *Columbia* drew level with the southern tip of the great Rock. The fortifications appeared, then the new mole protecting the harbour. Despite British and French trade embargoes, a crowd of ships rode at anchor. Behind massive stone walls, the town straggled along the shore at the base of the gentler western slopes.

"Look," said James, pointing up to the southern peak of the ridge. "That patch of red must be sentries' coats, I imagine."

"That's right, Redcoats," Carmichael confirmed, smiling, "even less popular with us Bostonians than tea. I guess you will be able to drink tea to your heart's content here, ma'am. You will be glad to set foot on British soil." He turned away to give orders for changing course and lowering sails.

British soil! Cordelia recalled the thrill of seeing the Union Jack flying at Syracuse, which was merely occupied by British troops at its monarch's pleasure. Gibraltar belonged to Britain.

Before she could savour the prospect to the full, Captain Barlow came up to supervise his ship's sailing into port. Seeing that all was in order, he addressed his unwanted British guests.

"We stay only to deliver my despatches to the American consul and to take on a few supplies," he announced tersely. "I trust you are ready to go ashore."

"Not quite," Cordelia admitted, and sped to her cabin to pack.

Since the captain went ashore with them, Lieutenant Carmichael had to stay on board. They were forced to snatch a hurried farewell under Barlow's impatient eye.

"Don't forget, now, any time your travels take you to America there'll be a welcome waiting."

"I have your direction," James assured him, "and you have mine. If you are ever in London, I expect to be the first person you call upon, or I shall be vastly offended."

Carmichael's round face turned expectantly to Cordelia.

Did he want her to say she hoped to see him soon in England? She could not, for the moment he arrived he would find out she was not really James's sister. Yet she did not want to hurt him.

"The pinnace is waiting," Captain Barlow pointed out.

"Thank you for all your kindnesses, Mr. Carmichael," she blurted out. "I wish you every success in your career."

Though a look of mild disappointment crossed his face, he

was not exactly heartbroken, to her relief. He was not so stricken by her charms as she had feared. Aware of a mild disappointment of her own, she held out her hand and he gallantly raised it to his lips, bowing.

From the pinnace she glanced back at the *Columbia* and saw him watching. She waved. At once a dozen hands besides his shot up to wave back, making her laugh. Bailly, who was one of the oarsmen, grinned at her, teeth white in his dark face.

"What's the joke?" James asked.

With the captain sitting there scowling at her, she just smiled and said vaguely, "Oh, nothing. What a great number of ships are here! Surely we shall soon find one to take us home."

"Heartless creature! Think of my sufferings."

The captain snorted.

"Perhaps if we ask at once we shall find one we can go aboard immediately," Cordelia suggested, "while you are accustomed to the motion."

James shook his head. "I must present my respects to the Governor first."

They reached the shore at that moment, so Cordelia did not ask why he had to call upon the Governor. A swarm of people awaited them: hawkers shouting wares from buttons to parrots; agents of ships' chandlers eager for the *Columbia*'s business, converging on the purser as he stepped from the pinnace; harlots jiggling their exposed bosoms as they ogled the sailors; porters nearly coming to blows as they swooped on James's and Cordelia's bags. There were faces of every colour, ivory, yellow, pink, brown, ebony. Spaniards, Turks, Africans, Maltese, Jews, Moors, Gypsies, a dozen other races, all in their own costumes, all gabbled in English of varying degrees of comprehensibility.

"Your papers, please." A scarlet-coated, ruddy-faced soldier shouldered through the mob. He flipped in a desultory way through Captain Barlow's ship's papers, then saluted. "Staying long, Captain?"

"As short as I can make it," Barlow snapped. "I've to see the American Consul and my men will pick up some supplies."

"No shore leave?"

"No!" The captain glared at a saucy Spanish wench in a black lace mantilla and not much else, who removed her hand from his sleeve as quick as if he'd bared his teeth and bitten her.

Winking at her, the soldier handed Barlow his papers. "Very good, sir. All in order." He turned to James and Cordelia. "You're with the *Columbia*, sir, madam?"

"Off, not with." James handed over their papers. "We are homeward bound to England. Is Lord Godwin Halsey still Governor here?"

"Yes, sir. You're bound for the Governor's Residence? You'll want a cotchy, as they calls a hackney here. There's a couple waiting."

Two men immediately jumped forward from amongst the remaining crowd, many having dispersed as the Americans departed. *"Señores, mi coche* is mos' fast, mos' comf'able, mos' cheapest!" they both screeched. Beyond them Cordelia saw two rickety open carriages painted in bright colours, each with a single bony nag waiting patiently with drooping head.

James shook his head. "I believe we shall walk, shall we, Cordelia? It's not far."

"Yes, I shall be glad of the exercise." She thought he had looked somewhat dismayed to hear that Lord Godwin Halsey was still governor. Was his lordship conversant with his more disreputable exploits? But if so, why did James still insist on paying his respects instead of just going to an inn? She would not be able to ask him in an open carriage with a driver who understood English.

"Perhaps, Sergeant, you'd be so good as to advise me which of these fellows is least likely to make off with our baggage?" James waved at the still squabbling porters.

Grinning, the soldier picked one. "Welcome to the Rock," he said, handing back their papers. The makeshift credentials provided by Major Saunderson had proved adequate. They set off for the town.

Up close, the protective wall was even more impressive than

from a distance. Like the fortress looming over the town on a spur of the Rock, it was originally built by the Moors a thousand years ago. Much of the oldest work remained, added to and patched over the centuries by the Spanish and the English. James pointed out the marks made by cannonballs during the Spanish-French siege three decades ago. They had chipped the wall but no more demolished it than a woodpecker demolishes a tree.

At present, Cordelia was more interested in the future than the past. "Why does it trouble you that Lord Godwin is still here?" she asked as they passed through an arch beneath the wall.

"Did it show?" He grimaced. "The trouble is not so much Halsey as his wife, Lady Millicent. She is a cousin of my mother's, and she knows very well I have no sisters."

"Need she find out we are here?"

"The place is so small—and its genteel society still smaller—that it's inevitable. She would be shockingly offended if I tried to evade her. Besides, I must speak to Halsey. No, I shall introduce you as my betrothed and we shall say—"

"Your betrothed! Oh, but we cannot. Sooner or later they will return to England and find out we are not married."

"We shall be. I told you it is necessary."

"We shall not." If only he spoke of love and not necessity!

"My dear girl, there's no time to argue about it now," James said impatiently. "For now we are affianced."

"Oh, very well. You can always tell her later you jilted me."

"Certainly not! A devil of a scoundrel I should look."

"Then tell her I jilted you."

"And look a fool? But never mind that now." He pointed ahead down the narrow main street. "The porter is already at the door of the Residence. Listen. You were travelling with a maid, an abigail—an Italian girl would be best, I daresay. What was her name?"

"Violetta," Cordelia said. "That was the name of my mother's abigail at Arventino. What happened to her? Why is she not with me?"

"Captain de Castilho told her such tales of the English climate, she stayed aboard the *Flor do Campo* to Sardinia, hoping to find her way home. So she was with you until just a few days ago when we joined the *Columbia.* We'll make much of Barlow's Puritanism. Quick, what is your father's name?"

"Sir Hamilton Courtenay of Hill House, Fenny Sedgwick, Norfolk, but why?"

"Sir Hamilton heard I was travelling to the East and begged me to escort you home. Pray that Lady Millicent is not acquainted with him."

"What was I doing in the East? How—"

"Oh lord, it's too late to work it all out." He stopped beside the porter and fished in his pocket for a coin. The sentry at the door stepped forward to ask their business. "Lady Millicent Halsey is my cousin. Please inform her or my lord that James Preston is here."

They were shown into a small, square anteroom to one side of the front door. The Governor's Residence was one of the few old buildings in the town, most having been destroyed by the Spanish-French bombardment. Once a Franciscan monastery, it seemed to Cordelia to retain an atmosphere which reminded her of the Orthodox monastery where they had been snowbound. At least she did not have to pretend to be a boy; she hoped she would not have to feign illness as an excuse to keep to her chamber to avoid awkward questions.

Inspiration struck. "I was never in Istanbul," she whispered to James. "I was sent for my health to a relative by marriage in Sicily, for the climate. I shall endeavour to look as if I recently recovered from a consumption."

"Splendid! Just transpose Arventino to somewhere near Syracuse."

She nodded, and drooped languidly on her chair as a footman in buff livery came in.

"We are still betrothed," James hissed in her ear, giving her his arm. "I fell in love at first sight."

No chance to protest as the footman bowed them from the room. Wishing it were true, she leaned heavily on his arm and they followed the servant along a stone-flagged passage.

Lady Millicent's sitting-room had nothing of the monastery about it. Elegant chairs in eggshell-blue and white striped satin complemented blue and silver striped wall hangings. The dark blue curtains and thick grey carpet were not striped, but her ladyship's modish sarcenet gown was, in buttercup and white. A handsome woman, she wore her dark hair arranged in ringlets beneath a cap of layered lace. Her complexion undamaged by the southern sun, she appeared to be in her late thirties.

Her glance raked Cordelia, who instantly felt horridly dowdy. The pink muslin was already faded from the sun and from washing in sea-water, and the hem had been dirtied in the pinnace. Her hair was still not long enough to do anything but pin it up roughly at the back of her neck. Even her beautiful straw hat now seemed drearily provincial.

Her ladyship would never believe James had fallen in love at first sight with such a perfect fright.

# Twenty-eight

"Miss Courtenay, Mr. Preston," announced the footman.

"Dear James," cooed Lady Millicent as he bowed over her hand. "How delightful to see you again. You will stay with us, of course, while you are at Gibraltar."

"It's kind of you, but we would not wish to inconvenience you, cousin." He had hoped against hope to be able to escape her prying with no more than a brief recitation of their story. "We can perfectly well go to an inn."

"I will not hear of it, I vow. You shall stay. But, la! do make me known to your companion."

"Allow me to present Miss Cordelia Courtenay, ma'am. We are affianced."

"Affianced?" Her ladyship's plucked eyebrows rose in a fine display of incredulity. "Indeed!"

Cordelia curtsied. "How do you do, my lady."

Lady Millicent nodded graciously. "Pray be seated, Miss Courtenay. Would that be the Kent Courtenays? Or the Berkshire Courtenays?"

"The Norfolk Courtenays, ma'am."

"Norfolk, hmm. I don't believe I am acquainted . . . yet there is something oddly familiar . . . Do tell me, James, how did you come to meet Miss Courtenay? The last we saw of you, you were eastward bound."

"Our meeting was arranged before I left England. Cordelia's father, Sir Hamilton, heard through my uncle that I was bound for the Mediterranean. He begged me to escort her home from

Sicily, where she had been sent for her health, to stay with connexions by marriage of her family." Too much unnecessary detail, he thought, bound to arouse suspicion. Keep it simple.

"I trust you are fully recovered, Miss Courtenay? La, but how silly of me, I vow! Your papa would not send for you until he heard of your recovery, and it is over a year since James was here with us so you have had quite enough time to regain your full strength."

"Yes, ma'am, I am quite well." Straightening, Cordelia abandoned her languid pose, unconvincing at best as her rosy cheeks and bright eyes were a picture of vitality.

"We have had an arduous voyage," James said quickly in an attempt to cover the sudden change. "Wait until you hear our adventures, cousin. We—"

"I am all agog, but first I must scold you, James. How shockingly inconsiderate in you to keep Miss Courtenay waiting so long! She must have quite despaired of ever returning home. I daresay it was quite impossible to find another escort, Miss Courtenay?"

"I-I expect it might have been possible, ma'am, but . . . but my relatives pressed me to stay and I was enjoying my visit. Once my health improved, of course," she hastened to add.

"Of course. You must have been relieved, however, when James did at last arrive."

"I came, I saw, I was conquered. It was love at first sight, cousin."

"On your part, also, Miss Courtenay? Nay, I shall spare your blushes. A prodigious romantic tale, I do declare." Her voice was full of malicious disbelief. "I only trust you did not set my cousin up in his own conceit by allowing him to see your partiality too soon! But then, you have had so little time. How long does it take to sail hither from Sicily, James?"

"I stayed a few days at the count's estate before we embarked." Dammit, more unnecessary detail to be remembered. "And the voyage was long enough, in all truth, on that confounded Portuguese tub, even before we were taken by the corsairs."

"Corsairs! My dear, you have had the most shocking adventures indeed. You must tell me all about it. But I daresay Miss Courtenay will not wish to hear a recitation which must revive painful memories. Your abigail must have unpacked for you by now, Miss Courtenay. I am sure you must be anxious to go up and . . ." she paused, looking Cordelia up and down, ". . . and tidy yourself."

James stood up as Cordelia rose, murmuring her thanks. "There is no abigail," he said. "The wretched girl—a Sicilian—deserted us after the affair of the pirates."

"No abigail? How very unfortunate!"

"Perhaps your maid might assist Cordelia?"

"By all means." Lady Millicent rang the bell and gave instructions to the footman who appeared. "And bring refreshments," she added. "I expect, Miss Courtenay, you will like a cup of tea. Do return as soon as you are ready."

Accompanying Cordelia to the door, James whispered, "Don't despair, you are not on your way to the scaffold."

With a disconsolate look, she departed. He turned back, to be poniarded by her ladyship's cynical smile.

"My dear James, there was no need to spin me that unlikely tale. You know I am no puritan. I am quite willing to put up your doxy as long as you are discreet."

"Cordelia is no doxy!" he said irately.

"Well, you cannot describe her as a Bird of Paradise! A drab would be closer to the mark. What the deuce do you see in her?"

"Enough to make me determined to marry her when we reach England. She is no lightskirt."

"If you truly mean to marry her—to save her reputation, I suppose—then why not do it here?"

"I should prefer to have Sir Hamilton's permission before we wed."

Lady Millicent laughed jeeringly. "No fear you will not get

it. A country baronet . . . Wait! Sir Hamilton Courtenay . . . Now I have it. She must be Drusilla Courtenay's daughter. Courtesan Courtenay! No, no, my dear, the girl's a harlot, and I do not take it kindly that you tried to mislead me!"

James had not the least notion what to say to persuade her of Cordelia's innocence. At the same time, he would give a monkey to find out what she knew of Lady Courtenay, yet he'd look a proper nodcock if he revealed his ignorance. Courtesan Courtenay? His heart ached for Cordelia, but not for a moment did he doubt her chastity. He knew her far too well.

To his relief, the footman returned with a tray of refreshments and announced, "His lordship is free to see you now, sir, in his office."

"Then why did you bring the tray, dolt?" snapped his mistress. "Take it away, and bring fresh tea when Miss Courtenay comes down."

"Be kind to her, cousin," James warned, "or I shall be very angry. Very angry indeed."

"I tremble in my shoes, to be sure," she said sarcastically, but she looked a trifle disquieted. "She may stay here, but do not expect me to introduce her about!"

Disquieted enough to take his tacit threat seriously, he hoped, leaving her. He could do her considerable social damage when he returned to London, if he chose. Not that he would, but she could not be sure of that. All the same, he wished he had suggested to Cordelia that she ought to lie down for a while before she rejoined her hostess. The less time they spent together, the better.

Upstairs, changing her gown in a chamber formed from two monk's cells thrown into one, Cordelia was tempted to plead exhaustion rather than face Lady Millicent again. The governor's wife clearly did not believe their hastily concocted story. Equally clearly, she was not an amiable woman. But as her reluctant guest, Cordelia would have to see her sooner or later, so she might as well get it over.

Besides, she refused to cry craven. After brigands and pirates,

Turkish Janissaries and French Lancers, snowstorms and precipices, she would not let a malicious female daunt her.

Her ladyship's abigail had brought hot water and taken the blue muslin to be pressed. Despite her uneasiness, Cordelia revelled in the scented soap as she washed her face and hands.

"Do you suppose I could have a bath this evening?" she asked the maid when she returned.

"Well, miss, fresh water's something of a problem here, but I'll see what I can do." Harsh-faced but kindly, the woman helped her into her gown.

Once the ribbons had been a darker blue than the muslin, but they had faded to much the same indeterminate hue. Cordelia regarded her image in the looking glass with despair. Above her dowdy dress, around her uncompromisingly round face, her unruly fair hair curled wildly in every direction.

"Let's see now what we can do with this," said the abigail.

"I had to have it all cut off because I was ill, and it's growing back slowly. *Very* slowly," she emphasized, remembering she was supposed to have waited forever for James to fetch her from Sicily after her recovery.

"Such a pretty colour, but I can see it's got a mind of its own, short as it is. We won't tame it, not without hot irons and you won't want to go to the trouble just now. If you'll let me, miss, I'll do it up in a knot right on top, give a bit of length to your face, like. And her ladyship has some white ribbon she'll never miss . . ."

"Oh, no, I would not for the world use Lady Millicent's ribbon."

Even without that simple adornment, Cordelia was pleased with the effect of pulling her hair up rather than back. Thanking the maid, she braced herself to go back down to the sitting room.

To her dismay, James was not there.

"He is closeted with my husband," said Lady Millicent, continuing with a sly smile, "Rest assured, only business could have torn him from your side. Of course, gentlemen invariably cloak a good gossip under the name of business. No doubt James is spinning the tale of your romance."

Her meaning was as plain as if she had said outright that she did not believe a word of it. She continued in this vein of roguish innuendo while they drank tea and Cordelia decided James had revealed that he was going to marry her only as a matter of honour. Lady Millicent was his cousin, after all. He must have invented the story less to deceive her than to save Cordelia from mortification. It was kind of him. He could not have foreseen that her ladyship would so spitefully tease her about it.

A footman rescued her, coming in to present a visiting card on a silver salver. "Lady Dodd and Miss Dodd have called, my lady. Are you at home?"

"Yes, yes, I shall receive them in the drawing room." She gave Cordelia a considering look, pursed her lips, and said smoothly, "The Rear Admiral's wife and daughter, Miss Courtenay. I'm sure you can have no interest in meeting them. Do, pray, make use of my sitting room." With languid grace, she glided out.

Cordelia glanced down at her dress and sighed. No doubt she was too dowdy to be presented to the Dodds.

Crossing to the window, she watched a flock of tiny birds cheeping and fluttering among palm trees, scarlet hibiscus, pink geraniums, and cascades of purple bougainvillea in a cloistered courtyard. Where was James? What business could he have with the Governor of Gibraltar, or had he really abandoned her to his cousin's tender mercies just for a gossip? She went to look at the book Lady Millicent had been reading when they arrived. It was a French novel, *Le Tombeau Mystérieux*. For want of anything better to do, she sat down and began to read it.

She read a couple of pages and had just realized it was the second volume when James came in.

"Alone?"

"I am not smart enough to meet Lady Millicent's callers."

He frowned. "Did she say so?"

"No, but why else should she not present me?"

James's mouth tightened, but he said mildly, "That must be

it. However, there's little point in buying new clothes before we reach London. Millicent is not my favourite relative, but she was not . . . uh . . . uncivil to you, was she?"

"Not precisely." Cordelia found she could not tell James of his cousin's veiled taunts. "I cannot be quite comfortable with her, though."

"I'm afraid we shall have to stay here. To remove to an inn would be to insult Halsey as well as Millicent, and quite apart from the fact that he's Governor, he's not a bad old fellow. Still, we shan't be here long."

"Let's go back to the harbour right now to seek out a ship."

"Unnecessary. Halsey expects a fast sloop from Malta any day now, on its way home. He will obtain passage on it for us. But let us go out, by all means, to see the sights."

Over the next few days they explored the Rock thoroughly. They climbed up to the sentry post on the southern summit and gazed across at the coast of Africa. Cordelia shuddered at the sight of that inhospitable shore where they had so nearly become slaves. They walked the galleries carved into the limestone massif to see the great cannon peering out from the shelter of its stony face. James persuaded Cordelia to overcome her distaste for natural caves and they visited the great cavern with its stalactites and stalagmites. Well lit by lanterns and lamps, it was a true marvel. They wondered whether the Greek brigands' cave might have been still more marvellous had they been able to see it properly.

Near the Queen's Gate, they fed the Barbary apes. An officer accompanying them had the gold tassel ripped from one of his boots as they stood there watching the golden-brown monkeys. "They always manage to steal something," he said resignedly. Cordelia clasped her new reticule tighter.

For the most part she succeeded in avoiding Lady Millicent. When obliged to be in her ladyship's company, she found the covert jibes had little power to hurt. The future deliberately ignored for the present, nothing could spoil the delight of the carefree days spent with James.

At last H.M.S. *Badger* sailed into the harbour and Lord Godwin ordered the sloop's captain to provide berths for James and Cordelia.

On their last evening the Halseys held a ball in the largest room of the Residence, once the monastery's chapel. "I fear you must be too tired to attend after all your gallivanting about, Miss Courtenay," Lady Millicent suggested suavely at dinner.

"Much too tired, ma'am," she agreed, half relieved, half disappointed.

"But you men are made of sterner stuff," her ladyship continued to James.

"You flatter me, cousin. We have been trotting too hard; I am quite done in, I vow. Besides, I know nothing more exhausting than doing the pretty to a crowd of strangers, and the *Badger* sails at dawn. We ought both to retire early."

Roused before daybreak, they took a *coche* to the harbour. Captain Bristow welcomed them aboard the sloop, a three-master of modest size and a single row of gun-ports, but with speedy lines. The captain was a dark-haired young man in his first command. He confided that "Captain" was merely a courtesy title as his actual rank was Lieutenant Commander. With the influence of his friends, however, he had high hopes of rising in his profession as long as Boney was there to be fought.

Shyly he offered Cordelia his own cabin.

"You need the space," muttered his first mate, irritably, as if he had said the same more than once before. A sour-faced, grizzled veteran—doubtless without influential friends, Cordelia thought with a wisp of pity—Lieutenant Duff added after a perceptible pause, "Sir."

A single glance around the cabin told Cordelia it was as much office as sleeping quarters. "I can see that you work in here, Captain," she said. "I must not dispossess you."

"If you are quite certain, Miss Courtenay . . ." Bristow said uncertainly. She nodded. "Then you shall have Duff's cabin, ma'am. See to it, please, Mister."

Duff looked furious. "Aye, aye, Captain," he said through gritted teeth.

"I'm going up to the bridge. It's time we set sail."

"Past time," the lieutenant grunted in a resentful undertone. To James he said, "You're in the second mate's cabin. Sir. He and I will be slinging our hammocks in the fo'c'sle." Which might have been the deepest pit of Hell to judge by his morose, foreboding expression.

James chose to go up with the captain to watch their departure. Cordelia would have liked to go too, but she felt it only polite to view her quarters. Tiny as the cabin proved, this took but a moment.

"Thank you, Mr. Duff," she said. "I believe I shall join Mr. Preston now."

"You won't want to be flaunt . . . showing yourself on deck overmuch, miss," Duff advised venomously. "There's lots of the men believe it's unlucky to have a woman on board, and it's best not to remind 'em."

Cordelia had no intention of being confined below all the way to England. "Thank you for the warning, sir," she said, chin raised. "I shall bear it in mind." And she went up to see the Rock of Gibraltar silhouetted against a glorious sunrise.

As it gradually shrank astern, James paled and started to fidget. However, the *Badger* cut smoothly through the waves, even beyond the Straits of Gibraltar where they met the great Atlantic rollers, and his queasiness failed to develop into full-blown sickness. Past Cape Trafalgar they sailed, across the Gulf of Cadiz, round Cape St. Vincent and up the Portuguese coast. After a brief stop in Lisbon to deliver and pick up despatches, another in Oporto (where several cases of Port wine came aboard with the despatches), they cleared Cape Finisterre and set out across the Bay of Biscay.

Notorious for its storms, the Bay lived up to its reputation. Beneath a charcoal sky, buffeted by a gale from the northwest, the little ship reeled and plunged as towering waves crashed booming over the deck.

Cordelia heard the furious elements, felt the *Badger* quiver in every timber at their assault. She caught only a glimpse through windows sluiced impartially by the sea and by squalls of torrential rain. Banished below, for observation she had neither desire nor opportunity: both James and Captain Bristow were laid low. Holding basins, wiping clammy foreheads, she scarce had leisure to wonder whether the end of all their adventures was to be a watery grave not five hundred miles from home. It seemed to go on for ever.

Suddenly a greater shock jolted the ship from bow to stern. The rolling, rocking motion ceased, though the spasmodic shuddering continued.

Bristow struggled to his feet. "We're aground," he croaked, his face ghastly. He staggered across the tilted deck to the cabin door. "Get to the boats. Any moment she may go down!"

# Twenty-nine

The *Badger* reposed upon a sandbank, a hundred yards from shore.

The shore of France.

Driven southeast by the gale, now dying, the sloop had passed the mouth of the Gironde estuary shortly before going aground. The lookout had seen the flash of the Cordouan lighthouse, beaming through a day storm-darkened to near dusk. And now true dusk was falling. In the west, between dark sea and lowering clouds, a band of primrose yellow promised fine weather—too late.

The sandbank broke the force of the waves so that the stretch of water between it and the beach was choppy but not tumultuous, practically a lagoon. The sandy beach stretched north and south to the limits of sight. Inland, dunes merged into marsh and scrubby pine forest: the barrens of Les Landes.

Enemy action from that quarter was unlikely, but nor could they look for help.

"We'll have to tow her off," Duff proposed.

"Aargh." Bristow clung to the rail, bent double, his sickness scarce abated by the lack of motion.

"Now, while the tide's at its height and before it gets dark."

"Aargh!"

"She may sink the moment we pull her off, if the keel's stove in. You'd best go ashore, sir."

"No," groaned the unhappy captain. "Duty to go down with ship."

"We'll put our passengers ashore, though. They'll be in the way on deck and it's not safe below. Don't want to risk their precious skins."

"Aaaargh."

James was in not much better case, and Cordelia's protests went unheeded. Duff was determined and, with Bristow incapacitated, he was in charge. A petty officer and boat crew rowed James and Cordelia to the beach.

"We'll be back soon as we see if she'll float," he said cheerfully, and they pushed off.

Overhead, seagulls wheeled, screeching. James dropped to the sand and sat with his head in his hands, moaning softly to himself. Standing beside him, wrapped in her Greek cloak, damp from the spray, Cordelia watched the gig bobbing back across the ruffled white-caps. By the time it reached the *Badger*, the rest of the sloop's boats had been lowered. Sailors straining at the oars, the four cockleshells headed out into the boisterous waves, trailing hawsers. Now and then Cordelia sighted one of the boats, like a beetle clambering up a grassy bank, but mostly they were hidden by the mountainous seas.

The *Badger* rocked, jerked, then slid smoothly backwards and floated free.

"Look, I believe she's all right," said Cordelia, straining her eyes to peer through the gathering gloom.

James raised his head, gulped, and put it down again. "All right! She's going up and down like a shuttlecock."

"At least she doesn't seem to be going more down than up. They're pulling her well away from the sandbank, turning her to face seaward. There, it looks as if one of the boats is coming back to fetch us."

She watched the gig slither down the side of a wave. That was when she realized that the return to the sloop would take them not just across the choppy lagoon but out among those heaving rollers that dwarfed the little boat.

"We could walk to Calais," James muttered disconsolately. "From there it's only three-and-twenty sea miles to Dover."

"We'd be arrested on the way, for sure."

"There are worse things than waiting out the war in a comfortable French prison."

"What makes you think it would be comf—"

*Boom!*

"Cannon!" James jumped to his feet.

Cordelia looked to her right just in time to see the flash accompanying the second *boom.* Two frigates flying the French *tricouleur* were swiftly bearing down upon the *Badger.*

The gig swung round and scurried desperately for the sloop. Abandoning the boat, the sailors swarmed up the ship's side on ropes as white canvas unfurled on all three masts. Like a swan stretching its wings and taking to the skies, the sails billowed in the still-boisterous wind and the *Badger* fled.

"It looks as if we'll be walking to Calais," said James philosophically.

"They'll come back for us!"

"If the French don't take 'em or sink 'em. If they can find this precise spot. We cannot wait to find out. We have nothing."

"I had no chance to bring my purse but I have my diamonds." Cordelia glanced around the wilderness of sea and sand, bleak in the twilight. "Not that they are much use to us here."

"Can't eat 'em, can't burn 'em—and it's getting deuced chilly." James, too, had on his Greek cloak. He pulled it tighter around him. "There's driftwood, but it's bound to be damp after the storm and I have no tinderbox."

"From the ship I saw pine woods inland. At least we'd have shelter from the wind."

"And at least it's not snowing." He grinned at her and offered his arm. "We've been in worse spots. Shall we walk, ma'am?"

It was not the sort of decorous stroll where fingertips on a crooked arm provide all necessary support. They hauled each other up the shifting sand of the dunes and slid down the other side. The sea now a muffled murmur behind them, they trudged onward across uneven, scrubby wasteland, skirting a reed-choked pond. As the last light faded, the forest ahead loomed black as pitch.

Noses and ears, more than eyes, told them they had reached the pines. The air breathed an aromatic scent and twigs snapped underfoot. Then Cordelia tripped over a fallen branch.

"Ouch!" she exclaimed, tightening her grip on James's arm to stop herself falling.

"Are you hurt?"

"I wrenched my ankle."

"It's not sprained, is it?" James said in dismay.

"Just ricked, I think, but I'm not walking any farther tonight," she said firmly. "We have no idea where we are or where we're going. There are no wolves or wild boars in France, are there?"

"I trust not. I refuse to spend the night in a tree. Let us just hope it doesn't rain."

Hunger and thirst and the ground for a bed were nothing new. Curled up in their cloaks, they slept.

The hoot of an owl roused James. He listened as it hooted again, farther off. Nearby something rustled among the dry pine needles. A fox, he guessed, or a badger. It didn't sound big enough to be dangerous.

He was cold. Rolling over, he put his arm around Cordelia's waist. Without waking, she snuggled back against him.

Astounded, he discovered that he was thoroughly happy.

A squirrel woke Cordelia. Four feet from her face, it sat with a pine cone in its paws, chattering angrily at her. She raised her hand to brush away a strand of hair tickling her cheek. The little rust-red creature dropped the cone and scampered off to climb the nearest tree, where it paused for a last burst of scolding before it disappeared into the branches.

Cordelia thought she and James ought to be moving, trying to find some sign of habitation, but she felt quite warm and safe lying there with his arm around her. Besides, he had had a hard day yesterday what with sickness and all. She did not want to wake him. In the gloom beneath the dark green canopy of the pines she could not tell how late it was. If only she was not so hungry and thirsty, like in Captain de Castilho's cabin . . .

She drowsed, drifting somewhere between memories and dreams of the peaceful time on the Portuguese ship between James's recovery from his sickness and the advent of the corsairs. In her dream, once again he put his hand on her breast, caressing, gently squeezing. Every nerve tingled. A fiery glow ignited in the pit of her belly. She turned towards him with a soft moan.

Someone called out, *"Mais où vas tu, sot?"*

*Where are you going, fool?* In French. In her dream? In all her wanderings she had never dreamt in anything but English!

She was awake.

*"Tu vas trop loin."*

At the sound of that voice—*you're going too far*—James's hand suddenly stilled, but it rested on her breast. Cordelia tried to sit up. His arm clamped around her, holding her down.

"Don't move," he breathed in her ear, his warm breath arousing a last flicker of desire.

"Let me go!" She whispered, though she wanted to shout. "We must catch them before they move on."

"Do you really want to spend the next few years in a French prison?"

"Do you really want to starve? We could wander round in circles for days!"

*"Il n'y a rien là-bas."*

*There's nothing there.* "I speak excellent French," Cordelia went on. "We'll tell them we're French, we're shipwrecked . . ." Drat, what was the word? ". . . *naufragés.*"

"They must be bandits. What would honest men be doing in this wilderness?"

"What would bandits be doing here? There's no one to rob."

"No one but us."

Cordelia turned her head to look at him and laughed. "Oh James, we hardly look like anyone worth robbing. You have pine needles in your hair."

"So do you." He drew his finger tenderly down her cheek. "But you have the diamonds on you, and I have not forgot—if you have—the Greek brigands' plans for you."

"I've not forgotten," she said soberly, "but I cannot see any alternative."

He sighed. "No, you're right. One does not last long without water, and I wouldn't care to drink from that marshy pond we passed. And my French is excellent, too. We should at least observe them to see what kind of men they are. With luck they may be on a path we can follow."

"Then come on. Hurry. I can scarce hear them now."

Deeper in the woods, the thick layer of old pine-needles deadened their footsteps despite their haste. The voices grew clearer. One said plaintively, *"J'veux mon p'tit déjeuner,"* and Cordelia's mouth watered at the thought of breakfast.

She and James came to the edge of a sunny clearing, overgrown with pink spires of rosebay willowherb. The sky above was blue, yesterday's storm vanished without trace. Quite close, three men in tattered, faded smocks and breeches sat on a fallen log. Two were elderly, with lined, leathery faces, greying moustaches, and grey stubble on their chins, one long enough almost to qualify as a beard. The third was a beardless youth with the flat, round, inexpressive face of a halfwit.

All three munched bread and sausage. Cordelia started forward. James grabbed her arm.

"Don't be a sapskull," she hissed. "They're harmless peasants."

The halfwit heard her. His face turned towards them, eyes and mouth round with alarm. Emitting an inarticulate squawk, he pointed.

James and Cordelia stepped out of the black shadow of the trees and approached, doing their best to look unthreatening. The old men stopped eating to gape, but they appeared more astonished than alarmed.

The youth's fright turned to wonder as he stared at Cordelia's fair hair, hanging about her ears since she had lost her hairpins in the night. *"Jolie dame,"* he said in delight. He held out his handful of food, as if coaxing a stray dog. *"Jolie dame veut de mon saucisson?"*

Tantalized by a whiff of garlic, the pretty lady certainly did want some of his sausage. However, she restrained herself while the proprieties were observed. As James explained their presence, Cordelia became aware of a pervasive odour underlying the garlic, like an intensification of the piny aroma which she had ceased to notice.

It was soon explained. The bearded peasant politely met James's shipwreck story with the information that he and his companions were employed in gathering resin from the pines for the manufacture of *"térébenthine."*

"Turpentine, at a guess," said James.

*"Not' résine,* it's the best," said the halfwit with pride. *"On l'envoie même en Angleterre!"*

*"Tais-toi, imbécile!* The English are our enemies. One does not trade with the enemy."

*"A bas les Anglais,"* the youth cried obediently. *"Vive l'Emp'reur."*

"Pay no attention to Jean-Marie, *m'sieur, 'dame,"* said the old man anxiously. "He is an idiot, not right in the head. If you please, be seated and share our meal."

James and Cordelia exchanged a significant look. As she ate dry bread and hard sausage, washed down with thin, sour, red wine, Cordelia racked her brains. How could they find out without giving themselves away whether Jean-Marie had indeed been talking nonsense?

Even the pungent garlic sausage was faintly tainted with a tang of pine. "Might as well be drinking Greek retsina," James muttered, "and we can't be more than a few miles from the best claret vineyards!"

The wine made Cordelia feel delightfully carefree. Heedless of discretion, she said to the old peasant, "We want to go to England. Can you help us find someone to take us there?"

The horrified shock on James's face mirrored that of the two old men. It made her giggle.

James seized the leather bottle from her hand. *"Petite ivrogne!"*

"I'm not a drunkard," she protested, pleased that the buzz in her head had no effect on her ability to speak French.

"The wine has risen to my sister's head. She is accustomed to drink coffee in the morning. Jean-Marie's words have muddled her. Please excuse her and don't take any notice of what she says."

Cordelia reached for the bottle. "I'm thirsty."

"This will only make you thirstier."

"We must conduct *mam'selle* to the village," the greybeard decided. He gave James a shrewd look. "And after, where is it that *m'sieur* desires to go?"

"To England," said Jean-Marie eagerly. *"Jolie dame* wants to go to England, like our resin, on the big boat. The *Alouette* will take her."

In silence the two old peasants looked at each other. The taciturn one turned his head and spat. They looked at James. All three shrugged.

"The *Alouette*?" said James cautiously.

"You see, m'sieur, we are Gascons. The king, the emperor, pah!" He too spat. "What do those *gros bonnets* in Paris know of our lives? Since forever the English are the best customers for our wines, our brandy. Shall we stop selling because a Corsican corporal says so?"

"The *Alouette* is a smuggling vessel?" James grinned. "Lead us to her!"

Of course it was not quite that easy. After a long walk in the shade of the pines, they came to a tiny, poverty-stricken hamlet inhabited by resin gatherers and charcoal burners. For several days they were hidden in an excessively smelly cowshed, until a wagon arrived from Bordeaux to fetch a load of resin and charcoal. The badly sealed kegs of resin among which they sat were even smellier than the cowshed. At first the odour seemed more acceptable, but soon the fumes made their heads swim. And the wagon—James was prepared to take his oath on it—moved even slower along the sandy tracks than that long-ago Greek oxcart on its stony road.

"We could walk faster," said Cordelia.

"But we'd be much more conspicuous. If we meet a troop of soldiers, they won't even glance at a couple of peasants in the back of a cart."

They had exchanged their comparatively fine dress for pale blue peasant homespun. An unnecessary precaution, it turned out. Not a sign of a uniform did they see.

As the sun sank behind them, they came to the bank of the Gironde, the estuary of the Garonne and Dordogne rivers. In the shelter of a spinney, their incurious driver stopped the wagon and told them to get down. He unloaded half a dozen kegs of resin. James helped him roll them into a thicket of bushes, briers, and brambles which miraculously gave way before them. The cleared centre was already stacked with dozens of barrels.

"You wait here," said the driver.

"When will the *Alouette* come?" Cordelia asked.

His shoulders rose and fell. "Me, I know nothing. I just follow orders." Without another word he plodded back to his wagon and drove sluggishly off.

They stared after him.

"We could easily run and catch him up," James suggested.

"We don't want to go to Bordeaux if we can help it. At least those barrels prove the smugglers really exist."

"You had your doubts? And I was carefully concealing mine!"

Cordelia smiled briefly. "They exist, but we have no idea when they are going to turn up."

"I doubt they leave their goods hidden here longer than they need, for fear of discovery."

"No, I daresay not," she said with relief. "All the same, let's eat just a bit of the bread and cheese the peasants gave us and save the rest for tomorrow. We may yet be glad the smell of turpentine in the wagon destroyed our appetites for luncheon."

They picnicked on the edge of the spinney, near a bank of sweet-smelling wild roses. The setting sun tinted the waters of the estuary as pink as the roses. Sails were few and far between, Bordeaux's once thriving trade destroyed by Napoleon's Continental System and the English blockade. Assuming that the *Alouette* would come from the great port city, Cordelia watched hopefully each vessel approaching from their right, but all stayed far out in the channel.

As darkness fell, they returned to the thicket. Finding their way to the centre was more difficult without the wagon driver to guide them, but at last, brier-scratched, they came to the secret clearing.

Wrapping her Greek cloak about her, Cordelia pillowed her head on her hands. "I do hope this will be our last night in the open," she sighed.

"Come now, it's better than a cowshed!"

"True, and it's not snowing, not even raining. There's absolutely nothing to complain about!" she said tartly.

She lay awake for a while, tense, wondering whether James would seize the opportunity to make another assault on her virtue. The atmosphere of the cowshed had not been conducive to desire. Here the air was full of the fragrance of the wild roses.

But he did not approach her and soon she heard his even breathing. She wasn't sure whether she was glad or sorry. On the whole it just went to prove that he was only attracted to her when emerging half-asleep from a dream, that his offer of marriage was purely a matter of honour.

A tear leaked from one eye. Fiercely she wiped it away and turned onto her other side. She must concentrate on her favourite fantasy, which was *not* of James loving her but of her father overwhelmed with joy at her return. So soon now . . .

The next thing she knew was lanternlight on her face. As she blinked up at it, a hoarse voice demanded, *"Que diable faites-vous ici?"*

For a moment she simply could not remember what the devil they were doing there. Then, before she could speak, the light glinted on a pair of pistols and another voice advised, "Shoot 'em!"

# Thirty

Blindfolded, gagged, their hands tied before them, James and Cordelia were hoisted aboard the *Alouette* in a net like a couple of barrels. At least, various inarticulate grunts and snorts made Cordelia assume James was suffering the same fate.

"They was with the goods, *mon capitaine.*" The hoarse voice. "Gaspard wanted to shoot 'em."

"You didn't say nothing about passengers, *mon capitaine.*"

"Monsieur did not warn me to expect passengers." A deep voice, slightly more refined. "Put them in my cabin. I'll deal with them when we're under way."

Rough hands hustled Cordelia across the deck. Then she was lowered, hands under the armpits passing her down to hands around the waist. She gurgled a protest as she was clasped to a brawny sailor's chest. He chuckled, but released her. A moment later she was shoved forward. She took two stumbling steps, then James—it must be James—blundered against her.

"Baw!" he said. Damn?

A door slammed, followed by the click of a key in a lock.

Uttering her own peculiar sounds, Cordelia felt for James's sleeve and tugged downwards. If they sat on the floor, they would not keep bumping into each other. Despite her tied hands, she herself subsided to a cross-legged position with the graceful ease of much practise. How long ago and far away Istanbul seemed!

James sat on her foot. "Oy." Sorry? He shifted. Then she felt his fingers on her face. He touched her nose, ran a fingertip down it, and tugged at her gag. "Ur ow."

Guessing, she turned around. He fumbled at the back of her head, and the gag loosened. Cordelia raised her bound hands and pulled it free.

"Oh, well done! Now I'll untie yours."

Either his gag was tied tighter or she was less efficient. She fiddled with the knot in the cloth for what seemed like an age. His hair was caught in it, and the several "Ow"s her groping elicited were probably not intended to express anything but pain.

At last the knot gave way. "Thank you," he said. "I trust you have not left me quite bald. Dare I ask you to tackle the blindfold next or will the scanty remainder of my locks go with it?"

"No, keep it on. Not because of your hair, but because they must have covered our eyes so we cannot recognize them. If they come in and find we can see, they may decide just to drop us overboard for safety."

"Good point," James agreed. "They would not have taken the trouble to blindfold us if there was not a chance they might let us go free."

Cordelia nodded into the darkness. "That is what I have been hoping. I daresay they might be nervous if they see our hands untied, too. Perhaps we should leave our bonds be, if you are not in pain."

"It's uncomfortable but not half so tight as the Greek brigands tied us. And even with our hands free, we could not possibly fight off captain and crew."

"I am sure they will be reasonable when they hear our story." She laughed, somewhat wildly. "Oh James, I believe I must be growing quite inured to danger! Here we are on a French smugglers' ship, bound hand if not foot, sailing towards a part of the sea where we were recently shipwrecked, yet I—"

"Don't remind me of the sea," he groaned. "I'd almost managed to forget that beyond the mouth of the Gironde the rolling waves await us."

She hastily changed the subject. "I wonder what Captain Hamid is doing now?"

"Patrolling the Turkish Empire in search of some other fugitives, I suppose, and keeping the roads safe for honest travellers. A few troops of Janissaries on the roads in England would soon do away with highwaymen, but the English continue to hold out against even an organized police force."

James continued to hold forth on the contrast between English and Continental notions of civil liberty. Cordelia scarcely heard a word. She rarely recalled that when she met James he had been a fugitive from justice. She had taken him for a criminal, but perhaps his crime had been something only the Turks regarded as such, something quite permissible in England.

Lord Godwin and Lady Millicent Halsey had accepted him as perfectly respectable. It was Cordelia whose respectability had been doubted.

How she longed to be safe in the bosom of her family, Miss Courtenay, daughter of Sir Hamilton Courtenay, Baronet, a young lady of impeccable, unquestionable reputation! Then, if James should come a-courting . . .

Impossible dream. "Who are the Bow Street Runners?" she asked, catching a phrase at random. She did her best to be interested in the answer, and soon found she really was.

She asked a question about Sir John Fielding, the Bow Street magistrate, and suddenly James started laughing helplessly.

"What is so funny? Did I say something gooseish?"

"No, no," he gasped. "A very sensible question. It's just that here we sit blindfolded with our hands tied, discussing the administration of the law in Britain while awaiting the judgement of a French smuggler! As you said, we have become perfectly accustomed to danger."

"Not quite perfectly." Cordelia's voice quavered just a trifle. "I wish you had not reminded me. I hate to feel so helpless."

"My dear girl, I'm sorry. Perhaps we should try to untie our hands after all, so that I can at least put an arm around you for comfort. Or, who knows, we might find something—"

A heavy tread outside the door told them it was too late. The key clicked in the lock.

*"Eh bien,* Gaspard, bring your pistols if you will, but remember the sound of a shot carries far over water. There are quieter ways to silence police spies."

A faint light leaked past Cordelia's blindfold. Her wrists ached as clenching her fists tightened the bonds about them. She forced herself to relax her hands.

*"Bon soir, monsieur le capitaine."* James sounded as insouciant as if he had just been introduced by a mutual acquaintance.

*"Bon soir, mon brave,* said the deep-voiced smuggler dryly. *"Bon soir, madame.* I see you have disembarrassed yourselves of the gags. You will forgive these little inconveniences, I hope. My men were perhaps overeager, but monsieur did not give me notice of your coming."

"Monsieur?"

"Ah, so you were not sent by a certain monsieur?" Now the captain's tone was distinctly threatening. Cordelia wished she could see his face.

Incredibly, James laughed. "I doubt you would grant the title of 'monsieur' to any of those who sent us. *Citoyen* is the best a peasant can expect."

"Peasant! Much as I dislike Monsieur Grignol, I should hesitate to describe him as a peasant."

"Grignol? Who is Grignol? Not the gentleman you thought might have sent us, I take it."

"What does it matter who Grignol is!" Cordelia burst out. *"Monsieur le capitaine* we are English. We were shipwrecked on the coast." Telling the story of the helpful, hospitable turpentine gatherers, she finished, "So, you see, we assumed they had arranged with you to pick us up." How she wished she could see his face!

"An extraordinary tale, madame, too extraordinary to have been invented by that pig Grignol. You can pay for your passage, I hope?"

*"Oui, monsieur."* All their money had been left on the *Badger*, but Cordelia still had a few diamonds left.

*"Très bien.* Gaspard, remove the blindfolds and untie their hands."

The captain turned out to be a black-bearded man the shape of one of the barrels in his illegal cargo. As Cordelia, her hands released, stood up, he bowed to her and invited her to take one of the velvet-covered chairs. The cabin's luxurious furnishings suggested that smuggling was a most profitable business.

Freed, James took another chair. "Who—excuse me, Cordelia, but I should really like to know!—who is Grignol?"

"He is the *préfet de police* at Bordeaux. Monsieur the owner of the *Alouette* is also a high official, and they are at drawn knives."

"So that's it!" said James.

"Monsieur, you understand, is a wine merchant since generations. In centuries the trade with England has never been stopped by a foolish matter like war."

"I was sure those barrels must be full of brandy."

"Cognac and the best wines of Médoc, besides a few bales of silks and some lace. Anyone might guess this, Grignol certainly, but it is of all things the most unlikely that he should find out that monsieur sends also *térébenthine,* to a good customer who has some use for it. This is why your story is credible, madame."

"Besides," muttered Gaspard, "it is now too late to contact *ces salauds de la police."*

The captain's laugh boomed out. "It is true. However, as a precaution you will stay below until we are past the Cordouan lighthouse and well out at sea."

James groaned.

"My brother suffers from *mal de mer,"* Cordelia explained.

"I'm surprised I'm not already suffering."

"There is little wind, the Gironde is smooth. We go with the tide and the current."

*"Peu de vent, voyage lent,"* said Gaspard, with a broken-toothed grin at James's grimace.

"If the winds are light," Cordelia consoled him in English, "perhaps you will not be sick. And a slow voyage makes no difference since you adjust after a few days anyway."

"I know. It's just that being so close to home I'm in a hurry to get there."

"What are they saying?" Gaspard asked suspiciously, fingering the butt of his pistol.

"Nothing of importance," the captain assured him.

"You understand English, Captain?" said James. "I suppose it is to be expected since you do business with English smugglers."

"Free-traders," said the captain in English, then switched back to French. "But I learned to speak from them and they tell me I have such an *accent de Cornouaille* that others cannot understand me."

"I shall understand you," James assured him with a smile. "I grew up in Cornwall."

They chatted together. Cordelia gathered that they were talking of the dangers of the Cornish coast, the rocks and cliffs and currents, and the hundreds of ships wrecked there. She was quite glad she could not follow much of what they said. Her head began to nod.

*"Eh bien,"* said the captain at last with a satisfied nod, "now I am sure you are truly English. Welcome aboard the *Alouette.* You are free to go where you will. Mademoiselle, if you will graciously accept the humble hospitality of my cabin, monsieur shall have a hammock 'tween decks."

The hammock turned out to suit James. As long as he stayed in it, out of sight of the ocean swells, he felt quite well. Of course, he had to leave it for certain necessary occasions, but he always hurried back.

As a result, he never did adjust to the ship's roll. Cordelia saw little of him, for there were always several off-watch sailors nearby, snoring in their hammocks or drinking and dicing, and she did not like to intrude. She spent a good deal of time sitting cross-legged on deck, watching flying fish soar over the sparkling waves, feeding scraps to squabbling seagulls, sometimes talking—in French—with the captain. She learned all there was to know about his family at home in Bordeaux, but still she had a lot of time with nothing to do but think.

Her thoughts ranged back over the past months, the dangers she and James had faced together, the triumph of obstacles overcome, the sweet moments of peace. She remembered arguments, laughter, desire. And the desire had not all been on his side, she acknowledged. In that she was her mother's daughter.

Yet she had not succumbed, not quite. What if she did, what if she let passion play, let James have his way with her? If she were no longer virtuous, would he feel himself released from his obligation to marry her to save her reputation?

Should she stop fighting his notion of honour and become his wife though he did not love her? Perhaps her love would suffice for both—but she could never take the marriage vows as lightly as had Mama. If James found no happiness as her husband, she did not think she could bear to see him stray.

*Mama,* she cried silently, *what shall I do?*

Mama had considered her "darling Dee" wiser than herself, yet now Cordelia would have given anything for a few words of advice. And still more for the comfort of her mother's arms about her. Tears trickled down her cheeks and burying her face in her hands, she wept. Whatever her faults, Mama had loved her.

Fortunately, Cordelia was not given too many days to brood. A brisk breeze took the *Alouette*'s sails. She skimmed around the Breton peninsula and into the English Channel. Soon the Cornish coast was a low, grey mass on the horizon.

England! Cordelia stood at the rail, staring. What need had she of Mama's advice? In no time now she would have a father to rely upon.

The sails came down. The *Alouette* rocked like a cradle on

the gently heaving waves, glassy-green in the golden evening light.

*"Je regrette, mademoiselle,* but I must ask you to go below. We have a rendezvous with my English colleagues, and they are naturally wary of strangers."

"Of course, Captain." With a last glance at the English coast, she went below.

James awaited her in the cabin. His face was rather pale and his knuckles were white where he gripped the arms of the chair. "I should have asked them to rig my hammock in here," he muttered, swallowing visibly.

"Go and ask them. The captain has been very friendly but he just might turn nasty if we don't pay him for our passage, so I need privacy to extract a diamond."

"I was told not to set foot out of the cabin. Don't worry, you could strip naked and do a belly-dance and I wouldn't be interested just now." He swallowed again.

Cordelia stuck her head out of the door and called, *"Holà!"* There was no response. Everyone must be up on deck preparing for the meeting with the Cornish smugglers.

James's face was now tinged with green. She grabbed the wash-basin and shoved it under his chin just in time.

The worst over, she made him as comfortable as possible on her bed. He lay with closed eyes, spent after the paroxysms of retching. Her back to him, Cordelia put on her Greek cloak and under its cover raised her skirts. The French peasant gown was shabbier than ever after daily washing in sea-water and hanging to dry overnight, and the petticoat and chemise bought new in Dubrovnik were not much better. She unwound the diamond cloth, frayed at the edges. The stitches held firm, a testament to Aisha's needlework.

"Bother!"

"What's wrong?" James asked in a feeble voice.

"No scissors. Why on earth did I leave my reticule in the cabin on the *Badger*?"

"We left in rather a hurry," he reminded her wryly.

"I wonder where she is now, whether the French ships caught up with her. I hope she got away, except that I shouldn't mind a bit if that horrid Lieutenant Duff was hit by a cannonball." As she spoke, she went to the captain's writing table. In a drawer she found a penknife. "Do you think one diamond will satisfy him? I haven't many left."

"We are nearly home."

"Not quite there yet, though." Putting the extracted diamond in the drawer with the knife for safety, she went through all the gyrations necessary to wrap the cloth about her middle again while preserving decency. "I suppose they mean to transfer us along with the contraband to the Cornish ship. It's going to be difficult with you sick as a dog."

She turned, to find him watching her. His cheeks were no longer green but tinted very faintly pink.

"Oh, I'm feeling much better." He grinned. "I kept hoping the cloak would fall. An absorbing interest is a great antidote against seasickness."

Cordelia glared at him. "You have absolutely no sense of propriety," she said bitingly.

"Not much."

Before she could utter a quashing retort, Gaspard came in. "Blindfolds," he said, waving a couple of kerchiefs. "I'm to tell you, if you take these off, you go overboard."

For some time they sat blindfolded in the cabin, listening to thumps and splashes and shouts in French and English. At least they were not tied up, but there was something horridly discomforting about being unable to see. Cordelia was glad when James found her hand and held it. To her relief he still felt quite well.

Then the captain and another man came in and spoke together in the thick Cornish accent she could barely understand. Papers rustled. She thought money changed hands.

"Ah, monsieur, mademoiselle, I find here your payment, for which I thank you. This gentleman will convey you the rest of the way. I wish you *bon voyage*."

"We'll drop off the cargo," said the other, "and then sail you into Plymouth as bold as you please."

The transfer to a boat and then to the fishy-smelling Cornish lugger, guided by invisible hands, was smooth if frightening. James and Cordelia were left blindfolded and warned that if they spoke above a whisper they would be gagged. Seated side by side on a coil of rope, they felt the changing motion as the lugger's sails were raised and she turned homeward.

She sailed in an eery hush, the only sounds the creak of rigging, the slap of water on the hull and bare feet on the deck, seagulls crying above. Like gunshots, voices carried across water, Cordelia thought.

At first a little fading daylight leaked beneath the blindfolds, but very soon it was pitch dark. Though her cloak kept out the chill of the breeze, Cordelia shivered.

James put his arm around her shoulders. "Frightened?" he asked softly. "Don't be. If they meant us any harm they have had plenty of time for it. We're nearly home!"

"I'm not frightened. I simply cannot believe I shall soon be safe on English soil."

An hour passed, perhaps two. Cordelia's excitement faded and she began to drowse, leaning against James.

He shook her awake. "We have stopped," he hissed in her ear. "They must be going to unload the goods. Listen."

An expectant stillness enveloped the lugger. Nearby, waves broke on a beach, each muted roar followed by the rattle of pebbles on the ebb. Somewhere in the distance a dog barked. An owl hooted thrice.

And from close at hand, on the ship itself, came a response: Tu-whoo . . . tu-whoo . . . tu-whoo.

At once the smugglers sprang into action. To Cordelia, unable to see, the thuds and creaks, the rumble of rolling barrels, splashes and low-voiced curses and oars squeaking in rowlocks seemed shockingly loud.

A thunderclap cracked open the night. A red glow seeped beneath the cloth over her eyes, then a white glare.

"Oh hell!" James swore. "A signal rocket."

As he ripped off her blindfold, from seaward boomed a voice amplified by a speaking trumpet: "Halt, in the King's name!"

"Revenuers!" someone yelled.

Already on his feet, James jerked Cordelia up and hurried her across the deck. By the rocket's fading light, she saw two men in dark clothes, with blackened faces, clambering over the side.

"Wait!" called James.

A moment later he dropped her into the midst of a huddle of smugglers. The boat was already moving off as he swung down beside her. Six men rowing like the very devil, they made for the line of glimmering surf.

As the keel grounded on the beach, another voice boomed—from landward: "Halt, in the King's name!"

"The Riding Officer!"

"He'll have dragoons wi' un."

The smugglers jumped out of the boat and ran, scattering, dimly visible against the pale beach by the paler light of the crescent moon. James hauled Cordelia out into ankle-deep water.

"Come on!"

"But we're not smugglers."

"Do you want to explain that to the dragoons? I don't. Come *on!*"

A ragged volley of shots rang out. He took her hand and they set off at a stumbling run across the sand.

# Thirty-one

Cordelia awoke to a buzzing noise and a heavy, over-sweet fragrance. She opened her eyes. Beside her James lay on his back, his hands linked behind his head, gazing up with a contented smile at a canopy of bright yellow flowers beset with wicked grey-green thorns. Bees zipped from blossom to blossom.

He turned his head to look at her. "Welcome to England," he said.

"Safe at last on English soil? Bah!"

"I can think of few things more delightful than lounging in a gorse thicket on a fine, sunny morning in May. Provided you watch out for the prickles," he added, too late, as Cordelia sat up, yelped, and clapped a hand to her neck.

"Not the prickles, a bee sting. It hurts! Welcome to England, *ha!*" Cordelia said bitterly.

"Turn around and let me take out the sting. Careful, now, or you will get caught in the gorse. Ah, I see it. Hold still."

In spite of the burning pain of the sting, his fingers on the back of her neck did strange things to her. Steadfastly she ignored the tendrils of sensation emanating from his light touch.

"It hurts," she repeated, "and I'm hungry. Do you think it's safe to leave this *delightful* spot?"

"My poor dear, you haven't had quite the best of homecomings, have you?"

"It's always nice to be greeted with gunfire! I cannot understand how we succeeded in escaping."

"Oh, that's easy. To start with our clothes are light-hued so they stood out less against the sand than the smugglers' black. Then, since both the smugglers and their pursuers knew all the ways off the beach, none of them was so muttonheaded as to enter that blind gully we got stuck in. We were saved by sheer ignorance. There, that's out." He kissed the bee-sting, a very wet kiss.

Taken by surprise, Cordelia exclaimed, "Oh!"

"My old nurse always said, if you haven't got any powder-blue handy, the best remedy for a sting is spit," James informed her cheerfully. "I didn't tell you beforehand in case you objected."

"What is a little spit after all we have been through? Can we go, or do you think the Excisemen are waiting to pounce?"

"Unless you have contraband concealed about your person, they have no grounds to detain us." He started crawling through the bushes. "Ouch! Mind where you put your hands."

"They are already scratched from last night."

They emerged on a hillside overlooking a wide bay. Clumps of pink thrift dotted the sheep-cropped turf, varied here and there with a drift of blue squills. As blue as the squills, the sea spread below. Shading her eyes against the rising sun, Cordelia saw green hills on the far side. Half way across a lighthouse rose from the waves.

James turned south, turned north, turned to look behind him, and gave a satisfied sigh. "I thought so. If I'm not much mistaken that's the tower of Maker Church. This is Cawsand Bay." He gestured towards the lighthouse. "And that is Plymouth Sound. If we were just a bit higher, we could see Plymouth to the north of us, across the water."

"Across the water? How shall we get there?"

"There's a ferry from Cremyll, a rowboat ferry. A couple of miles walk, at a guess. How lucky we landed somewhere I know."

"That's all very well, but a ferryman is not likely to accept a diamond in payment, and we haven't a penny between us!"

He grinned at her. "Don't fret, you are safe on English soil. Mount Edgcumbe is even closer than the ferry. Lord Mount Edgcumbe is probably in London at this season, but there is bound to be someone about who knows me and will lend us a shilling."

"You are acquainted with Lord Mount Edgcumbe?" Cordelia hurried to catch up as he set off.

"We used to visit here often when I was a boy. The earl is as much older than I as Valletort is younger, but . . ."

"Valletort?"

"Viscount Valletort, the heir. But Edgcumbe is a hospitable fellow and besides, the families are connected somehow. Through my great-aunt, I seem to recall—unless it's his great-aunt. Anyway, I know Mount Edgcumbe like the back of my hand, and someone is bound to recognize me."

"But we look like tramps!" she protested.

He stopped and looked her up and down, and laughed. "So we do, or rather, like singularly disreputable French peasants. We'll see if we can borrow some clothes, too."

Less sanguine, Cordelia refused to go with him to call at the great Tudor mansion. Since Lady Millicent Halsey called him cousin, perhaps it was true that the earl's servants knew James, but she was a stranger. Besides, the fewer people who saw them together the better, or she might find herself with no choice but to marry him.

He left her in a circular summerhouse with Grecian pillars—Milton's Temple, he called it—hidden by spring-green woodland from the house and looking out over the Sound to Plymouth. She had not seen so many ships since leaving Istanbul, fishing smacks, luggers, frigates, men-o'-war, sloops, ketches, merchantmen from every corner of the globe. Beyond, framed by green hills, rose the grey stone citadel and the town, with church towers rising above the roofs.

An English town, she thought, full of English people who spoke English. No struggle to communicate, no brigands, no pirates, no misogynistic monks, no French or Turkish troops—

but the bee-sting throbbing on her neck reminded her that she had woken this morning in a gorsebush, hiding from *English* soldiers . . .

A hand fell on her shoulder and she sprang to her feet, whirling round.

"James, you startled me! I was just thinking about the dragoons."

"We're safe. They have no way of connecting us with the smugglers."

"I hope you are right." Her hand to her still-jumping heart, she stared at him and giggled. His wrists protruded from the sleeves of the coat and the breeches sagged.

"His lordship is somewhat shorter and wider than I," he acknowledged, his lips quirking, "but after all, you have seen me dressed as a Turkish woman, a eunuch, a Greek fisherman, a French peasant, and goodness knows what else in between. Let's see how you look in Lady Emma's clothes. I always think of her as a little girl but it seems she's a grown-up young lady and presently doing the Season." He handed her a bundle.

"You did not steal them?" she faltered.

"What a low opinion you still have of me! I had hoped to have risen in your estimation by now." His hurt look made her flush and lower her eyes. Before she could apologize, he went on, "No, I did not steal them. Edgcumbe's housekeeper gave them to me and assured me they'd not be missed, though of course I shall return them when we reach Town."

"What did you tell her?"

"That I was just come from France after a secret mission for the government, and she must not ask questions nor breathe a word of it."

"Oh James, did you really?"

He nodded, a glint of amusement in his eye. "I'm afraid I left her with the impression I intended to dress up in Lady Emma's clothes myself. Put them on, there's a good girl, and let's get going."

Retiring into the trees, Cordelia shed the French peasant garb and donned Lady Emma's carriage dress. An elegant but serviceable garment of slate grey Circassian cloth, it was ornamented with black velvet ribbon and plaits of black gauze. Like James, she was somewhat taller and slimmer than the original wearer. However, it fitted well enough and a paler grey wrapping cloak would hide most deficiencies, including her hair, which she tucked well back under the hood.

When she emerged from the wood, James surveyed her and nodded. "Good enough." Actually, she was adorable, her round face peeking hopefully from the fur-trimmed hood like a Cornish piskie, but he would not tell her so. Her persistent doubt of his honesty rankled.

As they set off down the path to Cremyll, he jingled the borrowed coins in his pocket. "We'll take the ferry to Plymouth and find a quiet inn. Then to a jeweller. We'll buy a few necessaries—"

"Hairpins! A toothbrush!"

"— and take seats on the Mail."

"The Mail?"

"The coaches which carry the Royal Mail also take passengers. It's not the most comfortable way to travel, but we've endured a lot worse. It's fast and it will save a lot of trouble."

Cordelia frowned, obviously miffed. "What sort of trouble? What are the alternatives? You know England and I don't but I should like at least to be consulted."

James adopted his most patient air. "For one thing, the Mails are never held up by highwaymen because the guards are well armed and alert. As for alternatives, there's the common stagecoach. It's cheaper, but slower and still less comfortable. Or we could hire a post-chaise, fast and private, but no more comfortable and expensive."

"Very expensive?"

"Very expensive, and few postilions are willing travel at night. To stay overnight at an inn is to risk meeting someone I know, which means we should have to hire an abigail for you."

"An abigail! Why? I manage perfectly well without."

"Because, my dear, you're in England now. Being a virtuous young lady is not enough. The appearance of propriety is as important as the fact—if not more so!" he added sardonically.

She considered this in silence for several paces, then sighed. "I suppose so. If I had had a maid with me, Lady Millicent might have believed our story."

*"Might."* He was still out of charity with his beautiful but cynical cousin. "At any rate, to find a maid or chaperon in Plymouth could delay us for days, and would involve us in all sorts of explanations. On the Mail we shan't meet anyone who knows me, and as we shall travel through the night in company the question of impropriety does not arise."

"We will still need some sort of story."

"Any personal enquiries from strangers would be sheer impertinence, and I should treat them as such." He spoke with hauteur, eliciting a glance of surprise from Cordelia. Lowering his tone, he added more prosaically, "The most we need let drop is that we are cousins and I am escorting you home after a visit to relatives."

"Better relatives in Cornwall than in Sicily, I daresay!"

James grinned. "More credible, undoubtedly. When we reach Town we shall go to my uncle's house and—"

"No. Whatever we tell or don't tell our fellow-travellers, your actual relatives will require a proper explanation. I think it will be best if I go straight to Norfolk, alone."

"Not so fast!" Infuriating as she could be, James was not about to let her out of his sight while she persisted in refusing to marry him. "Your father is very likely in London with the rest of the Polite World. You cannot wish to throw yourself on the mercy of a house full of servants who don't know you."

"Oh, dear, I thought everything would be easy once I reached England." Her voice quavered.

He wanted to take her in his arms and hug her and promise all would be well, but he had decided he must observe the strictest decorum now until they were safely wed. It might after all be possible to keep their travels secret from all but their closest relatives—at least until Millicent returned to England, and her malicious tongue would be silenced by finding them man and wife. He'd much prefer Cordelia to marry him by choice, not because she was compromised in the eyes of the world. Very soon now he would be able to prove to her that he was not the good-for-nothing vagabond she thought him.

"Once we reach London, everything *will* be easy," he assured her. "I'll take you to my uncle and aunt, and we'll discover your father's whereabouts. If he is not in Town, you shall write him a letter so that he has time to kill the fatted calf before I deliver you to his doorstep."

She smiled at that. "Oh James, you cannot imagine how much I look forward to having a proper home!"

For once their plans proceeded smoothly. They were able to leave Plymouth that very evening, though James had to take an outside seat as far as Exeter. Cordelia marvelled at the splendid coach with its red wheels and undercarriage, maroon panels, and gold Royal arms, stars, and lettering. The public diligences she had seen on the Continent were always drab and generally dingy.

The four horses tossed their heads; the scarlet-coated guard, perched up behind atop the boot holding his mailbags, impatiently consulted his timepiece as the passengers took their places. The coachman gave James the coveted seat at his side on the box, to the loud envy of the two young squirelings off to see the world, or at least the sights of London.

Inside, Cordelia sat opposite an elderly couple who bade her good evening and then talked quietly together. Next to her was a middle-aged woman who merely nodded to her travelling companions as she took out knitting and embarked upon a muttered counting of stitches. This accomplished, the regular click of needles was periodically accompanied by such arcane mumbles as "Knit one, purl one, knit two together, slip one, pass the slipped stitch over." A pink baby-jacket took shape.

None of the three showed any interest in Cordelia. While daylight lasted, she gazed out of the window at the passing scenery. The English countryside, fields and woods golden-green in the light of the evening sun, enchanted her. Fat cows in the meadows, neat villages of thatched cottages with gardens full of flowers, everything so peaceful and prosperous, surely nothing could go wrong here. How could Mama have borne to leave?

But Mama had only recollected constant dismal rain and biting winds.

Now and then the guard sounded his post-horn to warn the toll-gate keepers to open. The Royal Mail passed free and must not be held up. At the bustling inns where they briefly stopped every hour or so, fresh horses were always waiting. As dusk turned to dark, Cordelia dozed, her dreams punctuated by the tantara of the horn.

Then the young fellows on the roof began to sing. Their rollicking hunting songs celebrated the pursuit of the fox and the village maiden impartially. At first Cordelia heard James's voice joining in the refrains, but as the songs grew less decent and more drunken, he dropped out. Soon the songs were interrupted by noisy squabbles about the words and tunes, until at last they fell blessedly silent. The coach rumbled on through the night. To the drumming of the horses' hooves and the snoring of the old man opposite, Cordelia sank again into intermittent slumber, hoping James would stay awake enough not to tumble from his seat.

At Exeter, in the small hours of the morning, the knitter departed and James took her place.

"It's getting chilly up there," he said, rubbing his hands together. "Those young rattlepates are drinking to stay warm. It wouldn't surprise me a bit if one or both came to grief."

"You are all right," Cordelia murmured drowsily. "That's all that matters. Besides, nothing dreadful can happen in England."

When the next stop roused her, her head was pillowed on James's shoulder. She was too sleepy and too comfortable to move.

The Mail stopped at Yeovil for breakfast. "Forty minutes," cried the guard, "then we're off, ready or not."

"Breakfast is served, ladies an' gemmun!" announced a waiter in a striped jacket with a white cloth over his arm. "This way, if you please."

The elderly couple climbed stiffly out and hobbled towards the inn. As Cordelia followed, one of the young men from the roof seat clambered down with the clumsy caution of the tipsy. He blinked at her with red-rimmed eyes.

"Tally-ho! A wench! A wench!" he cried. Seizing her around the waist, he aimed a sloppy, spirit-laden kiss at her mouth.

James promptly grabbed him by the collar and the seat of his breeches and tossed him in the horse trough, where he floundered, spluttering. The ostlers leading away the horses turned to laugh and jeer, and other by-standers gathered around.

Cordelia wiped her mouth. About to thank James, she saw the elderly couple hurrying back, their faces horrified. For a moment she wondered at their distress over a minor, if disagreeable, incident. Then she recalled that she was in England. No respectable young woman would casually disregard such an assault upon her person.

"Oh!" she cried hastily in a feeble voice, "I fear I am going to swoon." Checking that James was close enough to catch her, she raised the back of her hand to her forehead, closed her eyes, and crumpled into his arms.

"The brute!" said the old lady fiercely. "What modern manners are coming to I dare not contemplate. My dear sir, pray don't stand there. Carry her into the inn, do. I have smelling salts in my reticule."

James obeyed. The landlord had heard the commotion in his yard and bustled forward to hustle all four into a private parlour, apologizing for such dastardly goings-on on his premises.

"Forty minutes!" the guard called after them, "and not a moment longer."

As James deposited Cordelia full-length upon a cushioned wooden settle, she risked a peep up at him. His dark blue eyes were full of laughter. A giggle rose in her throat and she quickly closed her eyes again.

A moment later, pungent fumes filled her nostrils. Choking, she gasped for breath.

"There, she is coming round," the old lady said with satisfaction. "Poor dear, she will wish to rest quietly, I daresay, after such a horrid shock. Do you gentlemen go and take your breakfast in the coffee-room and I will stay with her. Richard, my dear, pray send in tea and a little thin bread-and-butter. You will feel better, child, after a nice cup of tea." She patted Cordelia's hand.

Cordelia shot a look of appeal at James. Correctly interpreting, he said, "Do you not think, ma'am, that my cousin is in need of sustenance to fortify her nerves?"

"After such a dreadful ordeal? Why, I doubt she will be able to swallow a morsel, but I shall endeavour to persuade her that a mouthful of bread-and-butter will do her good."

Gravely James thanked her, and left Cordelia to her tender mercies.

At least her presumed state of agitation preserved her from questions. Mrs. Piper—as she introduced herself—kindly seeking to distract Cordelia from her supposed vapours, rambled gently on about her own affairs. Her husband was a retired naval captain and they were going up to Town for a little holiday, to stay with old friends. Cordelia hoped Captain Piper was not subjecting James to a barrage of questions.

Though he deserved it, the wretch, leaving her here to starve!

"I'm ravenous!" she whispered as he supported her tottering steps out to the Mail coach. She covered her eyes with her hand at the sight of the shamefaced young squire already seated on the roof.

"You have been hungrier," James said callously. "Remember Montenegro. I must say your fainting was most convincing. After all our adventures, I'd have wagered you didn't know how to swoon."

"I did quite well, did I not? I thought in the interests of decorum I ought to show some strong reaction."

"Thank heaven you didn't decide to throw a fit of hysterics," he said with a grin.

He and the captain, on the most cordial terms, settled down to a game of travelling chess. Cordelia was charmed by the tiny, beautifully carved, ivory pieces, which had pegs that stuck into holes on the little folding board. James explained every move to her, thus averting general conversation. Mrs. Piper seemed quite content with some needlework.

At midday they stopped in Salisbury for luncheon, and Cordelia made up for her missed breakfast. Afterwards the captain dozed off, snoring softly, so they were all quiet so as not to disturb him. One way and another, despite their enforced intimacy, James and Cordelia managed to avoid telling the Pipers about themselves. Reaching London in the evening twilight, they parted with many expressions of good will, but no promises of future meetings.

The guard with his precious mailbags had already descended at the General Post Office in Lombard Street. As the Mail coach passengers alighted in the yard of the White Horse, a stagecoach arrived with ten passengers on the roof and six within. Amid the bustle, no one paid the least heed to a dowdy couple in good but ill-fitting clothes. James hailed a hackney, told the jarvey to drive to Arlington Street, St. James's, and handed Cordelia into the shabby carriage.

In a fever of nervous anticipation, Cordelia paid no heed to the busy crowds in the brightly lit city streets. What was she going to say to James's aunt and uncle? What would they think of his turning up unannounced with an utterly unknown female in tow? Would they even let her stay at their house? However amiable, they would surely consider her a dreadfully encroaching creature.

Miserably she wished she had insisted on going straight to Norfolk, where she belonged.

Perhaps she could put up at an inn tonight, and tomorrow James could come to help her discover her father's whereabouts. She turned to him to suggest it.

"James . . ."

"Cordelia," he said at the same moment, tugging at his neckcloth as if it was trying to strangle him. "Er . . ." he continued with unwonted hesitancy, "I . . . um . . . I daresay I ought to warn you."

Her heart sank. "Warn me?"

"I . . . well, the fact is my uncle is the Marquis of Wyvancourt. And . . . well, I'm afraid I'm his heir."

"You're what?" said Cordelia, incredulous. "You mean you are going to be a marquis one day? I suppose you will tell me next that you really were abroad on a mission for the government!"

"As a matter of fact," James said apologetically, "yes."

# Thirty-two

Far above Cordelia, the ceiling sported plaster garlands painted a delicate green, and bunches of gilt grapes. She turned her head. The walls of her bedchamber were hung with shimmering green silk. The elegant bow-fronted chest-of-drawers, the huge wardrobe, the dressing table, cheval glass, wash-stand, all gleamed from much polishing. A tall vase of yellow iris graced the small writing table.

Last night she had been too overwhelmed to take in more than a general impression of grandeur—magnificence, rather. This morning she was all too conscious that she had nothing to put in the drawers or the wardrobe. The cheap comb and hairbrush purchased in Plymouth lay on the dressing table beside the silver-backed dressing set provided by the house, like donkeys pastured with race-horses.

How could James have left it to the very last minute to reveal his identity? To say there had never been an appropriate moment was an utterly inadequate excuse! She would never forgive him.

He had been as relieved as she was, when they arrived in Arlington Street, to find Lord and Lady Wyvancourt out and expected home very late. Obviously, the longer he could put off presenting her to his aunt and uncle the happier he'd be. Why, oh why, had she not gone straight to Norfolk?

Her gaze fell on the clock on the mantelshelf, a pretty green-and-gold porcelain piece. Past eleven! She started to throw back the bedcovers, hesitated, reached for the bell-pull—and hesitated again. Last night the servants had greeted James with joy, even the supercilious butler cracking a smile. To Cordelia they had been politely hostile, though clearly bursting with curiosity. James's tale of a shipwreck to explain both her presence and their mutual lack of baggage lessened the hostility somewhat, but a chilly suspicion remained.

So Cordelia was reluctant to ring for a maid. On the other hand, the girl who helped her last night had removed her only clothes to be cleaned. She had no choice.

Half an hour later, clad once more in Lady Emma's carriage dress, she found her way downstairs. A blank-faced footman in olive-green livery directed her to the breakfast room, where, to her relief, she found only James.

He looked up from a large beefsteak, and rose to his feet, smiling. "Good morning. You look as if you have made up for lost sleep. What would you like to eat?" He gestured at a laden sideboard.

"Oh, tea and toast," she said distractedly.

"You will starve. Are you still furious with me?"

"What? Oh, no." Somehow it was impossible to go on being angry. He looked so handsome in a blue morning coat superbly tailored to fit his muscular shoulders without a wrinkle, his pristine white neckcloth contrasting with the sun-bronzed face she knew so well—and had come, much against her will, to love.

"Have some eggs," he said prosaically, "or some of this beef. There's nothing like English beef, though perhaps it's not exactly a conventional breakfast dish for a lady."

"I'm not hungry. I'm terrified. Are your uncle and aunt about?" Cordelia cast a nervous glance at the door.

"I expect they will be down any minute. Don't he terrified, m'dear. They don't bite, upon my oath, nor will they shoot at you, tie you up, blindfold you, arrest you, enslave you, or bury you in a snowdrift."

She managed a weak smile. "I wish at least I had some decent clothes. James, how long will it take to find out if my father is in London?"

"Shouldn't take long. I must report to the Foreign Office as soon as I've eaten and I'll make enquiries while I'm out. Then I'll come back to take you shopping."

"Thank you, but I'll take myself while you are out." Anything rather than be left alone with the marquis and marchioness.

"London's a big city," he reminded her. "You will never find . . . Aunt Maria!" He sprang to his feet as the door opened and Lady Wyvancourt came in.

"My dear boy!" Tearfully, the marchioness held out both hands. James thrust back his chair and strode around the table to enfold her in his arms and kiss both cheeks.

She was a small, fine-boned woman with silver-grey hair under a cap frothing with lace and pink ribbons. Behind her stood a lean, balding gentleman of middling height, in a sober black coat. A great grin split his lined face.

"James, my boy, it's good to have you home at last!"

James released his aunt and wrung his uncle's hand. "By Jove, sir, it's good to be home."

"I trust you mean to settle down at last. We feared the worst when the *Badger* limped home with a mast missing and reported you lost on the coast of France."

"She came home, did she?" He laughed. "That's a tale, though by no means the worst of my travails. But let me present to you the indomitable companion of the latter part of my travels. Aunt Maria, Uncle, this is Miss Courtenay."

They both stiffened and their expressions changed from rejoicing to resigned dismay. His lordship shot a glance of reproof at his nephew. Cordelia concentrated on performing her best curtsy with all the grace her mother had dinned into her.

"How do you do, Miss Courtenay," Lady Wyvancourt said coolly. "I trust everything has been done for your comfort."

"Yes, thank you, ma'am," she responded in a colourless voice. "I must beg your pardon for intruding. I shall leave as soon as I can discover my relatives' whereabouts. Mr. Preston assures me it will not take long."

"That's all right, then," said the marquis with forced heartiness, ushering his wife towards the table. "Now don't let us keep you from your meal, Miss Courtenay. James, we shall want a round tale of your adventures later, but I'm afraid I am due at the House shortly. The Prime Minister wants my advice before this afternoon's debate on the American question."

"And I am bound for St. James's Palace," the marchioness put in. "The poor Queen needs all the support and sympathy of her friends at this dreadful time."

"Dreadful?" said James. "What is going on?"

Over their breakfast, they spoke in hushed voices of the king's madness, leaving Cordelia to toy with her tea and toast in peace.

The Wyvancourts and James all left at the same time. James turned back at the door to say obscurely, "Oh, by the way, if you do go out, don't upon any account walk down St. James's Street. And don't fret." With an encouraging smile—which did not encourage Cordelia in the least—he departed.

Rather than sit and brood, Cordelia decided to go shopping by herself. She went up to her chamber for her purse, her diamonds, and Lady Emma's smart cloak. When she came down, finding a footman on duty in the domed, marble-floored vestibule, she asked him the way to St. James's Street.

His wooden face twitched. "St. James's Street, miss? I don't think . . . If you'll excuse me a moment, miss, I'll just fetch the butler." Dignity forgotten, he scurried off.

"St. James's Street, miss?" said the butler austerely, not twitching but looking as if he'd like to. "I fear it is not advisable for a young lady to walk down St. James's Street."

"Why?"

He lowered his voice. "The gentlemen's clubs, miss. I fear not all the gentlemen are gentlemen, if you understand me. There are those who are apt to quiz passers-by from the windows."

"Oh, I see." Cordelia bit her lip to hold back a smile. A dreadful hazard! "Well, you need not fear that I shall go there. Mr. Preston warned me not to. But I cannot avoid it if I don't know where it is."

"Very true, miss." Mollified, and struck by this wisdom, he unbent sufficiently to nod. "St. James's Street is the next street parallel to Arlington Street to the east."

"Thank you. Perhaps you can direct me to the nearest shops?"

"What do you wish to purchase, miss?" he asked cautiously.

"Gowns, shoes, hats, gloves, everything! But first, I need a jeweller."

"A jeweller!" he exclaimed, shocked.

Cordelia reminded herself that he was a servant and she a guest. Her affairs were none of his business. "Yes," she said firmly, "a jeweller."

Recognizing her change of tone, the butler resumed his proper demeanor. "I believe, miss, you will find everything you require in Bond Street, just across Piccadilly." He raised a finger and the footman materialized at his elbow. "George will accompany you, miss."

Cordelia, in turn, recognized that a young lady residing however briefly at Wyvancourt House was not to be allowed out unaccompanied. Bowing to the inevitable, she graciously thanked the butler and went off with George a pace to the rear.

By the time she returned to Arlington Street, several hours later, she was extremely glad to have the footman with her. His arms were full of packages and she carried two he simply could not fit in anywhere. She had even managed to find a modiste with a gown of lemon-yellow muslin sprigged with white, made up for a customer who could not pay for it. Lemon was not really Cordelia's colour, but the dress fitted quite well, and Lady Emma's must be returned.

"Is Mr. Preston home yet?" she enquired of the footman who had taken George's place in the hall.

"Yes, miss. He's in the library. Down the hall there, second door on the right."

Setting her two parcels on a side-table beside a bowl of columbines, she gave George a shilling and asked him to take the rest of her purchases up to her chamber. Then she turned towards the library.

She had to tell James that, reluctant to impose upon the Wyvancourts' hospitality a moment longer than necessary, she had taken a seat on that very evening's Mail coach to Norwich. She could always cancel it if he had discovered her father to be in London. Torn between hoping he had found out so that she could remove her unwanted presence, and wondering how she could bear to be parted from him, she walked slowly along the hall.

The door was an inch or two ajar. Her hand raised to push it open, she paused, hearing voices within. She did not want to see her host and hostess until she could bid them farewell.

"Happy as we are to see you, dear boy"—that was the marquis—"I really must protest. I daresay your travels were bound to induce a certain disregard for convention, but to introduce that female into your aunt's house is the outside of enough."

" 'That female' is an innocent young lady, sir, not to mention generous, resolute, intrepid, intelligent, and a host of qualities less easy to classify." The familiar laugh entered James's voice. "Independent and argumentative spring to mind."

"That is as may be, James," said the marchioness. "The fact is, Miss Courtenay has travelled with you unchaperoned for upwards of six months!"

"And without her I'd have come to grief a dozen times. Wait until you hear the full tale! Without her bravery, quick wit, knowledge of languages, and nursing skills, I doubt I'd have survived, not to mention that she franked my journey. I was practically penniless when I reached Istanbul. I owe her a great deal."

No more than she owed him, Cordelia thought. When it came to saving each other's lives and liberty, they were quits. She ought to leave before she heard any more, but she simply could not tear herself away.

Lord Wyvancourt was speaking. "Naturally you will repay every penny Miss Courtenay expended on your behalf."

"That's not the point, sir. And if it was, with the best will in the world I doubt we could ever separate my expenses from hers. From Istanbul to London is a long and complicated way."

"Istanbul is a very odd place to find a young Englishwoman," said his aunt. "Who *is* Miss Courtenay, James?"

"Her father is Sir Hamilton Courtenay, ma'am, of Norfolk. A baronet's daughter is, in the world's eyes, not a brilliant match for the heir to a marquisate, but by no means ineligible, you must agree."

"A match!" exclaimed the Wyvancourts in chorus. His lordship went on, "James, you surely cannot propose to wed the chit!"

"As my aunt has pointed out, sir," James said quietly, "she spent several months with me unchaperoned. Purely as a matter of honour, how can I not marry her?"

"Sir Hamilton Courtenay?" Lady Wyvancourt now sounded not merely shocked but horrified. "I knew the name was familiar. James, she is the daughter of a divorced woman. You cannot possibly marry her!"

"Are we all to be damned for the sins of our fathers, Aunt Maria?"

"I hope I am not so uncharitable, but you must admit there is bad blood there. Though Lady Courtenay went abroad with her lover, over the years the most scandalous stories trickled back to London . . ."

"Stories about her daughter?"

"No, to be fair, only about the mother, flitting from lover to lover. Courtesan is the *polite* word for what Drusilla Courtenay became! But the daughter lived with her and that is enough to damn her forever in the eyes of the Polite World. Miss Courtenay is no fit wife for you, or any gentleman. There can be no debt of honour, no duty to protect her reputation, for she has none."

Numb to the heart, Cordelia crept away.

In the library, James was silent for a long moment. It went against the grain, against both upbringing and instinct, to talk of his emotions, even to these two who had been like mother and father to him.

He held them in deep affection, and had never doubted their affection for him. He knew them to be sincerely fond of each other. But love? What a feeble little word to be thrown into the balance against the weight of propriety and convention, Society and good breeding!

A feeble little word, yet more important to him than life. Without Cordelia, his life would be empty, aimless. What did he care for estates and titles if she was not beside him to share them?

He stood up and went to the window. In the walled garden, the earliest roses were only just in bud. He remembered her at Arventino, surrounded by roses and children, smiling at him, making his heart turn over in his chest—the moment he knew he must have her for his wife.

"I love her," he said softly, half to himself. He turned and spoke aloud, in a tone of quiet reason. "I have explained badly. You see, it's not a question of a debt of honour, nor a debt of money or even of my life. I love her."

"Love!" The marquis seemed more bewildered than contemptuous or disapproving. "But Miss Courtenay is not even beautiful. If she were a diamond of the first water, the *Haut Monde* might be persuaded to make allowances."

"You will never be happy with a wife who is ostracized," his aunt pointed out gently, "and nor will she."

"Come now, Aunt Maria, do you really believe that a future Marchioness of Wyvancourt, presented to the Ton by the present Lord and Lady Wyvancourt, is in the least likely to be ostracized?"

"James, you *cannot* expect me to lend countenance to the daughter of Courtesan Courtenay!"

"No?" An icy calm overtook him. "Then, much as I shall regret any breach between us, I must tell you that I have every intention of marrying Cordelia with or without your approbation. If she will have me."

"If she will have you!" His uncle barked out a dry laugh.

"She has already refused me more than once." This was not the moment to reveal that at the time she had thought him a penniless rascal. Though James had his hopes, he was still far from certain of her true feelings towards him. Was the note he had left in her chamber presumptuous? "If she will not be my wife, I shall accept the new mission I've been offered. England will hold no charms for me; I'll be off to Japan."

Enveloped in a cold mist of misery, Cordelia had packed half her new belongings in her new valise before she saw the note on the dressing table.

> Dear Girl—As far as I can discover, your father is not in Town. Tomorrow I shall procure a Special Licence, and then we can be married at a moment's notice, here or in Norfolk, as you choose.
>
> Ever your most humble, devoted servant—J

Humble! James! It was only a form of words, of course, like the "devoted," yet she couldn't help smiling. Her lips trembled so she pressed them tight together. If only he had not started "Dear Girl"—but after all, he often called her "my dear girl" when he was annoyed with her.

She put the note in the valise, piled the rest of her things on top, and closed it.

She had rejected him when she believed him to be an outcast. How could she accept him now she knew herself to be an outcast? Even if he loved her . . . but the talk had all been of debts and duty and his wretched sense of honour.

Haunted by her mother's scandalous behaviour, she was no fit bride for a gentleman. Well, she had no desire for marriage, she thought defiantly. The Polite World might damn her with her permission. She would go and live quietly with her father in the country, where London gossip could not reach her.

As she trudged down the stairs, the footman in the vestibule was called away to perform some chore. Cordelia slipped out of the house unseen.

At the inn, she had over two hours to wait before the Mail coach was ready to pick up its passengers and proceed to Lombard Street to collect the mail and its guard. Sitting in a retired corner of the busy coffee-room, she sent for pen, ink, and paper. With much thought and crossings-out, she wrote to James. She glanced often at the door, unsure whether she dreaded or hoped that he would guess her plans and somehow find her.

Inexorably the hands of the clock marched onward. The Mail passengers were called. Cordelia hastily signed and sealed her latest, briefest effort, which said all—and nothing—that was in her heart.

Dear Sir,

I am going to my father's. I cannot marry you, but I shall never forget you. Thank you for everything.

Ever your most humble, devoted servant,

Cordelia Courtenay.

Perhaps he would smile when he read that last line, echoing his. He could not know how humble she had become in the past few hours. He would never know she was too devoted to ruin him by becoming his wife—not that it mattered. The marquis and marchioness had given him reason enough to withdraw his offer.

Giving a boy sixpence to deliver the letter, she stepped wearily into the coach.

It was raining when she reached Norwich next morning, and it continued to rain as the gig hired from the Rampant Horse carried her east. The land was flat, almost treeless, and unspeakably dreary under the relentless drizzle. The ostler driving the gig spoke with an accent quite different from the French smuggler captain's Cornish, but equally incomprehensible. He soon gave up trying to be friendly.

After a while, they turned off the Yarmouth turnpike. The lane ran along the top of a dyke, with water-meadows and marshland on either side, criss-crossed by drainage channels. The rain stopped, but the grey clouds stayed and a cold wind blew from the north-east. Ahead, a hill rose from the fens.

Little more than a hummock, it was crowned with a building. As the gig approached, Cordelia saw a four-square house in the starkest early Georgian style. The ochre brick and flint walls were pierced by uncompromisingly regular rows of windows, many false to avoid the window tax, and roofed with slate-grey pantiles. No trees broke that inflexible outline, though sombre yews and hollies ringed the base of the mound. The rest of the slope was grass, except for a cluster of dark, flowerless rhododendrons half way up on the southern side.

No garden. Had her mother's desertion so grieved her father that he dug up all her roses? Or was she mistaken? Perhaps this was not her destination.

"Hill House, miss."

This time, Cordelia understood him all too well.

She must not let mere appearances dismay her. King Lear's Cordelia had been faithful to her father through thick and thin. If Sir Hamilton was wrapped in gloom, still mourning his faithless wife, it was his daughter's duty—would be his daughter's joy, she vowed—to cheer and comfort his declining years.

She paid the ostler and dismissed him. After all, she was not a visitor who might be turned away. She was coming home.

Squaring her shoulders, she knocked on the door. The butler who opened it stared at her, stony-faced.

"I have come . . . I'm . . ." Oh, why had she not waited to write rather than arriving out of the blue? "Please tell Sir Hamilton Miss Courtenay is here. Cordelia Courtenay. His daughter."

He left her in the hall, stone-flagged and almost as chilly as outside. The only furniture was a heavy oak table with a silver salver and a horsewhip on it, so she stood. Several minutes passed before the butler returned, still expressionless.

"Please to come this way, miss." He led her along a passage, opened a door, and announced, "Miss Courtenay, sir."

Dark panelling, dark furniture, dark-bound books, lowering clouds outside, Cordelia's eyes took a moment to adjust. Then she saw a tall, thin man with thin grey hair. He stood by the bookshelves, open book in hand, perusing it. She waited, hands clasped tight, for him to notice her.

He turned. His face, too, was long and thin, his eyes cold, his thin-lipped mouth a straight line. He looked Cordelia up and down. "So you're Drusilla's brat." His tone was utterly indifferent. "What do you want?"

"I've come home, Fath—sir!"

"Home?" Dispassionate enquiry. "Is it not rather late to call Hill House your home?"

"I have no other, sir. My mother is dead." In spite of her efforts to keep it even, her voice quavered on the last word.

"Gone, is she?" He still sounded uninterested, though a corner of the rat-trap mouth twitched. "I suppose I can hardly throw you upon the charity of the Parish. You may tell your aunt I shall permit you to stay." He crossed to his desk, sat down, picked up a quill, and started writing.

*Mama!* Cordelia cried silently, closing the door softly behind her, *is this what it was like? Is this what you ran from?*

# Thirty-three

"I trust you realize, Cordelia," said Aunt Tabitha coldly, "that nothing you can do will wipe out the stain of your mother's behaviour. You may hope, if you conduct yourself henceforth with the utmost propriety and circumspection, to avoid open censure."

Sir Hamilton's sister was quite unlike him in appearance, short and plump, with a round face and rosy cheeks. However, a second glance at this comfortable exterior revealed tight pursed lips and eyes every bit as icy as her brother's. Worse, Cordelia soon discovered that whereas her father ignored her—thank heaven he had not asked about Mama's death, for she simply could not have told him the true story—her aunt actively enjoyed browbeating her.

"Answer when I speak to you, miss!" From her, "miss" was a slap in the face.

"Yes, Aunt. I beg your pardon."

"And you had best call me ma'am, not aunt. Hamilton chooses to recognize you so I am forced to, but I cannot wish to stress so mortifying a relationship."

"Yes, ma'am." Cordelia bowed her head over her needle. She *hated* the drab brown stuff she had been given to make herself a few new gowns.

"I am at home on Friday mornings. News of your arrival will undoubtedly have spread, so the busybodies will come. Drusilla was wont to chatter on in a lamentably frivolous fashion whenever we had callers. You will preserve a dignified silence unless spoken to. Do I make myself plain?"

"Yes, ma'am."

"Drusilla was—unfortunately!—the lady of the house. You are not. If I see anything amiss in your manners, you will be sent to your room."

"Yes, ma'am. May I walk in the shrubbery until your visitors arrive?"

"I suppose so." Aunt Tabitha's beady eyes surveyed her. "It will not do to have you fall ill, with all the fuss and the expense of a physician. Be sure you tidy your hair when you come in, though, to be sure, it is too short to look anything but unkempt."

Cordelia swallowed a sigh of relief as she left the stiffly formal parlour. To escape for half an hour into the sunshine was the most she could expect. Her aunt had informed her that genteel young ladies did not roam about the countryside.

The sun shone, the rhododendrons kept off the wind, but Cordelia felt chilled to the bone. Tears rose to her eyes as she recalled the warm affection in which *Zio* Simone, a mere honorary uncle, had always enveloped her. She had felt more human warmth from James's Uncle Aaron—even from Captain Hamid—than from her own relatives. She blinked back the tears. Drusilla, Aunt Tabitha said, always burst into tears at the least rebuke, thus proving herself irremediably childish and unworthy of being the wife of Sir Hamilton Courtenay of Hill House.

Why had she married him? The portrait on the stairs of the baronet as a young man showed a tall, well-built form, a devastatingly handsome face. So young herself, scarce out of the schoolroom, poor, pretty, loving Drusilla would not have recognized the insensitivity, the lack of humour in that face. And then, to have Miss Tabitha Courtenay as a constant companion . . .

No wonder she had fled to the arms of a lover! Cordelia no longer felt the slightest urge to condemn Mama. Instead, she was deeply grateful not to have been left to grow up at Chill House.

If she had a lover, if James came after her, she would go with him without a backward glance, whether he still offered marriage or not. But he would not chase after her just to make her his mistress—especially now she was at her father's house—and the Wyvancourts had talked him out of marriage.

The Reverend Mr. and Mrs. Turley arrived. The vicar's wife gave Cordelia a look of sympathy and squeezed her hand while welcoming her kindly to Fenny Sedgwick. Then she meekly subsided with her workbasket and said no more. The vicar, striding about the room with his thumbs in his lapels, preached an impromptu sermon on the sin of lust and the virtue of obedience to one's father. Of mothers he made no mention.

Next to arrive were the Misses Browne, unmarried sisters past their first youth who lived in the village with their bedridden mother. They found it quite impossible to address a single word to Cordelia, turning red and fanning themselves when she made her curtsy. Thereafter, chatting with the elder Miss Courtenay about domestic matters, they sent her niece frequent sly glances followed by giggles behind the fans.

They were still present when Mrs. Swathely-Connaught surged in. A massive woman upholstered in mustard satin, she announced that Mr. Swathely-Connaught had taken himself off to speak to Sir Hamilton about cattle. "And I did not bring the girls today, Tabitha." She turned a bright, curious, unwinking gaze on Cordelia. "Young girls are so impressionable. One must have a care whom they meet."

Giggling, flushing, fanning vigorously, the Misses Browne took this stricture to themselves and departed. Cordelia only wished she could do likewise.

So much for being the respectable daughter of the respectable Sir Hamilton Courtenay, Baronet. That longed-for goal was as unattainable as her father's love.

She could go to James, since she was certain he would not come to her. She still had money enough for her fare back to London, and a few weeks' lodging if he had gone out of town. But after that she would be penniless. Pride rebelled against throwing herself on his mercy. What would he say if she told him she was willing to be his mistress because the only other choice was the living death of Chill House?

She knew him too well to imagine he would laugh at her, at least not unkindly, nor would he spurn or abandon her. If he still wanted her, he might accept, however much he despised her. More likely his desire had been a passing whim, a result of unavoidable proximity, and he would offer her money to go away.

The pain and humiliation of that would be a hundred times worse than anything her father and her aunt could inflict.

Only a few days had passed since she arrived in Norfolk, she reminded herself. There was still an outside chance James had been delayed by his duties at the Foreign Office and would come to beg her to marry him. But the days continued to pass without a word from him. The fragile hope withered and died.

And then the letter came, a letter with the unknown name of Rothschild on the outside, and a London address: New Court, St. Swithin's Lane. Braving Aunt Tabitha's wrath—"I, or your father, should read all your correspondence, miss, and decide whether it is fit for your eyes"—Cordelia hurried up to her tiny, bleak bedchamber to read it.

> Madam,
>
> It is my pleasure to inform you that we are in receipt of a considerable credit forwarded to your account by Mr. Aaron ben Joseph of Istanbul. In view of the amount, we hesitate to forward the funds to you directly. Please inform us of the name of your bank, or otherwise advise us of your wishes. If you find yourself in this vicinity, be so good as to call in and Mr. Rothschild himself, in consideration of Mr. Aaron's personal recommendation, will be happy to discuss possible investments.
>
> Please find enclosed a receipt and statement of your account, and a letter from Mr. Aaron.
>
> I beg to remain, madam, your most obedient servant . . .

The signature was a squiggle, with "Chief Clerk, Rothschilds' Bank" neatly printed below.

Cordelia burst out laughing She had forgotten that Aaron the Jew owed her half the value of Mama's jewels. Or not quite forgotten, but having convinced herself she must not rely upon ever seeing a penny, she had long ago pushed the memory to the back of her mind. She should have known she could count on James's uncle.

Sitting cross-legged on her hard bed, Cordelia rocked with laughter. She could not stop. Tears ran down her face and her throat ached and still she laughed. Until Aunt Tabitha marched in and slapped her cheeks.

Cordelia smiled at her. "Thank you, ma'am. I fear I was growing a little hysterical."

"The best cure for hysteria is bread and water for a week," said her aunt grimly. "Give me that letter."

"Oh, no, Aunt, it is mine." She felt quite serene now. "And I shall not live on bread and water for a week, not even for a day. I am leaving at once, you see, or as soon as I can procure a carriage." Though she'd walk if necessary.

"Leaving! Going to your lover, I presume? A harlot, just like your mother."

"Yes, Aunt."

Yes, she was going to James. She was not a beggar now. If he wanted her, she would be his harlot. If he spurned her, she would go and hide her broken heart in a cottage in the country—under an assumed name, and anywhere but Norfolk.

But oh! please, let him want her!

Sir Hamilton's farewell was a frigid statement that he washed his hands of her and she need not expect to be taken in a second time. Aunt Tabitha called her a wicked, ungrateful slut, and a great many other epithets. By the time the hired gig carried her down the drive, Cordelia was passionately determined to scrub floors for a living rather than ever again set eyes on either of her nearest and dearest.

Not that it would ever come to that, thanks to dearest Mama's foresight. She felt the bank's letter in her pocket, and wished she still had the ill-spelled letter Mama had left with the jewels, so full of humble love. All these years she had betrayed Mama in her thoughts. No more.

When she reached Norwich it was too late in the day to set out for London. She took a comfortable chamber at the Rampant Horse and settled in a wing-chair by the window to read Aaron's letter. Writing in the Turkish language with the Roman alphabet, he hoped she had had a pleasant journey—that made Cordelia giggle. Next she breathed a sigh of relief: Amina and Aisha were safe at Aaron's house and he had already found a possible husband for the lively Amina. Ibrahim had evaded the pasha and taken ship for Alexandria, determined to set up as a barber in the great *hammam* at Cairo.

In closing, Aaron begged her to convey his kindest regards to his nephew, James, who he trusted had been helpful on the voyage.

Cordelia leaned her head back against the chair. Yes, James had been helpful, she thought dreamily, when he had not been utterly infuriating. Sometimes both at once. She would convey his uncle's regards. Could she possibly pretend—just to start with—that that was her purpose in seeking him out?

Now she came to think of it, she was absolutely terrified of facing him, of making the offer which would confirm the world's opinion of her as her mother's daughter. When James told his aunt and uncle she was intrepid, he had not envisaged anything like this.

She was going to do it, though, because a few more months with James, a few years if she was lucky, were worth fighting for.

Next day, the journey seemed to go on forever, yet it was over all too soon. Cordelia had decided to stay a few days at an inn, to call on Mr. Rothschild and to have at least one pretty, fashionable dress and pelisse made up before she saw James. But now she was just a mile or two from his side, a quarter of an hour in a hackney, she could not wait.

The lemon muslin would have to do. "Arlington Street, St. James's," she told the jarvey.

The pillared, Portland stone facade of Wyvancourt House was much grander and more intimidating than she remembered it. She paid the jarvey, then stood on the front steps, wavering. Considering her errand, should she have sent a note asking James to meet her elsewhere?

Too late. She must go through with it now or she might lose her courage entirely. Raising her chin, she took a deep breath and knocked.

George, the footman she knew, opened the door. "Miss Courtenay!" His eyes widened before his training took over and he schooled his features to impassivity. Cordelia could not make out whether he was horrified or merely surprised.

"I should like to see Mr. Preston," she said, with all the aplomb she could muster.

"Yes, miss. I shall enquire whether Mr. Preston is at home."

She nearly said that if he was out she would wait, then she realized that "at home" was a polite fiction. The footman knew very well that James was in, but not whether he wished to see her. If he was "not at home," she might just as well start looking right away for a cottage in the country.

Several black-and-white striped chairs stood against the walls of the vestibule, but Cordelia was far too agitated to sit down. She paced. She went to smell the roses on a side-table—their fragrance brought a sorrowful flash of memories of her mother. She studied portraits of former Prestons, without noticing anything except the men's resemblance to James.

He would see her, she told herself, if only to find out whether she was in need.

The stately butler came to her. "Miss Courtenay," he said, his tone kindly—or was it pitying?—though his expression preserved the proper imperturbability, "Mr. Preston is dressing for dinner, so . . ."

"Oh, dear, I did not realize it was so late!" Was he going to tell her to come back tomorrow? Would she ever be able to screw her courage to the sticking point a second time?

"Mr. Preston will be down shortly. May I suggest that you wait in the Blue Drawing Room?"

He showed her into a small sitting room, comfortably furnished. Trying to still her fluttering nerves, Cordelia bent over another bowl of roses, red and white, breathing deeply of their perfume. Her nerves continued to flutter. She crossed to a gilt-framed mirror on the wall, took off her bonnet, and tried to tidy her hair. It was still too short to pin up easily, and she had lost several pins in the coach.

She froze as the door opened behind her. Reflected in the mirror, a slim, elegant gentleman hesitated on the threshold, his head hidden by her upraised arm. Black buckled shoes, white stockings, black satin knee-breeches, black evening coat with white waistcoat, glinting ruby pin in his neckcloth—a guest, or Lord Wyvancourt come to tell her to go away?

She moved a trifle and saw his face. James! In her mind he was still a ragtaggle rover, dressed in whatever costume suited the moment. This polished perfection made him a stranger.

Then she noticed that his hair was uncombed, a corner of his snowy cravat had somehow escaped to stick up beside his ear, and he had cut himself shaving.

"James, you're bleeding!" Fumbling in her reticule for a handkerchief, she hurried towards him.

"I was shaving when George came to tell me you were here." He stepped into the room, shutting the door behind him. As she dabbed at his chin, his hand closed over hers. "No, dash it, Cordelia, it's no good doing it that way, you have to press till the flow stops."

"You do it, then." She extricated her hand, burning from his touch, and moved backwards, away from his unsettling nearness.

He stared at her as if he could not believe his eyes, the hand clutching her handkerchief gradually lowering as he forgot about the cut. "You came back."

"Yes. I . . ." Cordelia fixed her gaze on her clasped hands, half aware of the white knuckles, the nails digging into her palms. "James, if you want me, I should like very much to be your mistress." There, it was out, unrecoverable.

The stunned silence rang in her ears. Then he said, odiously patient, "My dear girl, that's quite impossible."

Hope and energy drained from her. "I've left it too late," she said in a dull voice. "Now you have your pick of any number of Paphians much more beautiful and desirable than me." She looked up, pleading just as she had promised herself not to. "But James, you would not have to give me expensive jewels. Your Uncle Aaron sent me the rest of the money from Mama's jewels and I am quite rich."

"Rich, beautiful, desirable, what more can a man ask for?" He was laughing at her, the wretch!

"But I'm not—"

"You don't believe you are desirable? Come here, I'll show you."

He swept her off her feet and carried her to the nearest sofa. Sitting down with her in his lap, he cradled her head in one hand and feathered a kiss across her lips, while his other hand fumbled at the buttons of her pelisse.

Cordelia tried to protest that someone might come in. In her own ears her protest sounded ineffectual, chiefly because she could not find the breath to finish the sentence. James ignored it completely. His mouth had found a spot just below the tip of her ear and was doing something to it that made her feel most peculiar inside. His fingers had mastered her buttons and were now mastering her breast as if the thin muslin did not exist. Her nipple tingled.

The pelisse was in the way. Impatient, James helped her shrug out of it. The buttons on the back of her gown took a moment longer, and then her breasts were exposed. Weighing one white globe in each hand, he gently squeezed and Cordelia moaned. He shifted her off his lap, onto the sofa, lying on her back while he knelt on the floor. His mouth closed on the tip of one breast. His hand found its way beneath her skirt, ran up her leg, caressed her naked thigh. The liquid throb inside her became an agony of tension urgently demanding release.

And then, with a gasp, he sat back on his heels. Breathing heavily, he said in a rough voice, "Well, do you still think you are not desirable?"

"But if . . . then why . . . ?" Her lips quivered.

"You were right, it's too late." He pulled her skirt down, the bodice up. "Sit up, dear girl, and turn around so I can button you. It's nothing to do with the birds of Paradise queuing to . . . Well, never mind that. It's too late to make you my mistress because I discovered months ago that what I wanted was not merely to seduce you but to make you my wife. I did keep asking you," he added in an injured tone.

"Oh James, I thought you were just being noble. Are you sure . . . ?"

"Quite sure."

"But I cannot marry you!" she cried tragically. "I shall never be respectable. People will never forget poor Mama."

"You'd be surprised what people will forget when they know you're going to be a marchioness. Besides, have you forgotten I myself am a criminal wanted by the law?"

She turned to him, knowing before she saw it that he was grinning. "Only the Turkish law. In England you are a hero—and I am a pariah. Lord and Lady Wyvancourt will disown you if you marry me."

"On the contrary, they have promised to help establish you in Society."

Cordelia stared. "They have? How on earth did you persuade them to accept me?"

"I told them all about our adventures, and how many times you saved my skin. And I told them if you were not to be my wife I should be off very shortly on a mission to Japan. The next heir is an unsatisfactory sort of fellow, much what you thought me . . . You have changed your mind?"

"You know I have!"

"But more important, they are rather fond of me. They want me to stay safe at home and settle down to start a family."

Cordelia took his dear face between her hands. He encircled her wrists in a light clasp. She gazed into his eyes, trying to discern the truth. "You will really go to Japan if I don't marry you?"

"Yes. I don't wish to force your hand, but without you my life will be meaningless. At least another mission would give it some meaning. You see, I love you."

"Oh James, I love you too!"

She was in his arms, held close to his heart. "Why did you go away?" he demanded in a choking voice. "I thought I had lost you."

"I overheard your aunt and uncle telling you . . . Don't they say eavesdroppers never hear good of themselves? I knew I wasn't worthy of you, and I was sure they would convince you. Then you didn't come to Norfolk, and that confirmed it. Why didn't you come?"

"Partly just to give you time for your reunion with your father." He hugged her closer. "But that was really just an excuse. You had refused me several times. I hoped you would think better of it when you discovered I'm not a good-for-nothing adventurer, but then you ran away. It seemed to mean you didn't want me for a husband even though I am quite respectable after all."

"My darling sapskull, how could anyone not want you for a husband? Yes, please, I will marry you."

He kissed her, and the kiss—cut off before it could reignite the smouldering embers of desire—was a promise of long years together.

"Strict propriety until we are wed," James said firmly, "and a very short engagement. Dash it all, I suppose I ought to post to Norfolk first to beg your papa's permission."

"No! He has washed his hands of me, and I am glad. James, he was perfectly horrid, cold and unkind, and my aunt was even worse. At last I understand why Mama ran away. I cannot be angry with her any longer. It helped me to realize that respectability is less important than being with the man I love."

"Then I must bless her for that, and for making you the woman I love." He kissed the tip of her nose. "Though you shall have me and respectability too! So much for your father. I must write and tell Uncle Aaron."

"Yes, how surprised he will be."

"Not he." His voice laughed at her, but she didn't mind anymore. "When he sent me to you, Aaron said you were far too respectable not to marry a gentleman after travelling so far alone with him. And he wrote to me asking me to convey his respects."

"He did? He wrote to me asking me to convey his kindest regards to you!"

"The crafty old fox! He wanted to make sure of us. He knew we were made for each other."

"Ahem!" George stood in the doorway, red-faced and rigid, his gaze fixed on the far side of the room. "Her ladyship wishes to know if . . . erhem . . . if 'the two of you' will be joining her and his lordship for dinner. Her ladyship told me to point out that dinner has already been held back half an hour and Cook will have the hysterics."

"Tell her ladyship we shall be there any minute."

The embarrassed footman bowed and thankfully vanished.

James smiled down tenderly at Cordelia, smoothing her tousled hair. Then he picked up her reticule from the floor. "I trust for once we have a comb between us, dear girl," he said. "Otherwise we shall both have to go without our dinner."